P9-DMK-359

"It is time," I informed Vanin, keeping my sword point low. "You spoke earlier of warriors, therefore allow me to introduce myself. I am Jalav, war leader of the Hosta, foremost of all the clans of Midanna—who are *warriors*. I spit on your concept of warriorhood, on your concept of honor. Face me if you dare, for I mean to have your life."

"War leader?" Vanin scorned, reaching for her sword and unsheathing it. "Of the Midanna? What a fool's tale you tell, wench. *I* am of the Midanna, chosen favorite of Mida the Golden. I shall soon have your blood upon my sword, dedicated in whole to the glory of Mida."

**"Such is to be seen," I said, advancing. . . .**

**SHARON GREEN**

has also written:


**THE WARRIOR WITHIN**
    (DAW Book UE1707—$2.50)

**THE WARRIOR ENCHAINED**
    (DAW Book UE1789—$2.95)

**THE CRYSTALS OF MIDA**
    (DAW Book UE1735—$2.95)

and will be writing more novels
in both these exciting series.

# An
# Oath
# to
# Mida

*Sharon Green*

**DAW BOOKS, INC.**
DONALD A. WOLLHEIM, PUBLISHER

1633 Broadway, New York, NY 10019

COPYRIGHT ©, 1983, BY SHARON GREEN.

All Rights Reserved.

Cover art by Ken W. Kelly.

FIRST PRINTING, JUNE 1983

1 2 3 4 5 6 7 8 9

DAW TRADEMARK REGISTERED
U.S. PAT. OFF. MARCA
REGISTRADA. HECHO EN U.S.A.

PRINTED IN U.S.A.

# TABLE OF CONTENTS

# DEDICATION

For my sons,
Andy, Brian and Curtis,
true males all.

# 1.

## A meeting of enemies—
## and the tears of Mida

The fey was more than cool despite the brightness of the skies, yet I would not allow the discomfort of it to touch me. My warriors and I wore naught save the clan covering of the Hosta about our hips, each of us standing within small, silent sets not far from the platforms which had been set upon the grass within sight of the entrance of the immense dwelling of Galiose. The High Seat of Ranistard had declared a feast that fey for those who would soon arrive in the city, yet my warriors and I planned a greeting of another sort. I sat cross-legged upon the grass, watching the slaves both male and female prepare the provender for the feast, and Gimin and Fayan came to sit beside me.

"All are prepared, Jalav," said Fayan, her brown eyes arove among my warriors. Then a small laugh escaped her, and she tossed her heavy, golden hair. "The males insisted to all Hosta that they be present at the feast for the Silla. Soon shall such demands be regretted by them."

"Males must ever be demanding actions of warriors," I murmured, my eyes, too, unable to rest. "The damned Silla shall be welcomed as Hosta are ever wont to welcome blood enemies, and I regret only the loss of our weapons. Yet shall we make do without. How goes the time for your slave, Fayan?"

Fayan's eyes came to me, and laughter was there in them as well as in her voice. "The slave Nidisar finds his lot a hard

7

one." She grinned, her hand going to her life sign where it hung
upon its leather about her neck. "I have had him secured in the
room of feeding in his own dwelling, and there have I used him
each time desire has come to me." She paused to laugh again,
with true pleasure. "Truly has he been repaid for his actions with
me, and great anger is ever upon him—most especially when he
must swallow his slave gruel, or have it forced upon him by
Galiose's males. My enjoyment of him is great, and I shall not
see him released till my revenge is complete."

"I do not envy you your enjoyment," said Gimin sourly as
she lay upon her side by us. Her hair, as black as mine, fell
about the arm she leaned upon, and her gray eyes watched the
grass. "The male will not forget your treatment of him," said
she, "and if ever you release him, you may be sure he shall see
to his own revenge. I do not care for the revenge of males."

Fayan and I exchanged a glance, for easily might it be seen
that Gimin yet felt the punishment given her by the male who
had claimed her. The Hosta, once free, had all been taken
captive by the males of Ranistard, and now were we expected to
tend to the males and obey them, and serve them in their
pleasure. Gimin had joined Fayan, Larid, Binat and myself when
we had escaped from Ranistard to seek the third Crystal of Mida,
yet had we been recaptured by the males, the Crystal taken from
us, and we, ourselves, returned to Ranistard. Much angered had
Gimin's male been at her attempt to regain freedom, and much
leather had he used upon her in punishment. After having given
her humiliation and pain, he had used her as though she were
slave and unable to deny him, saying he would teach her clearly
what her actions had brought upon her. Gimin continued to ache
from his anger, yet she had joined us as we grouped against the
coming of the Silla, for true Hosta warrior was she. The pain
given by males was not to be considered against the duty a Hosta
owed to her clan.

Fayan was no longer amused, and she, too, stretched out upon
the grass in thought, her unbound hair amove about her. Once
before had she angered Nidisar, and the male had not been gentle
with her. That was doubtless now in her thoughts, although the
time was past when the predicament might be avoided. Galiose
had given Fayan the gift of Nidisar as a slave, for Fayan had
demanded such in exchange for her assistance in using the device
of the gods. That the use had not brought the males the results
they had desired made little difference, for the gift had not been

disclaimed by Galiose. The High Seat Galiose was at times capable of a certain honor, and Fayan had retained her gift.

I shifted in the grass and raised my eyes to the blue of the skies with a sigh. Such great difficulty had the Crystals of Mida caused, pain and death the like of which only full battle might produce, yet had it all gone seemingly for naught. The males had not spoken with the gods as they had hoped, and were greatly distressed. We had been told that we were lost kin to those who spoke from the depth of the golden air about the device, and that soon would come others to take from us our ignorance and lack of knowledge, to be replaced with the great benefits of those who are truly civilized. Deep shock had been felt by the males, caused in great part by the knowledge that those who came to teach the ignorant were female, and the past two feyd had been spent by them in almost constant discussion, seeking a means by which those who were to come might be returned from whence they came. Fayan and I, who had been present when the threatened invasion had been spoken to us, had yet, nonetheless, been barred from the discussions of the males, first having been cautioned to speak no word to others of what had occurred. Most annoyed had Fayan and I been; however, we had other matters of import to discuss between ourselves. We had withdrawn to the dwelling which had once been Nidisar's, and there had we drunk renth and spent many hind in an attempt to make sense of what had occurred.

We, who were Hosta of the Midanna, followed the teachings of Mida, and Mida, too, had been spoken of by her whose voice came from the golden air. The female had denied the divinity of Mida, saying Mida was naught save a joining of theirs, yet was such not to be believed. I, myself, had been spoken to by Mida in dreams, and had often seen things that only occurred by the will of Mida. Fayan and I agreed that the female who had spoken did not know the true nature of Mida, and then we discussed how to halt the strangers when they came. The Midanna would require little urging to ride forth upon their gandod, bravely draped in their clan colors, each warrior eager for battle, yet would it be necessary for word to reach them of our need. Although the males would surely lose if they engaged the strangers in battle, the Hosta were kept close behind the walls of Ranistard, not being allowed to return to our lands beyond the Dennin river. Once we had escaped the walls to ride in search of the third Crystal, but our escape had been known to and approved of by the males, who had wished that we fetch the

Crystal for their use. Not again would escape prove as effortless as it had been then, and the Hosta would need a greater effort to ride free once more.

The cramps came again to my middle as they had done so often in the past two feyd, therefore I lay back in the grass, one hand upon the pain, till the aching would cease. The pain brought Ceralt to mind, and deep anger filled me at thought of the male. Much pain had Ceralt brought unknowingly to me, yet this pain that now was mine came from his desire to see me with child. That a war leader of the Midanna, such as I, was forbidden to have life within her meant naught to the male, for he had claimed me as his own, to do with me as he pleased. Many strange feelings had I had for the light-eyed, dark-skinned hunter, and by cause of these feelings had he been able to send me seeking the third Crystal, thinking I rode to aid him in dire need, when in truth he and the other males had merely followed the track my warriors and I left, and then took the Crystal from us when we had secured it. Many times had I been betrayed by the hunter Ceralt, yet now he would see me further betrayed by placing his seed within me. The leaves of the dabla bush, which had kept me childless, were then in battle with a potion given me by Phanisar, a thing done by the aged male at the urging of Ceralt, and Phanisar had said that the potion would have bested the dabla leaves in a matter of feyd. Quite pleased had Ceralt been with his actions, yet had I been able to locate dabla bushes within Ranistard, and had, each fey since the potion was given me, chewed the leaves to increase its strength against the potion. The taste of the leaves was not unpleasant, yet even were they foul enough to curl the tongue, still I would have chewed them with a will. Not again would the hunter Ceralt have opportunity to betray me.

"Jalav, I have had a thought," said Gimin from where she lay. "The High Seat will not be pleased by the manner in which we greet the Silla. Think you his anger shall reach out to the war leader alone, as once before? That would be an unfair burden upon you."

A sudden breeze blew my hair about my thighs, and I brushed it back before shrugging. "There is no knowing, Gimin," said I, "yet have I little care for the anger of males. Should they so dislike the doings of Hosta, they may release us and have done with it for all time. Hosta have ever been free, and I, for one, will retain my freedom even in captivity."

"It is difficult for one to be free beneath the lash," said

Fayan, sitting straight once more so that she might look down upon me. "Thus far has Ceralt kept you from it, yet the patience of Galiose runs thin in these times. The Hosta have given over darkness roving so that they might prepare themselves for the Silla, yet our attack may well bring the lashing Galiose promised in revenge for the roving. Think you Ceralt shall once again find himself able to dissuade the High Seat from his purpose?"

"Do not speak of that male to me!" I spat, raising myself, too, from the grass. "Should the hunter Ceralt be taken by Mida before my eyes, I would do naught save laugh! The battle will soon be upon us, Hosta! Have you no means by which to prepare for it save by chatter about males?"

My warriors appeared shame-faced and subdued before the anger of their war leader, though Fayan looked at me strangely. Fayan had found revenge for what had been done to her by Nidisar, and I was unable to revenge myself upon Ceralt in a like manner. The male had used the darknesses of the past two feyd to fill me well with his seed, and had refused to hear why I wished to remain as I was. Jalav will no longer be war leader to the Hosta, he had said, therefore might Jalav now be given a child to bear. The first of many, he had said, and then had he forced his way within me, using the accursed strength of males to overcome my denial. Deep pleasure had I found in the past through the touch of Ceralt, yet little pleasure had been granted me of late. No word would I again address to Ceralt, though he as yet was unaware of that. Much concerned had he been with the discussions in the dwelling of Galiose, and had returned to his own dwelling only for sleep and the use of Jalav.

"The nilno seem nearly done," said Gimin, her eyes upon the hand of nilno aroast upon the fire beyond the platforms of provender. "Surely the time will not be long before the Silla are brought. Think you they have chosen a war leader to stand for Zolin, Jalav?"

"Undoubtedly Zolin left one to direct matters in her absence," said I, again smoothing down my hair. "Though the Silla know not yet that Zolin has been bested, they shall still be led by a war leader. Would that her blood, too, might cover my sword as Zolin's did upon that fey long past."

My warriors made no answer to my words, for no sword had any of us to wield. The males of Ranistard had taken all from us, as they would have taken all from the Silla before approaching the city with them. In truth, I felt less loathing toward the Silla than for Ceralt, since the Silla had not betrayed me as Ceralt

had. My freedom and pride had Ceralt taken, my will and desires
ignored by him, and then had he caused me to feel such things
that a warrior was not meant to feel. Having nearly destroyed me
as a warrior, he had then betrayed those feelings he had caused
within me, giving me shame for ever having felt them. Once had
I delighted in the feel of the male's arms about me, once had his
lips been the sweetest of touches, once had I longed for the
gentleness of his presence. Not again would desire for those
things come to me.

The sound of a kan's hooves upon the broad way caused my
warriors to turn, and they and I beheld the hasty arrival of a male
in the leather and metal of Galiose. The male drew rein before
the large, pink-stone dwelling of the High Seat, then jumped
from his mount and climbed the steps rapidly, to disappear
within the entrance to the dwelling. The large grin upon his face
spoke of the arrival of the Silla, for the males of Ranistard were
sorely in need of females to tend them. Few females had there
been left by cause of the doings of the traitor Vistren, therefore
had the males decided to replace the lost with captured Hosta and
Silla. The Silla, through dealing with Vistren, had hoped for the
trade of their Crystal for many male slaves to serve them. With
the death of Vistren had gone their hopes, and soon would they
be urged with leather to tend to the needs of males they had
wished for slaves. No less had the Silla earned by their actions,
yet the Hosta had not done as they. The Hosta had displeased
Mida with their failure to recover her Crystals, therefore were
the Hosta held as well. Perhaps the coming battle might in some
measure ease the wrath of Mida, so that her Hosta might be
forgiven their failure. Could I but raise the host of Midanna from
beyond the Dennin to face the coming strangers, surely would I
also find a means to return the Crystals to their rightful place.
The Hosta would then be free to return to their own lands, where
naught of males might touch their lives with pain.

An ache again ran through my middle, and I wrapped my arms
about myself and willed the pain to be gone, for soon I would
need all my strength. No sound did I make against the pain, yet
Fayan saw and frowned.

"Jalav, I fear the pain comes more often to you than previous,"
she said, her hand upon my shoulder. "Perhaps it is unwise to
continue with the dabla leaves in the presence of the potion. Can
naught of council be gotten from Phanisar upon the matter?"

I forced a breath of air through my lungs, and then looked
upon Fayan bleakly. "Phanisar is male, and moves in the cause

of another male," I rasped. "As the warrior Fayan should know. Perhaps the warrior Fayan becomes too concerned with males and their aid. Has she yet decided upon a time when her war leader may have use of her slave, as was previously promised?"

Fayan's hand left my shoulder, and her gold-maned head rose high. "The war leader may have use of Nidisar whenever she chooses," she answered, her dark eyes unblinkingly upon me. "Yet do I feel that Jalav seeks not to punish Nidisar for his treatment of her while she lay chained as a slave, but seeks instead to cause hurt to another. Has he touched you so deeply, Jalav, that you are no longer able to speak as one sister should to another?"

Fayan did naught to betray her hurt, yet was I able to see its presence in her eyes. Of all my warriors had Fayan been the truest, and no cause had there been for me to speak to her as I had. My head lowered in silence, and one hand left the ache in my middle to cover my eyes, so that I might not look upon the shame I had brought to myself. Again her hand came to my shoulder, and her words were soft and concerned.

"Jalav, I do not care to see you so," she said, though I looked not upon her. "I feel certain the potion has done you an illness which was not meant to be. Speak with Phanisar and question him upon the matter."

"I cannot," I whispered, shaking my head. "Should he learn that I have again chewed dabla leaves, the other, too, would know. The pain shall soon pass and leave me free once more."

A short silence was there, and then Fayan grasped my shoulders. "Jalav, can you not even speak his name?" she demanded. "What has he done that burns so within you? Many times has Ceralt kept you from the wrath of the High Seat, to his own jeopardy! That he cares for you may easily be seen by. . . ."

"He has betrayed me!" I snarled, disallowing the balance of her words as I brushed her hands from me. "The male uses me in all things, forever an item of trade! The pain—!" My words, too, ended abruptly, for no wish had I to discuss my pain. I looked again upon Fayan, and then rose to my feet. "Soon shall the Silla be among us, sister. Let us make ready."

Fayan sat saddened, Gimin silent by her side, and then they both regained their feet as sounds came to us from the beginning of the broad way which ran past the dwelling of Galiose. Chill was the air, and chill, too, was the grass beneath my feet, yet all matched the chill within me as my hair blew about my thighs. Completely unbound was the hair of my warriors, for I had

disallowed the placing of war leather upon it. Many of the males
knew the use of war leather, and foolish, indeed, would it be to
give warning of our intent. The Silla would be well aware of
where they had been taken, for the drug used for their capture
would no longer be with them, and sight of waiting Hosta would
be warning enough.

Many males began to drift within sight of us, each looking
back toward the body of the city and the sounds of joy and
greeting coming faintly therefrom. The dwellings were hung
with many-colored silks as they had been hung about for the
fetching of the Hosta, yet no more than two colors would find
preeminence that fey. The green of the Hosta and the red of the
Silla would merge in battle, one to prove triumphant above the
other. Mida willing, the grass of Hosta would prevail as ever it
did when Hosta and Silla met.

The sounds of male voices raised in triumph reached us more
clearly, and then appeared the first of the males, a Silla held
bound before him. The Silla twisted about, attempting escape
from the male who held her and the leather which bound her
wrists, yet were her efforts to no avail. Nearer to the dwelling of
the High Seat was she brought, others behind her, and the red of
their clan colors reached to my warriors and caused them to stir.
No more than a stir did my Hosta allow themselves, no more
than a stir would the males perceive. Later, with the Silla
unbound, would they perceive further.

Not long was it before the Silla were brought to the platforms
of provender, their eyes no longer looking about. They gazed
upon the waiting Hosta, knowing full well of the battle soon to
be brought to them, not one of their greater than twenty hands in
number doubting such. We, too, numbered greater than twenty
hands, therefore would the battle be of much pleasure, although
no weapons were at hand. The males dismounted, reached the
Silla down to stand beside them, and then Galiose approached
from his dwelling, the males who had been in council with him
moving in his wake. Large and broad was Galiose and dark of
hair and eye, his well-made body clad in a short blue covering of
city males, with blue leather and metal covering of protection
above that. His feet, like those of the other males, were encased
in leather, which was bound up his legs, showing he cared
naught for the touching of Mida's sweet ground by his own
flesh. Those of the cities have no souls, and by their each and
every action do they proclaim it. My hand went to my life sign,
that of the hadat, the guardian of my soul, and there it rested as

Galiose and his males drew nearer. Behind was Ceralt, and the large, dark hunter moved his light eyes about, searching for the presence of Jalav. Jalav had been bidden to attend the feast, and as Ceralt's eyes touched me, a small smile of satisfaction appeared. Jalav had obeyed Ceralt, so he thought, yet never would Jalav obey Ceralt. Beside Ceralt, Telion walked, and the great, red-gold-haired male warrior also seemed pleased. Telion, as Ceralt, cared little for disobedience, and therefore had Larid, my warrior whom Telion had made his own, been refused permission for attendance. Larid, who was with child, had not been deemed strengthened enough from her illness to bear the exertions of a feast time, yet had it been my word that had kept Larid within Telion's dwelling. Indeed had my warrior not the strength for battle, and this had I proclaimed above her protests. A true Hosta warrior, Larid had wished to join her sisters against the Silla, yet had she obeyed the word of her war leader, as do all Hosta.

Many murmurings were there from the males all about, and then Galiose paused before the gathering to hold his arms high. Much pleased was the High Seat with the look of Silla, and slowly did his eyes move among them as a silence covered the waiting throng. When full silence had fallen, Galiose raised his voice.

"We, the men of Ranistard, welcome the Silla wenches to our city," he shouted, his deep voice carrying to all. "The Silla have been found pleasing to men, therefore have they been taken by men as mates. No longer shall the Silla find need to do battle, for we shall now stand their protection. We open our city to you as we have already opened it to the Hosta, and you may explore as you please, so long as you remain a distance of two streets from gate or wall. I feel sure the Hosta will inform you of the penalties for being found nearer, for the Hosta have already incurred those penalties." He paused briefly to grin about himself, and the listening males chuckled in rueful remembrance. Again the Hosta stirred, also in remembrance, yet naught was said. "Now, wenches," Galiose continued, "you may join us at the feast prepared for you. Ranistard welcomes her newest citizens in such a manner."

The males beside the Silla began to unbind them, and other males began to approach the platforms tended by slaves. As previously instructed, each of my warriors watched her war leader closely, and then began her approach as I did. The Silla twisted about, desperate to be released before the arrival of Hosta. No battle would there be with bound Silla, and as the leather fell from them and they turned to face us, I gave the signal for attack. Hosta battle cry merged with Silla as males were shouldered from our path, and then were our two groups met, nails and teeth and stones doing that which should have been done by sharpened metal. Shouts were there about us, and cries of victory and defeat, and she who had closed with me found a scream in her throat for the pain which my teeth brought to her. Her hair, a pale gold of a length like mine, merged with mine in the struggle of battle and the breeze which had grown to wind. Naught save a single silver ring in her ear did this warrior wear, showing that she had attained full warrior status in battle, but I wore the second ring as well in my left ear, showing my attainment of war leadership. In true battle, each war leader sought out the other so that skill might match with skill; now, though, that was impossible. The true Silla war leader lay dead by my sword, and no other yet have been chosen for the second ring. I faced only a simple warrior but was not reluctant.

A chaos and cacaphony surrounded the area, the blood lust rose high within me, yet no time was there to dedicate my enemy's blood to Mida, nor to partake of it. Blood flowed freely from the Silla's shoulder when I was pulled from her by the hands of males, and each of us was held well out of reach as other warriors were separated. My left arm bore the marks of her painful reprisal, yet I had no feeling for the touch of pain. High was my pleasure at having closed with Silla trash, and deep was the snarling coming from the Silla as a male attempted to examine her shoulder. All about were warriors held from what they had been about, and high was the anger of the males, yet was their anger as naught when compared to that of Galiose. The large male roared about himself, ordering the separating of warriors, and Telion and Ceralt each held a struggling Silla, attempting to keep them from the Hosta who struggled toward them, held by yet other males. Galiose, in his anger, did not await the silence as he had before, but strode toward where I stood, held in the grip of males, and then took my hair in his fist and shook my head by it.

"So!" he hissed, his blazing eyes not far from mine. "The Hosta war leader would turn my city to a battleground, spitting upon my words of welcome to these others! Never before have I seen wenches act so, and never again shall I see its like! This time shall Jalav feel the lash of punishment!"

"No!" shouted Ceralt from where he stood, and quickly did he pass the Silla he held to another male so that he might stride to where Galiose glowered, my hair held in his fist. "Galiose, do not have her lashed!" he insisted, his light eyes disturbed beneath dark brows. "I shall punish her for this affair, you have my word!"

"As she was punished by you upon previous occasions?" Galiose demanded, his anger not lessened. "Look about yourself, man, and see how effective your punishments have proven to be! She has not obeyed you, nor shall she! The lash, I will wager, she shall obey! In any event, we shall soon see the testing of the matter." His eyes left Ceralt to come to the males who held me, and he ordered, "Escort the wench to the holding cells in my Palace, and have the guards see to her locking away."

"Galiose, I will not permit it," Ceralt growled low, his hand upon the High Seat's arm. His light eyes, so startling in the dark of his face, had become hard and cold as they never before had been. Galiose's fist left my hair, and he turned completely to Ceralt.

"Hunter, you presume too far upon my patience," said he, his voice as hard as Ceralt's gaze. "The wench shall be lashed for her disobedience, and no further shall be spoken upon the matter."

Then Galiose walked from Ceralt, his bearing stiff, his head held high. A brief, glaring flash of anger was sent to me by Ceralt, then he followed the High Seat, his wide shoulders set in determination, yet no farther was I able to see, for the males who held me propelled me toward the dwelling of Galiose. Through the sets of Hosta and Silla and Ranistard males was I taken, across the way lined with stones, and up the steps of smooth, pink stone, and within. The fingers of the males went deep into my arms as their anger hastened their pace, and roughly was I taken between them up the flights of steps within the dwelling. No time was there to fully see the blue cloth upon the floor before the entrance, no time was there to frown at the silks upon the walls, no time was there to observe the startlement upon the features of males and city slave-women who stood about in uncertainty, astare at the males and the Hosta held between them. To the first landing above was I hastened, a landing of many rooms for taking repose, to the second landing, a place of polished wood on walls, rooms with strange, unwholesome smells, and the like, to the third landing, a place of no floor coverings, bare stone walls, and rooms doored only with lines of metal. It was there I had once before been placed, and it was there I was placed again, the lined metal being closed firmly upon me once the males had thrust me within a room's confines. I stood

straight with head held high as the males glared upon me, then
when they had withdrawn, I walked to a wall of gray stone and
sat myself before it.

Truly great was the anger of Galiose, yet I cared naught for
the male and his anger. Twice before had I felt the touch of a
lash, and still did memory of the flaming touch hold sway within
me, yet was Jalav war leader of the Hosta. To no male would
she show pain, to no male would she give obedience, for Midanna
were warriors, not slave-women of the cities. Galiose would use
his lash, and then would Jalav feign great fear and assure the
male of future obedience. When once the male's back turned,
Jalav would be gone, over the wall and to the south, to fetch the
waiting clans of Midanna. Upon my return would Galiose learn
the extent of my obedience, and should he live through the
ensuing battle, great pleasure would I take in naming him sthuvad
for my warriors' enjoyment. A use tent would be his dwelling
for many feyd, and should he also survive his use, he would then
be given to the Harra, sister clan of the Hosta, who hold slaves
as the Hosta did not. Ceralt, too, would join Galiose in bondage,
and never again would I lay eyes upon the accursed male. The
pain came again to my middle, allowing in its distraction a
memory of dark, unruly hair above light eyes, yet I thrust the
memory from me, placing my shoulder to the gray stone of the
wall as I bent to the ache in my middle. No further pain would
Jalav be given, had said Ceralt, and Jalav, a fool truly made, had
believed. Not again would Jalav heed a male's false words.

Some few hind passed in the waiting, and I did naught save sit
by the stone. A cloth-covered platform was there within the
enclosure, of a sort called "bed" by those of the cities, yet
would I have naught to do with such. Sleep is properly taken
upon sleeping leather or bare ground, a thing unknown to those
of the cities, yet were Hosta not of the cities. The enclosure
contained no window, therefore I didn't know what had befallen
my warriors, and that disturbed me somewhat. I had given them
no word of my intentions, for surely most would have attempted
to join me beneath the lash to promote their own escape, and I
had no wish to see such. Escape would be brought to them
through the pain of their war leader, and their pain was unnecessary to ask. None other had felt the touch of a lash and, Mida
willing, none would need to do so.

Then came the sound of male footsteps, heavy upon the bare
stone of the floor, and to the lined metal of the enclosure came
Telion, his broad face angered, his eyes disturbed. He stood by

the metal a moment to study me, then shook his great, red-gold-maned head.

"Never before have I seen so foolish a child," he growled, looking at me. "Have you any idea of the pass matters have been brought to, girl? Know you the trouble you have caused?"

"Telion may save his words for another," said I, turning my head from him. "Jalav finds no interest in the babblings of a male."

"The babblings of a male!" Telion echoed with outrage, his large hands grasping the metal. "Truly meet would it be for a child such as Jalav to receive a sound hiding at the hands of this male! And so it would go, had Jalav not worse to come to her! Will you never find the good sense to avoid the lash?"

"All is as Mida wished," I informed him, seeing him only from the corners of my eyes. "Should Mida wish it so, the lash shall be avoided."

Telion made a sound of disgust, and then removed his hands from the metal. "Your Mida sleeps soundly and does not hear your call, wench," said he, once more coldly angry. "The lash awaits you now, and shall not be avoided. Galiose has had your wenches bound in leather, till they have witnessed your punishment. Ceralt gave challenge to the High Seat for possession of your overly desirable body, and for that was seized by the High Seat's guard. Galiose, in unexpected generosity, merely had him beaten somewhat before expelling him from the city in exile. Once you are lashed, you shall be given to another whom Galiose shall choose."

"To no male shall Jalav be given!" I snarled, rising to my feet. "Jalav is no city slave-woman, to be given away at the whim of Galiose!"

"Jalav is female!" Telion shouted, lost again to his anger. "A black-haired, black-eyed female child too lovely to long go unclaimed by a man!" With no further words, he removed the metal from before the door, and then took my arm to lead me forth. Silently we passed the males in leather and metal, and the eyes of those males found pleasure in the appearance of Jalav, yet the looks held more than mere pleasure and desire. Jalav was to be given to a male for his use, and the eyes of the males imagined themselves as he to whom she was to be given. These males knew not the true meaning of taking a Hosta war leader, and I held my head high to scorn their foolishness. Let the chosen male of Galiose beware, for I would have none of him.

Beside Telion did I stride, allowing my fury full rein, and therefore was I able to think of Ceralt not at all.

Again were there large numbers gathered before the dwelling of Galiose, yet had the fey grown clouded, Mida's light grayed cold as it reached us. A murmur arose when Telion led me forth from the entrance, and many were the Midanna and males astare below the height of the steps. Silla stood in great satisfaction, Hosta stood angrily bound in leather, males stood covered with grim approval, all eyes upon Jalav as her hair blew in the chill wind. Galiose and a hand of males stood to the left of the entrance, where a contrivance of wood had been erected, and to this contrivance Telion took me. The dark eyes of Galiose fell upon me as I approached.

"Pleased am I to see the matter nearly done," said he to a male who stood beside him. "We have little need now for distractions such as these." Then his eyes went to Telion. "She has been told?"

"Aye, Galiose," Telion nodded. "She has been told."

"Good," Galiose approved, also with a nod, and then those eyes came to me again. "Ceralt dared my displeasure once too often," said he, "and now he finds himself without city and without wench. You shall go to him whom I deem most suitable, for I shall have no further disobedience from you."

I folded my arms beneath my life sign, and returned Galiose look for look. "Jalav shall go to no male," I said. "Galiose shall one fey find himself sthuvad to Hosta warriors, and then shall he learn the foolishness of his actions. Jalav shall never be his to give."

Galiose looked amused. "Jalav is mine to give on the moment," he snorted. "Once the punishment is done, I shall make my decision. Take her to the frame, Telion, before the clouds empty upon us."

"How many is she to be given?" asked Telion, making no move to obey.

"The wench has earned twenty-five strokes," said Galiose in his deep voice. "She will receive what she earned. Take her to the frame."

"Relinor, take her to the frame," said Telion. The male beside him nodded in obedience and grasped my arm, and then was I led to the contrivance of wood. Upon a base of heavy timber stood two high poles, one to each side of the base, yet were they forced to bend toward each other, so that they might be joined at their meeting place with heavy leather. Upon each of the poles had cuffs been placed, one to each pole, and no further adornments. The male Relinor pulled me to the base of the contrivance and upon it, then he saw to the fastening of my wrists within the cuffs.

As in Bellinard, where first I had learned the touch of a lash, I found myself unable to stand flat when cuffed. Surely those to be lashed were meant to have attained a greater height than I, though there were few Midanna who had my size. Perhaps it was males who were meant for the cuffs, yet had I, for the third time, come to such a pass. Little time had I to note the smoothness of the wood beneath my toes, as though many feet had stood there before mine; Relinor captured my flying hair and brought it forward across my shoulders so that it might be knotted below my chin and give the lash no interference, then he stepped away from me. Already did my arms twinge from the strain of the cuffs, and the ice fingers in the wind reached to me and touched my blood to freezing, and then was I touched in another manner. A gasp was forced from my throat as the lash set my back afire, and my hands clawed at the poles to which they were fastened as I rose yet higher on my toes to escape the flames. Worse, far worse, was the actuality than the memory, and I writhed in silent agony as a voice proclaimed, "One." A sound arose from the watching throng, a sound which rose about in waves, lapping with growls and shouts and peals of laughter. Amid the noise the word "two" was lost, yet the stroke itself remained. A second trail of fire marked me, setting down in my flesh a guide way for agony to follow to my soul. Well marked did the trail become, and soon was the ache in my middle a mere nothing, easily overlooked and forgotten in the face of its larger kin of the lash. No sound did I allow to escape my lips, yet my body writhed and sought a means of relief, relief which would not soon appear. Surely did I wish to cry out when no more than "eleven" was to be heard, yet I clung to the memory of being a warrior, and did no more than cry to Mida in my soul. The skies lit to sudden brilliance, blasting the ears with screaming sound, and then the tears of Mida struck together with "twelve," a blessing and damning at once admixed.

In some manner the remaining count advanced itself even in the face of Mida's fury, all sounds from the throng lost to hearing as the rage of Mida roared about and upon those below her skies. The lashing done, still was I pelted by the rain and wind, and when at last I was permitted to crumple to the base of the contrivance, through merging sheets of rain and pain I saw

that none had moved from their place. Nearly awash were Midanna
and males, yet they stood braced against the winds, making no
sounds, their eyes upon a Jalav who could no longer stand erect.
The male Relinor reached toward me where I lay upon the
smooth base of wood, my cheek bruised by too rapid a fall, yet
was he halted by Galiose, who slowly approached and knelt
beside me. The tears of Mida covered his expressionless visage,
and so, too, did they soak within his long, bound hair and blue
covering. A moment he gazed upon me, a large guardsman with
bloodied lash silent behind him, and then his arms reached
toward me, to take me from the wood. Surely had I felt the
touch, I would have been shamed by voicing my pain, yet Mida
spared me such. Quickly, softly, before the male, Mida touched
me with darkness.

# 2.

# A male to be given to—
# and an encounter in the woods

Returning to the light and pain was not pleasant. Mere breathing restored the agony, and my fingers grasped the cloth beneath
them in desperate reflex, wishing the darkness to return. No
darkness came, therefore I attempted to move myself on what I
lay, to perhaps ease the pain in such a manner. A grunt accompanied my effort, and immediately was a hand placed upon my
head.

"Lie still!" came the sharp voice of Phanisar, a surprising
amount of unsteadiness to it. "You are conscious too quickly,

wench. It would have been a greater kindness had you remained insensible."

My eyes opened slowly to the sight of blue cloth beneath me, and in a moment I saw that the cloth covered a platform called "bed." Once before had I seen such blue in such unvaried amounts, and clearly then did I know myself to be in the sleeping room of Galiose, though I knew not why. The silk beneath me was cool and smooth, still possessed of the faint odor of a male. My hair was no longer tied about my throat, but lay piled above my head upon the cloth of the platform. All these things was I aware of but partially, for the raging of my back denied other sensing. The hand of Phanisar removed itself from me, therefore did I turn my head to relieve the pressure upon my bruised left cheek, thereby bringing the males into view. Phanisar stood closest, tall and grayed in his lengthened green covering, the silver sign of an opened eye upon its chain about his neck. Sharply did his dark eyes touch me, strong disapproval upon his long, thin face, and beyond him stood Galiose, still adrip from Mida's tears. The High Seat also inspected his handiwork, for it has been truly said that should one wish a thing done, one must also find the will to look upon it.

"Far too excessive," muttered Phanisar in his disapproval, his gaze unblinking. "Blessed One, the thing should not have been done. A wench is not a man."

"Never was it meant to reach such a pass," said Galiose, also in disapproval. "The lashing was to have ended when she cried out begging it. The stubborn she-lenga refused to cry out."

Galiose grew angry at this further disobedience of mine. I had not wept and begged release as I should have, therefore was the fault of the lashing mine. Unbidden, the laughter began in me, at first a chuckle, then rising and swelling to great gasps and roaring, covering me with amusement without humor. The pain in my back increased as the laughter gained in strength, yet was I unable to halt it. Phanisar came quickly close, as did Galiose, and achingly then did my head ring as Phanisar slapped my face. As quickly come was the laughter gone, and barely was I able to lean my head from the platform before my stomach emptied itself upon the blue floor cloth. Over and again did all heave from me, till at last it was done and I was able to lean back from the vile roundness below and close my eyes. No strength does the lash leave behind it, no more than a trembling in the limbs, a quivering in the soul. I lay still, wishing it were possible to halt the need to breathe for a time, and again a hand touched my hair.

"I have sent for a salve," came Phanisar's voice, moving my hair away from my back. "Once applied, I shall also give you a potion for sleep."

Again his potions. Had I been able, I would have thrown his hand from me. "I wish none of what males offer," I whispered, pained. "Keep what you have for use upon each other. I did not ask to come here. I do not wish your aid."

Deep silence greeted my words, and from it came a dizziness to surround me so that I fairly fainted away.

My wrists were bound with leather when I next opened my eyes. Still I lay face down upon the blue silk, yet had my wrists been bound, separately, to the metal of the platform. Never shall I find ease upon a platform, for the proper place for taking one's rest is upon sleeping leather, flat upon Mida's ground. No more than an ache was there left from the lashing, therefore did I attempt to free my wrists from the leather.

"Lie still," came a voice, yet this time was it Galiose rather than Phanisar. Then came a creak, as of one rising from a seat, and heavy steps approached me. Galiose came to view upon my left, and no longer did he show the signs of Mida's tears, though the sound of them came clearly from beyond the window. Briefly he studied me, then folded his arms across his chest.

"You must lie as you are for some time yet," said he, "for Phanisar would see the salve undisturbed. With his permission shall you be unbound."

"I would be unbound now," said I, of a sudden aware that my hair was held well away from my back by some device. "I do not care to lie here so, nor do I wish my hair as it is."

Annoyance flickered across his broad face, and he looked at me sharply. "You shall remain as you are till Phanisar wishes otherwise," said he, his voice nearly a growl. "How long have you been war leader for your wenches, girl?"

"Nearly three kalod have passed since I slew her who was war leader before me," said I, wondering why he would know. "I do not wish to await Phanisar's pleasure, and would . . ."

"You shall not be released!" he snapped, greater anger growing within him. "Too long have your word and your wishes been unopposed, and such bodes not well for a female. Men have little patience for willful wenches, and a female would be wise to recall the fact, should she wish to avoid punishment!"

"I see little reason to associate with males other than with a sword," said I, my annoyance growing at his. "Does Galiose still refuse to meet Jalav so?"

"Galiose regrets having met Jalav in any manner!" he shouted, fists on hips. "On the morrow shall you be given to Nolthis, a Captain of my Guard, who is foolish in no way save that he wishes the possession of a she-lenga! Then, the Serene Oneness willing, I shall be rid of you!"

"Jalav shall not be given to a male!" I shouted in return, pulling at the leather. "Jalav and the Hosta shall ride free!"

"Jalav goes to Nolthis," he repeated, his anger grown deep and cold. "Inala and I shall pass the darkness elsewhere, for I would not have her disturbed seeing you so. For some cause beyond reason, my woman has a fondness for you. My chamber is now yours."

A final glare did he send before moving from the platform, and then came the sound of a door aswing, interrupting his footsteps. My fury at his words lasted till I recalled my earlier intent, then I groaned most feelingly. The lashing was to have been to a purpose, and now had my foolish tongue seen the purpose undone. Galiose would not take his eyes from me till his male had come, and as surely as Mida ruled her warriors would the High Seat then caution his male to do as he did. Ah, Mida! Is there no way for you to silence your warrior when silence would be best? Perhaps by use of a hand to mouth, as Ceralt had so often— The thought had not come by volition, and quickly did I banish it. No longer had I to think of that male, for he was truly gone. Telion had said so, and no call had Telion to lie. Ceralt was gone, and soon Jalav, too, must be gone. I heard the door swing, yet none entered, therefore did I know that Galiose had left one to see that his word was obeyed. I had thought upon the wisdom of chewing through the leather which bound me, yet now would the effort prove wasted. Mida's tears continued to strike the window in anger, yet was there naught save weariness within me. I rested my head upon the blue silk, and awaited what would come.

Despite all things, the darkness passed most rapidly. Sleep would not stay from me, though I yet lay upon the platform, and no more than a single time did I waken to the ache in my middle. The pain passed quickly, and again sleep took me, allowing no time for thought. Then was there a hand at my hair, and my eyes opened to see the leather and metal of a male quite near. My hair fell free once more, and the male backed a step or two, the better to study me. Large was the male, of a size with Galiose who was also present, possessed of gold-hued hair worn long and bound, green eyes astare at me where I lay bound upon the blue silk. Faintly did I recall the male, having seen him about the dwelling of Galiose, yet I knew him not. Heated indeed was the look he gave to me, yet I turned my face from him in complete disinterest. A chuckle came, and the faint creak of leather.

"High spirited, as I knew," said a voice, presumably that of he of the gold-hued hair. "She shall be a source of amusement and delight. My thanks are boundless, Blessed One."

"Do not be hasty with your thanks, Nolthis," came the voice of Galiose, dry and annoyed. "The wench is completely undisciplined, and stubborn beyond belief. May you have more success with her than Ceralt had."

"I am not Ceralt," came the reply of the male Nolthis, with amusement. "May I take her now?"

"Aye," replied Galiose. "She will be sore from the lashing for some time, yet there is little reason for her not to learn what manner of man she is now the possession of. Phanisar would not have her worked overmuch till her back has begun to heal."

"I shall see to it," said Nolthis, and then were there hands by the leather at my wrists. The leather was removed from the metal, yet left upon me, and then was I pulled from the platform to my feet. There was some slight dizziness in such abrupt movement, as well as familiar pain, yet I gave sound to none of it. Straight did I stand before the grin of Nolthis, the leather to my wrists in his large hand, his eyes arove about me. Behind him, past the window, the tears of Mida continued to rage, yet was his laughter unaffected by it.

"I have wished possession of this wench since first I saw her," said he to Galiose, his eyes unmoving from me. "See how her black eyes flash with hatred and challenge. Those long legs carry fire between them, those large, jutting breasts were made for a man's teeth, that face was meant to be tear-covered, begging a man's favor and mercy. So do I wish to see her, and so shall I see her become. It will not take long, Blessed One."

Galiose made no answer, his broad face expressionless, his eyes seemingly lacking the pleasure he no doubt felt. The male Nolthis was his choice, willing to give that which Galiose would see me have, yet was Jalav no city slave-woman. Jalav would be free of Nolthis, and gone from the Mida-forsaken city. No further did Nolthis speak, and with a bow for Galiose he pulled me from the room by my leather-bound wrists. Through the corridor to the steps was I taken, Nolthis' stride forcing haste upon me, and then down the steps to the lowest level of Galiose's dwelling. Upon this level, I knew, were the places of many males, the males of leather and metal bound to Galiose. To the left of the steps Nolthis went, and great was the amusement of those males we passed. With laughter they hailed Nolthis, remarking upon the sight of the wench hurrying in his wake, and to all he replied with a laugh that the wench hurried to her first proper bedding. The leather s knotted too tightly upon my wrists to allow me to free myself, and so was I taken by the male Nolthis to that place which was his.

The room revealed by the swing of the door was not large, muddy reds and blues and greens and browns darkened still more by the lack of brightening light from the window. Here and there upon the floor cloth lay discarded coverings, weapons belts, strapped footgear, and the like, well-tended weapons alone covering the walls. Much did I wish even one of the weapons within my grasp, yet was such a wish idle. Quickly did Nolthis slide a bar of metal across the door to prevent its swing, and then I was pulled to his sleeping platform, where his foot cleared a space upon the thinning floor cloth. With various sized pots and soiled coverings aside, I was forced to my knees upon the floor cloth, and quickly were my wrists bound behind me.

"We have some hind yet before I must report for duty," said this Nolthis with a grin, straightening from my wrists and beginning to remove his covering. "I shall not take the time and begin slowly with you, for too much time has already been wasted so. Within a matter of feyd shall you obey me completely, for I shall have little patience with you."

I made no answer to the male, fighting the fury within me silently, so that I might find myself unbound the sooner. Instead, I attempted to regain my feet, but this was contrary to the will of the male. With his foot, he knocked me to my side upon the floor cloth, and then was he free of his covering. Broad and hard was his body, scarred with marks of battle, and eager indeed was his maleness for Jalav. Quickly was he upon the cloth beside me, and his muscled arms nearly brought a gasp from me as they circled my back.

"Still feel the lashing, do you?" he chuckled, his hand going to my clan covering without removing it. "A good lashing it was, too, and well deserved. I shall have to procure a lash for my own use, should the need arise. Best you hope you never earn it, wench, for a lashing at my hand will not be as light as that which you received from the High Seat."

His fingers moved below my clan covering, teasing my blood to stirring, yet I felt a quivering of another sort within me. Not again was I willing to face the lash, not again did I wish the agony of its touch, yet was I possessed by one who would joy in its use, one who was eager to see me writhe beneath it. Within my soul a wail began, and the face to whom the wail called was not that of Mida.

"I have heard that you wenches made practice of capturing men and using them for your pleasure," said Nolthis, his hand leaving my body to slowly remove my clan covering. His green eyes looked close upon my face as he spoke, and my covering gone, his hand returned to my body. "I do not care for the sound of such," said he with a grin, "therefore shall I show you that your pleasure is no longer of consequence. You are not yet ready to receive a man, therefore shall the lesson be sharp."

On the cloth was I forced flat upon my belly by him, and then were my hips raised. In such a manner was I first taken by him, his hands hard to my breasts, and naught save pain did he seek to bring to me. My body, unknowing, attempted to respond to his, yet was this not as he wished. No response but resistance did he seek, his strong fingers clamping tight to my nipples to force upon me the need to attempt escape. There was no escape from his driving maleness and determined hands, though in desperation I made the attempt, and much amused was the male by the actions he produced.

"Good," he panted, moving upon me with strength. "Try your will against mine, wench, and learn that much sooner that my will shall prevail. Now shall you be shown another thing."

His maleness left the place he had brought to heat, and then was I stabbed at in another place, a place no male had ever gone to before. In pain and shock I cried out against such use, yet he forced himself within me with laughter. No escape was there from such shaming and pain, no escape from his raucous laughter, no release from the burning need he had begun. The male found full release where he battered against me, not once but twice, yet no relief was I vouchsafed. When sated, he lay back upon the cloth by me, his fingers toying to increase the aching need he had brought, his chuckle filled with full satisfaction.

"I knew the fire burned within you," said he, his other hand holding to my arm to keep me within reach of his fingers. Moaning was I in my need, yet no interest had the male in such. "The fire shall continue to burn, till I see fit to extinguish it," said he. "Come closer now, wench. I would sample the taste of you."

Easily did he pull me to him, so that his teeth and tongue might touch me. No breath had I left in the gasping he produced, and I could not resist the feelings he forced upon me. The moaning would not cease, and when he placed me upon him as he lay upon his back upon the cloth, I attempted to take his reawakened manhood with me, yet he prevented such with great laughter. The hairy belly of him pressed to mine, he kept me from his maleness with his fists in my hair, disallowing more than the faint touch of its end against me. At first, he allowed me to believe I might attain my goal, watching as I, bound tight in his leather, writhed about upon him, yet had he no intention of allowing me to take him. When the strain grew too great upon him, again was I thrown to the cloth upon my belly, to be used as previous, in a manner which gave pleasure solely to him. At long last was his play done, and when once again he was within his coverings, I could not look upon him. Never had I felt such hate for another, never had I so wished to see a male's blood puddled at my feet, to be spat in and left for the children of the wild to relieve themselves in. I lay upon my right side upon the thinning cloth, knowing naught save pain, my knees pressed close to my chin, the male's laughter heavy in my ears.

"Such will have to do us for now, my lellin," said he from where he stood, buckling on his swordbelt. "Later I shall return to continue with your lessons—and my own pleasure. Let us make certain that you shall not fly from my grasp."

With such words he fetched further leather with which to bind my ankles, and then he placed a length of it about my throat, the other end of which was knotted to the metal of his sleeping platform. With a final pat was I left so, bound near to choking, to await his return. No slack was there in the leather, no edge was there to cut it upon, no strength had I to fight its confinement. No more was I able to do than listen to Mida's fury beyond the confines of the room, and ask how I had this time failed her. Truly must her anger with her warrior be great, to allow such a male as Nolthis to possess her. I prayed that the capture was no more than punishment, a matter to be endured till at last it was done. In no other manner would I allow myself to think of it, for I was Hosta, and Midanna. I closed my eyes more tightly and held fast to the memory that I was yet Midanna.

Three further feyd did I pass with Nolthis, each worse than the last. The tears of Mida continued to fall, which brought him

quickly to a foul humor. His hand lashed my face harshly when I
refused to beg his favor, and little liking had he for my lack of
speech to him. Much of the time was I unbound and loudly
challenged to try my strength with him, although Mida taught me
that my strength was not meant to match a male's. When I did
not try him, he laughed aloud and threw me to the cloth, there to
use me in the manner he most preferred. Once, I attempted to
reach a weapon, a thing he had taunted me to try. I had no hope
of reaching it, yet had the trying been necessary, for much did I
wish to send the accursed male to Mida's chains. When caught, I
was beaten with the swordbelt I had nearly had in my hand, a
thing which brought such ill to my unhealed back, yet I cared
not. As I still wore my life sign about my neck to guard my soul,
the thought came that perhaps the male would succeed in ending
my life, an action which would free me from his capture. No
more than pain unending was there from his touch, and high
grew my hatred of all things male.

Dark had come upon the third fey when at last he left me,
bound as always, with a parting kick. Much displeased was he
that duty called him to the ways which ran with mud from rain
without halt, and in his displeasure had he much shamed me.
Though I gave him not the full satisfaction he craved, still was I
continually shamed at his hands, treated as less than slave. Never
had he used me upon his sleeping platform, saying comfort was
not for the likes of me, yet there had he taken his rest as I lay
bound in leather upon the cloth. No word did I dare to speak to
him, for surely had I allowed myself free rein, again a lash
would have touched me.

Upon the third fey, I lay in near darkness with but one small
candle left aglow, and gave thanks that the male would not
return for some hind. Only then and when he slept was I free to
do no more than breathe to my own urging. Upon that instance
was breathing somewhat difficult, for again was the leather
knotted tightly about my throat, yet was breathing so preferable
to the presence of the male. No sound was there but that of the
rain for a number of reckid, and then I heard the slow swing of
the door. My eyes closed, thinking the male had returned to
torment me further, yet was there naught save the sudden indrawing
of breath, and a moment later was a gentle hand placed upon my
shoulder.

"Jalav!" came a voice I knew even in a whisper. "What has
been done to you?"

My head turned and my eyes opened to the face of Inala, she

who had once been slave in Ceralt's dwelling, she who was now chosen woman of the High Seat—and free. Small was Inala, as are all city slave-women, and possessed of dark hair and eyes, yet large were her eyes as she looked upon me, and filled with horror.

"Jalav, what has he done?" she gasped, moving aside her long, slave-woman's covering of green so that she might kneel beside me. "Your face—and your back has not yet even begun to heal! I shall fetch Galiose at once!"

"Inala!" Though I was capable of no more than a croak, the word stayed her. Quickly she returned to my side, and took my face gently in her hands. "Inala, if you would aid me," I whispered, "do not fetch another male to my sight. A dagger hangs upon the wall by the door. Should it be your wish to free me, such would serve."

But a moment did she stare in upset, and then she was gone, immediately to return with the dagger. In three strokes was I freed, and shakily did I raise myself to sit upon the cloth. My wrists were marked from repeated use of the leather to bind me, as were my ankles, but that was nothing beside the constant burning of my back. Again Inala studied me, and then she hastened to fetch the pack she had brought and left by the door. Within was a large leg of roast lellin, cuts of nilno, dark bread still warm, and a small skin of renth. My stomach knotted at sight of the provender, and quickly did I fall upon it.

"Slowly, Jalav!" Inala cautioned, her hand upon my arm as she sat beside me. "Has he kept food from you as well?"

I took a moment to drink from the skin before I made reply. "No food was I given, yet twice was I made to drink of the slave gruel." My eyes went to her shadowy form where she sat, looking upon me with pain, and a thought came. "Inala," said I. "For what reason have you come here?"

Her indignation grew, and her small shoulders squared. "I came knowing Galiose a fool!" she flared angrily. "Often have I asked his permission to visit you, yet has he refused, saying Nolthis had asked that his training of you not be disturbed and undone! Nolthis assured us all that you were well and healing, and that you had begun to obey him! Perhaps a man may be told such fantasies, but not I! This darkness I determined to visit you, and awaited no more than the departure of Nolthis." Again her hand came to my arm, and tears showed in her eyes. "Jalav, are you able to forgive me for not having come sooner?"

Small amusement was there in the place of Nolthis, yet such

brought something of a smile to me. "Inala, my sister," said I quite softly, "I merely thank Mida for allowing you to come as soon as you have. And you, also, do I thank for touching me with your thoughts."

The eyes of Inala filled further with tears. "Ah, Jalav," she sighed. "How may I not think of you? Has not my freedom come about solely because of you? Am I to allow the memory to slip from me as though it never was?"

"Such has occurred many times previous," I murmured, gazing upon the provender with regret. No more than a hand of tastes had I been able to take, yet the renth did best by warming and invigorating me, therefore I pushed the provender away, yet retained the skin. I sat cross-legged upon the cloth, for long had it been since I had been able to do so.

"Jalav," said Inala, "much has occurred since the arrival of the Silla. Would you hear of it?" At my nod, she composed herself to speak further. "No other clashes have occurred between Silla and Hosta," said she, sober-faced, "yet all believe that once the weather clears there shall be further battle. Galiose intends to instruct Nolthis to bring his well-trained Jalav to speak before the Hosta, bidding them to accept the Silla as sisters, and such, I believe, is the why of his taking the word of Nolthis. Galiose craves control of the Hosta through their war leader."

"He shall not have it," said I, drinking again from the skin. "Jalav would stand before Mida in shame sooner than betray the Hosta."

"Galiose does not understand," said she with a sigh of sadness. "No woman has ever dared to disobey him. Even I—" Again she sighed, and then she shook the thought from her. "In any event, the Silla are not pleased to find themselves in Ranistard, and wish only the opportunity of meeting with the Hosta with weapons in hand. Galiose thought to impose his will upon the Silla war leader, yet has the one who was looked upon as war leader in some manner departed from the city with perhaps ten others, having taken the lives of a number of men in their going. The weather does well to cloak one's movements, and the Silla are not without skill."

Wordlessly I nodded, thinking upon the Silla. Less than faith are the Silla trash, yet are they not unskilled.

"The Hosta have been disciplined for the incident of the feast," continued Inala. "None may appear in public now, save upon a leash held firmly by her man. Many have felt the leather for their doing, yet harshest has been Fayan's lot. Galiose has once again freed Nidisar, and has given her punishment to him to see to. Nidisar proved unreluctant to accept the commission, and Fayan was most upset.''

Inala's eyes seemed disturbed, but that was not unexpected. Ever and again is the spear cast, and at each new cast is one's lot in life in peril of abrupt reversal. Such was known to Fayan, yet had she acted as circumstances demanded, thinking naught of future consequences. In such a manner must all Midanna conduct themselves, meeting action to circumstance, for easily might they be beside Mida before a consequence might presume to touch them. I offered the skin for Inala's use, yet she refused it with a shake of her head.

"There is one further matter which is most disturbing," said she, large dark eyes upon me. "Galiose does not speak of it, yet has his sleep been marked by it. Telion has not left his house since your lashing, and has not replied to Galiose's order to attend him. He does not refuse the order, he merely ignores it, and Galiose seems loathe to press the matter.''

"Galiose, by his actions, should have been Hosta," I remarked, and then rose to my feet. Much of my strength was still lacking, but the renth had aided me to attempt that which must be done.

"You now leave Ranistard," said Inala, gazing up at me from where she sat. There had been no questioning to her tone, for she knew what I must be about.

"There is Mida's work yet to be done," said I, looking about. "Should Mida smile upon her warrior, I shall one fey return.''

"In truth?" asked she, rising also to her feet. "I would not care to believe that we should never see one another again.''

Most anxiously did the small female stand, looking to me for an assurance that she would find herself able to believe. I smiled in memory of our odd, short friendship, and placed my hand upon her shoulder.

"We shall surely meet again," said I, "for Galiose has not seen the last of me. Once he called me a trial imposed upon him for his sins, and such shall I prove myself to be.''

At her smile of amusement, I walked to where my clan covering lay, thrown aside by Nolthis three feyd earlier, and donned it. Clan colors give a Midanna a sense of belonging, the knowledge that her sisters shall ever stand by her side. In clan colors do Midanna enter battle eagerly, for they fight to Mida's glory and to the glory of their clan. No sword was there in Nolthis' place, therefore I took no weapons save the dagger, which Inala had used to free me, placing it in the leg bands about my right leg. Snuggly did the dagger fit so, and so it should have. For many kalod had I worn a dagger so, before the coming of the males of Ranistard. A long length of leather lay in a corner, seemingly forgotten by Nolthis, and such did I also take, for there were yet the walls of Ranistard to scale. As I turned from coiling the leather, I saw that Inala had replaced the provender and the renth within the pack.

"You must eat upon your journey," said Inala with a smile, "and no need is there for you to begin upon uncooked meat with such as this available. Care for yourself, Jalav, for I feel that your journey will not be an easy one."

She looked upon me with true friendship, and such did I also feel for her. Small city slave-woman though she was, easily might she have been welcomed as true Hosta. I placed the coiled leather within the pack, and then looked upon her most sternly.

"Speak to no one of your coming here this fey," I ordered as war leader to warrior. "Galiose would not be quick to forgive such an action, and Nolthis would surely seek revenge. Should you find yourself at the mercy of Nolthis, with Galiose, in his anger, uncaring, little comfort would the thought of my freedom bring you."

A shiver made her small frame quiver, and a brief look of fear crossed her features. "I had no thought of the matter in such a way," she replied unsteadily. "I shall be sure to say naught of my visit."

One last time did we each place a hand upon the other's shoulder, and then I took the pack and went toward the door. It's swing revealed the darkened corridors free of life, therefore did I see Inala upon her way before taking to the shadows. Upon a previous occasion had I left the dwelling of the High Seat unobserved, but the difficulty then was slightly greater. None were there about within the pink stone of the dwelling, no other foot trod the blue floor cloth, yet when I had passed sufficient torches in silver sconces and sufficient blue silk upon the stone of the walls, the window twice left ajar was ajar no longer. Firmly had it been shut against the tears of Mida, and firmly did it remain shut against my efforts to open it. Nearly had I decided to seek another means of egress from the dwelling, when my eyes fell upon a small bit of metal upon the window. The metal pushed down against the window, refusing it movement, and no further effort than a touch of a finger freed the window from its grasp. Easily, then, I climbed through to the bushes without, and no longer saw Jalav a captive to males.

Long was the way to the vicinity of the city walls where they nearly touched dwellings which might be stood upon, and much difficulty did I find with the tears of Mida. Cold and penetrating were the rains, immediately soaking my clan covering and hair, and quickly setting me to shivering. Never before had I felt rains of such a coldness, for beyond the Dennin river to the south was the air sweet and warm, the rains gentle and refreshing. The north held much cold within it, the rains contained small bits of ice, and my back howled from coming in contact with such. Some protection did my hair provide, yet not enough to bring an easing of pain, and with difficulty I pulled myself and pack to the metal-topped city walls, and thence to the ground below. Nearly did I meet the ground more quickly than I had intended, for the rains turned the leather slick and difficult to hold, yet the knots I had placed within the leather proved themselves worthy, and at last I stood in rain and darkness, without the walls of Ranistard. Regretting the need to take the time, yet nevertheless taking it, I coaxed the leather down to where I stood, then moved away from the city of hate.

The driving rains disallowed even Hosta eyes to see what lay about, yet had I memory of the area from when my warriors and I had gone seeking the third of Mida's Crystals. Many hind travel to the south lay the forests which stood between Ranistard and Bellinard, and such was the direction in which I wished to travel, yet would it be unwise to be found in the open, should Nolthis come upon kan-back hunting me. I, afoot, would have little chance of remaining uncaptured, and surely would the males ride directly south in pursuit of me. Wiser would it be to walk north, to the beginning of forest there, for in that direction safety lay no more than a hin or two away. Easily might I observe Ranistard from there, for the gate lay clear to its view, and should the male Nolthis ride forth, I had only to await his return to begin my journey in greater peace. So had I seen the matter, and so would I see it done.

Many hind was it before I had attained the first of the trees. Keeping true direction in the raging storm had proven well nigh

impossible, and quickly had I lost all sense of where I stood. My
strength, far from adequate, had imposed a further burden, and
surely would I have been completely lost had not Mida lit the
skies before me in an instant of anger, showing that the forests I
sought lay well to the left of my direction of travel. Cold, wet,
aching and weary, I stumbled toward my briefly revealed goal,
and at long last were there the looming shadows of giant trees
about me. Some distance farther did I force myself before I
sought shelter, and then Mida truly smiled upon me. In the
darkness and rain, I tripped upon an unseen obstacle, and slipped
to my hands and knees in the mud. Unsure of whether I possessed the strength to rise again, I put my hand out to the trunk
of the tree beside me, discovering a small hole in the trunk, with
hollow behind it. Easily had the rains found all beneath it, yet
was the hollow surprisingly dry, offering shelter from the elements.
No sooner had I lain myself upon the ground in the hollow, than
all things faded from sensing.

The sounds of the children of the wild roused me, and achingly I peered out of my shelter to see that the rains had ceased,
and a thin golden light streamed down through the trees. The
light stood close to its highest, and by that did I know that I had
not slept, but lay unconscious the time. Hosta do not sleep past
first light, yet had I lain as though dead the while, and perhaps
such was not far from truth. Still did I feel the cold most sharply,
and to my greater pain had some strands of my hair attached
themselves to my back. With one motion, I wrenched them free,
then groped with shaking hands for the skin of renth, and drank
deeply. Then, and only then, was I able to force myself to feed
upon a small bit of the nilno.

At last I crawled from the hollow, marking its location as I
looked about, for there had I left the pack, and there would I
return come darkness. In no way had my strength grown, as I
had hoped it would, however that could not deter me. Ranistard
had not been watched as it should have been, and such would
delay me yet further. Feyd must I now spend watching for the
return of those who might have already gone, yet perhaps the
time might be spent restoring myself. The way to the lands of the
Midanna was long, and no easy trek would it prove to be. Best I
begin when most able, for many of the children of the wild give
no more than a single chance at survival. Only those who are
able may take advantage of the chance.

To my surprise, I found that I had come farther into the forests than I had at first thought. Marking my way as I went, I began to search for the forest's edge, for all track of the previous darkness had been washed away by Mida's tears. The feeble glow of the light did little to warm me as I went, and little did I know how deaf and blind I had grown in the city. No more than three hands of reckid did I move through the trees before they stepped out to view, surrounding me without my having had the least idea of their presence. Two hands of Silla warriors were they, and one who had not yet had the silver ring placed within her left ear, though she stood nevertheless as war leader. Swords they wore, and daggers, and each carried a slim-shafted spear such as males of the cities were fond of. I had only a dagger in my leg bands and little taste to appreciate the pleasure of battle. The Silla grinned in pleased anticipation, weighing spears in hands, yet I only folded my arms beneath my life sign, awaiting an indication of their intent. Silla were not known for their love of single combat, yet the possibility of such remained. Should it be Mida's will, still might I enter her realm with sword in hand.

She who was war leader in place of Zolin stood perhaps seven paces from me and studied me with something of a smile upon her face. Red of hair was this Silla, of a red like that of Larid, and eyes also of a similar blue. Her height did not match mine, yet was she far from the puniness of city slave-women. Full Midanna was the Silla, well-versed in the weapons she wore, proud of the red of her clan colors. A moment did she study me, and then she laughed in full amusement.

"You looked well beneath the lash, Hosta," she called, causing her warriors to join her laughter. "Hosta are fit for naught save the lash of males—or Silla swords. Should you have followed us to betray us to your city-male masters, you shall not live to do so."

"Jalav is no slave," I called in return. "All save Silla have the wit to know this. I come to the forests upon my own affairs."

The Silla's face had darkened at my words, then she snorted. "City slave-women such as the Hosta have become do not belong in the forests," said she, her head held high. "For whatever reason you have come, Helis will see that you regret it."

She began to gesture to her warriors. "Should Helis wish true leadership of the Silla, she may choose to face Jalav," I called.

The attention of all centered upon me, and more firmly did they grasp the spears which they held. No closer than four paces

did any of the Silla stand. Helis gazed upon me sober-eyed and
stiffly, for Zolin had been a warrior of repute, and great would
be the fame of Helis among the Silla, should she slay the one
who had bested Zolin. Surely did I know that I would not
survive such an encounter, for I was not as I had been when I
had faced Zolin, yet I could not choose simple slaughter above
holding a sword in hand once more. Helis continued to study me
a moment, and then she drew herself up.

"The Hosta are well known for their empty boasting," said
she in disgust. "Never would Zolin fall before one such as you,
and there shall be payment for the suggestion! Yet I choose to be
generous. You may have your throat opened upon the instant, as
the low sednet you are, or you may walk the lines. Choose!"

About to demand that Helis face me, I saw that all words
would be futile. In opposition her spoken sentiments, Helis
did indeed believe that Zolin had fallen before my blade, and
therefore had no stomach to do the same. That she would
undoubtedly triumph she did not know, and I could not inform
her of the fact. Perhaps alone she might have been swayed to
place a sword in my grasp so that she might say with truth that
we had faced one another, yet with these others about, the effort
would indeed be futile. Angrily she stood, awaiting my decision,
yet little choice was there to the matter. A Hosta does not seek
an easy death, and with the walking of the lines would my fate
be placed in the hands of Mida.

"There is naught else to choose save the lines," I informed
the Silla. "Thought you I would choose otherwise?"

Her eyes held mine for the moment, and then she laughed
shortly. "Who may know what the Hosta are capable of?" said
she, a low grin upon her face. "At the end of the lines shall I
await you, Hosta war leader. Come to me if you are able."

Then she stepped back a bit farther as her warriors moved
forward to form the lines. Two hands of Silla warriors were
they, one hand to each side of the aisle formed between them,
their leader placed at the far end, awaiting me with folded arms.
A pace before Helis was a sword placed, point in the ground and
hilt up, also awaiting me. Should I survive the walk well enough,
the sword would be mine to take, and then might I earn the
honor of death in battle. No matter of survival was the walking
of the lines, yet was it a means of choosing the manner of one's
death. A warrior strong enough would die with glory, yet had
my strength been severely drained. Only through Mida's will
would I find myself able to reach the sword and Helis, yet are

not all things done through Mida's will? As the Silla warriors lowered their spears, I prepared myself to meet them.

"Begin your walk," called Helis from the far end, and in truth there was naught else I might do. To the lines of waiting, grinning warriors I walked, and then slowly between them. The first warrior on my left chose to put the point of her spear in my left thigh, the warrior on the right choosing my right arm. The touch of sharpened metal was full, true pain to my body, and nearly did I stagger as the spears were removed, giving free run to my blood. The second warriors in line reversed their choices, and the golden light danced before my eyes, rippling in a cadence with the beat of my heart and the pain washing over me.

"Excellent, Hosta!" called Helis with a laugh, as I nearly went down to the touch of metal in my sides. "You are almost here, and have but four more spears to pass!"

Still could I see the sword I so desperately wished to reach, yet it seemed to recede with each step I took. My blood flowed swiftly to Mida's ground, for though the wounds were not meant to kill, neither were they gentle, meaningless scratches. A spear entered my right calf, breaking my staggering pace, and then I fell, coming to Mida's ground upon hands and knees. The Silla laughed in deep amusement as I gasped for breath which would not come, crawling toward the waiting sword, and those toward the end urged me on in turn, their prodding nearly unfelt in the vast agony surrounding me. Mida's light glared in my blurring vision, damp and stony was the ground beneath me, uncaring was the breeze upon the wet of my wounds, and then had I nearly reached the sword, my sweat mingling with blood and dirt. No more had I to do than put a hand out to claim the sword, yet I was unable to lift the hand. My red-stained, straining fingers grasped the dirt as I attempted to force my body to my will, yet no farther could my body go. Slowly I collapsed to the ground entirely, the sword completely beyond my ability to possess it, and the Silla laughter came strange and distant to my ears.

"A pity," said the voice of Helis, a voice which echoed about the swirling mists before my eyes. "Now must the Hosta be ended without glory, though truth to tell, I believe she may already be ended. Linid, see if there is yet life within her, and if so, remove it with your dagger."

No steps did I hear approach me, yet a hand touched my throat, seeking sign of life. That I yet lived would not long continue as a state, yet no touch of a dagger came. Naught was I able to see through the mists, little did I hear; I suddenly felt abandoned, and then the ground trembled to the urging of many hooves. I knew then that a large force had come, sending the Silla to the cover of the trees, yet I was unable to know to whom the force belonged. In my heart, I wished it to be sister Midanna, come to free the Hosta from the grip of Ranistard, yet the mists swirled too thickly for my senses to pierce them. Too low had my strength gone, too faint was the spirit yet within me, and then I felt the touch of hands, by the size and shape of them, male hands. A laugh bubbled in my throat, knowing the males too late to once again possess Jalav, too late to attempt to work their will upon her. A murmur of deep voices came, no words clear to my hearing, and then Mida came, to wrap me in final darkness.

# 3.

# An awakening—
# and a tale is told

Strange are the dreams a warrior finds before entry to Mida's Realm. Much darkness was there, and a sense of searching, for something never found, no more than darkness again appearing. I felt movement, and surprisingly also pain, then the pain receded to throbbing, yet the movement continued. Once I saw the form of the male surrounded by darkness, his entire demeanor one of disapproval and anger, and I laughed at his displeasure, pleased that I need no longer be troubled by males. The form stiffened in anger at my laughter and began to raise an arm in menace, yet was he restrained by another presence, who was amused. No part of the second presence did I see, yet was I made curious by its amusement, and then both male and presence faded from my perceiving. No understanding had I of what had transpired, then the darkness came once more, ending speculation.

At last my eyes opened to find that it was not Mida's Realm which met my gaze. To accompany the feeling of movement, I saw the wood and cloth of a conveyance of those of the cities, a conveyance which was taken about by kand pulling upon it. Brown and old was the wood, stained and fraying was the cloth which enclosed the conveyance, and great was the creaking as the conveyance protested its movement. Belly down I lay in lenga pelts, the warmth of the long, silky fur keeping the chill at bay, and not far from the pelts I lay in were other pelts, just then untenanted. Wide enough was the floor of the conveyance to hold the two sets of pelts with perhaps a pace between them; I was unable to see the length of the thing, nor anything more. I was disturbed that I had not yet attained Mida's Realm, yet when I attempted to turn in the furs, surely did I think that attainment was not far from me. Pain and weakness tore at me so, that I was unable to keep from voicing a groan, and then the dizziness came again, bringing with it the darkness.

When the darkness did not recede all the way, I knew that it was not within me, but all about. The conveyance stood at last at rest, and more urgently did I wish to know in whose possession I was. Not those males of Ranistard could it have been, for the city did not lie so far from the woods where I was taken that a conveyance would be needed to bring me to it. Others, strangers, had found me, and faintly I heard the small sounds of the movements within a camp. In determination I moved my leaden limbs, slowly and painfully yet with purpose, till at last I had turned from my belly to my back. No lessening of pain was such a position but an increase, yet I wished it no other way. The first of movements was most painful, yet without the first of movements were all others lost. If I were to escape these males who had found me, a beginning must be made. Lightheaded did I feel, and my insides lurched about, yet had I made something of a beginning.

Once my breathing had slowed, I also made certain discoveries. Bound in cloth was most of my body, principally upon the tracks of the Silla spears, and damp did certain of the cloth seem, as though my blood yet flowed beneath it. A wide, uncomfortable lump beneath my right shoulder proved to be my hair, twisted together in some manner to contain it and all I could do was pry it from beneath me, the action again leaving me breathless. No strength at all had I, with the wounds from the spear thrusts added to my previous weakness. I knew not why I yet lived, save that such was Mida's will. That Mida was not yet done with her warrior seemed of little comfort, but I was unable to argue the matter. Even had I the strength, Mida was not one who was easily approachable.

In my new position I was able to see the sky, tiny lights atwinkle in the frosty darkness, for the cloth gapped about an opening at the far end of the conveyance. For a number of reckid I lay silent and unmoving among the shadows, my eyes upon the sky, my grasp upon consciousness a frail thing, and then I saw a stronger glow than the tiny lights, which approached the gap in the cloth from without. The leather-clad form of a male appeared.

"What have you done?" snapped the male, looking upon me with severity as he placed a metal-enclosed flame upon the floor by my furs. "As I placed you, so should you have remained! Have you not the wit to know how sorely hurt you are?"

"Jalav asks the aid of no male," I whispered creakingly, seeing the surprise in his light eyes. "Return me to the care of Mida, and my actions shall not disturb you."

The male stared, and then his sternness turned to a chuckle of amusement. "By the enlightening glow of the Serene Oneness, you are a handful indeed," he grinned. "I now no longer doubt your survival, and look forward to the journey to the Snows. Foolish was I to question the signs, for never have they been so clear." His touch upon my face could not be avoided. "Good," said he in satisfaction, withdrawing his hand. "The fever is gone, allowing one less matter for concern. Now let us see what you have done to the wounds."

He moved aside the lenga pelt, allowing the chill to draw all warmth from me, and a frown displaced his amusement.

"Again does the blood flow from three," he growled, bringing those light eyes to pierce me with disapproval. "I shall change the bandages upon them, wench, and then are you to remain unmoving till they have had opportunity to heal! Do you think you body's blood unlimited that you waste it in such a manner?"

The cold made me shiver and the male quickly replaced the lenga pelt upon me, then rested his forearms upon his thighs.

"You, I know, are Jalav," said he, "and now do I see why

the sign of you was so fitting. Indeed do you seem a hadat, all teeth and claws and temper. I shall expect no thanks for healing you, just as I would expect none from a hadat, yet shall I expect something of respect and obedience. Though hadat is your sign upon the Snows, you are only female in flesh.''

"Jalav is a warrior," I whispered, teeth still ashiver. "Even should I survive the walking of the lines, you shall not own me, male.''

Lightly did he laugh at hearing my words, and his head shook in negation. "You mistake me, warrior," said he with a grin. "I am merely here to see to your healing and the reading of the Snows. Your ownership belongs to another, one who shall have it no other way. Best you understand that, for his humor has been rather dark of late. He dislikes what the Snows have told him, yet he may do naught save follow their beckoning. Are you hungry?''

Indeed my insides felt as though they touched at all points, yet were there other matters to be discussed first. "I wish naught from males," I rasped, disliking his grin. "Who is this male who presumes to call me his?''

His grin widened, and he laughed. "The male is one who is fond of hadats," said he, rising out of his crouch. "He rides now to see to our backtrail with a number of our Belsayah, yet shall he present himself upon his return. First shall I fetch nourishment for you, then shall I change the bandages.''

With those words the male turned from me and left the conveyance, also leaving behind much to think upon. I knew naught of males called Belsayah, nor did I know the meaning of the word, "snows", which the male had spoken a number of times. Seemingly, the male knew of me, yet how could this be? These thoughts occupied me till the return of the male, who then carried a pot of metal from which the aroma of nilno arose. Carefully did he carry the pot, showing the contents spillable, and then was it brought to me. The meaty aroma caught me so, no resistance did I make to the male's arm about my shoulder, raising my head for the easier reach of the pot. The taste and warmth of the nilno broth more than compensated for the discomfort. Down my throat it slid, filling my hollow insides, though I was unable to take it all. Much too quickly did I reach the limit of my capacity, and regret was mine when the male had lowered me once again to the furs.

"When you are strong enough to hold meat and vegetables,

the healing shall progress at a faster pace," said he, putting aside the pot. "Now for the wounds."

From a place behind the other lenga pelts, he took a pot and a pack which proved to contain cloth, and both things did he bring to where I lay. Then he withdrew my left arm from beneath the furs, and began to remove the bloody cloth upon it. Little pain was there till but one layer of cloth was left upon the wound, and then the cloth attempted to cling to the flesh of me.

"Steady," said the male, compassion clear in his tone. "The rest shall be easier to bear." Scraping sounds did I hear then, and cool smoothness touched the flaming ache upon my arm. "My name is Lialt," said he as his fingers did their work. "How did you come by wounds such as these, girl? Never have I seen their like not made by a spear."

"Indeed it was spears which made them," I gasped, fighting dizziness. "I walked the lines for the Silla trash, yet was I unable to take the sword." I spoke of my shame without giving thought to it.

"Spears?" echoed he called Lialt, his fingers unmoving upon my arm. "Sword? What might a female have to do with such things? And who are these men called Silla who would so misuse a woman?"

Through the dizziness laughter arose within me, thinking of the fury the Silla would feel had they heard themselves called males. "The Silla are not males, but warriors such as I," I informed Lialt weakly, yet with the remembrance of a grin. "Silla shall ever do a Hosta so when they may, for so would Hosta do them, had we the opportunity. Silla and Hosta be blood enemies."

"Blood, indeed," muttered this Lialt, again bending to his task. "Never have I heard of females acting so, and never would Belsayah allow such. My brother must truly be a child of the Snows that he takes such a woman as you for his own. With scores of proper Belsayah women aburn for him—" Abruptly did his words end, and he sighed. "Yet, how may a man avoid his path through the Snows? I, better than any, should know the futility of such an attempt. Brace yourself now, wench, for I must see to the other wounds."

Again was the lenga pelt moved from me, and his hands banished all thoughts of the cold. The last I saw was his dark head bent over me, a frown creasing his face, and then the light was no more.

I awoke to the jostling movement of the conveyance, the light of the fey having returned as I lay within a darkness of my own. Again was I belly down within the furs, and annoyance touched me that I had been turned so once more. I would know as much as I might of where the males took me, for the return trek would be mine alone. Slowly and carefully, I turned to my back, and this second movement was much the easier. Nearly gone was the pain in my back, and the spear wounds troubled me less as well. Soon would Jalav again be fit to travel, and then would the males seek her in vain.

To my disappointment, there was as little to see upon my back as upon my belly. I moved my toes about within the pelts as I studied the skies, and quickly the sway and creak of the conveyance caused my eyelids to grow heavy. I must have slept heavily all fey, for the next I knew, all was silence about, and the flame within the metal again approached. As the instance previous, Lialt carried the flame to where I lay, his light eyes examining me closely.

"I know not whether to be pleased or not that you are again awake," said he with familiar disapproval as he crouched beside me. "Though two feyd have passed since your last awakening, you should not be moving about so. Have I not said this to you?"

Quite sternly did the male look upon me, and easily might it be seen that my position must be made clear to him. Although the male had been of some assistance, I no longer wished the bother of him. With some small difficulty I removed my arm from beneath the lenga pelts so that I might move the pelts away from my face.

"Jalav thanks you for your previous assistance, male," I informed him with curtesy. "Now shall Jalav see to herself, and should it be possible to return the favor, it shall be done."

"Shall it," he murmured, and then he snorted in amusement. "Jalav is far from able to see to herself, wench, and she shall obey Lialt till she is up and about. Let us first see what damage you have done to the wounds, and then we shall see to your feeding."

His hands moved toward the lenga pelt, yet I closed my fist about it, disallowing movement. "I have said that I shall see to myself!" I snapped, disliking his manner. "Have you naught else to occupy you that you must remain where you are unwelcome? Leave me, and we shall say no more upon it! The war leader of the Hosta of the Midanna demands to be left in Mida's peace!"

"No," came a deep, calm voice before Lialt had found his tongue. "The former war leader Jalav may no longer demand. In future, she shall ask for that which she wishes, and in a proper manner more becoming to a wench."

Surely did I know to whom the voice belonged, and surely had I known for some time that it was he, yet had I refused to admit my knowledge as I then refused to look upon him. My eyes upon the leather covering of Lialt, I shook my head and whispered, "No!" and then attempted to raise myself from the pelts. Lialt's large hands were immediately upon my arms, forcing me down, and my small store of strength was uselessly spent.

"She is the spawn of Sigurr, Ceralt!" said Lialt in vexation, astare upon my face. "See how she has paled through overtaxing herself so! This darkness I shall read the Snows again, for surely she cannot be the one they speak of!"

"She is the one," replied Ceralt, coming nearer to where I lay. Still did I keep my eyes from him, and the cold of the darkness entered me more fully. "She is the one," said he, "and I knew of it even before the Snows spoke of it to you. How does she fare?"

Lialt made a sharp sound of annoyance. "How may I know?" he demanded. "She will not allow me to look upon her! What is this matter of war leader of which she speaks? What means it?"

"It means naught," said Ceralt, "for the condition no longer applies. Jalav. Remove your hands from the lenga pelt so that Lialt may see to you."

My fingers gripped the pelt, holding it to me, my weakness a curse upon my will. Slowly, with reluctance, my eyes raised to him. He, too, wore leather of the sort which Lialt wore, and strange did he seem without the city-male covering of cloth. Such strange feelings did the sight of him bring to me, feelings which a warrior was not meant to know. I shook my head once more and again whispered, "No!" and my meaning was not lost upon him.

"You may not deny it," said he, crouching beside Lialt. "You are mine, and shall ever be so. Had you not left Ranistard by your own devices, I would have taken you from there."

Then his hands went to mine and gently removed the pelt from the clutch of my fingers. I had the will to attempt to pull from his grip, yet was I even more lacking in strength than usual. Lialt removed the pelt and looked upon the cloth bindings, grunting in approval when no blood was to be seen upon them, and after considerable inspection, he replaced the pelt. Ceralt's eyes had been upon me as well, the set of his jaw and the tightening of his grip speaking well of his disturbance, and then his eyes moved to mine.

"Never again shall such a thing occur," he vowed raspingly, my hands yet in his possession, his anger clear. "Not again shall Jalav take weapon in hand, for whatever reason!"

Slightly did I move in his grip and return his lowering look. "Jalav had no weapon in hand," said I distinctly. "Think you such would have come to be, had I a sword to wield?"

"No sword, no spear, no dagger shall Jalav again touch," spoke Ceralt, light eyes cold, not to be swayed from his purpose. "Remember my words, wench, for they shall not be told you again." Then his gaze went to Lialt. "How does she fare, brother?"

"Better than I had expected," replied Lialt as he studied me. "She heals with a rapidity which is gratifying, though rather difficult to understand."

"It is the doing of Mida," I informed him with sureness. "Easily might it be seen that there is yet work she would have me see to."

The last was for Ceralt, so that he might know that the possession of Jalav was Mida's alone, yet the miserable male smiled faintly and placed my hands beneath the lenga pelt. "Indeed there is yet work for Jalav to see to," said he, anod at Lialt. "Jalav shall learn humility, and curtesy of manner, and the ways of the proper woman. And Jalav will also learn the pleasing of Ceralt."

Lialt's laughter joined Ceralt's smile, and the fury rose within me. So sure was the male, so sure that again I might be taken and held by him, yet I clearly remembered that which had gone before.

"Jalav shall learn naught save the return path to the lands of the Midanna," I choked out in the midst of their amusement. "Not again shall males find opportunity to betray her. Not again!"

"What number of times did the lash touch you?" came Ceralt's voice, soft with deadly menace. "What is the size of the thing between Galiose and me?"

No answer did I make to him, for Galiose would find himself repaid by my hand, should Mida allow me such pleasure.

"Perhaps it is unwise to speak now of such matters," came the voice of Lialt. "She has not sufficient strength for memories such as those—which by the looks of her, must be painful indeed. I shall fetch her a bowl of broth, and then she must sleep again.''

''The matter is yours to determine, brother,'' replied Ceralt amid the sounds of movement. ''She must be recovered before the Snows indicate the time for the journey, else I shall not allow her to accompany us.''

A pause was there, and then Lialt said, ''Yet without her presence, the journey shall not succeed. Clearly was this shown me, Ceralt. Should she remain behind, our lives may well be forfeit.''

''Then it shall be so,'' said Ceralt, a final inflexibility to his voice. ''Should she lack the strength to survive the journey, she will not go. Her life shall not be thrown away.''

''Many are the lives at stake,'' said Lialt with a softness, ''yet the decision is yours to make, brother. I may do no more than search out the paths in the Snows. It is your lot to choose among them, and pleased am I to have it so.''

With those words did Lialt depart, and strange did such words seem. Was Ceralt not a city male of Bellinard, as all had supposed? For what reason would a male present himself so, speaking not of those from whom he came? Perhaps the male felt shame at his beginnings, a thing truly fitting for males. Midanna felt pride in their clans, and never would they renounce their roots through shame. Soulless did all males seem to be, whether of cities or elsewhere.

Though Ceralt yet remained, no longer was I able to lie upon my side. The spears of the Silla had touched deep in arm, leg and side, and the pain flamed with increased anger as my weight pushed the wounds to the lenga pelt. Reluctantly, I turned again to my back, left hand going to right arm, yet naught did my fingers come upon save the rough cloth which bound the wound. No strength had I left to deny the pain, and it set me begging to Mida for the surcease of darkness.

''In time the pain will ease,'' said Ceralt, his voice soft yet echoing the ache, his hand moving to the moisture upon my brow. ''Only in childbed was a woman meant to know such pain, for only then has the pain meaning and purpose. I would know what befell you.''

My head, beneath his hand, turned somewhat to find his eyes soberly upon me. Such pleasure had I had from him, the pleasure of his manhood and the simpler pleasure of his presence, yet must I thrust the memory of all such from me, for males were evil and sought naught save the betrayal of warriors.

"Jalav wishes naught of your presence, male," I informed him huskily, seeking the strength to take my eyes from his broad, familiar face. "No word shall Jalav address to you, no word and no thought. Much would I have preferred to have been left where I had fallen."

Deep hurt flashed briefly in his light eyes, and then those eyes studied me a moment before his hand withdrew from my brow. "You are much wounded and sorely in need of rest," he said quite softly, a small catch to his voice. "We shall speak again when some measure of strength has returned to you."

Then he rose from his crouch and left the conveyance, his step slow and heavy, his eyes not again turning toward me. Swiftly did I close my eyes to erase all sight of him, yet was there a trembling within me. Naught might a male mean to a warrior, naught did Ceralt mean to me! Pain had the male given me, and betrayal in all things, and none save a fool would allow the memory of strong arms and soft lips to wipe meaning from what had gone before! Weakling wetness seeped from between my closed lids to roll to my cheeks, shaming me by their presence, yet was I unable to stem the flow.

"Has the pain worsened?" asked the voice of Lialt from beside me, startling in its nearness. Large fingers brushed at my cheeks, spreading the wetness, and then his hand smoothed my hair. "The wench Jalav is as brave as she is beautiful," he murmured in a soothing manner. "Surely so brave a wench will not allow the pain to best her when soon it shall be gone completely? Weep as you must, wench, but do not despair. Lialt will see that you grow well again."

My eyes opened to see his face but blurrily, and angrily I wiped at the weakling wetness. "Jalav does not weep!" I snapped, yet the words emerged hoarsely, in a whisper. "Warriors of the Midanna do not weep, male, and easily shall I grow strong again without your aid!"

"Certainly you shall," said he in a manner most conciliatory, his hand yet astroke upon my hair. "Soon shall my aid be unnecessary, yet now must I continue to supply it, for I would not have Ceralt grow angry with me. Come, the broth will strengthen you, and prepare you for the meat which will quickly replace it."

Again he lifted my shoulders and brought the metal pot to my lips, and in no manner was I able to deny his wishes. My belly ached for the warmth and satisfaction of the broth, and easily might it be seen that I was unable to do so simple a thing as hold the light metal pot. My hands shook in the attempt even as I swallowed all that came past my lips, and Lialt's voice murmured soothingly and with encouragement, calling me a good, brave girl, and a beautiful wench. Filled with indignation, I attempted to berate him for such terms, yet the broth did not cease to fill my mouth, making speech impossible. At last was the bottom of the bowl to be found, and Lialt lowered my shoulders to the lenga pelt with much of a large grin.

"I am pleased to see that your capacity increases," said he as he put the bowl aside. "Such is ever a good sign. We shall now put you upon your face again, so that I may tend to your back."

His hands reached toward me, and my annoyance grew even higher than it had earlier been. The word of a war leader meant naught to males, yet had it been many kalod since any had sought to oppose me, and never had any attempted to order me about. Greatly displeased was I with the way of males, and this, I felt, should be made known to Lialt.

"This back you speak of," said I, halting the motion of his hands. "Undoubtedly it is your own back you refer to, is this not so?"

A frown creased his face, and puzzlement entered the light eyes of him. "Certainly not," he replied, his tone filled with lack of understanding. "Have you forgotten, wench, that it was you who felt the lash? The back which needs tending is yours."

"Ah," said I, nodding quite soberly. "The back in discussion, then, is mine and not yours. And yet I have no memory of being asked my wishes in the matter. Does this not seem exceedingly strange?"

Closely did I look upon him, and comprehension was not long in reaching him. The puzzlement faded from his eyes, to be replaced with something of annoyance, and wryly did he shake his head.

"I see," he said, resting his forearms upon his thighs. "Again you seek to be difficult. Have you never been taught simple obedience?"

Again this preoccupation with obedience. All males seemed to be obsessed with the matter, and totally did I lack understanding of their views.

"A Hosta war leader need be obedient to none save Mida," I informed him, and then looked upon him with curiosity. "Lialt, for what reason does a male ever expect obedience? Never have I demanded obedience from a male, save when he was captive to my clan, yet do all males demand obedience from me. The why of this I am unable to fathom."

He laughed. "You speak as though you have almost no knowledge of men," he mused, his eyes upon my face. "Surely your father demanded obedience from you, and taught you that you would one fey obey the man who chose you, as well."

"I know naught of the sthuvad who served she who bore me," I shrugged, seeing that my words disturbed him. "A mere captive was he, and gone about his business the moment he found release from the leather which bound him. Such is the way Hosta wish it to be, and your words hold no meaning to me."

"Nor do your words hold meaning to me," he murmured with head ashake. "That you have had no teaching from men is clear, yet the why of it is beyond me. However," and deeply did he sigh, "I shall do my best to explain whatever is unclear to you."

He shifted from his crouch to sit cross-legged upon the wood of the floor, and then he briefly smoothed my hair before taking my face in his hand.

"You," said he, as though he spoke to one who had little understanding of our common tongue, "are a young, female member of this our race. With infinite wisdom did the Serene Oneness decree that females must be obedient to males, and so would all men have it. Perhaps when you have grown old and gray, younger men may heed what wisdom you have attained from your kalod of life, yet is such a state far from that which you may now expect. For the moment you are a female child who must learn to obey the word of men, else shall you ever find punishment at their hands. Has the matter been made clear to you?"

So serious did Lialt seem, that I could only laugh. "Such is foolishness," I informed him with amusement as his hand left my face. "Never have I heard of such a decree, nor would it apply to one who follows Mida. Now do I see it as the foolishness of males, fit only to be laughed at by warriors. My thanks, Lialt, for having given me the explanation which I sought."

Greatly vexed was Lialt then. "You have heard naught of what was told you!" he growled angrily, his face stern. "The wench before me is no more than that—merely a wench! You shall obey as do other wenches, else shall you be punished as they!"

His anger caught greater confusion within me. "For what reason are males to be obeyed?" I asked. "Why should females not be obeyed in their stead?"

Open-mouthed he stared at me, and then his mouth closed in outrage. "Men are ever obeyed by their women!" he snapped, one hand agesture in vagueness. "Females are emptyheaded and filled with nonsense, and ever unable to decide upon questions put to them! Should men find cause to obey females, never would the females have wit enough to direct them properly!"

"What difficulty is there in directing others?" I asked, feeling sure there was some matter still beyond my comprehension. "For three kalod have I directed the actions of the Hosta, and only twice did I find the need to answer disagreement with a sword. Your objections do not seem valid."

Much pained did Lialt's expression grow, and his hand ran through his hair in the gesture Ceralt had so often used.

"Never before have I had such difficulty in expressing myself," he muttered, his head ashake. "I think it best, Jalav, that these matters be discussed with Ceralt. I feel sure he shall find the answers you seek with much less difficulty than I. There remains but one further matter to be discussed between us, and the answering of it should not prove difficult to one of your exalted standing. Your back must be tended if it is to heal properly, and I shall see it tended to. Should you not wish to assist in your turning, I believe we shall both find that I am possessed of more than enough strength to see the thing done without your assistance. I will know this moment how you would have it: are you to turn or be turned?"

Amusement had once again returned to him, yet was I not of a humor to share it. Ever do males see their will done through naught save greater strength, reason finding itself totally beyond them. Bleakly did I look upon the grin he gave me, and had I stood, I would have held my head high.

"Jalav has little choice in the matter," said I quite frostily. "Yet shall it not ever remain so. Lialt had best learn to sleep lightly."

With difficulty, I began to turn to my belly, yet was I able to see the grin fade abruptly from the face of the male as I struggled, and the breath of him drew in sharply.

"By the fetid breath of Sigurr the foul, I do believe the wench has threatened me!" he muttered. No further attention did I pay to his ramblings, for movement proved itself more difficult than I had anticipated. Sharply did the spear wounds stab at my efforts, and I felt the moisture break over my face as I panted and nearly gasped. Abruptly were there two strong yet gentle hands to assist my scrabbling, and then I lay belly down, drained of everything within me, yet untouched by the darkness which would have been most welcome.

"I had not meant for you to do the thing yourself," said Lialt softly, and then was there a cloth at my face to take the moisture. My eyes had closed of their own, and little desire had I to open them once more, therefore did I naught save lie as I was as that about me slowly returned to awareness with the ebbing of the pain.

Lialt sat upon the other lenga pelts and began to remove the furs from about his legs. Each did he draw from him, then he stood the two upon the wood beyond the lenga pelts. With this done, he stood to remove the leather shirt of him, the belt of metal, the leather leg coverings, and lastly, the leather breech, and easily might it be seen that Lialt was well made as a male. Faintly did my interest stir, as ever is a warrior's interest stirred at sight of an acceptable male, yet was such interest considerably curtailed by the presence of my wounds. Lialt tossed the breech upon the pile of the other of his coverings, and then his eyes crossed mine as I looked upon him in contemplation. Amusement showed at the corners of his mouth, and he folded his arms upon his broad, dark-haired chest.

"Have I been found acceptable?" he asked with faint laughter in his tone. "I should dislike to think that sight of my body has displeased you."

"Lialt need have no fear," I murmured, the shadow of a smile of appreciation touching me. "Should you ever be taken as sthuvad to Midanna, your body shall not displease them."

With full truth did I speak then, for Lialt was made much as Ceralt was. Tall and broad, firm muscled beneath the dark of his skin, flat-bellied, slim-hipped, possessed of a manhood much in evidence even when unaroused. Easily did I recall the look of Ceralt when first he and his hunters had fallen to my Hosta, the heat that had come to him at touch of my body upon his, the heat that he, too, had caused to rise in me. Before my eyes stood the memory of Ceralt, disallowing sight of all else, disallowing banishment from my thoughts, the light eyes of him holding my gaze as none other was able to do. Again was I touched by feelings which a warrior was not meant to know, and the lenga pelt beneath me became a broad, dark-haired chest, rising and falling in rhythm, warm with life, precious by cause of the shortness of the time I had been allowed to hold to it without bitterness. Slowly, I rubbed my cheek upon the chest that was not, and again it was naught save a lenga pelt, warm yet lifeless, too soft and too smooth to be that which I had briefly imagined it. Sight, too, returned, and I saw that Lialt was now between his lenga pelts, having moved himself there without my having seen.

"So you are returned," he murmured, his eyes upon me as he lay upon his side. "What other did you see when you looked upon me? And where did he take you that you return with such sadness clear in your eyes? Had I my pipe to hand, I would have journeyed with you."

I looked upon him with little understanding, yet did I know that I wished to keep my thoughts my own. Deeply did Lialt gaze upon me, so deeply that surely it seemed he would soon be as deep within my mind, and such was not that which I wished. With deliberation, I pulled my eyes from his, breaking some link before it might grow to strength, and shakily I drew a breath.

"Fascinating," he breathed, though he made no movement within his pelts. "Few indeed are those who are able to dismiss the demands of my call so. A child of the Snows are you in truth, a fitting mate for my brother. I am now even more pleased that our arrival in your need was so timely."

Strange, again, were his words, of a strangeness to make my head whirl, but I did understand one thing.

"From whence do you come?" I asked, raising my eyes once more to his shadowy form. "And how did you come to be near Ranistard when you were?" Also did I wish to ask of Ceralt, yet was I unable to speak his name without faltering. Lialt smiled faintly, and then he reached toward the flame within the metal and drew it to him.

"The tale is an odd one," he said, "yet I shall be pleased to tell it to you—though not with the lamp alight. We are both of us in need of sleep, and should one or the other succumb to its lure, the tale may be completed at another time."

In some manner did he then open the frame and with his single breath the darkness surrounded us completely. Then came the sound of the metal returned to its place, and Lialt's voice resumed.

"Nearly a kalod ago," said he, "the Snows gave sign of a strange insistance. We were told, it seemed, that our High Rider must travel from us, and take residence for a time with those of the south. No understanding had we for the why of this, and none cared overmuch for it, yet were we unable to delay and question. All signs, all indications, insisted that our High Rider leave at once and without explanation. Ceralt asked my estimation of the importance of the journey, and I was able to add naught to what I had already read—he must leave for the south immediately.

"Ceralt was not pleased; however he knew that all men must go as the Snows reveal, therefore did he leave me as temporary High Rider, and take himself off to the south. He chose the city of Bellinard as his destination, for he saw some small attraction in the name—Bellinard for a Belsayah Rider— and naught did we hear of him for some time; then the Snows brought to me a further message—concerning the need of our High Rider.

"Ceralt would require the presence of his riders, said the Snows, and therefore were they to ride at once to the southern city of Ranistard. Yet Ceralt had gone to the city of Bellinard, all protested, wherefore the need to go to Ranistard? None knew, least of all I, yet was I sure of what I had read. Immediately, I mounted fifty riders, and we all took ourselves toward the city spoken of by the Snows, the city of Ranistard, yet was I somewhat unsure of an open approach, therefore did we leave the road for the woods when yet a fey's ride from our destination. It was then that we came upon Ceralt."

A sigh escaped him then, almost unnoticed by me, for the soothing sound of his voice had caused my eyelids to grow extremely heavy. No thought was I able to give that which I was told, merely was I able to hear the words and possibly remember them, and difficult was it to resist the softness and comfort of the pelts about me. Afloat in the darkness, the voice disembodied continued.

"Ceralt had been in the woods for three feyd and more, afoot yet attempting to reach the Belsayah. Easily might it be seen that he had been beaten, and all our riders called for the blood of those responsible, yet Ceralt quieted them, saying there was more important work to be done. There was a possession of his yet to be found in Ranistard, said he, and such was he bound to fetch from there, no matter who would stand in his way. I wished to halt for a time, to see to Ceralt's bruises, yet he would have none of it. No further time did he take then to don proper clothing, and then we were off once more.

"Through the darkness we rode, and through a good portion of the new light, still within the woods, and then we glimpsed that which seemed a group of people. Immediately we turned toward the group, yet they vanished into the trees all about—all save one. That one lay upon the ground, giving her lifeblood to quench the thirst of the soil, and then we learned that before us was the one whom we sought. Ceralt sent two of our riders to purchase a wagon from Ranistard, instructing them to say naught of their origins nor purpose, and when they returned, we began the homeward journey. Shortly shall we reach our village once more, and then must we prepare for the journey spoken of to us so long ago. The journey set in the Snows even before our birth. Much danger. Yet we must go.''

Slowly, Lialt's voice ceased, and soft breathing spoke of his having been taken by sleep. Warm and compelling were the furs and darkness about me, more compelling than thoughts of that which I had been told. Deeper did the darkness grow, and I, too, was taken as Lialt.

# 4.

# A struggle for motion— and a destination is reached

The new fey was well begun before I became aware of it. Again were Lialt's furs untenanted, and again was the conveyance about me in creaking motion. Having first seen to the matter of turning to my back—an exertion becoming increasingly less difficult—I then spent considerable thought upon that which I had been told. Much of it held little or no meaning, for still did I lack knowledge of that which Lialt had termed, ''Snows,'' yet it seemed that Ceralt, who stood high among his people, had been sent from them by cause of duty. I knew not what such duty entailed, nor did I know what manner of journey both he and Lialt saw for me, yet had I the thought that again I was of value to Ceralt as an item of trade. That he had said I would not undertake the journey spoken of save that I had regained my strength meant naught, for often did it appear that my value to Ceralt was a many-sided thing, one side to be weighed against another, that side of most value ever prevailing. The light of the fey came weakly through the opening in the cloth of the conveyance, bright yet much thinned from that which I knew in the lands of the Midanna. Soon indeed would I grow strong once more and then would I leave the lands of males who ever sought for value, never again to return, never again to ride from that place where Mida smiled upon her warriors. Would that I could have left upon the moment.

That fey and four others were spent upon the trail, yet was I unable to put further questions to Lialt. Much of the first fey I spent in sleep, yet when I had finished the broth brought by Lialt at darkness, again he instructed me to attempt sleep. Much annoyed, I refused to do so, wishing instead to put my queries, yet the male refused as well, saying that *he* wished sleep and would have it though I remained awake the entire darkness. No further words would he address to me, merely removing his leathers silently and with purpose, yet it seemed that much of his amusement at my appreciation of the male sight of him had gone. In annoyance did he look upon my appraisal, and then he frowned.

"Have you never been taught the impertinence of such inspection?" he demanded, wide fists upon slim hips. "At first I had thought you looked upon me in curiosity, never having seen a man naked before you, yet do I now perceive a difference. Much does it seem as though you stare with practiced eye, though that would not be likely. In future, you will turn your head when I disrobe, as a proper wench should."

Quite disturbed did Lialt seem, and quickly did he place himself within the pelts, yet I felt considerable confusion.

"For what reason must I turn my head?" I asked, moving to my left side to see him more easily. "Lialt does not possess a body of ugliness, therefore it is unclear to me why I may not look upon it."

Such a strange expression grew upon the face of Lialt that surely did I feel concern for his health. Full flushed his face became to underscore the unnamable expression, and wide-eyed did he stare upon me.

"In the name of the Serene Oneness, am I fated to ever have the wench put such questions to me?" he demanded of the air about us. "Perhaps it would be best to put the matter thusly,"

said he to me in a manner most precise, his light eyes seriously
upon me. "Would it please you to stand bare before me when I
have not so much as smiled upon you, not to speak of drawn you
from the circle?"

Again was my confusion increased, yet had I learned time and
again that confusion was ever the preferred circumstance of
males, and a warrior did well overlooking strange utterances.
Therefore I sought not to give meaning to the meaningless, but
gave answer to what I might.

"It is the purpose of a male to be pleasing in the eyes of a
warrior," I explained as precisely as had he, moving some small
bit in the furs to ease the wounds. "Should a male please a
warrior, for what reason would she object to his also finding
pleasure in the sight of her? It is only when the male is displeasing
that she might object. Do you feel yourself displeasing to me,
Lialt?"

Naught save a deep groan greeted my words, for Lialt had put
his head down upon his furs, his arms afold upon his face, his
body unmoving. Then came mumbling sounds, as though Lialt
spoke to the arms upon his face, yet naught intelligible came to
me. Abruptly, then, he removed arms from face and turned to
reach for the flame within the metal. Again a single breath
pitched us to full darkness, and only then did Lialt speak so that
I might hear him.

"Wench, I shall say no more than one further thing upon the
matter," came his angered voice, "and then there shall be
silence! It is the place of the female to be pleasing to the male,
not the other way about! You shall obey my wishes as I put them
to you, and I shall have no further questions of the sort you have
already attempted! In time shall you learn all which was never
taught you earlier, and now we will sleep!"

There came the soft sound of Lialt's movement within his
furs, but no further words. In annoyance, I moved within my
own furs, for Lialt's words did not sit well with me. No call had
there been for him to speak so, yet what reasons do males
require for what they do? All warriors know well the lack of
reason behind the actions of males, and as Lialt wished no
further questions, so would he also receive no further explanations.
Upon such a decision did I seek my own sleep within the
darkness, and despite all, had little difficulty in finding it.

Upon the following day, with the light at its highest, the
conveyance halted a short time, and then Lialt brought to me a
bit of nilno, cut small and awash in broth. Both did I feed upon

with great pleasure, and no notice did Lialt take to the fact that I spoke no word to him. When I had finished with the nilno, the journey once more resumed, halting again at darkness. A larger portion of boiled nilno and various vegetables, principally soft, white fellin tubers and green gemild, was this time presented me, and much strength began to flow from the provender to my body. Still was I weak as a lenga cub, yet was I able to know that my wounds were on the mend. Ceralt made no further appearances; Lialt seemed pleased that I spoke not, and so did it go, for two further feyd. No more than twice did Lialt look upon the wounds beneath the cloth, and each time he grunted in satisfaction, saying no word, yet seeming pleased. Jalav attempted no denial of such treatment, for Jalav had not the strength to hold sword in hand, yet such would not continue forever. When Jalav was well, Lialt would speak words of apology upon his knees, a point of sharpened metal resting upon his throat. So had I seen it, and so would it be.

With the light of the fourth fey came an awakening to a feeling of renewed ability. Much did I feel that Mida had once again smiled upon me, for greatly lessened was the pain in both limbs and body. The conveyance once more creaked upon its way, and easily did the solitude tempt me to try my new-found strength. Slowly, for otherwise would be foolishness, I raised myself to sitting upon the lenga pelt, and though some effort was necessary, the position was at last mine. Some dizziness visited me, and also was the ice-tinged air a discomfort, yet I sat where I had formerly lain, the pain increased nowhere save within my legs and thighs. Gingerly, I touched the cloth upon my right leg, debating the wisdom of removing it and the rest so that the wounds might be bared to the sight of Mida, allowing her to better promote their healing, yet did I see that such a course of action would be unnecessary. Well did Mida know of my wounds, for how else had I thus far healed? Far better to leave the cloth as it was a time, and see first to other things.

Too chill was the air to move about bare as I was, therefore did I wrap myself within the top lenga pelt before I began to make my way to the gap in the cloth at the far end of the conveyance. Somewhat littered with dirt and leaves was the wooden floor of the conveyance, yet I pulled myself through it, one fingerlength each time, sweat forming upon my forehead and between my breasts from the effort. The distance had not at first seemed far, little more than half the entire six pace length of the conveyance, yet when I halted to rest and judge my progress, no closer than two paces was I to the opening. Resolutely I lowered my head once more, and resumed my crawl.

Many long, painful reckid later, I lay at last beneath the opening in the cloth. My breath came in gasps, shaking my now aching body with its violence, my arms and legs flaming with angry pain which turned them leaden, yet had my goal now been reached. My back, too, throbbed somewhat, yet not as badly as it once had, and such gave me great encouragement. I know not how long I lay unmoving beneath the opening, setting my attention upon the creaking movement about me. Only do I know that quite some time passed before I was able to force my cheek from the dirty, vibrating wood. One hand holding the lenga pelt about me, I used the other to pull myself to my knees by the raised wooden side of the conveyance, and at last was I able to see what was about me.

Through deeply forested and untenanted lands we moved, the gray-blue skies bright above tall, shedding trees. Of red and gold and orange were the leaves of those trees, those that yet hung upon branches, yet vastly more lay upon the ground beside bushes of bare branches, cold fire in the chill of a land with warmth gone away. Beside and behind the conveyance, at some small distance, rode more than four hands of males, clad as Lialt and Ceralt had been, in leathers and belts of shining metal. Little notice did I take of the males themselves, for their mounts quickly grasped my attention. Warriors rode scaled and clawed gandod, city males rode long-maned and hoofed kand, yet these males, called Belsayah riders by Lialt, rode great beasts whose like I had never before seen. Fully half again as large as kand and gandod were the beasts, of a white so pure that nearly did one's eyes burn to look upon them, and long was the fur upon them, thick and silky and magnificent. No leather seats such as those used by city males were upon them, these Belsayah males making do with single, broad straps about the beasts' bellies and backs, and also there were no reins. A single length of thin leather, looped about the beast's nose and thereupon leading back to the rider's hand, sufficed as control. Highly spirited did the mounts appear, yet their riders controlled them with small difficulty.

Aching were the wounds in my thighs as I, upon my knees, gazed out at that which surrounded me, but I did not go back to my place. Bright was the light which shone down upon the males and their mounts and the landscape all about, yet bleak was the feeling within me, for I knew naught of the strange land through which I moved. Far distant were the lands of the Hosta, the lands of my sisters and my birth, and greater grew the distance with each pace and length we traveled. Long would it be before I once again looked upon the face of Rilas, Keeper of our clans of the Midanna, and I wondered if ever I would again look upon her. Against the chill, I pulled the lenga pelt closer so that I might huddle within it, alone as a Hosta had never before been, alone and helpless among enemies. Was I destined to once again ride free, or had I been given into the hands of males forever? The cold put a great shuddering upon me, and the bleakness of the fey in my heart rose to overwhelm me.

In no more than a hand of reckid was my new-found strength gone, and wearily I lowered myself to the wooden floor once more, and lay where I had not the ability to move from. Great was the ache in which I was wrapped, and deep was my despair, and surely did I wish to give myself over to hopelessness and defeat; however surrender was not possible while I yet lived, no matter how enticing the idea. With difficulty I attempted to regain what I might of strength.

Quickly must exhausted sleep have claimed me, for the first I knew of the halt of the conveyance was the sound of Lialt's voice, raised in outraged exclamation above me. Slowly, I opened my eyes to see his angered face, hanging within the opening above where I lay, the balance of his body still without the conveyance.

"What have you done?" he demanded, stepping across me to enter the conveyance. In his hand was a metal bowl, and quickly did he place it beside the other lenga pelt which was mine before returning to where I lay. With no effort was I lifted in his arms, and a moment later was I placed again upon the pelt which I had left so long before. Lialt seemed angry as he unwrapped me from the pelt I had taken with me, and examined my wounds. When all was done and the pelt again placed upon me, Lialt's light, accusing eyes moved to my face. Though there had been no blood beneath the cloth, still was the male grim with disapproval.

"Now I shall know what foolishness possessed you to attempt such a thing!" he growled, a fist upon his knees. "The Serene Oneness alone must have kept the wounds from opening, and I care little for seeing my work so casually undone! For what senseless, female reason do you move about the wagon, wench?"

Much did Lialt's words anger me, and much would I have joyed in deriding his actions as he did mine, yet was I still not of

a mind to address him. Stonily, silently, I returned his glare, and
greatly did his anger grow.

"I will have an answer!" he shouted, taking my face in his
large hand. "What did you think to accomplish other than your
own destruction? Even one so clearly marked by the Snows as
you are cannot be thought to be indestructible! Speak to me,
wench, else shall I see you soundly punished!"

"What has happened?" came Ceralt's voice, and then the
second male entered the conveyance and approached us. Still did
Lialt look upon me sourly, and with much anger did he turn his
head to Ceralt.

"Brother, the wench's stubbornness is not to be borne!" he
snapped. "At the wagon's entrance did I find her, insensible
from the effort necessary to reach it, yet does she refuse to speak
of her purpose in doing such a thing! Am I to labor at restoring
her, merely to see her spit upon my council? So willful a child
surely begs to be punished, and wise would you be to see it
done!"

Ceralt did not immediately reply, yet his eyes came to me,
sharp with displeasure and disapproval. Many times had the male
looked upon me so, and each time had I in some manner
regretted the look, for Ceralt had not hesitated to make his
displeasure known. Uncomfortably, I moved within the lenga
pelts, and slowly Ceralt nodded.

"Indeed she shall be punished," he murmured thoughtfully.
"First must she be made well. Has she eaten as yet?"

"No," responded Lialt, having been reminded of the bowl he
had fetched. Immediately was the bowl retrieved, and then were
its contents fed to me, Lialt's arm tight about my shoulders.
Little stomach had I for the thin nilno stew, yet was I made to
take all of it, Ceralt's low-browed eyes not moving from me the
while. Sternly did I berate myself for allowing such treatment to
be done to a Hosta war leader, yet Ceralt was not Lialt, and well
did I know this. With the stew done and Lialt's arm gone from
around me, I turned to my right to take my sight from the males
till they had gone, yet such was not quickly forthcoming.

"I shall ride with her till we have reached our village," said
Ceralt amid the sounds of rising. "Once there, she will not have
further opportunity for disobedience."

"I feel you are much too optimistic, brother," Lialt returned,
a sour dryness to his tone. "The wench is one who will make her
own opportunity."

No further words were exchanged, Lialt departed, and Ceralt

settled himself in broad silence. Heavy was the stew within me, causing discomfort, yet greater was the discomfort of Ceralt's presence. Fully did I feel his eyes upon me, and much did I wish to rise and leave, even would I have crawled willingly to escape, but such an attempt would have brought his hands to me, a thing I could not bear. As the conveyance again creaked to motion, I set myself upon my belly, my face turned away from him, and begged Mida for the release of sleep. Surely must I have at last found favor in her eyes, for quickly did the sleep come.

The halt of the conveyance wakened me to find that darkness had once again fallen, yet was the darkness filled with much sound and movement as had not heretofore been the case. Torches blinked in movement in the darkness, voices called one to another, laughter flowed in greeting, footfalls approached and moved about. No longer uninhabited was the darkness without, and I moved myself to sitting, hoping for some view of those who surrounded us.

"Stay as you are," came the voice of Ceralt from the near darkness, and then was the sound of his movement. "You shall have sight of your new home soon enough."

"My place is with Midanna," I muttered, more to myself than to the male. It was a thought I must keep firmly with me, one to hold to in the presence of this male. No answer did he make, and no time was there for the heavy cold to enter my uncovered backbone, for then came Lialt to the opening with a metal-enclosed flame, and quickly did I learn the reason for his remaining without the conveyance. In one motion was I lifted in Ceralt's arms, both furs surrounding me, and then was I carried toward where Lialt awaited us.

"There is no weight left to you," muttered Ceralt in disapproval as he moved carefully to the opening. "The stronger you grow, the more I shall see you eat to return the flesh to your bones. I do not care to see you so."

His light eyes did not look upon me, for he studied his path, and most grateful was I for that. Even in the dimness was I able to see the cords in his neck, unstrained by my weight, leading to his shoulders, one of which I now rested against. Surely had I the choice, I would once again have walked the lines rather than remain so near to him, yet was the choice not mine. One broad hand rested against my side, not far from where a Silla spear had touched me, and surely was the touch of that hand the more painful of the two. Nearly lost to such thought was I, therefore did I turn my gaze to where we went, if only to save my sanity.

Lialt retreated a step to allow Ceralt exit, and many were the
folk who stood all about us, gazing with approval upon the male
who held me. Many dwellings were there about us also, difficult
to see in the darkness, and then were there many males moving
near, cutting off view of all else. Large were these males, dark
of hair and skin as Ceralt and Lialt, and also clad as they, in
leathers and belts of silver, yet none others seemed to have the
light eyes of my captors. Dark-eyed were they, as dark-eyed as
I, and the eyes of one seemed to be dark with anger as well.
Fully as large as Ceralt was this male, though with many more
kalod to his age, and angrily did he push forward before the
grinning welcome of the others.

"What means this?" demanded the male of Ceralt, his hand
awave toward the conveyance and myself. "Has our High Rider
become so fond of city ways that he must return with tainted city
women? For shame, Ceralt! I had thought better of you!"

Very slightly did Ceralt's hold upon me tighten, though his
gaze upon the other male held naught save mildness. "In truth,
Uncle, I had not known I held such esteem in your thoughts,"
said he, and the skin of the other darkened in the torchlight.
"Nevertheless," continued Ceralt with mildness, "I would set
your mind at rest. The wench is no city woman, but is the one
spoken of by the Snows. Should her health return with sufficient
rapidity, she shall ride upon the journey of the Snows, in company with Lialt and myself."

"Indeed, she has not the look of a city female," the uncle said
low, his forehead awrinkle. "Should she truly be the one spoken
of by the Snows, she shall be welcomed," the male allowed
stiffly. "Such, however, remains to be seen. In whose halyar is
she to dwell till the time of questioning?"

Again Ceralt's grip upon me tightened. "She shall dwell in
my halyar," said he, nearly as stiffly as the other had spoken.
"The wench now belongs to me."

Much muttering again arose with the announcement, and many
gasps from the females who stood behind the males accompanied
it as well. Defiantly Ceralt stood in the face of all, and near to
explosion did the male before him seem.

"I shall do no more than ask the required questions," choked
the male, his fists clenched tightly at his sides, perhaps to keep
them from the knife at his belt. Greatly disturbed was he, for no
reason easily apparent. "From what circle was she drawn?" he
demanded. "Before which elder was this accomplished? With
what approval did her father look upon these acts?"

With teeth clenched Ceralt stood before those demands, angered yet voiceless. Little understanding had I of what eventuated between these two, yet I knew the look of one who was an enemy. He called uncle was not fond of Ceralt, and surely did Ceralt mean to defy him in some manner, yet Lialt approached his brother and placed hand upon arm before further words might be spoken.

"Ceralt, it is not wise to gainsay custom," advised Lialt softly, a compassionate look to his eyes. "All may be properly seen to with the blessing of the Serene Oneness. Surely, there is little need at the moment to defy the oldest custom of our people? The girl will not be prepared to receive you for some time."

Unmoving was Ceralt, seemingly unhearing as well, and then his eyes came to me. Much had I disliked his claimed ownership of me, and such must he have seen in my own eyes, for capitulation came to him then, and slowly he nodded.

"Very well," said he, his voice weary. "It shall be as custom demands, and I shall draw her from the circle in due time. Now must we find a halyar for her as quickly as possible. I would have her out of the cold as she is not accustomed to it."

"Desslar's halyar is as yet untenanted," offered a voice from those males who stood about. "With a bit of cleaning, it should do her."

"The cleaning is not immediately necessary," said Ceralt with a nod. "Do you go now, Cimilan, and light one fire." The male nodded and left at a run, and Ceralt turned his gaze to the male called uncle. "In this shall matters go as you wish, Uncle," said he to the tight-lipped male. "Do not presume to think it shall ever be so. I am High Rider in my father's place not merely through birth."

Such coldness was there in Ceralt's tone that the male before him did not attempt to give further voice to his outrage. For a moment the two stood eye to eye, and then the older male reluctantly backed a pace. He who held me took the path silently, with shoulders straight, and many males with torches accompanied us, leaving he called uncle to stand within the darkness. With deliberation was I carried to a small dwelling, all of dark-appearing wood, and then inside. He who had been called Cimilan had begun a small blaze in the fireplace in a corner of the room, and little was there to be seen by it, save the bare surrounding of the single room. Stale and musty was the air in the dwelling, speaking clearly of its previous emptiness, and all in all, I liked it not. The tents of the Hosta gave none of the trapped, closed-in feel that this dwelling did, and much like the dwellings of those of the cities was it, soulless and not for those who are fond of freedom. Despite the cold of the air of the darkness, I determined that I would not long stay in a dwelling such as that.

Gently did Ceralt place me upon the wooden floor not far from the fire, and a moment later Lialt appeared, a wooden bowl in his hands, a skin of water hung over his shoulder. First I drank from the skin, for a great thirst had overtaken me, and then I fed from the contents of the bowl. Undoubtedly not nilno was the meat cut up therein, yet was it edible to some small degree, being much too well cooked by the fire. Somewhat discomforted was I as I fed, for the males with torches stood about silently, eyeing me with an interest I could not fathom. No more than my shoulders and cloth-bound arms were visible about the lenga pelt, yet did they stare upon me where I lay against Lialt's arm, being fed the cuts of meat. At last, I would have no more of such stares, and firmly refused the balance of the meat, thinking to be rid of the males along with the remnants of the meal. Lialt was not pleased with my decision, yet he accepted it, spilling the meat from the bowl before taking a thin fold of cloth from his leather chest covering, and emptying its contents in the place of the meat. When water was added to that which had been in the cloth, I grew apprehensive, recalling the many potions given me at various times by males, and attempted to deny the drink, yet Lialt and Ceralt would have none of it. Easily did they force the drink upon me, holding me unmoving as I choked and sputtered, and then a great weariness came up from my feet, covering me heavily till at last I knew no more.

# 5.

# A new place of capture—
# and a questioning by males

Foul was the taste in my mouth when I awakened to the new light coming through dingy windows. I lay upon my back a moment, recalling with anger the potion which had been forced upon me, wondering as to its purpose. Though the fire burned high and hot not far from where I lay, no other remained within the room to feed it. Perhaps the potion had merely been meant to cause sleep to take me, yet I could not fail to remember the slave-potion Ceralt and the other males of Bellinard had used to capture the Hosta in their own home tents. Devious are males, and seldom forthright, and unhappy was the fey that first saw their paths entwined with those of warriors.

Crossly, I moved myself to sitting, and then found the air within the dwelling much less chill by cause of the warmth of the fire. I threw the covering pelt from me, firstly to increase my comfort, and secondly to examine the state of my wounds. As soon as my legs were again able to bear my weight, I would find some manner of escaping the hold of these males and returning to my own land.

Slowly and clumsily I unwrapped the cloth from about my right calf. The wound upon my leg showed itself only partially healed, a raw, red slash still clear evidence of the one-time presence of a Silla spear. Easily might Helis have allowed me a sword, yet the Silla war leader had not chosen to do so, choosing

instead to await me at the end of the lines. Should she and I ever
face one another again, sorely would she regret her former
actions. All do act through the will of Mida, yet ofttimes Mida
does no more than allow us our choice of actions—and their
consequences. Helis had had her choice of actions, and one fey,
Mida willing, the consequences would also be hers.

Abruptly, then, the door to the dwelling opened, allowing in a
gust of cold air along with the form of a young female. Dark of
hair and eyes was this female, of a size slightly greater than
other city females, and strangely clad was she. No cloth was her
covering but leather, closed to either side of her body by long
leather ties, and about her waist was a belt of copper-colored
metal, hugging the leather to her and displaying her form beneath it. The covering itself fell only to her knees, for below it,
rising from her feet, were fur wrappings of the sort Lialt and
Ceralt had worn.

"But you are not to sit up!" the female blurted, her pretty
face distressed as she stepped the closer. "And what have you
done to the bandage? Oh, Lialt will be furious!" Quickly she
glanced at the door. "Lialt will be here in no more than a
moment," she fussed, seemingly in consternation. "Come, I
will assist you in replacing the furs before his appearance."

"Jalav does not care for the orders of strangers," I informed
the female, my eyes holding her once-again widened ones. "Jalav
shall replace the covering when it is her wish to do so."

Though my tone had held naught save mild annoyance, surely
did the female behave as though faced with sword-threat. Carefully,
her hand left the pelt I yet held, and in a slow scrabbling manner
she backed away from where I sat. Her face, though she had the
kalod to be a fully blooded warrior, appeared to be that of a
child, frightened, unsure, open and vulnerable.

In a thin, quivering voice she began, "I did not mean to—"
and then her eyes fell upon my wound. Pale she grew, and even
more unsteady, and again the large, dark eyes returned to me. "I
had not known what manner of hurt you had sustained," she
whispered, clearly touched. "The pain must hold you in constant
grip. How might such a thing have come to be?"

Little understanding had I of the female's actions, yet did I
feel as though I spoke with a child of the clans, one far from
knowledge of warriorhood and the ways of Mida. No warrior
might honorably feel anger toward one such, nor does a warrior
heap upon such a child knowledge which it is unnecessary for

her to have. Never would the one before me prove a warrior, therefore had I little reason to give detail which would frighten.

"The manner of arrival of such things is unimportant." I shrugged, attempting a soothing smile. "Rest assured that the wounds heal well and rapidly, and soon shall be no more. How are you called, girl?"

"I am Tarla," said she quite eagerly, her face brightening. "I am most pleased to know you, Jalav, and I shall come each fey to see to your comfort. May I do you some service now?"

This female appeared as eager to please as my male Fideran had been, and surely did the thought cause me to smile in amusement. Not often is a Hosta warrior served so by a female, and never had I known such service till it became necessary to move among the places of males. Males are ever unable to fend for themselves, ever in need of one to do for them. This Tarla seemed well suited to the needs of males, and had undoubtedly been trained by them to be so. Child though she was, still was she a slave-woman to males, as are most city females, and now had her services been offered to me.

The thought came that a water skin might be well received by my throat, and just as I began to voice the thought the door opened once again, bringing a breath of cold and Lialt within side by side. Lialt quickly closed the door behind him, and as he did so, the female Tarla gasped in upset and rose to her feet.

"You must not enter, Pathfinder!" Tarla exclaimed, one hand extended before her as though to keep Lialt away by main strength. "Jalav is not yet prepared for you, and your presence now is improper!"

"My presence now is necessary, wench," Lialt snorted, striding forward toward where I sat. "Jalav shall not be allowed the time to prepare as she most wishes to. And what has been done here?"

Sternly did the male look upon me with renewed anger, for he had seen the cloth I had removed from the wound. His light eyes flashed with disapproval, much as Ceralt's were wont to do, and his broad, dark face creased in a frown. Deliberately, I reached out toward the cloth upon my left leg.

"All know that a wound kept from the sight of Mida cannot be thought to heal as rapidly as one exposed to her vision," I murmured as I loosened the cloth. "Lialt need have little concern, and may now go about his business— elsewhere."

Lialt knelt immediately and grasped my wrists in large, angry, male hands. "I grow exceedingly weary of a wench who doesn't

restrain her tongue!" he snapped, the strength of his grip tightening about my wrists. "Lialt's coming and going may be dictated
by the will of Ceralt, but none other may so direct him, and most
certainly not a girl child! You will lie quietly in accordance with
my wishes, and will not touch the bandage I place upon you,
else will you be well punished! Heed my words, Jalav, for I have
no further patience to spend upon you!"

Much did Lialt's anger cause my own to blaze, and truly did I
attempt to escape his grip. "Jalav is no slave-woman to be
spoken to so!" I hissed, twisting at his hold. "Jalav may be
directed by none save Mida, for Jalav is proven war leader of the
Hosta! Should Lialt wish her obedience, he may face her with
sword in hand, and thereby earn final obedience—or find that he
has pledged his own! Choose now, male, and rest assured that
your blood shall be dedicated to Mida in a proper manner!"

Numb had my wrists grown beneath the pressure of Lialt's
fingers, yet the male seemed unaware of the state he caused. His
features seemed in some manner shadowed as he stared without
movement at my indignation. No sound was there save the snap
of the fire and the breathing of the two city-folk in my company,
and then did Lialt think to bestir himself.

"I do not fail to note the sincerity in your offer," said he quite
softly, though something of anger yet remained. "I am appalled
that a wench might be raised so, to fancy herself the match of a
man with a man's weapons, yet was it clear long ago that much
must be taught you. The greater part of your teaching will come
from Ceralt, yet there is that which may be supplied by me. I
shall not shirk my duty."

With those words I was forced flat upon the lenga pelt, and
kept so as Lialt replaced the cloth about my right leg, also
tightening that which I had begun to loosen upon my left leg.
Much did I rage and call down Mida's wrath upon his head, yet
were my words unheeded by the male, he uncaring as he went
about that which he wished done. The blows I rained upon the
arm and back of Lialt were as naught by cause of my weakness.
Tarla stood atremble with distress, fearful of the male's anger as
a warrior would never be. Had it been Fayan or Larid who stood
there, quickly would Lialt have found himself struck upon the
head with firewood, or the object of merciless attack, but were
my warriors far behind me, unable to aid their war leader. Alone
among enemies was Jalav, subject to the whim of males. However Jalav was on the mend, soon to be well and strong again.
Such thought sustained me as Lialt turned from my legs.

"I shall see you fed before I go," said he as though I had never raised hand to him, and then his eyes moved upon me as they had never before done. Widely did he grin at that which took his eye, and much approval did he find in the sight of my breasts, his eyes leaving them reluctantly to come to my face. "You are a well-made wench, that I'll grant," said he with a lightness which caused my teeth to clench. "As you find the covering of your body unnecessary, I shall recommend to Ceralt that he display you so before the elders this fey when they call. Perhaps they shall be sufficiently distracted to cause less difficulty than they currently propose to do."

With a snarl for his words, my hand immediately reached for the cast-off pelt, but he held it where it lay against my outraged pull.

"Ah, no," said he grinning. "You may not now cover yourself. Perhaps I shall allow it later, should I be pleased with your conduct. Tarla, warm some falum for Jalav, so that she may properly invest her halyar with her presence."

I lay in helpless outrage as the girl Tarla hurried to obey the word of Lialt. With nervous fingers did she take a small, metal pot and hang it over the fire. Quickly an odor arose from the pot she tended with stirring wood, an odor of grains admixed with salt, and I knew I wished none of it. In a hand of reckid, Tarla dipped out a wooden potful of that which had been called falum, and then brought it to where I lay.

"With Lialt's permission, I would offer falum of my own self, Jalav," said the girl as she knelt beside me. "Ever do Belsayah partake of falum as their first true meal within the walls of a new halyar, thereby asking the blessings of the Serene Oneness upon themselves and their undertakings. I offer you welcome to our village, sister, and also offer up a prayer for your well-being."

She was smiling, and soft were the words she addressed to me, for she spoke clearly of custom one did well to accept and abide by—yet I had not come to her village of my own accord. Many times had I followed custom of others, accepting that as the duty of a war leader, yet Lialt's knee upon my hair showed well that I was prisoner rather than guest, and therefore free of the requirements which bind a guest. I turned my face from her, saying, "One does not extend hospitality to captives. Your actions are mistaken, girl."

"She is naught save a child of savages, Tarla," said Lialt with great gentleness, speaking across to me. "To feel pain from that which she does in ignorance is futile, for one cannot instruct when obscured by tears. Each of us must instruct her as best we may, and perhaps one fey she, too, shall feel tears for that which she has done.''

Lialt took possession of the wooden pot, turning his attention to me. I lay upon the pelt I had lain upon so long, feeling within me the echo of the word, ''savage.'' ''Savage'' had the slave-guards of Belinard called me, as a ''savage'' had Ceralt once looked upon me, and much loathing did I feel for the word. Not warrior was I to them, nor war leader, but ''savage,'' one to be looked down upon and scorned. And I sought memory of the lands of Midanna, a land fraught with danger, yet one which was mine.

''The falum should be eaten while still warm,'' said Lialt, and his arm began to circle my shoulders. ''Come, Jalav. You may sit the while you eat.''

In such a manner did the male speak to me. You are to feed, Jalav. You may sit, Jalav. No matter my will in the matter, Lialt would see his own will done. As the male's arm raised me, I reached out and knocked the pot from his grasp, sending it to the dirt-covered floor, where its contents might spill and spread. A low curse escaped the male's lips as his eyes followed the path of the pot, his hand futilely areach for that which was already lost, and then was his anger sent toward me once more.

''Indeed are you the spawn of Sigurr!'' he spat, as his arm tightened about me. ''As you wish it, so shall it be!''

Then did he let me fall once more to the lenga pelt, causing sharp pain to stab at my sides and arms, and quickly did he gain his feet. Though no sound had passed my lips to give evidence of the pain, still had Tarla seen its track across my face, and compassion took her features as she moved the closer, extending her arms as though to offer aid. Surely would she have touched me had Lialt not returned, two lengths of leather from a wall peg in his hands, determination in his manner, and brusquely did he reach past her to me, and roughly was I thrust to my belly upon the furs, Lialt drawing my wrists behind me to fasten them there with the leather, then doing the same to my ankles. Such a doing twisted my wounded skin as it should not have been twisted, and my stomach heaved from that and from the odor of the pelts beneath my face, yet I made no protest nor outcry, for how may a captive protest the doings of her captors? With some difficulty did I grapple with the queasiness as Lialt bade Tarla fetch further falum, yet when Lialt turned me to him once more, a fresh pot of falum in his hand, no sign of my battle did I show to him.

Overwarm was the room and the air within, and moisture touched my body at many points, and the arm of Lialt was most unwelcome. Firmly, I attempted to refuse the heated grain, yet this Lialt would not accept, forcing the pot to my lips. Much of it spattered my body, Lialt's leathers, the furs and the floor, yet much of it entered me as well. Coughing and choking, I was made to feed as Lialt wished, and with the pot emptied, he did naught save return me to the pelt beneath me and take himself from the dwelling, his low-muttering voice reviling all womankind. Urgently did my stomach insist that it would soon empty itself of all placed therein, but I only lay as I had been placed, upon my bound wrists, and refused to hear the protestations of my innards. The sweat of illness ran between my breasts, finding smears of falum which must be circled, and my eyes closed in near defeat, for how may a warrior fight the strength of a male? From a great distance off, I felt the touch of a hand upon my brow, yet the words of a question spoken by Tarla did not reach me, flowing low and slow about the whirlpool in which I spun. Then the hand withdrew and the voice as well, and the darkness came in their stead.

When once again my eyes opened, no longer did the leather hold me, no longer did the falum cover me, no longer was the cast-off pelt apile beside me. A moistened cloth touched my face, held by a sad-eyed Tarla upon my right, and to my left, cross-legged, sat Ceralt. Beyond Ceralt, by a window through which he gazed, stood Lialt, no victory apparent in the slope of his shoulders, no joy visible in the bend of his head. Slightly did I move beneath the fur which covered me, for its presence was discomfort, and immediately Ceralt looked at me, keenly questioning. No wish had I to meet his gaze, yet his hand came to my face and turned it to him, his fingers gentle and warm upon my skin.

"How do you fare?" he asked, his voice overly soft as though at the urging of great anger. I could not take my face from the hand in which it was held.

"I fare as do all captives," I made answer, no longer avoiding his gaze. "My value in trade is not much diminished, therefore may you set your mind at rest."

"As I thought," growled Ceralt, the anger ablaze in his eyes as he released me and rose to his feet. "See you now my meaning, Lialt?"

"Ceralt, it matters not," protested Lialt, his face full to his brother's. "None know as well as I how sorely she was wounded, yet I bound her in leather, increasing her pain. I did not inform you of my doings to have you place the blame upon her!''

"The blame must be placed where it most belongs,'' said Ceralt, his hand upon Lialt's shoulder. "Ever has she been so, able to tear at a man's pride so that he wishes to do naught save show her her vulnerability. She knows not where she stands among men for none have taught her. When I have drawn her from the circle, she will begin to learn, yet now her manner must be borne. Are you able to wait for full punishment to come to her?''

Lialt shook his head and turned away. "I know not,'' said he, his back to Ceralt, his hand arub upon his neck. "Sooner would I tend a true hadat, for she seeks ever to oppose my will. Is there naught you may do, Ceralt?''

"I may do no more than take some part of the burden from you,'' replied Ceralt, turning once more to study me where I lay. "I shall assist you with her feeding, and shall also seek a punishment which might be given her now. In such a manner might we all survive her healing.''

With dry humor had Ceralt spoken, yet no humor was there in his eyes, as though I had not the right to protest my captivity. Odd are males in their thoughts and beliefs, yet no males had I known as odd as Ceralt and Telion and Galiose and their ilk. As a child, I had been told that for three or four to fall upon one was cowardly and evil, for one grants single combat even to blood enemies, yet large numbers are used in the capture of males to keep the males from harm. Should one wish to challenge a male, one warrior would suffice, yet it is the male's seed, not his blood, that one seeks from a sthuvad. What, then, might a male seek from a warrior whom he takes captive, one who wishes naught of him? To live with the hatred of another seems ill to me, yet so do males choose to live when they take an unwilling female. In confusion did I shake my head, finding great frustration in lack of understanding, yet naught was there I might do for it.

"Truly I, too, shall soon require healing,'' said Lialt, the beginnings of a grin upon his face as he turned once more to me. "She tries me sorely, brother, and I cannot see what interest she holds for you.''

"Were she in her normal dress,'' laughed Ceralt, "her attraction would be more visible, yet even such bounty is not the reason I desire her.'' He crouched slowly then, to put his hand upon my face, his eyes searching deep within me. "There is some lure, some need acalling, that draws me," he murmured, his nearness and the smell of his leathers nearly overwhelming me. "I knew her for mine when first I laid eyes upon her, knew then, too, she would never escape me, but knew not for some time the manner in which she might be approached. Now that knowledge, too, is mine, yet it may not be used as she is. All must wait upon her healing, yet the will of the Snows may refuse to wait. Have you seen aught further?"

"No," replied Lialt, his hand upon Ceralt's shoulder. "The Snows blow with great turbulence, showing the approach of much of importance, yet naught with definition have I seen. Would you have me search further?"

"I do not seek to bring the time upon us," said Ceralt with a shake of his head, a sigh in his voice. "I feel it best that we refrain from prodding at the sleeping torcho, lest it waken prematurely and devour us all." His eyes met mine. "And you," said he, a touch of asperity to his tone. "Captive have you named yourself, yet you are mistaken. No captive are you but an unclaimed wench—till I choose to have you otherwise. Do not give me further cause to seek punishment for you. There shall be no pleasure for you in such an undertaking, nor shall your pride find further salve in pain. Should you wish to avoid humiliation, do not set yourself against me."

With such words did Ceralt rise and gesture Lialt with him, both taking leave of the dwelling with no further look for me. Much relieved was I at his departure, for greatly did the presence of the male disturb me, and I knew not how to deal with the weakness. I turned to my belly in great upset, barely noticing the remnants of my body's aches, deeply concerned with those feelings which held me in their grip. I had no fear of Ceralt, although I much feared that which sight of him brewed within me. Well did I know that he cared naught for me, thinking only and ever of my value, yet I knew not why I could not keep his acts of betrayal clearly in mind when he stood before me. With the capture of the Hosta had he betrayed me, with the recovery of the third Crystal of Mida had he betrayed me—yet his broad chest and dark, unruly hair drove such thoughts from me, his light eyes and caressing hands filling my thoughts with naught save the feel of him against me and within me. Truly did I wish myself city slave-woman, so that I might run and hide from that which I feared. Mida allows no fear to her warriors, a law I had never before found fault with, yet I knew not the manner in which I might face this fear.

"Do not upset yourself so, Jalav," came Tarla's hesitant voice from behind me. "The High Rider will not allow harm to come to you, for he means to draw you from the circle. That he smiles upon you is your good fortune."

I raised my head to gaze at her across my shoulder, and saw that she knelt not far from me, her dark eyes wide and worried. No longer did she wear the fur wrappings about her feet, they being stood neatly beside a wall, and she knelt back upon bare heels, her hands at rest in her lap. Much of the slave was there in Tarla the female, but worse than useless would it have been to remark on it. I turned again with a sigh, coaxing my abused arms to raise me to sitting, and then looked bleakly upon her.

"I have noticed few smiles of late from Ceralt," said I. "What is this circle of which all speak, and in what manner is one drawn from it?"

"Surely you jest." Tarla smiled in disbelief. "Do not all men everywhere draw their women from the circle of choice?"

Again I sighed, for ever must it seem to those who do not travel that their ways are followed the world over. Much had I, myself, believed so in some part, yet had my wandering taught me otherwise. With a patience I did not truly feel, I smiled upon the female.

"Never have I heard mention of the custom," said I, drawing my bound hair across my left shoulder so that I might loosen it. "Would you care to instruct me in the matter?"

"With great pleasure," said she, eagerly. "I know not why your people fail to know of it, yet shall I assist you in your learning. The matter goes thusly: In the fall of her sixteenth kalod, each girl of the village must begin to place herself within the circle of choice, where the men of the village might lay claim to her. The circles are formed each time the darkness is unlit, an event which occurs each thirty-fifth fey, and all girls eligible are required to circle. Should a girl circle undrawn as many as six times, she is then withdrawn and sent to circle in a neighboring village. Many girls, with their father's permission, are sent to the circle sooner, for they have caught the eye of a man who does not care to wait for their sixteenth kalod, yet is the decision one for the men involved. Should the girl, at the younger age, be unprepared to receive a man, her father will not allow her to join the circle till the law directs his choice."

That males should have such sway over their slave-women came as no surprise, yet the matter sat ill with me. Surely did they mean to extend such treatment to me, hoping to see me become slave to them, yet sooner would I stand beside Mida, though my work for her was as yet unfinished.

"Entering the circle is a time of great excitement," continued Tarla. "Should a girl have been smiled upon by a man of the village, he will surely claim her then before all of the village. Some girls are of interest to more than one rider, and then does the claiming leather of each of them fall upon her, each attempting to draw her to his side, and then do the riders challenge one another, the winner taking the girl as his own. Surely, in such an instance, does the girl hope for the victory of the rider she prefers, for should the other prove victorious, it would be him she must serve." She sighed deeply then. "Can you not feel how marvelous it would be, Jalav, to be won by the man of your heart? To be his despite the attempts of others? Ever do I dream of being won so, of being carried to my father's halyar and first claimed there, and then taken to the halyar of the man of my heart, there to serve his every need. Upon my knees would I serve him, and gladly, yet must I wait a kalod longer, for my father will not see me within the circle sooner. But what shall I do if he does not wait?"

Carried off by a male indeed! Surely would Tarla have thought the capture of the Hosta by the males of Ranistard "marvelous." Hosta knew naught of such custom as she had described, being properly unconcerned with the wishes of males. At no time were the wishes of the males consulted, for such would have been foolishness. I drew my fingers through the tangle of my unbound hair, and thought with annoyance upon the matter of the circle of choice.

"Your hair is very long and beautiful," said Tarla with her usual shyness, her previous distress seemingly overcome. "I shall comb it for you so that you may feel more presentable at the appearance of the elders."

She rose from her place and went toward a small, round platform beside the wall to the right of the fireplace, and drew therefrom a thick comb of wood. The small, round platform had not been there when I had first been brought to the dwelling, and then did I see that much of the dirt of disuse had been removed from the room as well. The wooden floors were now without rubble and dust, the fireplace had been cleared before a new fire had been laid, and some layers of grease and dirt had been removed from the windows. Still was the room quite bare, with only the round platform and my furs, a few large metal hooks on the walls, yet had it been cleaned. Undoubtedly Tarla had been set to the doing, and without protest must she have obeyed.

I made no refusal as Tarla set the comb to my hair, for I still had not the strength to move my arms so. Instead, I attempted to question the girl upon the matter of the forthcoming visit to those who had been called elders, yet naught did she know of their purpose, save that they would attempt to dispute the claims of Ceralt. Much interest had I in such news, for were it possible to deny Ceralt's assertions, then might I be released to go my own way. Naught would be lost in such an attempt and much might be gained, therefore did I resolve to do what I might to see it so.

Tarla was nearly done with her combing when Ceralt and Lialt returned. I sat with my hair spread out about my arms and thighs as the door opened, and looked up to see the entrance of the males. Lialt frowned in usual disapproval over some matter, yet Ceralt halted a pace or two from the door, an odd, indescribable look within the deep, light pools of his eyes. With longing did those eyes hold to me, a longing well mixed with hot desire, and sharply did I recall the manner in which his heat used me, ever with strength, never to be denied. My fingers found the ends of my hair and grasped them nervously, for surely he meant to take me then to quench his heat. I, too, felt the stirrings of desire, yet would his use of me be most painful with the presence of my wounds, more painful even than the use of Nolthis had been. Quickly I lowered my gaze so that my eyes might not betray and shame me, and nearly did I miss the voice of Lialt.

"Again she disobeys!" snapped Lialt, his annoyance clear even through my upset. "Have I not told her, again and again, that she is forbidden to sit so? Now would I see her punished, Ceralt, as you have promised!"

No immediate answer was made by Ceralt, yet the sound of his step upon the wooden floor caused me to twist more vigorously at the ends of my hair where it lay upon the lenga pelt which covered me. Sooner would I have had his punishment than his caress, for his caress was true pain, yet his hand came to smooth my hair, and then the backs of his fingers touched my cheek.

"Is a wench to be disallowed the combing of her hair, brother?" Ceralt asked most softly as he stood beside me. His hand went to a strand of my hair, and he drew it gently through his fingers as he crouched beside me. My cheek burned where he had touched it, and surely did I wish for the strength to draw away from him. "See how lovely she looks, Lialt. Her health and beauty return through your efforts—and those of Tarla. Never have I punished a wench for seeing to her appearance, yet should you ask it—''

"Enough, brother!" laughed Lialt, no longer with anger in his voice. "Willingly do I grant the girl time for her beautifying, if only for your sake, yet does she now seem weary. I would see her rest a time, and then may the ministrations continue."

"As you say, brother," Ceralt agreed, also with laughter. His hands took me by the arms and pressed me back toward the pelt beneath me, and surely did I think the thudding of my heart would be heard by all in the dwelling. Now would he use me, causing me to voice my pain, giving me shame before the others in my weakness. My eyes sought his, seeking a sign of when the thing would begin, and the laughter left his broad, dark face.

"Lialt, see how pale she has become." Ceralt frowned, his eyes concerned. "And feel how she trembles beneath my hands. What ails her?"

Lialt, too, came to crouch beside me, his hand upon my brow, yet was I unable to take my eyes from Ceralt. A silent moment of consideration did Lialt pass, and then he spoke.

"I know not the why of it, brother," said Lialt somewhat in puzzlement, "yet does it seem that the wench fears you."

"Fears me!" echoed Ceralt, shock and disbelief in his light eyes. "For what reason would she fear me?"

The words of Lialt touched me with shock as well, and then indignation came, more strongly than the earlier apprehension. "Jalav fears no male!" said I with heat, attempting to twist from the hands of Ceralt. "Use me as you will, give me pain as you will, yet shall I look upon you with hate rather than fear! Do your worst; I do not fear you!"

"Of what does she speak, Ceralt?" asked Lialt in confusion, his eyes turning toward his brother. "She is not yet strong enough to be drawn from the circle and used. For what reason would she believe you meant to use her?"

Ceralt took a breath unto himself, and then he shook his head with a good deal of annoyance. "The wench knows me well, Lialt," said the male whose hands yet held my arms, whose eyes yet held mine. "I do indeed feel great desire for her this moment, yet does she know me less well than she believes. Despite the urgings of my desire, I shall not bed her till she is able to reply with the small amount of expertise I have thus far been able to teach her. Use of her now would be less than adequate, and I have not the patience for it."

"Less than adequate!" I sputtered, full outrage upon me.

"Small amount of—that *you*—!" Words failed me then, so great
was my indignation, and the laughter of the males did naught to
cool my outrage. Furiously, I struggled against the strong hands
which held me, for many males had felt themselves honored to
be allowed the sharing of my sleeping leather long before the
appearance of this prancing he-wrettan, Ceralt! And now does he
calmly announce—!

"Gently, Jalav, gently," laughed Ceralt, greatly amused as he
held to me. His light eyes danced with laughter, and Lialt
crouched, forearms upon thighs, also widely agrin. Truly drained
was I from the struggle, yet never would I allow males to laugh
at me so. My hair twisted and caught beneath me, Tarla's
combing totally undone, yet the males' amusement knew no end.

Then came another, unexpected voice, the voice of Tarla, yet
was this a Tarla I had not earlier seen. With great anger, she
grasped an arm of Ceralt in her two small hands and attempted to
loosen his grip upon me.

"For shame, High Rider!" she cried, drawing the eyes of the
males and their surprise as well. "Never had I thought to see one
such as you torment a helpless woman! Is not the pain of her
wounds enough? Must you add to it? Can you not see what your
amusement has cost her?"

"Truly am I now able to see that which is so clear to you,
Tarla," said Ceralt, his voice as soft as the look in his eye as he
gazed upon me. "I am pleased that the well-being of my wench
is so firmly seen to by you, for she has great need of wise
protection. Her protection must be yours till I am able to claim
her."

"I *shall* protect her," asserted Tarla, pink-cheeked with flus-
ter over that which she had done, yet attempting to maintain a
great dignity. She knelt beside Ceralt, her hands now returned to
her lap, her head held high, true dedication in her large, dark
eyes and upon her youthful face. Still feeling anger, I turned
from them, for they continued to make sport of me. How was a
child such as Tarla to be the protector of a war leader of the
Midanna? In no way might this be done, save through the
shaming of such a war leader. Some small dizziness attempted to
claim me as I lay with my cheek to the fur, yet this I would not
allow. The wounds inflicted by the Silla had done me considerable harm, yet would I overcome these wounds and all that my
enemies might do to me. I, a Hosta warrior, would not be kept
forever from earned vengeance and the freedom of the forests!

"Now must I see further to Jalav's protection," said Tarla,

and there came the sound of her rising. "Falum, though traditional, cannot by itself return her to strength. I shall prepare a cut of vellin for her, for her hunger must be great."

"Excellent," said Ceralt, approval clear in his tone. "I would see her fed before the arrival of the elders, for they mean to question her closely. And I would also see her boniness replaced with her former roundness. There is little pleasure in taking a wench in your arms, only to be stabbed at by her ribs."

Lialt's chuckle joined Ceralt's, yet Tarla, who had moved to the fire and therefore within my sight, reddened with embarrassment at these words, and hurried about her self-proclaimed task. I, in the furs, my back to the males, uttered no word, yet my hand stole to my side. Still was there cloth about the wound there, yet was there also no difficulty in perceiving the truth of Ceralt's words. Through the efforts of Nolthis and the Silla, much of my body weight had gone from me, leaving naught save an ungainly gauntness in its wake. Not since the time before I had become a warrior had I been so thin. Again I lay upon my back, turning my head to see Ceralt and Lialt, sitting cross-legged not far from me, conversing lightly, and the thought came that perhaps I had not been blessed by Mida with a full figure, but rather cursed. Perhaps, to avoid further pain and shame, it would be best if Jalav remained unpleasing to males, to be scorned by them rather than coveted. In such a manner might freedom be more quickly regained and thereafter kept. A sthuvad need not be pleased with the warrior who uses him, and once free, such was the only male whose use I would seek.

The males continued to speak with one another of unimportant things, such as the doings of their village and the trade engaged in with other, similar villages, and quickly was the room filled with the odor of meat aroast. Tarla stood by the fire, slowly turning a spit which was part of the fireplace, carefully awatch upon a cut of meat which she had placed thereon. Vellin she had called the meat, and though I knew not from which of the children of the wild it came, still its aroma had the power to tempt me even though Tarla did as other city folk and allowed the meat too long a time with the fire. When at last she removed it from the spit and placed it upon a square of wood, the juices ran but feebly from it, and much of its lure had gone as well. Such was not the disappointment it might have been, for it aided me in the decision I had made. Little would I feed upon in my captivity, no more than enough to restore my strength and health. Few males would find me pleasing as I was, and none would seek my detainment or capture. Little knowledge had I of males and their thoughts, yet was it easily seen that most preferred a female with great beauty. Though there was naught I might do upon the matter of my femaleness, perhaps seeing to the other would suffice till I once again held sword in hand.

Tarla brought the meat, upon its wooden square, to Lialt and he, with the dagger which hung at his belt and a three-pronged device carved from wood supplied by Tarla, cut the meat into tiny pieces.

With the meat cut, Tarla knelt beside me and attempted to place a portion of it in my mouth with the sharpened wood, yet this I would not allow. With some small effort, I once again sat erect upon the furs, and with slightly trembling fingers took the meat through my own efforts. Disapproval stood clear in the features of Lialt and Ceralt, yet they did not voice their disapproval, and Tarla saw it not. The girl merely smiled with pleasure that I took sustenance, content to allow me my own wishes, and answered my query with a small laugh. The meat did not derive from a child of the wild, said she, but from one of the herd animals kept by her people. Vellin were raised for the purpose of feeding and clothing the villagers, and were never willingly allowed the life of the wild, for they might injure themselves or feed less than was desirable. I made no answer to these words, and concealed my upset from the female's eyes. City males, in their vileness, refused freedom to all, enslaving all within their reach. Midanna looked upon herding as an affront to Mida, for the children of the wild were as much the children of Mida as were the Midanna. That we fed upon each other in turn was proper, for in such a way might the strong continue to exist, yet one did not enslave a sister. Such were the actions of the weak and fearful, those who would not try their strength in the forests. Of little worth were city males, and long had I known this.

With half the meat consumed, my hunger was no more, therefore I refused the balance of the offering and lay down upon the furs once again. Tarla's frown joined those of Lialt and Ceralt, yet the closing of my eyes precluded argument. Should they believe that weakness and pain had once more taken me, I would not disabuse them, for in truth I had not the strength for disagreement. In a moment or two, Tarla urged me to my belly, so that she might see to my hair. Once again was it twisted about itself, yet I said naught upon the matter. When I regained my freedom, my hair, too, would fall free as was proper.

The males continued to converse quietly, Tarla moved about

by the fire, and weariness brought sleep to me for a short while. The hum of voices caused strange dreams to surround me as I slept, yet I remembered no more than their strangeness when I was awakened by the sound of a fist upon the wood of the door. My eyes opened to see Lialt rise from his place and approach the door, then open it to admit more than a hand of males. He who had been called Uncle entered first, the others following deferentially behind, and his eyes swept the room and its contents quickly, to rest upon a suddenly wide-eyed Tarla. No word was spoken to the female, yet she hurried to where her leg furs stood, donned them rapidly, then slipped to the door and out. No swing was allowed to the door of the room, and as Tarla pulled it to behind her, so it remained without the aid of a bar. Briefly, then, were the eyes of uncle upon me, dark and calculating, before turning to a still seated Ceralt. The elder male performed a small, stiff bow, duplicated with more enthusiasm by the others, and Ceralt's hand moved to gesture about him.

"Take seat and join me, Elders," said he, a relaxed tone to his voice. "You have many questions, I know, and perhaps I shall be able to answer them all. You may question the wench as well, but only with gentleness. She is not yet well enough to stand an inquisition."

The face of the one called uncle darkened with anger; then another male stepped forward before the first might speak.

"We do not come in hostility, Ceralt," said this male, mild reproof in his tone. "We come in curiosity, asking no more than the reasons behind the doings of our High Rider. Do you believe we mean harm to the wench?"

Ceralt gazed soberly upon the male who spoke, then he rose to his feet. "No, Garrim, I do not believe you mean her harm," said he, "yet I have found that words of caution must be spoken when one has dealings with this particular wench. Her manner is such that it is ofttimes difficult to recall that she is sorely wounded. Come and seat yourselves, men, for I have a narrative I would have you hear."

With many odd glances for me, the males took seat upon the wood of the floor, ranging themselves to either side of him called uncle, all facing Ceralt where he sat. Ceralt sat alone before them, Lialt having taken a position behind his brother and to his right, toward me, and no indication did Ceralt give that he saw the continuing though unvoiced displeasure of him called uncle. Ceralt settled himself in comfort, and then was his tale forthcoming.

"You all know the reason for my having left the village," said he to the others, "yet was I, at the time, quite displeased. I knew not why the Snows directed my path in such a manner, yet was I required to comply. I journeyed from the village of my birth, and in time came to the city of Bellinard, a place whose ways are easily learned. We all of us dislike the ways of cities, yet are we somewhat familiar with them, therefore was there little difficulty in securing acceptance in the brotherhood of hunters. I labored among the men of the brotherhood, and in time was I given the leadership of hunting parties, the others not having acquired my level of skill.

"For some time, I hunted with the men and sported with their slaves, yet even in sport I wondered as to my purpose in being there. Time spent with slaves is most amusing, but surely that could not have been the reason for my presence." The other males chuckled at this, though he called uncle did not join their amusement. Again his gaze came to me, then was it quickly withdrawn. I lay within the furs, listening to Ceralt's tale, awaiting the time I might work toward my release.

"And then a thing occurred which was most unexpected," continued Ceralt, his light-eyed gaze sliding to me. "I and my hunting party of some twenty men were taken captive by females, large, armed females who called themselves warriors and bore arms as though they were men."

Lialt joined the other males in exclamations of surprise and incredulity, yet Ceralt did not allow an interruption. "These females," said he above their voices, "were led by one called Jalav, a wench of great beauty and ability, one who had never known the restraint of a man's wishes. Wild and untutored was she, a true child of savages; she stood nearly the height of a man, was possessed of black hair and eyes, did not deign to cover her large and tempting breasts, and had been born beneath the sign of the hadat."

No sound now came from the males, yet the eyes of one and all rested upon me in something much like shock. Lialt alone was sober of face, as though he knew the meaning of Ceralt's words, yet the others continued to stare in shock.

"Aye," said Ceralt, nodding as his eyes fixed upon me. "In such a way were we told of a wench who would toil with us to save our people, and though the Snows spoke of her many and many a kalod ago, still do we all easily recall the admonition that we must seek her, for she would not seek us. At once, I knew the wench for what she must be, and determined to return her to our village so that the wish of the Snows might be fulfilled, yet the deciding and the doing were not accomplished with equal ease."

The eyes of the males returned to Ceralt as he sighed and shifted about. "The wench," said he, "was not one who might be expected to obey the wishes of others. She was first and unchallenged among her wenches, and though I succeeded in securing her as a slave, still was there much difficulty with her. At last, she and her wenches were brought to the city of Ranistard, a city which had lost most of its women, and there I attempted to civilize her so that she might have an easier time of adjustment in our village. This attempt, too, was a failure, for she insisted upon incurring the wrath of the High Seat of Ranistard, a man with little understanding of the manner in which a wench should be disciplined. Galiose and I disagreed as to how she was to be treated, I was ejected from Ranistard, and the wench was lashed."

A familiar hardness and coldness had entered the tone of Ceralt, and those males who looked upon him did so with discomfort. Lialt studied the floor beneath his folded legs, not caring to lift his gaze, and all was silent as the males awaited the continuing of Ceralt's words. Ceralt took a breath to banish the anger which had held him, and then he continued.

"I was determined to retrieve the wench," said he, "from the rubble of Ranistard if necessary, yet arrival at the woods near the city showed that the wench had effected her own escape, though not as successfully as one would have wished. Not only had she been lashed to the bone by Galiose, but she had also been set upon by enemy savage wenches, who had touched her many times with their spears. Lialt felt she would die of her wounds, though she did not, and we both feel that her survival is but another indication that she is indeed the one the Snows have spoken of. As I am the one who was sent to fetch her to us, I also feel that the wench was meant for me. As soon as she is well, I shall draw her from the circle of choice, and no man may come between us save at the peril of his life."

Again was the hardness in Ceralt's voice, and those before him made no denial of his words. He called Uncle also sat in silence, yet the stiffness of his shoulders spoke well of his anger. He was not pleased with that which he had heard, and it took but a moment for him to find a basis for argument.

"That the wench is the one spoken of by the Snows may well be," said he, his voice giving the statement no support. "However, I find difficulty in understanding your other contention, Ceralt.

Surely it was the High Rider of our village, not a man called
Ceralt, who was sent to fetch the girl. Why, then, do you assume
that she is to be yours? Perhaps she was meant for another, such
as Lialt, our Pathfinder, or Hamiral, my son, who is first among
your riders. That it was you who brought her to us proves little.''

"On the contrary, Uncle," replied Ceralt, holding the attention of the other male. "My having brought her must be proof to
all that it is my intention to keep her. I determined that she
would be mine when first I saw her, and will allow none to deny
me. She is not to be Lialt's or Hamiral's, but *mine*! Are my
words clear to you?"

He called Uncle once again fell to anger, yet this time his
anger was not contained. "And what of my daughter Famira?"
he demanded in a shout, one fist held up before his darkened
face. "It was she you were to draw from the circle, not some
draggled she-savage! Is she now to be shamed in such a way,
discarded before being claimed? Have you no honor?"

"Honor!" echoed Ceralt, rage claiming him as well. "And
when, Uncle, was it my announced intention that I would smile
upon Famira? The announcement and hope were yours, thinking
to see the son of your daughter in the place your own son could
not claim! Famira does not tempt me, nor would I have chosen
her merely to quiet your insolent tongue! Famira will be chosen
by another one, hopefully, who possesses much leather to use
upon her! Then might she prove a fitting mate!''

Wordless with outrage, he called Uncle rose to his feet and
stormed from the room, causing the door to fall closed behind
him with much of a thunder. Ceralt and Lialt and the other males
watched him gone, then he called Garrim took a deep breath and
chuckled somewhat.

"I, for one, do not regret your words to him, Ceralt," said he.
"He presumes upon his postiion as your mother's brother, and
such does not sit well with any of us. Perhaps he thought respect
for his age would keep him free of your wrath."

"I do not respect age," said Ceralt, settling himself in comfort once again. "It is wisdom I respect, Garrim, and only now
do I feel that I am in the presence of wisdom. Do my Elders
wish to question their High Rider?"

The males before Ceralt looked upon one another soberly,
each considering the question put to them, yet it was Garrim who
continued to speak.

"As I see it," said he, "the matter before us is not who the
wench shall belong to, but rather to ascertain as thoroughly as

possible if she be the one the Snows have spoken of. Are we agreed?''

The others nodded and murmured, no sign of dissention among them, all pleased that Garrim spoke for them. The male was tall and dark, thinner than the others, yet possessed of a dignity that was not lost upon one who saw him. Some gray appeared in his hair, as it did in the hair of the others, yet was his gaze steady rather than infirm. Ceralt nodded in approval of their decision, and smiled warmly.

"Wisdom might ever be counted upon to seek the heart of the matter," said he. "If it is your wish to speak to the wench, please do so."

Garrim nodded his thanks, then turned dark, inquiring eyes toward me. A smile lit his thin-boned face, and gentleness entered his tone.

"We have not, as yet, properly welcomed you to our village, girl," said he, speaking as though he addressed one such as Tarla. "We do not wish you to fear us, for we mean you no harm and shall ask no more than a very few questions. Do you understand me?''

Nearly did I laugh scornfully as I moved myself to sitting upon the furs. "I understand naught at what you say, male," I asserted with as much vigor as I possessed. "For what reason would one give welcome to a captive in his midst? And for what reason would I fear you? Males have done much to Jalav, yet Jalav fears none of their doing! And should you wish your questions answered, you may first see to the restoration of my freedom!"

Loud exclamations from the males greeted my words, some appearing shocked, others angered, and still others outraged. Lialt coughed gently and without sound, his cupped hand covering his mouth; Ceralt alone sat as he had, his calm unruffled, his light eyes undisturbed. Garrim turned from his startled examination of me, and cleared his throat.

"Of what does she speak, Ceralt?" asked he, nearly in dismay. "What foolishness would prompt her to think herself captive and in need of release?" Again his eyes came to me, and he added, "Have you not heard the words spoken here, girl? Your life remains yours solely through the efforts of Ceralt and Lialt! Had they not found you and tended your wounds, you would surely have died!"

"In no manner did I ask their aid," said I, my chin held high. "Had they left me as they found me, Mida alone would have seen to my safety, had that been her wish. I now demand release, so that I might return to the lands of my own people. No wish have I to remain among city males.''

Much loathing filled the last of my words, yet the males took them as I had not expected. Knowing looks grew upon their faces, and heads nodded in approval.

"Such feelings are well understood by us," said one unnamed male. "City men are not the sort we, ourselves, care to associate with, and you may set your concern to rest. You now dwell in a village, girl, where you will be properly cared for.''

"Aye," said another, his smugness thick as a shield's breadth. "And have you not heard that you are to be claimed by our High Rider? It is a great honor he does you, an honor many another wench would be awed to receive.''

Many nods of assent came then, yet had I no doubt as to what my responses must be. My right hand upon my left arm to still the throbbing beneath the cloth, I looked most solemnly upon the male who had spoken.

"I wish no part of your concept of honor," said I, "nor do I wish your High Rider. Both may you keep to bestow upon another, and grant me no more than a cloud's path.''

Silence surrounded all, heavy silence weighted with deep stares and light breathing. The elder males gazed upon me with disbelief, one or two bridling with insult, most frowning at my choice of words. To ask to be granted a cloud's path was something of an insult to the dwellers of a land, for a cloud moves lightly above all and at a distance, never deigning to partake of offered hospitality, if any. It was thought by some that clouds were the breath of giants who dwelt upon that rising called Sigurr's Peak by males, giants who scorned the lands and company of mortals. I, too, wished naught of males and their ways, no more than sthuvad use of them, and such, I believe, was seen by the males before me. My gaze swept them all with a good deal of coldness, bringing stiffness to them and an increase in anger.

He called Garrim studied me closely in his anger, then slowly nodded his head. "Your words were truth, Ceralt," said he, not moving his eyes to the other male. "Indeed, she knows little of the manner in which men are to be addressed. I know not why you would wish to draw one such as her from the circle, but I see a difficulty in your intent. That the wench is unwilling would mean naught were her father here to give his approval, yet her father is not here. How is such a lack to be overcome?''

"Easily, Garrim," replied Ceralt in such an untroubled voice that my gaze went to him. He sat at his ease, grinning slightly, his light eyes resting upon my face. "The wenches of her clans have no true fathers, yet I have spoken to one named Maranu, who looked upon himself as her father. Gladly and willingly did he grant her to me, pleased that she had at last found favor in a man's eyes. She goes to the circle with her father's approval."

"Maranu is naught to me!" I snapped, irritated beyond bearing by Ceralt's grin and the light laughter of the others. "The male is naught save one who once stood beneath the protection of the Hosta! Jalav shall not remain in this Mida-forsaken pesthole to be slave to males! Let her freedom be granted now, lest she find the need to seek it later with a sword!"

My words did well to counter the laughter of the males, yet it was not respect for my wrath which then claimed them, but their previous anger. Many growls and mutterings were produced by them, and most stirred angrily where they sat, yet he called Garrim drew himself more fully erect and looked upon me with great disapproval.

"I do not care for your manner, girl," said he, "nor do I care for your choice of words! Were you not already taken with pain from your wounds, I, myself, would find great pleasure in taking the leather to you! Your comings and goings are the decision of those about you, and the decision has already been made! You have naught to do save answer the questions put to you, civilly, obediently, and promptly! Now! Describe to me the land from which you come, and describe as well the beasts which dwell therein!"

The male sat with blazing eyes, awaiting his answers, the other males also silent now so that my obedient words might be heard. These males, I saw, were no different from others, ever demanding their will from warriors. No fear had I of males, no more filled me at sight of them than a great weariness, for now I must find the need to free myself, as always. I lay back upon the lenga pelt, drawing the covering pelt closer to my chin, raising my eyes to the wooden heights of the dwelling so that I need not gaze longer upon those who cared naught for any save themselves. Another moment of silence was there, and then once more came the voice of him called Garrim.

"Ceralt, her actions are intolerable!" he spat, great agitation upon him. "Order her to reply to me at once!"

There came the sound of leather stirring, and then Ceralt's voice, no more disturbed than previous. "I doubt that she has the strength to reply," said Ceralt, and I knew that he looked upon me. "She has already done more than Lialt would have her do, and rest is essential if she is to grow well again. I shall answer your questions if you wish, else it must be left for another time."

Again a stirring, as though the males turned to look upon one another, and then a sigh, as of resignation. "Very well," said Garrim, no longer agitated. "The questioning of the wench shall await another time. There are some few questions we may put to you, Ceralt, and we shall have to satisfy ourselves with those."

The males returned to the time Ceralt had spent away from them, eliciting details to add to that of which he had already spoken. Ceralt answered without hesitation, giving much time to that which he had observed of the Hosta. The voices, soft and even, refused to hold my attention, and easily did I drift into a light sleep, seeing again the feyd I had spent in Bellinard. I rode free for a time, then great chains were upon me, and males stood about staring at me, each calling, "Slave! Slave!" I writhed and panted in the chains, attempting escape from the hungry eyes of the males, and then the male Bariose and the female Karil came forward, he with the coiled leather whip in his hands, swung gently against his leg, she with her hands clasped before her, a smile of satisfaction upon her face. All about in the great room were metal enclosures filled with slave-women, some whimpering silently, some crying out with arms stretched through the lines of metal, yet none paid them heed. I, and I alone, chained in the center of the room, held their eyes, and there was no escape. She called Karil stepped forward to stroke my hair, and in a voice of silk proclaimed, "Test her heat, my friends! See how great her need is for the touch of a man! Buy her and make her yours!" "She must be punished!" announced Bariose, his eager hands caressing the lash. "Speak words of apology to your mistress and myself, slave, else shall you feel the kiss of the lash!" All surrounded me, closer and closer, the males with hungry eyes reaching forward to touch me, to bring an agony of desire upon me, and I could not avoid the caress of their fingers. In misery, I threw myself about, moaning from their efforts, and then but one stood before me, a lash in his hand, his fingers hard upon my breast. "You will be mine," said Nolthis, his fingers tightening to give me pain. "I will use you and use you, and then I will lash you till you obey me. You are mine to do with as I wish." "No!" I cried, bending in the chains with the pain so cruelly given. My warriors were gone, and I alone was left among the enemies of Hosta. I writhed and again cried, "No!" and then there was a form behind Nolthis, a form in tan leathers and silver belt, and I cried, "Ceralt!" as the form reached a hand toward Nolthis. Nolthis snarled and whirled toward the form, his hand going to his dagger, and then was I taken by the shoulders and shaken, and my eyes beheld the small wooden dwelling in the village of my capture. Tarla bent to me with great concern, her large eyes troubled, her hands yet upon my shoulders, and easily did I feel the moisture upon my brow and the shakiness in my limbs. My breath came rapidly and with much effort, and I found I must blink before the mists of sleep retreated in entirety.

"Jalav, you cried out!" said Tarla, removing her hands from my shoulders so that she might wring them. "You called so desperately for the High Rider that surely did I think you in true jeopardy! Do you wish me to fetch him?"

"No," said I, my voice no more than a croak, memory returning of that which had disturbed me. "It was no more than a dream, sent by one other than Mida. The males have gone?"

"Indeed," she nodded. "Hind ago. You slept soundly when I returned, therefore I took care not to disturb you. Your meal is nearly done, and I shall shortly bring it to you."

The female Tarla rose from where she had knelt beside me, and returned to the fire where meat and vegetables awaited her attention. Beyond the dwelling's windows was full darkness, showing that another fey had gone to naught. Wearily, I turned to my belly in the furs, little refreshed by the sleep I had had. Evil dreams and presentiments dogged me in the places of males, as evil as the actions of males themselves. In truth, I knew I had cried out for Ceralt, yet I knew not why I had done so. Ceralt was male, no different from the rest, and foolish indeed would I be to think him otherwise. Often had he betrayed me, often had he brought me pain, and naught did he wish from me save use. My cheek to the furs, I closed my eyes, attempting to ease the throb which had returned to my wounds.

Shortly indeed did Tarla fetch my provender, a mixture of vellin meat, green gemild, fellin tubers, and other, unfamiliar vegetables. All had been cooked as one, a thin broth containing it, and little stomach had I for the concoction. I raised myself to sitting, grimacing inwardly, and proceeded to eat no more than half of that which had been given me. Tarla showed dismay that I would not use the shallow-bowled wooden stick with which to feed, yet I felt little concern over her dismay. To touch with

one's fingers that which Mida provides is no offense, a thing
which city folk seemed not to know. I fed as I wished upon that
which I wished, and said no word on the matter. Again Tarla
showed dismay when I returned the wooden pot to her, still
partly filled with that which she had prepared. Earnestly she
attempted to wheedle my acceptance of the balance, and desisted
at last only when I took my attention from her to examine the
bare room in which I lay. No more than the blaze of the fire lit
its dimensions, shadows throwing themselves about the walls
with its movement, and truly did I dislike the chill feel to the air
and the odor of mustiness. Sooner would I have been without, in
the cold and dark, than remain the longer in such a place, yet
those about me would not see me freed. Anger stirred within me,
anger that others ever sought to pen a Hosta, though Hosta had
never sought to keep others beneath their sway. Perhaps, when
all were freed of male restrictions, the Hosta might add the
bondage of these others to the vengeance that was theirs. Such
would indeed be fitting.

The door to the darkness opened, admitting Lialt and Ceralt,
who came within with naught save silence about them. Little did
I need the sight of the cloth packet to know their purpose, yet
struggle availed naught. Ceralt held me as Lialt mixed the potion,
and again the two males saw the flat, chalky liquid within me.
Grimly, with teeth and fists clenched, I attempted to deny the
potion, yet denial was not possible. Within reckid, the males
had had their way, and deep, dreamless sleep was once again
mine.

# 6.

# The coverings of a slave—
# and a taste of freedom

The new fey was already begun when next I wakened, finding Tarla prepared with falum for me. Much angered was I by the actions of the males, so angered that I spoke no word to Tarla lest I give to her the venom which was others'. The young female took no note of my silence, instead chattering away upon all matters that took her mind and tongue. Little heed did I pay the chattering, thinking only of the time my wounds might heal sufficiently to allow my departure. The light of Mida would guide me south once more, and much pleasure would I feel when I stood upon the banks of the Dennin. There, the light of the fey was full and strong, warm and invigorating, not thin and cold as that in the lands of males.

Little of note occurred that fey, nor were matters improved upon by the passage of two feyd further. Tarla fluttered about constantly, seeing to the dwelling and to the cooking of meals, yet once had she gone so far as to chide me for refusing the greater part of her offerings. No word did I speak upon the matter, yet when her gaze met mine her chiding ceased, and her eyes grew large and frightened. Quickly, then, did she scurry from my sight, for not for naught was Jalav war leader of the Hosta. Many were the warriors who had thought to stand against me and win for themselves the second silver ring of war leader, yet few were those who had retained their resolve beneath my gaze. A war leader who must face constant challenge is not a good war leader, for it is her place to see that her warriors do not spend themselves uselessly against her sword. Many were the Hosta who had wished to be war leader, yet few were the number who had stood before Jalav with drawn sword. Willingly had I faced those who truly would not be swayed from their purpose, yet the others I had saved for battle with the enemy. Such was the way of a proper war leader, and such had been the way of Jalav.

Lialt, usually in the company of Ceralt, came many times to add to my anger and annoyance. They, themselves, were in good humor, and neither felt concern over the fury they bred in me. The first fey, Lialt insisted upon examining my wounds, using Ceralt's aid when I refused his wishes. Much pleased was the male with the progress of my healing, yet did he find himself less pleased when the following fey showed him that I had removed all of the cloth bindings from my body. Much did he rage and storm about, sending Tarla to shiver in a far corner in fear of his anger, yet I merely lay myself back in the furs, pleased at the absence of the cloth. Ceralt had not accompanied him that fey, and from his raging, I surmised that the High Rider had left the village upon some matter, yet I cared not that the male would be informed upon his return. I had determined that I would do as my warrior Fayan had once done with the male Nidisar, and refuse to acknowledge the existence of the male Ceralt. Perhaps then the male, in disgust, would seek another to torment, and leave Jalav to go her own way.

Lialt, after vowing punishment for my actions, took himself from the dwelling, leaving Tarla to creep about as though it had been she who had caused the anger in him, yet in a short while he had returned and silently seated himself not far from the fire. Though he seemed to have words for none in the dwelling, his eyes fixed themselves to me and did not stray, causing even greater upset in the young village female. I, however, had been looked upon many times by males who had been mine in the Hosta home tents, and the gaze of Lialt meant naught to me. I sat or lay in the furs as I wished, finding comfort difficult to attain, and fed upon as little of the provender offered by Tarla as ever. Tarla turned anxious eyes to Lialt as I returned the still-filled wooden pot to her, yet Lialt did naught save narrow his own eyes thoughtfully, then take himself off again. That darkness, a stranger aided Lialt in forcing the potion upon me, showing that Ceralt had not yet returned. Till then, it had been none save they two who had visited each darkness with the chalky liquid which brought sleep, an action I had as yet to understand. I knew not why the potion was given me, yet no darkness had passed without it.

Upon the fourth fey, after having fed upon almost none of the falum, I was displeased to see the return of Lialt. The male entered the dwelling, closing the door quickly as always, yet when he turned from the door, his left arm showed itself to be laden. Tan leather lay folded across the arm, and in his hand the male carried wrapped furs of the sort which Belsayah villagers wore upon their feet. I frowned at his burdens, not caring for the sight of them, yet the male took no note of my displeasure. With firm step he approached the furs where I lay, and looked down upon me.

"Your appetite has grown as pale as your features, wench," said he, frowning. "Close captivity works ill upon all wild things, therefore must you now be allowed a certain freedom from this halyar. A hin or two beneath the open skies will return you some measure of strength and appetite. Tarla will assist you with the clothing and boots."

With which words did the male throw his burdens to my feet, the movement revealing the presence of a copper-colored belt as well. Tarla, all asmile, began to walk toward me, yet I cared not for these new events.

"Jalav requires naught save her clan covering," said I, raising myself to sitting in the furs. The leather, I was now able to see, was like that which Tarla wore, a slave-woman's covering. Truly did the male wish to see me slave, yet Jalav was no slave.

"The chill in the air is too sharp for one unused to it," said Lialt, crouching down beside me, sober-faced. "As weakened as you now are, you would surely fall ill were you to leave here with naught save that bit of cloth. The leather and furs will protect you, Jalav, and keep you safe for Ceralt."

So, I was to be kept safe for Ceralt, protected as though I were city slave-woman in truth! Rage rose once again within me, straightening my shoulders and lifting my chin high. Heatedly, I regarded this male Lialt, and my tone was not kind.

"Had Mida wished her Midanna to don leather and furs," said I, "it would have already been done! It is the clan covering which Midanna are to wear, and naught else have I ever worn! All things are as Mida wishes them to be!"

Though I expected to see Lialt enraged, the male showed naught of anger. Still sober-faced, he nodded slowly.

"All things are indeed as the gods wish them," said he, "yet one may not know the will of the gods till an event has transpired. It is my intention to see you in the proper clothing for this time of the kalod, and I shall not accept your refusal. I allowed you your will in the matter of the bandages; in this matter, my will shall prevail. Do you don the clothing with Tarla's aid, or with mine?"

No rage had yet claimed him, no anger, nor impatience. Merely did he crouch beside me, calmly awaiting his will to be done. Again I felt my lack of strength, my helplessness in being wounded and unarmed among males, and briefly I shivered, touched by the fear that Mida had meant such a fate for me forever. Was I destined for the lot of slave-woman, ever to bend to the will of males, never again to ride free? My hand crept to my middle, seeking to still the rolling illness there, and I dared not think upon the number of times I had failed Mida. Surely, had she wished to find reason to abandon her warrior, she need not have sought far.

"I do not wish to leave the dwelling," said I to Lialt, lying again in the furs. Once before had I been prisoned beneath the skies of Mida, kept from freedom by the metal of an enclosure, seeing that which could not be mine. Should it be true that I must now be slave to males, never again would I seek to leave the dwelling. I attempted to turn from Lialt and lie upon my side, yet the male moved swiftly to take my face in his hand and turn it toward him once again.

"No, Jalav," said he quite gently, his light eyes full upon me. "You shall be clothed in the leather, and you shall be taken outside. Not again will I fall to anger over your willfulness, for I shall not allow you your willfulness. Is Tarla to aid you, or am I?"

There were no words which might be spoken then, for the male wished to hear none, therefore I spoke not at all, merely returning Lialt look for look. There was naught then that the war leader Jalav might do to free herself, yet was it not the way of Midanna to heed the will of their captors. Much pain had the leather of Bariose given me, yet it had all gone for naught, for I had not obeyed him as he had wished. Never would I obey the will of males, never would I bow before them! This must Lialt have seen in my eyes, for his lips tightened and his nod became stiffened.

"Very well," said he, releasing my face. "As it is my aid you desire, you may have it. Should your modesty be offended, you must recall with whom the decision rested."

Then did Lialt take up the leather covering and quickly remove the lenga pelt from my grip, throwing it to one side. Tarla gasped in distress clearly disturbed by Lialt's doing, yet no more was accomplished by the female than the wringing of her hands. In full disgust, I took my sight from her, thinking again upon how matters would have gone had one of my warriors been in the place of the slave-woman. Lialt struggled to raise me from the furs, at the same time attempting to place the covering over my head, yet matters were not of a mind to aid him in his doing. Lialt might have raised me, or he might have placed the covering upon me, but with Jalav unmoving, he could not do both. Furiously, he struggled to accomplish his aim, seemingly forgetting that he was not again to fall to anger, and I smiled at his fruitless struggles, seeing the will of the gods being done. Then a thought came to me, a thought possibly sent by Mida herself. How, asked the thought, was Jalav to make her way from the village and the land of males, when Jalav knew naught of that which surrounded her? Surely it was at Mida's behest that Lialt sought to take me from the dwelling, and I, a mindless fool, attempted to deny this. Had I continued in my blindness, surely Mida, in disgust, would have permitted me to remain in the capture of males forever. If I were to find my freedom, amends must quickly be made.

"Hold," said I to a red-faced, panting Lialt. "I do not wish your aid with the covering. I shall do the thing myself."

Lialt, astare in disbelief, allowed the covering to fall from his hand. "Now she wishes to do the thing herself," he murmured, wiping at his forehead with the back of his hand. "First she will not hear of it, now she must do it herself! A man must indeed be insane to enmesh himself with a woman!"

Angrily, Lialt rose from his crouch, stalked to the door, threw it open, then pulled it noisily shut behind him, the trail of his mutterings being abruptly ended by the closing of the door. I knew not what his muttering pertained to, nor did I care, for there was much I must be about. Again, I sat upon the lenga pelt, bringing the leather covering closer so that I might look upon it, yet I could not determine the manner of its donning. One's clan covering merely wrapped about one's hips, yet the leather covering was not meant to be done so. I turned it about, seeking a means of entrance, a frown and impatience covering me, and Tarla knelt to my right and sighed.

"Allow me to aid you, Jalav," said she, an unexplained unhappiness clear in her tone as she reached for the covering. "Men know little of the clothing of women save its removal."

The female took the covering from me, and at once began to loosen the leather ties to each side of the thing, causing the garment to grow larger than it had been. Too, the small leather tie at the throat of the covering was loosened, thereby enlarging that part of it, and then, seemingly, it was ready to be worn.

"Raise your arms," directed Tarla as she gathered the leather in both of her hands. I did so, curious as to how one accomplished such a thing by oneself, then watched as Tarla slid the leather upon my arms, then raised the rest for the entrance of my head. There was some pain in the adjustment of the garment, for my wounds, uncovered, were touched by the leather, yet the leather was soft and the pain was not great. Gently, Tarla smoothed the leather down to my hips, then seemed somewhat perplexed.

"The thing is properly done while standing," said she, nearly to herself, looking thoughtfully upon me. "Perhaps it may also be done while you lie flat upon the fur. Let us make the attempt, Jalav."

With some misgivings, I lay back upon the fur, for I cared little for the feel of the leather upon me. Its smell was not offensive, yet the feel of it seemed wrong and much against the ways of the Midanna. At Tarla's urging I raised my hips, bringing twinges to my leg wounds, and the female gently tugged the covering to my knees, then began tightening the leather ties to each side of the covering. When at last the tie at my throat was closed, Tarla reached the copper belt about my middle and secured it by means of a curved bit of metal holding to one of the links. With all seemingly done, I again raised myself to sitting upon the fur, yet did I experience some difficulty in doing so. The leather, though soft and supple, was most confining in its presence, a limitation upon one's body's freedom. Much did I dislike the entrapped feeling it engendered, but it was necessary that I bear the torment. Without the garment, Lialt would not see me without the dwelling, and I knew I must be away from there and about Mida's work. Slowly, I moved my arms within their new leather coverings, considering what adjustments one would find the need to make, should it be necessary to use bow, spear or sword, and Tarla busied herself with the placement of the wrapped furs upon my feet. Strange indeed were the sensations caused by the furs, so strange that nearly did I overlook the deep misery of the girl who aided me. A tear of two touched Tarla's cheek, quickly brushed away as she adjusted the leg furs, her shoulders rounded as her body bent forward over my legs. No more than a moment did I consider her, and then my hand was upon her arm.

"What ails you, girl?" I asked in a gentle manner, not wishing to cause her further upset. Although the leg furs had already been placed, she did not turn her face toward me, but lowered her head to regard her hands.

"He no longer desires me," she whispered, a catch coming to her voice as the tears returned. "Did you not hear him? He wishes naught to do with a woman!"

This seemed, to me, an excellent state of affairs, yet the female before me obviously did not see it as such. Lialt, then, was he upon whom she looked with favor, he whom she had spoken of earlier. Again I moved my arms within the leather, feeling the small bite of the wounds, regarding Tarla with some curiosity. Perhaps a word or two of suggestion might suffice the female.

"As he pleases you," said I, "why do you not take him as sthuvad? Such is not the way of city females, I know, yet might it be accomplished should you feel yourself determined."

"Sthuvad?" said she, raising her head and eyes to regard me. "What might be sthuvad, Jalav?"

About to reply, I hesitated, seeing the large-eyed female child and her close attention, true innocence seeking an answer which Mida had not meant her to have. No more could Tarla take Lialt as sthuvad than Mida be made to serve the wishes of another, and foolish indeed would I be to attempt the instruction of one such as she. Deeply, I sighed, and then gave to the girl a smile of encouragement.

"Perhaps we had best forget the matter of sthuvad," said I, shifting my legs with the fur coverings upon them. Much weightier did my legs now seem, an added burden to the soreness of my wounds. "One might recall, however, that males are ever prone to shifting about in their beliefs, now here, later there. That Lialt has once looked upon you fondly may mean that he shall do the same again."

"Never have I seen him so angered as when he must speak with you upon some matters," said she, her large eyes yet upon me. "It often seems that you take enjoyment from his anger, yet I know that this cannot be. There is no enjoyment for a woman in a man's anger."

"Perhaps a warrior may see that in a male's anger which city females do not," I murmured, stretching gently to ease the stiffness in my muscles. Tarla regarded me with greater curiosity, yet I was not of a mind to pursue the comment I had made. Should Mida wish the bereft to know of the true life, she shall undoubtedly send many warriors to assist with the attainment of their freedom. One warrior alone may do naught.

No further opportunity was there for discussion, for it was then that Lialt returned. The coldness which entered with the opening of the door was much lessened, yet this did naught to alter my dislike of the garments I had been given. Lialt, leaving the door ajar, came toward me, and again his anger had been replaced with a grin of amusement.

"Ah, Jalav," said he, "now do you seem the picture of a proper wench. Ceralt will be much pleased."

His amusement was as distasteful as ever, therefore I folded my arms and regarded the male coldly. "I know of none called Ceralt," said I, "nor have I desire to meet one such. And Lialt shall not know the true meaning of 'proper' till he has served Midanna as sthuvad. Then shall all things again be proper."

"No," denied Lialt, crouching down beside me, a deep satisfaction added to his amusement. "All is proper as it now stands, and such shall Jalav learn well, taught to her by Ceralt. Well am I able to understand that you do not wish to know Ceralt, for his lessons will not be gentle, wench. Yet it matters not, for you shall not escape your due. Come. The outer air awaits you."

With such words did Lialt then put his arms about me and lift me from the furs. Little effort was required to do so and I liked it not, neither the ease with which I was carried about, nor the words which had been spoken to me. Much like Ceralt was Lialt, dark-skinned and light-eyed, broad and strong. Lialt's arms about me did not bring the pain which Ceralt's brought, yet was there a shadow of his brother within him, a shadow which did much to disturb me. How was it that one male might easily be ignored, while another caused himself to be remembered even in his absence? I knew not the why of it, to this fey know only that it is so. There are males about who are beneath one's notice, and also those who may touch a warrior deeply, causing her great pain. Perhaps Mida may explain the matter; I am unable to do so.

Through the opened door was I carried, Tarla replacing the furs upon her own feet so that she might follow behind, at Lialt's bidding, with the lenga pelts which were mine. Mida's light shone down upon us, thin and without vigor, yet bright to the eyes of one so long within a dwelling. Chill was the air, as I had known it would be, as though Mida had withdrawn the warmth of her favor from the land. Thin grass and few trees appeared to the eye within the village, yet not far beyond the dwellings, to my right, lay the beginnings of the forest through which we had travelled. No more than twenty paces from the dwelling in which I had lain stood a tree, large yet nearly leafless, and to this tree was I carried, Tarla hurrying before us to place the pelts upon the ground. With the pelts placed as Lialt wished them, I was then returned to sitting upon them by the male who held me.

"There shall you stay till I come for you," said Lialt, straightening to standing. "Should you feel the chill too keenly, you may draw the second lenga pelt about you. As for us, the fey is lovely, and I have not seen enough of Tarla of late to satisfy me. We shall return when we return."

Lialt had turned to gaze upon Tarla as he spoke, extending his arm so that the female might approach him and be held. Eagerly she did this, her body flowing to his as she looked up to the face of him, his arm wrapped tightly about her, holding her close. Deep were the feelings which these two shared, yet as they walked from me, seeing naught save each other, I found that understanding had not touched me. What were these feelings which caused Lialt to look upon Tarla so fiercely, so strongly? For what reason did Tarla glow in such a gaze rather than shiver with fear? The girl knew little of the ways of males, never having been touched by any, even Lialt, for much had the female told me in the feyd of her time in the dwelling. Yet she had no fear of Lialt, merely of his displeasure, while I—I shook my head as I breathed deeply of the air, finding no understanding even in reflection. The matter was beyond me, beyond all I had known. It was necessary that I trust in Mida, and do no more than await her will.

I moved about upon the lenga pelt, sending my gaze to the left, where lay the largest part of the village. Although it had not seemed so in the darkness, the village now proved itself to be much larger than the Hosta home camp. Many hands of dwellings stood, one beyond the other, about a great circle, in the midst of which moved and worked large numbers of males and females. Children, too, played about the dwellings and across the circle, yet were there male children as well as female. Such a thing seemed odd, that male children would be kept and raised, and then I realized that these were city folk and not of the

Midanna. Strange were the ways of others, and not for a warrior to spend thought upon.

Across the great circle from where I sat was a large enclosure of wood, a thing of wide logs lashed tightly together with much leather. Within the enclosure moved the furred, white mounts of these village males, some standing quietly, some pacing restlessly about. In such a manner did city males keep their kand as well, yet the gandod of Midanna were not kept so. A warrior allowed her gandod to feed well, and then was it bound about the jaws and legs before being tied to a line of leather strung between trees. Should a warrior ever find the need to enter such an enclosure filled with gandod, there is little likelihood that she would find her way out again. The temper of the gando being as it is, the undertaking would not be one I, myself, would care to consider.

Voices drifted across the large circle, voices of males calling to one another, of females scolding children, of children raised in laughter. Sounds accompanied the voices, sounds which blended with and muted the voices so that few of the words were intelligible. Many smells reached me as well, smells of cooked meat and the sweat of beasts, and the trees of the forest and traces of the children of the wild. Mida's skies were blue above, something I could easily see as I leaned back against the leafless tree I had been placed near. Freedom was before me, my line of travel clearly marked by the movement of Mida's light, yet once again I was unable to avail myself of that which had been shown me. I was captive to the village and my wounds, a captivity which must not be long allowed to continue.

For more than a hin, I sat before the tree, none approaching nor giving indication that they were aware of my presence. The lack of attention pleased me, assuaging, somewhat, my annoyance over the garment which had been given me. True, the garment kept much of the chill of the air from my body, yet within it, I was unable even to sit cross-legged, as is my preference. No longer did I wonder why Tarla knelt as she did, for now I knew. There were few other positions possible to one in such a garment.

As a larger and larger number of reckid passed, I grew more and more firm in my need to know freedom once more. Determining that there were no eyes upon me, I cast about for a means of holding myself from the ground, and saw at once the branch which lay nearly at my feet. Clearly had it fallen from the tree against which I leaned, and clearly would it serve as that which I needed to brace myself to standing. I drew the branch to me, feeling the dryness of its dead husk, leaned it upright against the tree, then turned my body till I knelt upon hands and knees, my head nearest the tree. Many aches assailed me, pain from my wounds and from my back and from long inactivity, yet pain was no stranger to me. Despite the pain, I reached a hand to the tree, and then a second hand, and finally was I able to pull myself erect, to cling to the tree as though it were Mida herself. Dizziness swam about in my vision, attempting to raise my insides, a thing which caused me to give solemn thanks that I had not fed much that fey. My cheek against the leafless tree, I stood beneath the thin blue skies till the chill air had once again cleared my sight, then gave my full weight to my legs. Much did I experience a tearing sensation where the wounds lay, as though the healing skin strove to pull apart about the forming scars, yet no blood came to sight beneath the leather nor upon the leg furs. With great pleasure, I gave thanks for this to Mida, adding also a request that she still the trembling in each of my limbs, then reached the dead branch to me, holding to it with a double grasp as I looked about. Still were there no eyes upon me from those of the village, and though a new-born nilno was gainlier than I, I felt it an excellent time to take my leave. Should it be Mida's wish to see me survive in the forests, I would surely do so.

Slowly, I began moving to my right, each lifting of a fur-clad leg an effort. I leaned heavily upon the tree branch, disgusted with the weakness which sat leadenly upon me. Wounds were not unknown to a warrior, yet no warrior would welcome such wounds, nor their aftermath. To be unable to swing a sword or vault to the back of a gando is a great loss, one which has been known, upon occasion, to be fatal. Had there been Silla or other enemy Midanna about, I might have confidently looked forward to joining Mida forever. Without enemy Midanna, however, it might prove possible to attain the forests of freedom.

I had gone perhaps four hands of paces from the tree, watching carefully for that upon the ground which might cause a misstep, and therefore knew naught of those who awaited me till their feet and legs came to view. I paused in my forward movement, raising my eyes to their faces, and beheld three village females, somewhat of an age with Tarla, perhaps a bit older. All were dark of hair and eye, all were clad in the leather garment and leg furs which I, myself, wore, all had caused their hair to be plaited as Tarla had done with mine, and two were of a size with Tarla, that is to say, perhaps a head less than my height. The third female was larger than the other two, standing no more than four fingers below me, her head haughtily high, her eyes cold, her right fist arrogantly upon her hip. Well made and fair of face was this female, yet it seemed that she had little liking for the warrior who stood before her, and this I could not understand. I wore no clan colors, nor did she, therefore I knew not why her gaze was one which would be used for none save blood enemies. As she inspected me with contempt, I thought that perhaps the females looked so upon all who were not of their village. The other two seemed filled with as little warmth as the first, giving support to the thought, yet there also seemed more amiss than such an outlook might call for. Undoubtedly they had been told that Jalav was a captive within their village, and such coldness was their manner of facing captives, yet I had not thought that city females were allowed proximity to captives by their males. Within the leather I shrugged somewhat, knowing again that understanding of city ways was not yet mine and perhaps would never be. Those within the village went about their own affairs, too distant to hear the larger female as she spoke.

"So," said she with a coldness to match her gaze. "I am at last allowed the privilege of seeing the one who has taken the eye and heart of our High Rider. With due courtesy to his exalted station, perhaps he would do well to see to the healing of his vision—and his wits as well. There is naught before me save a ragged savage—bone thin and without stance or presence."

The two females beside her laughed in amusement, and she to the left of the larger nodded. "Indeed, Famira," said she, "it is as you say. See how she hobbles about as though from extreme age. Perhaps she is not as young as she at first appears."

"Undoubtedly she is lame as well as naturally ungainly," laughed the third, letting her eyes move over me. "Long have we wondered as to Ceralt's preference in women, and now we know. To catch his fancy, Famira, one must be a bent stick."

The amusement of the three increased with these words, yet I was unable to concern myself with insult. Dizziness had returned to me, causing beads of moisture to form upon my brow and body, increasing the trembling in my limbs, draining what little strength I had. No purpose was served in standing about with three witless females, and the longer I continued to do so, the shorter would be the distance I was able to put between my final step and the village. I turned from the females who yet stood in laughter and began to circle to their right with small, painful steps, yet she called Famira stood herself before me, keeping me from my chosen path. Again I raised my eyes to hers, yet this time the humor had gone from her, leaving naught save hate and loathing.

"Your life here will be a horror," she hissed, bringing her face closer to mine so that I might more easily see the twisting of it. "No woman of this village shall befriend you lest they face *my* displeasure! Errands given you by men shall find no assistance in their completion! Should you find yourself alone and far from your halyar, there will be sticks with which you are beaten, and should you cry your misery to Ceralt, there will be further beatings! You will heartily regret having been brought here, Savage. For this you have my word!"

Nearly foaming was the village female, so deeply did she feel her hate, and the war leader who was Jalav was unable to turn from her challenge. Aswim in dizziness and deepening pain, I forced my body to straighten itself so that I might stand tall and proud before her, answering her challenge with agreement to meet any manner of attack. No word was I able to speak, so great was the pain, yet my eyes said that which my tongue was unable to utter. Gasps came from the two females who accompanied her called Famira, their eyes widening as they looked upon a war leader who showed no fear, no uncertainty. The third female, startled, took herself back a step from my presence, yet her rage returned immediately, greatly intensified, and her foot lashed out, catching the limb which I still used to support a great deal of my weight. The limb flew from my grasp, destroying the delicate balance which I had accomplished, forcing my body's full weight onto my legs. Well had I known that I could not support myself without the aid of the limb, and I was not proven wrong. As the branch went from me, I went to the ground, finding it hard and cold and unwelcome. A stone met my side, bruising my flesh, the pain adding itself to all the rest. I gazed at the thin grass beneath my hands, attempting to breathe against the weight upon my chest, and again the laughter of the females came to me, thinner than it had been, yet heavy with scorn. Footsteps sounded upon the ground, and I raised my eyes to see the three females walking from me, pleasure and unconcern in the set of their shoulders. So casually would they have thrown away their lives had they been among Midanna, for one does not turn one's back upon a living enemy and expect to retain her own life. Much did I wish for the presence of a sword or dagger or spear, yet even more did I wish my strength returned to me, so that I might avenge myself upon these puny city females who dared, in their ignorance, to oppose themselves to a war leader of the Hosta. Briefly I attempted to rise again to my feet, yet my first effort showed the futility of the attempt. Barely could my arms support the presence of my shoulders, and my legs seemed totally useless. I sank back to the ground, bathed in the moisture of dizziness, and then came the sound of hurrying footsteps, and a hand grasped my arm.

"Jalav, what have they done to you?" demanded Lialt, his eyes flashing over me as his arm supported me from the ground. "Ceralt shall hear of this, I swear it!"

"That Famira!" spat Tarla furiously, bending to me. "She should have been made to circle long ago, for had she been drawn by a rider, her temper would long since have been seen to! It is high time she felt the leather for her actions!"

"No longer shall she be exempt," said Lialt grimly, and then was I lifted in his arms. "Tarla," said he, his steps leading back to the dwelling from which I had so briefly been released. "Bring the furs quickly, for I must examine her wounds."

Obediently, Tarla nodded and sped to the tree where the lenga pelts lay, and in but a handful of reckid, I again lay upon them in the dwelling. Tarla, with Lialt's assistance, removed the leather garment and fur wrappings from me, then Lialt carefully examined the tracks of the Silla spears. Angrily red did the tracks show themselves to be, throbbing and aching so that surely I thought movement would be visible upon them. Lialt cared little for the look of the wounds, and fetched a salve which he rubbed gently upon me. The salve eased the ache and throbbing somewhat, allowing me to rest, and the two village folk took themselves from my side to stand by the fire and speak to one another in murmurs. I closed my eyes in the comfort and warmth of the lenga pelts, reflecting that Lialt had not questioned the why of my having been found so far from the tree. Perhaps Mida had seen to this omission, or perhaps the presence of the female Famira had accomplished it, yet it mattered not. Lialt did not know that I had attempted escape, therefore he would not, in future, be on his guard. I smiled somewhat, knowing that though the time had not been proper

for escape, the opportunity would come again, when I was able
to avail myself of it. Then Jalav would retrace her steps to
the Midanna, and find the means by which the Hosta might be
freed. So pleasant was the thought that sleep came easily to
cure my exhaustion.

# 7.

## *The white land—*
## *and a punishment for escape*

In the next three feyd, I was not again allowed alone from the
dwelling, yet twice each fey was I placed before the leafless tree.
At these times Lialt sat beside me, speaking little yet ever
present, a thing I cared little for. When in the dwelling, either
alone or with none save Tarla about, I had worked much toward
restoring my strength, flexing arms and legs and thighs, placing
my full weight slowly yet completely as it should be. A dozen
times had I walked the length of the dwelling, Tarla seeing none
of this, at first stiffly and with much pain, at last nearly as easily
as I had done before my meeting with the Silla, and greatly
pleased was I that my strength had returned so quickly. Yet there
was another thing which disturbed me, a problem I had no
solution to, a problem first spoken of by Ceralt upon his return,
two feyd after she called Famira had approached me. At his
arrival, I sat upon the lenga pelt in my dwelling, again seeing to
the removal of knots from my hair, and his grin was large indeed
as he approached.

"Your ability in healing has my greatest admiration, brother,"

said he to Lialt who had accompanied him. "Her skin has again
the look of life to it, and her body seems even this soon to have
regained a deal of flesh. She will look well in the circle with my
leather about her, of this I have no doubt."

"Indeed," nodded Lialt, also agrin. "She regains her vitality
so quickly that even I am amazed. Perhaps she may be circled
the next moon—with Famira to accompany her. Your riders
seem pleased that Famira may now be looked upon."

"They are extremely pleased," laughed Ceralt, his eyes yet
upon me. "My uncle has too long presumed upon the lack of a
woman of his own to keep his daughter from circling. Should he
need his halyar tended to, there are sufficient females about who
have been left without a man, and he may choose from among
those. Famira goes to one who shall not be a father to her."

"A thing she does not care for," chuckled Lialt, his eyes, too,
upon me. "Much did she rage and carry on when your decision
reached her, for she hoped to be the one to choose to whom she
would go. Drimin would have been her choice, for he is unusually shy with wenches and would have easily been controlled by
her, yet Drimin shall not return from the rounds of trade till
after she has been circled. A full rider shall have her, and not she
him."

"Such shall prove best for her," murmured Ceralt, bending to
me to put the backs of his fingers to my cheek. "A strong wench
requires a stronger man if she is to find happiness and pleasure."

In anger, I struck his hand from me, yet he did no more than
laugh and stand erect again. His eyes were filled with great
desire, and once he had gone, I examined my ribs in misery. In
truth, my appetite of late had been immense, and the gauntness I
had been so pleased with was nearly gone. No more than three
feyd had passed, yet the gauntness was nearly gone! I took the
wooden comb in my hand and threw it from me, watching in
great anger as it struck the wall of the dwelling and fell to the
floor. A warrior had no need to understand the doings of Mida,
merely had she to accept them, yet the acceptance of what had
been done to me was difficult indeed. In no way save through
Mida's intervention could I have regained my former appearance,
and much did I wish to rail at such a doing. Now I was again
pleasing to males, again the object of their desire, a thing
which would make escape much more difficult. I lay upon my
belly in the lenga furs, angry, hurt, miserable. Was it Mida's
wish that I again be punished for some error or omission? Had I
failed again to obey her commands, or was I still condemned for

earlier failures? I knew not which it was, and very nearly cared
naught for the meaning. Much had I striven to obey Mida, and
much had I been punished for my failures, yet now it seemed
that I might not be given further opportunity for obedience.
Again I feared that I had been given into the hands of males
forever, and I fretted the point till sickness filled me, yet when
Tarla brought my provender at darkness, I could do naught save
fall upon it. A warrior's strength, it seemed, was to be returned
to her, yet not without a price. I fed upon the provender, seeing
little else which might be done, and thought only of the time
when I might find escape.

Upon the fourth fey, seeing that little had been accomplished
by pretense of weakness—the males had continued to force the
potion of sleep upon me—and driven nearly mad by the long
confinement, I determined that that fey I would walk about my
place of capture. When Lialt arrived to carry me to the tree, he
discovered Jalav erect upon her feet, prepared to walk about
wherever needful. Tarla had been startled by my mobility, yet
Lialt appeared to have expected some such. No more was needed
than a small amount of argument before it was established that I
might go where I would with none save Tarla accompanying me.
Such a decision pleased me, for Tarla was neither warrior nor
male, and should the opportunity arise, escape from her would
not be difficult.

With Lialt gone upon his way, Tarla and I emerged from the
dwelling into a fey which was lacking in brightness. Gray were
the skies above us, high yet seemingly not far distant, and the
cold of the air was quiet, with no wind to disturb it. I shivered in
my leather garment, smelling a smell upon the air which I knew
not, and Tarla also looked about herself.

"Perhaps this winter the snows may come early," said she,
her nostrils flaring slightly, showing that she, too, was aware of
the smell in the air. "Lialt has said that the snows shall not this
soon be upon us, yet this fey may prove him wrong."

"Tarla," said I, looking upon her, "what might 'snows' be? I
have heard mention of it, yet never have I been told the meaning
of the thing."

The female's dark eyes left off their roving and came to me
with surprise strong in them. "Have you never seen snow,
Jalav?" she asked, her head to one side. "Your land must be
strange indeed never to have produced snow."

"My land is ever warm," said I, somewhat annoyed with her

tone, "not bleak and lifeless as the land hereabouts. Sooner would I have the warmth."

"And I would not have missed knowing snow," said she with a shrug. "Perhaps you may judge more accurately when once you have seen it. Snow, Jalav, comes from the skies in the manner of rain, yet it is white and light and silent and able to fill the entire land with its presence. It lies upon the ground, often in mounds, and is very cold to the touch. Children joy in playing in it, yet it is difficult to travel about in it. Such is snow—both a joy and a difficulty."

"I see," said I, moving slowly across the ground as I thought upon her words. Snow, then, was Mida-sent, yet I was unable to visualize what the occurrence must be like. Surely Tarla must partly be in error, for how might the substance fall lightly yet lie heavily upon the ground? Deeply did I sigh then, wishing myself more than ever back among the Midanna, where a warrior might know the why of things about her. The lands of males held naught save questions without answers, problems without solutions, ills without cures. Even Mida's ground lay hard and cold beneath one's feet, bringing about the necessity for furs upon one's legs, garments upon one's body. Much did I dislike the presence of such things yet, in the lands of males, they were necessary.

Tarla and I walked from the vicinity of my dwelling, yet I was not yet of a mind to enter further into the village. Many village folk were about, as seemed to be usual, and no wish had I to join them in their movings about. Rather, I walked toward the enclosure of the white beasts, wishing to see more of them, feeling my curiosity aroused. Within the enclosure were a number of males, they being watched by a number of females who stood beyond the confines of the enclosure, and much pleased did the females seem to be. Their voices rose in great excitement and laughter, their hands clasped or pounded upon the wood of the enclosure, and clearly were they unable to keep from jumping about where they stood. Tarla, too, laughed softly as she looked upon them, yet I saw naught which might call for amusement.

"Let us hurry, Jalav," said Tarla, taking a grip upon the leather of my sleeve, her eyes yet upon the enclosure. "The riders are about to break more of the lanthay to the rein, and we are in time to watch. Hurry, Jalav, hurry!"

Such was the urgency in the young female's tone that I quickened my pace as she had asked, though I knew not the reason for haste. Shortly we stood before the enclosure, which was made of logs hewn from trees, they then being bound with much leather to upright posts at each end. These logs stood my height from the ground, a height which allowed the beasts, apparently called lanthay, to place no more than their heads and necks above the obstruction to their freedom. The village females, in high good humor, peered between the logs at that which was occurring within the enclosure, yet I, taller than they, found the position uncomfortable. I gazed a moment at the logs before me, then, with some noticeable protest from my healing wounds, climbed the logs to their top, thereby obtaining an unrestricted view of the goings-on within.

Perhaps two hands of males stood within the enclosure, most with the short, heavy twisting of leather usually worn at their belts now in their hands, their attention upon the greater number of lanthay which had been herded toward the far end of the area. As I settled myself atop the highest post, two of the males cracked their twisted leather whips toward the herded lanthay, causing them to move backward from the line of males. The balance of the males looked toward three who stood closer to the post I sat upon, they three being engaged with a single lanthay which obviously had not yet been shown the superiority of two-legged beasts. The lanthay stood much as unbroken gandod do, four legs spread wide against the bending of its neck by two of the males, its head and ears firmly in their grasp, its entire body attempting to pull loose from that which held it. The two males strained to keep the beast still while the third placed a wide leather strap about its middle, just above the shoulders. The third male worked quickly, and when the strap had been set he grasped a leather lead which led to the beast's mouth, mounted in one smooth leap, clutched the strap with his right hand while keeping the lead in his left, and shouted to the two males who held the lanthay. At his shout, the two males moved as one, throwing themselves from the sides of the lanthay, running rapidly in opposite directions. In Midanna lands, there had sometimes been gandod who had not realized that they had been freed, gandod who stood with jaws bound shut yet otherwise free, but unmoving as though they were still held. The lanthay before me had no such misconceptions, for as soon as it was released, it screamed its rage, throwing its head back in an attempt to strike the puny annoyance upon it and free itself completely. The male wisely avoided the thrust of the white, furred head, which further enraged the beast. It reared high and smote the air with battering hooves while screaming its challenge

to all within hearing, then began jumping about and kicking out
with its rear hooves. The male upon its back clung with hands
and knees, clung through the trumpeting challenge and bone-
jarring leaps, clung through the shaking and twisting, already
beginning to use the leather rein to curtail and guide his mount.
The lanthay jumped stiff-legged toward the wall of the enclosure,
blazing rage in its large, red eyes, and the females who stood
there screamed and backed hurriedly away, fearful lest the beast
come through the wall at them. The male attempted to force his
mount back toward the center of the enclosure, yet his efforts
were in vain. I, having seen such behavior from gandod many
times, merely gripped the log I sat upon as the giant lanthay
hurled itself against the logs of the enclosure, attempting to crush
the life from the male upon its back. The logs trembled to the
onslaught, too sturdy to sway as a lighter wall might, yet not
untouched by the attack. The males within the enclosure, those
keeping the herd of other lanthay at bay, called out to the rider
with laughter and encouragement and advice, all watching
attentively, none seeming concerned. Tarla, who had joined the
watching females, now stood back from the wall with them,
alarmed, as were the others, and then, amid the screams of
fright, the male upon the lanthay behaved foolishly. The beast
had been twisting toward the wall, hoping to scrape the male
from his seat, and the male, fearing that his right leg would be
crushed between the beast and the wood, shifted his weight and
knee grip. As swiftly as lightning strikes from Mida's skies, so
swiftly did the lanthay see the meaning of the movement upon its
back, and immediately it, too, moved to advantage. Its head
went down as its hind quarters erupted toward the skies, and the
male, no longer deeply seated, was thrown to the ground over
the lanthay's head. He struck the ground heavily, pain flashing
across his face as the metal of his belt was driven into his back,
yet this was not his most pressing problem. The lanthay, knowing that that which lay before it was the enemy which had dared
to mount it, sounded its challenge once again, then made for the
male. He upon the ground knew well that the lanthay wished his
blood, for he made haste to roll from the path of the thundering
hooves which were meant to take the life from him, his effort
taking him to safety by no more than a finger's width. Upon the
charge of the lanthay, those two males who had aided the third to
mount, raced forward with twisted leather flails cracking, and
drove the lanthay from him upon the ground. Such foolishness
caused me to laugh softly, for among the Midanna there would

have been none to chase the gando from him. A warrior knows that should she show weakness before any gando, even one broken to the rein, the gando will strike immediately, taking her life if possible. A warrior who wishes to teach a gando mastery does so alone, for there may not be others about should the gando, one fey, revert. A Hosta who has taken seat upon a new mount is then alone, to overcome or be overcome. In no other way might Midanna use the gando with confidence.

The male upon the ground looked about himself, then rose to his feet and brushed the dirt from his leathers, also putting a hand to his back where the fall had hurt him. His eyes slid past the knot of anxious females, who still gazed upon the retreating, trumpeting lanthay with fear, then came to rest upon me where I sat atop the wall. The garment I wore was a great annoyance, nearly too tight to allow me my seat upon the wall, yet I paid it little mind as I gazed upon the male. He, large and strongly made, dark of hair and eye as were the others, frowned as he looked upon me, then moved the closer.

"Your amusement is offensive, wench," said he in a rasp of a voice, looking up to where I sat. "Should you be made to take seat upon a wild lanthay, your own self, you would find little to amuse you!"

"It was not the ride which was amusing," said I, the still grinning. "Males must ever seek the aid of others, unable to do a thing themselves. Should you have been alone with the beast, upon a plains, perhaps, would you also have allowed it the opportunity to reach you as you did just now?"

The male stood angrily, fists on hips, face raised toward me, yet he made no answer, for the answer was clear. Had he been alone, his effort would have been greater; he had allowed the presence of others to lull his achievement from him. No warrior would have behaved so, and his skin darkened with annoyance and perhaps humiliation.

"Who are you?" he demanded, his brows creased in a frown. "What village do you come from that you feel free to speak to a rider so?"

"I come from no village," I replied, raising my head somewhat. "I am of the Hosta of the Midanna, a people far superior to those of any village. The males hereabouts would find little patience for their lacks in the land of the Midanna."

I spoke with some annoyance, for I tired of the manner in which males addressed me. No respect had they for a war leader, and much would I have joyed in leading my warriors against them. The male before me frowned further, then his features cleared as a malicious grin touched him.

"You are the savage wench fetched here by Ceralt!" said he, his large hands reaching forth to grasp the logs of the wall as he pulled himself up to sit beside me. His eyes moved about me in a manner he had not used before, and he laughed as my chin rose high in insult. "I now see why Ceralt is eager for you to circle," said he with a chuckle. "You are indeed a beauty, made to inspire a man to high achievement in the furs. Perhaps my leather, too, shall await you from without the circle."

I cared little for the words and look of the male, and less for the intimidation that I would soon be chosen by any who desired me. Bleakly I looked upon the male and shook my head.

"Jalav has ever chosen her males," said I. "A thing which those of the villages shall learn. I am not to be chosen as though I were slave, male, and I shall not remain prisoned here forever. With Mida's aid, I shall once again ride with my warriors, and then shall those of the villages beware."

"Female warriors!" laughed he beside me, striking his thigh in high amusement. "Such a battle would indeed be enjoyable, nearly as enjoyable as the following victory celebration. I would pierce many of you wenches with my sword—but not the sword carried in my hand—and then would you be made to serve me on bended knee, a fitting punishment for wenches who dared to try their strength with men!"

Others of the males had joined us, and they, too, raised their voices in laughter and derision. I looked upon the males as they stood about, recalling a time when strangers—males—had entered the lands of the Midanna, from whence, none knew. Hunting parties of Helda and Hitta had been taken by them, the males using ropes of leather to snare the warriors from the backs of kand, allowing some warriors to escape as though their freedom were of no consequence. Quickly had the escaped warriors alerted their sister clans, and many Midanna had ridden forth, the Hosta, being closest, the first to arrive. Much had the males abused the warriors they had taken, and great was the rage of the Hosta upon seeing this. With deliberation were the males encircled, and then the Hosta, on foot, showed themselves. The males, large, armed, in numbers equal to the Hosta who had ridden forth, had grinned and risen to their feet, intent upon drawing the Hosta, too, within the forest clearing where they held those previously taken. The males had drawn swords negligently, laughing, thinking to take the Hosta as easily by sword as they had taken the Helda and Hitta with leather. Upon seeing their advance, I had signaled the attack, and Hosta warriors, joyfully shouting their battle cry, had fallen upon them. Quickly, then, had the males' laughter ceased, and they fought desperately for their lives, for they were not as well versed in swords as they were with leather. He who had stood before me had had hair of red, his pale skin paling further as he attempted to keep my point from him. With kill-lust burning high within me, I struck at him with my sword, right thigh, left arm, head and chest. He had had attempted to meet the movements of mine, yet his sword had failed to do so, crying out when my edge had opened his arm and leg, losing precious moments to pain and fear as I moved in for the kill. When he lay in spreading blood at my feet, my sword adrip with his life essence, when all the males had been done so, the Hosta had raised their arms to Mida, dedicating the blood and males to her who watched over her daughters. Well did Midanna know the use of a sword, and perhaps, should it be the will of Mida, these males before me would, to their sorrow, learn this as had others before them.

I looked again upon the male who sat beside me, and smiled in fond remembrance. "May Mida hear your wish for battle and grant your plea," said I to him, much pleased with such a thought. I then began to climb down from the wall, seeing glancingly that the humor had left a number of the males who had heard my words, yet he who sat upon the wall was not one of them.

"My sword would seek you first, wench," he called after me, laughing yet in great good humor. "Now that I have seen you, I think the time is ripe to show Ceralt that there are other men in this village."

The words he spoke had no meaning for me, yet they seemed to affect the others who stood about. The males, in their leathers and silver-chased belts, looked quietly upon one another with looks which seemed to hold meaning for them, while the females, some yet laughing delightedly over that which had been said to me, gazed solely at me with an insolence which brought a great deal of annoyance. Tarla stood apart from them, showing much distress upon her child's face as she looked upon him astride the wall. The thought came that perhaps she knew the male's meaning, yet it mattered not. He upon the wall was merely male, of no great consideration nor concern. I took myself toward Tarla and past her, wondering yet again how one walked any great distances in the fur leg wrappings. The weight of them dragged

one's feet to the ground, slowing the step and destroying the
pace that is able to take one so far. In a scant moment, Tarla's
hurrying footsteps brought her in my wake, leaving the laughter
and strangers behind us.

The fey remained gray about us as we walked further toward
the heart of the village, and a small wind had begun which blew
my unbound hair about my arms and thighs. With the wind, the
cold had increased, and I quickly saw the value in drawing the
leather ties of one's garment as tightly as possible. Tarla, by my
side, glanced with dismay at my flying hair, for she had not
approved of my having unbound it. Women of the village ever
wore their hair bound, she had said with pleading in her eyes.
Men did not care to see them unkempt for it detracted from their
beauty, she had said. I said naught and merely continued to
unplait my hair, and Tarla had bitten her lips and had not
broached the matter again. As I walked, I briefly became aware
of my life sign, that of the hadat, which hung between my
breasts beneath the covering. Tarla had often gazed upon the
carved wood of it, and had once suggested that I ask Ceralt to
make me another, one which would lack the flat brown stain of
the one I wore. The stain marred one's sight of the wood grain,
and she had felt that a new carving would give a better appearance.
I had smiled at her words, recalling my first battle as a warrior,
how proudly I had worn the life sign which I had carved from
the tree marked like mine from birth. Then my life sign had been
unstained, yet at battle's end, with an enemy Semma lying still
at my feet, I had removed the life sign from about my neck, held
it by its leather tie, and had dipped it thrice into Semma blood.
Once in thanks to Mida, twice to give thanks that I was of the
Hosta, thrice in thanks for the glory of battle, asking that I be
granted such glory many times before being called to Mida's
side. Then the life sign had been replaced by my war leader,
proclaiming to all that I had become a blooded warrior of the
Hosta. The Semma blood had felt warm and sticky against my
breasts; the life sign had spread the blood upon me; my pride and
pleasure had been so great that I had barely felt the stab of pain
from the silver ring of a warrior as it had been forced through
my ear. Never does a warrior forget the time of the staining of
her life sign, and I had laughed well at Tarla's suggestion. Ask
Ceralt for another indeed!

The folk of the village seemed not to notice the chill of the air,
and some few of the males were bare-chested, wearing no more
than the leather breech and leggings, silvered belt, and fur leg

wrappings. One male seemed to have recently arrived, for he stood before a dwelling unburdening a lanthay, three small children jumping about beside him. A female appeared in the doorway of the dwelling, her leather garment unbelted so as not to bind her slightly swelling belly, her face wearing a look of radiant joy. The male turned to her and she hurried to him from the doorway, his arms bringing her close to his chest and lips. Much did the male drink from the lips of his female, she standing contentedly in the circle of his arms, and then he laughed and took a leather pack from the lanthay, left the beast standing tied by the dwelling, sent the children about their business of play, and drew the female into the dwelling with him. Much hunger had been in the eyes of the male, and long would be the use of the female. As she already carried a child within her, I wondered that the male did not seek the use of another female. All know that males care only for their own pleasure and the getting of their offspring, therefore it seemed odd that the male would take a female who had already been quickened and would not, in such a state, afford him the pleasure of one not so quickened. Indeed the matter seemed odd, yet, as I have said, understanding was not mine in the land of males.

Large was the number of females I saw as I walked about, and many were the tasks which they had been set. Some cured hides for the leather of garments, some skinned small, furred children of the wild, some sat before their dwellings, binding leather together for garments. Some spoke to one another as they passed in and out of the dwellings, and I noted that those who went within emerged again in a very short time. Children ran about everywhere, children of all ages, male and female alike, though there seemed to be many females who had shortly before reached womanhood and few males who were no longer boys. Through the shouting and laughter of the children, I questioned Tarla on the matter and was informed that the young males had been taken by their elders to learn that which a village male must know. Though there were many smells of meat and vegetables aroast on the air, and smells of leather and beasts and all manner of things unguessed at, no trace of the pungent oil for swords did I find in their midst, no sign of weapons of any sort among the females. I looked again upon these slave-women, one of whom, bent over, took a bluish-white liquid from the teats of a small animal, allowing the liquid to fill a deep pot, and attempted to fathom the why of their remaining slave to males. Had they no desire to ride free as Midanna did, had they no yearnings for the glory of battle? For what reason had Mida spurned them, turning her back upon their plight? Had they sinned so greatly then, that they were forever lost? Would such a fate be given a warrior who failed in her compliance with Mida's demands? Deeply did the chill of the wind touch me, setting my bones ashiver, and bleak indeed was the fey I looked upon. The grass beneath my feet yet held to its place, though soon it would be no more, and none save mindless slave-women might find joy in the midst of a lifeless land. Wounded, nearly dead, I had been brought to such a land by males, males who would take all from me without thought to any save themselves. My gaze rose to the thick, gray clouds above, seeking a sign from Mida that I had not been abandoned, yet no such sign was forthcoming. For long moments did I stand so, yearning toward Mida's skies, and then I felt a gentle touch upon my arm.

"Jalav, you seem weary," said Tarla, her voice soft yet concerned. "Let us return to your halyar."

I shook my head, leaving the searching of the skies for another time, and again began walking past the dwellings. I had somehow thought that perhaps there might be a weapon among the village females which I might make mine, yet I had seen none where there had not also been males. Each of the males wore a dagger at his belt, some bore spears, some bows, yet none of these things had been left in the possession of a female, and I saw no swords. Perhaps the males feared that a female with weapon in hand would attempt escape or battle, or perhaps it was merely that slave-women feared the touching of weapons. Whichever the truth of the matter, I saw naught which Jalav might take and use as her own.

As I continued to look about, I grew aware of a lessening in the sounds about me. The females, in groups and alone, all seemed much interested in the look of Jalav. They stared with odd expressions upon their faces; those who sat or stood with others whispered animatedly, many were wide-eyed, some were amused. The older children, seeing the interest of their elders, also emulated their stares, attempting to pierce the mystery of she who walked among them. Only the looks of the males was I able to fathom, for they looked upon me as had the males who came to the slave enclosures of Bellinard, where I had once been pent. Their eyes showed great desire and hunger, yet none attempted to approach me and make his desire known. Most of the males I had seen were tall and strong, broad of shoulder and chest and lean of waist. Many would have been quickly taken and put to sthuvad use in the lands of Midanna, yet none approached and made his desire known. Briefly, my thoughts touched the memory of Pileth, a male of Bellinard, called Captain of the High Seat's Guard, one who had not hesitated to make his desire for me known. Much had Pileth and I pleasured one another, seeing to our mutual needs, yet these males about me said naught of their desire. Strange were males in their various ways, truly strange, and a warrior did well to keep her thoughts from them.

Tarla, too, saw the looks about us and grew exceedingly anxious, yet she made no further suggestions that we return to my dwelling. My legs, though yet with the strength needed to carry me, nevertheless felt greatly wearied and had begun to throb a bit about the wounds. Leaves now flew about the ground above the dying grass, leaves of many colors which gave a false feeling of life to the land. The dwellings in their places, each of wood of a weathered brown, the village folk, each in leather of tan and furs of gray, all seemed part of the death of warmth, yet the scattering leaves reminded one that life remained elsewhere, among a people freer and happier than those about me. I continued to walk among the stares and whispers, Tarla unhappily by my side, and kept my thought with those in other lands.

A number of reckid passed in silent walking, and then Tarla again grasped my arm. "There is Lialt's halyar," said she, much relief in evidence as she pointed toward a dwelling which stood among the others and yet also apart. Beside it stood a second dwelling, also among the others yet also apart, and Tarla saw my eyes upon it.

"That is the halyar of Ceralt," said she, something of a smile upon her lips. "It is forbidden that you now enter therein, else I would show you where you shall dwell, yet you may enter Lialt's dwelling, where I may not. Go within and see if Lialt is about, for I would not face the return walk past the others alone if there is no necessity for it. Much would I have preferred the presence of snow upon the ground, for snow shall drive those tongue-waggers within their halyars." She turned about to look angrily toward the females who yet stood about and whispered, then returned her gaze to me. "Hurry, Jalav," said she, making motions toward the dwelling with her hands. "There is naught improper in your entering. You have my word!"

I looked upon her in curiosity, caring naught for matters of propriety nor the stares of others. "You may not enter Lialt's dwelling?" said I, my head to one side. "For what reason is this so?"

Impatience flashed in the large, dark eyes before me, and Tarla took a breath before replying. "Lialt has said that he shall draw me from the circle," said she, the patience in her tone of the sort one uses with those who know little. "I am now forbidden entrance to his halyar till he has fetched new lacings to me in my father's halyar, and has led me within himself. So do matters stand between you and Ceralt, yet there is naught between you and Lialt, therefore may you enter his halyar—with haste!"

Again words spoken to me held no meaning, and I felt myself fool for having asked. It is truly no wonder that city folk know so little, for how may one learn Mida's ways when all one's time is spent upon foolishness of the sort Tarla was ever concerned with? I shook my head, brushing a strand of hair from my face, well aware of Tarla's anxiety. Her eyes were now pleading as she looked up at me, therefore I shrugged in resignation and turned to Lialt's dwelling. Much pleased was I that it was not Ceralt's dwelling which I must enter, for I had no desire to go where the male dwelt. Tarla was much mistaken in believing that I, too, would dwell there, yet I had not corrected her in her ignorance. When the time came, my actions would instruct her more fully than any words.

A strip of leather hung through a small hole in Lialt's door, and a pull upon the leather caused the wooden bar within to rise and allow the door its opening. Why these villagers used naught of doors which swung both in and out I knew not, yet the matter was so. To enter a dwelling within the village, one must pull upon leather. The interior was much the same as my dwelling, yet there was more within to show the presence of an owner. Here and there, upon the walls, were woven mats, yellows and reds and blues and greens, all mixed about and blended as though the falling leaves had been captured and formed. To the left of the door were leather cases, piled one upon the other, a set of fur leg wrappings astand beside the cases, as though recently left. Thinking that Lialt perhaps lay sleeping within I entered further, allowing the door to fall closed behind me, yet the closing of the door left no place where Lialt might be. To the right of the door, in the near corner, stood the dwelling's unused fireplace, a fire blazing only in the hearth to the far left. Below a window in the right wall stood a low platform, a full lenga pelt

upon the floor before it, and strung between the right wall and
the far wall, suspended from heavy metal hooks of the sort
which were also to be found in my dwelling, was a thick, tightly
bound length of leather, a length which exceeded the height of a
tall male. To what purpose this length of leather might be put I
knew not, nor did I care. That which village folk do holds little
interest for a warrior.

About to retrace my steps to Tarla, I halted as movement of
some sort past the window caught my eye. No more than a flash
of tan had there been, yet the thought came that perhaps Lialt
was to be found without the dwelling to its rear. In truth, I had
little wish to find the male, yet Tarla had seemed most anxious,
and Hosta shall ever repay assistance to those to whom it is due.
Tarla had served me well in the weakness of my wounds, and
now might I, in some measure, return her aid. I strode to the
window, feeling the warmth of the dwelling caused by the fire,
and looked through to the outside. Beyond the woven window
cover lay naught save a clearing, beyond that the beginning of
the forest. Trees now waved gently in the wind which had
sprung up, yet they waved to emptiness for naught living appeared to my sight. The window cover, made fast to the frame
with rebal sap and woven from the clear thread of the commonly
found tree maglessa, took very little from the true view of that
which lay beyond the window. Midanna themselves have no
need of the light thread produced by the maglessa, yet often is it
found in use by village males and their slave-women. Those of
the village of Islat, a place in the lands of Midanna, also make
use of the thread for their windows, yet the woven cloth is
placed upon a frame which may be swung wide from the window
itself. In such a manner do Islat folk make use of the cloth to
protect their dwellings from the rains of Mida, and at other times
swing the frames wide to allow entrance to the sweet, warm air
of our land. Water and air find no easy passage through the
thread, a thing to be thankful for in the village of those called
Belsayah, a place where there is little in all to be thankful for.

There being no further reason to stand before the window I
began to step away, yet my gaze was immediately taken by that
which lay upon the small, low platform beneath the window. I
had not earlier seen the contents of the platform for my gaze had
been for that which lay beyond the window, yet now I saw with
great pleasure that Lialt had left a pipe and sack to hand, a
fire-maker within easy reach of them. Long had it been since last
I had filled a pipe, and surely had I thought that those of the

cities knew naught of the pleasure a well-filled pipe might give.
The pipe, carved from the black wood of the binda tree, lay
smooth and inviting upon the platform, its very presence proclaiming its availability for use. Should one not wish one's pipe
used, one puts it beyond the sight of others.

Eagerly I took the pipe up, admiring the rubbed smoothness of
its bowl, then opened the leather sack from which it might be
filled. The grains within appeared odd, small, coarse and brown
as they should have been, yet also with some bits of yellow well
mixed within it. I considered the mixture briefly, then shrugged
and filled the pipe. That Lialt used the mixture proved its
acceptability, for what may a male do that a warrior may not?

The lenga pelt at my feet seemed equally as inviting as the
pipe, therefore I seated myself before putting the flamemaker to
its use. The discomfort of the garment I wore tempted me to call
Mida's vengeance down upon it, yet I refrained as I puffed the
pipe to life. The taste of it was not unpleasant, a sweetness
seemingly added by the yellow substance, and I leaned back in
comfort, shaking my hair from my arms as I drew further upon
the stem, the aches and strains of the fey draining slowly from
my body and mind.

Not long had I lain there, full upon the lenga pelt, drawing
upon the pipe, when a great lethargy came over me. My arms
and legs, no more than normally weary earlier, now felt possessed of great weight and little strength, much as though I were
once again chained beneath the ground in Bellinard, and my
vision swam about as though seeking a new viewpoint. Hand and
pipe dropped as one to the wood beyond the pelt, my head fell to
the pelt in a cloud of sweet-smelling smoke, and my hearing,
keen as only that of a hunter and warrior might be, no longer
touched the sounds of the world about me. Great clouds of white
billowed, at once within as well as about me, and I no longer felt
the warmth of the dwelling nor the discomfort of the garment.
More thickly did the clouds swirl, thick as bits of leaves from the
trees, yet lighter, as light as down from the feathered children of
the wild. Well I knew that I lay upon the lenga fur in Lialt's
dwelling, more helpless than when I lay beneath the spears of the
Silla, yet I felt that I stood elsewhere, a distant land that was not
a true land, a place where none save shadows dwelt. A feeling of
menace caused me to stare about, to see what stood beyond the
concealing clouds. No longer was my body constrained by the
presence of garment and fur leg-wrappings, a thing most
pleasurable—yet more than disturbing in its unexpectedness. I

felt as though there were eyes upon me from out of the white,
eyes sober with intensity, hard with deep-seeking interest, a
feeling which caused me to move even farther from where I had
first found myself. An unmeasured time I moved so, gaining
very little distance as movement through the white was difficult,
and then with unsettling suddenness the whiteness thinned to
where I might see farther than my hand before my face, yet that
which I saw was no comfort. The white was deeply piled upon
the ground beneath my feet, stretching far into the distance with
naught to obstruct it, yet was it plain to see that many tracks ran
through the mounds, tracks which led in many hands of directions.
I stood upon the soft whiteness, staring about at the tracks, and
then my eyes went farther, to where the tracks led. Most tracks
disappeared from sight into the distance, yet some seemed to
lead, a long way off, to tiny movement of tiny forms. Much
curiosity filled me as to what the movement might be, and
despite the remaining sense of presence, I wished to go closer to
the movement. There was a ripple in the unseen presence about
me, disapproval strong and clear, yet the call of the movement
ahead was strong, as though I were bound to it in some manner. I
took a step forward, feeling the disapproval increase though I
cared naught for it, and the call of the movement increased as
well. I would go to the place which lured me so, for there, I felt
sure, lay knowledge which I would do well to have.

No more than three steps did I take when Lialt abruptly
appeared from nothingness, a hand of paces away, and his eyes
found me where I stood.

"Jalav, return with me at once!" said he, angrily though I had
not heard his voice. His lips had moved, forming the words he
had wished to speak to me, yet no sound had traveled between
us. The meaning of his speaking alone had come, deep within
my head, and I saw that he, too, was unclothed. His very
presence was annoyance, for I had no wish to share that place,
nor was I yet prepared to return. Without speaking I turned from
him and began to move toward my goal, yet the movement was
still as slow as it had been—for me. Lialt, somehow, had not the
difficulty that I found, and within three paces he had come far
enough from where he had stood to place an arm before me.

"We shall now return!" said he without sound, his light eyes
nearly wild with anger. "Come of your own volition, or be
forced to my will!"

"I go elsewhere," said I, also without sound as I returned his
gaze. "Your will means naught."

Surely did my meaning reach him, for his eyes began to blaze as I turned my face once more toward the movement which I wished to approach. His arm, still held before me, seemed a slim barrier to my purpose, for an arm is easily avoided, yet this conclusion proved to be an error. With no further words and more quickly than I would have thought possible, the arm encircled me, and immediately upon contact all about me vanished.

In the blackness which I next found myself, breathing proved nearly as difficult as motion. The weight of all things seemed to be upon me, and only slowly did I become aware of that which surrounded me. The sweetness in the air was very faint, a last lingering memory of that which had been, and my sight returned with the awareness of Lialt's arm about me, holding my shoulders from the lenga pelt and forcing a pot of liquid to my lips. No more than three swallows of the liquid was I allowed before the pot was taken from my lips, yet those three swallows proved sufficient to restore me somewhat. Again was I able to lift my arms and legs and no longer did my back require Lialt's support. I sat upon the pelt, Lialt's dwelling about me, and gazed most bitterly at the male who crouched beside me.

"We shall one fey have a reckoning between us," said I to the male as he gazed narrow-eyed upon me. "I had no wish to return to this place as yet, and care little for having been forced here. What land was that, and how may I return to it?"

Lialt crouched beside me without movement, his gaze as narrow-eyed as it had been, his forearms resting upon his thighs, no response to my questions upon his lips. Again were we each clad as we had been, somehow accomplished without my notice, and the warmth of the dwelling had caused moisture to form about my feet beneath their fur wrappings. Much did I wish to remove the wrappings, yet the slow head-shaking at that moment produced by Lialt stayed my hand.

"You know not even where you were," said he, an odd tone to his voice, "yet you wish to return there. Were you born without sense, or have your recent wounds merely robbed you of what little you were given?"

So quietly were these words spoken that a moment passed before I felt insulted. For a male to speak so to a warrior was great foolishness, yet I had no weapon to hand with which I might wipe out the insult. There was much between Lialt and myself which needed seeing to, and each time I had dealings with the male, the differences grew greater. I shifted upon the lenga pelt, knowing that the fey upon which these differences were settled would be bloody indeed.

"Again your chin rises in stubbornness," said he, the calm tone rising to anger. "Though you be a child of the Snows, do you not know how close you came to being lost? By whose permission did you make free with my pipe? How dared you refuse to obey my will upon the Snows? In the name of the Serene Oneness, should Ceralt fail to punish you this time, I shall do so myself!"

His anger had risen to great heights, and again his light eyes blazed as they had done in the strange white land. Forever was this Lialt becoming angered, and I had long since tired of it. No Tarla was I, to be spoken to so.

"Lialt forgets that Mida watches over her warrior," said I quite coldly. "No danger was there in my being lost, save by the will of Mida. Should Mida wish one lost, that one will be lost no matter what her place might be. Your pipe lay in the open, a clear invitation to any who chanced by, and the war leader Jalav was pleased to accept the invitation, thereby honoring you. The will of a male means naught to a warrior, and less than that to a war leader of the Hosta. Lialt has now been answered, and Jalav, too, would be answered. What land have I stood in, and how may I return to it?"

"By the fetid stench of Sigurr the dark!" shouted Lialt, rising to his full height so that he might glare down upon me. "I grow exceedingly weary of being told of Mida, warriors, and war leaders! Know you, *wench*, that one must walk the Snows many times with one who has often done so, before one may walk there alone! I, a Pathfinder, know the manner in which one may return from there, yet you, no more than a child of the Snows who has never been trained in the ways of a Pathfinder, would become lost till your body died from lack of tenancy! The thread is thin between flesh and spirit when the spirit walks the Snows, and had I not been there, even your Mida would not have been able to return you! Had I known that your spirit would find release through the Clouds of Seeing, never would you have been allowed entrance to my halyar! From this moment on, you are forbidden entrance here, and should I again find you within, you shall be chained to the wall in your own halyar! Have I made matters sufficiently clear for you?"

"Indeed." I nodded, rising also to my feet so that I might gaze more directly into his eyes. "Lialt has shown that he fears the presence of Jalav in the white land, and for this he cannot be faulted. There are few lands which would not fall sooner to Midanna than to males.''

I folded my arms beneath my life sign as I spoke these words, and regarded the purpling of Lialt's visage with great interest. Seldom had I seen such anger directed at me before I had begun moving among the lands of males, and the occurrence yet held fascination. From the fey I had become war leader of the Hosta, none had dared attempt the direction of my behavior, nor had any spoken to me in the manner of males save with sword in hand. Of those who had faced me, none survived to give insult a second time, for quarter in battle is not the way of Midanna. It was a thing Midanna had yet to teach these males, for Lialt knew not what his words and actions might bring when directed toward a warrior. His purpling visage well displayed before me, he yet felt the need to draw himself up to an even greater height, and placed a large, grim hand upon my arm.

"I cannot speak with you," he choked, great anger tightening the grip of his fingers. "Each time I speak with you, the urge for violence claims me! I shall return you to your halyar and leave you for Ceralt to see to!''

Rudely was I then taken, by the arm, from the dwelling, a large-eyed and fearful Tarla awaiting without as we emerged. Lialt spared her no more than a glance as he strode past, hurrying me from the vicinity of his dwelling, and much did my anger match the male's. In no manner was I able to release his grip from my arm, nor was I able to slow his pace. Much did I wish to put the question to Mida as to the why of males having been given such strength, the while warriors were made to do with lesser. Tarla, seeing my anger and Lialt's and growing even more frightened, nevertheless hurried to match our pace so that she might walk to the far side of Lialt.

"Lialt, what has happened?" she ventured in a low voice, glancing about herself at the great interest shown by those males and females of the village who had earlier looked upon us. They now stood and stared with disturbance clear upon their features, the males with frowns, the females close to fear. A moment Lialt remained silent, and then, grudgingly, he spoke.

"She enveloped herself within the Clouds of Seeing and walked the Snows alone," said he, his eyes touching neither the girl beside him nor the folk all about. "I should have known from her ability to close me from her mind that the Paths would be open to her, yet the thought had not touched me. Had she been lost, the fault would have been mine.''

Tarla had gasped and paled upon hearing his words, yet at the end of them, her hand reached out shyly to touch the arm of the male.

"You could not have truly known," said she, her voice soft and comforting, her dark eyes upon the tightened jaw muscles so clearly to be seen upon his cheek. "The High Rider shall see that you could not have known."

Lialt's headlong pace slowed somewhat, yet the grim look he had adopted did not lighten.

"I shall place the matter before Ceralt when he returns," said he, in no manner comforted. "Her safety was given into my hands, and it is the place of the Pathfinder to know another who might walk the Snows. My brother shall not be as lenient as you, Tarla mine."

No answer did the female make save a lowering of her head, and we continued through the village in silence. The chill of the fey had grown deeper with the rising of the wind, and as my hair blew about my arms, I attempted to understand where Mida's light had gone. When I had first left my dwelling, the light had not yet reached its highest point, yet as I walked I saw that the light now lessened toward the darkness. No less than three hind had been lost in my visit to the white land, yet the passage of time had not been evident there. Strange was this thing, as strange as Lialt's speaking of it, for the male had said, that I had "walked the Snows." Perhaps the tracks I had seen were the paths he had previously spoken of, and he the chief tracker of the white lands. From the little he had said, I felt sure that not all were able to reach the land I had visited, and this I could find no reason for. I had reached the white land without effort, and where one may go, might not others thereafter follow? Confusion was high within me, and annoyance as well, for Lialt might have cleared the clouds from my understanding had he wished to.

We came quickly within easy sight of the lanthay enclosure, and a glance toward the males who yet stood within caused Tarla to draw her breath in sharply.

"Nearly had I forgotten," said she to Lialt, her hand agrasp his arm. "Earlier, in the corral—Jalav was seen by Balinod. When he learned her identity, he smiled upon her openly, before the other riders!"

An amusing indignation and anger were in the girl's tone, yet Lialt's features darkened rather than lightened.

"Ceralt shall see to Balinod's insolent manner," said he, a

grimness in the glance he sent me. "In this matter, he shall not find his High Rider willing to overlook his actions due to the blood we three share."

"First Famira, now her brother Balinod," said Tarla with a shake of her head. "A pity one cannot choose one's blood relatives."

"Indeed a pity," nodded Lialt, his dourness only then lifting somewhat. He looked down upon Tarla, who walked by his side, and his arm moved to encircle her, a true fondness appearing on his features. Much gentle feeling did Lialt have for the small female, yet this gentleness had not loosened the grasp of his fingers upon my arm.

In no more than a hand of reckid farther, we again stood within the dwelling which was mine. At last was my arm released, yet the look given me by Lialt contained as much inflexibility as had his grip.

"You shall remain here till Ceralt's return," said he, his brows drawn down in deep disapproval. "There is little time left till you may be circled, and I shall suggest that you be kept within till that time comes."

He began to turn away from me, prepared to leave, yet I could not allow matters to be left so. Though I burned with anger at his words, I pushed the anger from me and touched his arm to halt him.

"Lialt, I must know," said I, speaking to him as though he were the equal of a warrior. "What is the meaning of the movement I saw, and why did it draw me so?"

Lialt turned again to face me, expressionlessness covering him, yet in a moment he nodded.

"Very well," said he, his light eyes looking deep within me. "I shall have to school you at some time for your own protection, and perhaps this is the best way to begin. You saw, I wager, many paths upon the Snows, yet there was movement at no more than one or two points."

The words were less question than statement, and at my nod, Lialt nodded as well.

"I know this only from memory of my own first walk," said he, folding his arms upon his broad, leather-clad chest. "All paths have movement upon them in many places, yet much time must pass in study before one is able to see this. The movement is ever an event of importance, usually containing much violence, yet not always. The birth of a man of importance is shown as clearly as the death of a city. When one first begins his walks, only those events of great importance to the walker are perceived, should there be any. Many Pathfinders do not see themselves upon the Snows, for they are searcher only, never participating in the events which are shown them, yet you are yourself a child of the Snows, as Ceralt and I also seem to be. The movement you saw drew you because of your own presence in the event of importance, yet had you gone closer, you might not have known yourself in the seeing of it. The shadow you cast upon the Snows is that of the hadat, and Ceralt's shadow is that of the lanthay. Of these two things I am sure, yet I am not yet sure of my own shadow. I think perhaps I am the revro, flying above all upon wings of vision, yet there is also a scaled sednet and a red flame bound about your doings. It is also possible that I am one of these.''

Lialt paused, as though to give me opportunity to speak, yet there was naught I might speak of. That which I had been told contained much to be thought upon, and my silence, in some manner, gave the male satisfaction. Rather than pressing me for comment, he turned quietly and drew Tarla from the dwelling with him, leaving me to my thoughts. The warmth of the fire gave discomfort in the dwelling, therefore I removed the fur leg wrappings, then went to seat myself upon the lenga pelts before submerging myself in the words Lialt had spoken.

Surely no more than a hin passed before Tarla's return, yet I paid her no mind as she removed her leg wrappings then took herself to the fire. Much had I thought upon the white land, and much did I wish to visit it again, this time seeing all there might be to be seen. I had come to understand that the white land was a part of Mida's realm, a part that few were allowed a vision of. This, perhaps, was that which Mida wished me to see in the land of males, a thing which had been kept from Midanna yet was now to be made theirs. I would return with this knowledge to my home lands, and then would my sister warriors ride forth behind me, to first free the Hosta, and then wrench from these males the means by which the white land might be reached. Lialt I would carefully keep from death so that he might be made to speak of all he had learned upon his journeys, and then would I again go forth to study the movement I had seen. The call of the movement continued to burn within me, and something of urgency was now apparent in the call.

''Jalav, here is your vellin,'' said Tarla from beside me, startling me with the unexpectedness of words and movement. She knelt beside the lenga pelt I sat upon, a cut of vellin upon a square of wood, held invitingly in her hands. Her eyes were unaccountably sad as I took the provender from her, and abruptly she could no longer keep her sadness within.

"Jalav, I feel your coming punishment as you do!" she blurted, putting a gentle hand to my cheek. "Ceralt shall be exceedingly cross with you, yet perhaps the weight of his arm might be lessened should you weep at first sight of the leather. I have been told by others that the ploy is sometimes effective, and I shall ask my elder sister what else you might do!"

The agitation in the female was great indeed, yet I, with my thoughts yet floating about the white land, knew not what she meant.

"Of what do you speak?" said I, examining the condition of the vellin. Tarla's upset had happily spared the cut as much exposure to the fire as was usual with her, and the blood ran upon the wooden board in a most satisfying manner.

A moment of silence followed my query, and then Tarla's hand withdrew from my cheek as she sighed heavily.

"Ah, Jalav," said she, her eyes sad. "You pretend to unconcern, yet how may a woman be unconcerned with the anger of a man? Does she not see the anger upon his face, does she not feel the anger in the weight of his leather upon her? Lialt has said that Ceralt now deems you well enough to punish properly, and you shall not this time escape your due. I know you have been fearing Ceralt's return, for I saw the deep preoccupation upon you as I entered earlier, yet perhaps he may be swayed from his purpose." Here she hesitated, a bright flush coloring her cheeks as her voice lowered in embarrassment. "As you have already shared Ceralt's furs, it would not be unseemly for you to beg his use of you before the punishment. I have heard it said that a man is gentle in his satisfaction, and generous after release. Perhaps he may then punish you only a little—if at all."

Her words had fallen upon one another in her haste to release them, and her cheeks had grown so bright that one might think her fevered. Young Tarla, it seemed, had never taken a male as would have a warrior of her kalod, and the thought of male and female together caused her embarrassment. Little understanding had I of why this was so, yet my curiosity upon the point was pushed aside by anger. It was expected by the village slave-women that I would fear Ceralt and his punishments, and it was also expected that I attempt to placate him in some manner to ease the pain he would bring. I raised the vellin to my lips and tore a bite from it with my teeth, feeling the warm blood drip from the corner of my mouth. Much pain had I felt in my kalod as a warrior, some brought to me by Ceralt in various ways, yet never had I cringed before the promise of pain, never had I crushed my dignity underfoot to keep the pain from me. I bit again at the vellin, anger rising to fury in its towering strength, and the taste of the vellin grew ashes in my mouth. I threw the meat back to its board with strength, causing a gasp of alarm in Tarla, and looked upon the now-frightened female as the war leader I was.

"Never shall I fear a male," said I to her, though I wished to shout the words. "Ceralt may lash me if he wishes, yet never shall I beg his use! Never!"

Tarla cringed back in fear, so strongly had my anger come to her, yet my anger was not yet done. Unbidden came the memory of a time with Ceralt, a time when my desire for the male had been so great that I had begged his use as he had demanded. Shame filled me that I might be so weak before the male, as weak as a slave-woman in all her helplessness. I cast the wooden square and the vellin to the floor, rose quickly to my feet, then strode to the window, leaving a frightened Tarla locked in place behind me. Without the dwelling the fey had darkened, strong wind blowing the trees about in anguish. I, too, felt anguish over the place of my capture, and knew that I must soon put the village well behind me.

Silence filled the dwelling for many reckid, then, at last, Tarla again found her voice. "Jalav," she whispered with a tremor. "I did not mean to . . ."

"Leave me!" I snapped, my eyes unmoving from the grayness beyond the window. No longer had I patience for the folly of the girl. With no more than a pause for the replacing of leg furs, the female left as she had been bidden to do. In scant moments, I saw her hurrying toward the other end of the village, her head low, her hand to her mouth. Undoubtedly there were tears in her eyes as well, yet such a thing meant naught to a warrior. It was well past the time for Jalav to be on her way, and as the chill winds seemed to have driven the village folk within their dwellings, I turned from the window, replaced my own leg furs, then went to the door.

No eyes were upon me as I moved toward the trees beyond the edge of the village. Those within the lanthay enclosure had been well wrapped in the business they were about, and females no longer stood about regarding their doings. The wind blew my

hair to a frenzy of flying, yet it came from before me so my
vision was unobscured. The hard ground was nearly like rock, so
faintly did my trail show in it, yet I, myself, would have
followed the track with ease. No need was there to announce my
direction of travel with others undoubtedly coming behind me,
yet there was no well-leafed branch to hand to cover the track. I
paused once I was well among the trees so that I might look
about, yet naught met my eye that might be of use. The chill of
the air and the greater chill of the wind made me reluctant to
accept the sole course of action left to me, yet I had no choice.
Amid the swaying branches of leafless trees, I loosened the
leather ties of the covering I wore and removed it, then turned
with my back to the cutting wind so that I might brush lightly at
the ground over which I had walked. Once this was done, I
turned my line of march to the south, walking and brushing with
as much care and speed as possible.

Some few hind was I able to continue so, my hair held in one
hand, my covering in the other, before I was forced to replace
the leather garment. My body had first been chilled by the
exposure, then warmed somewhat by walking and brushing,
yet the passing hind had left naught save a numbness upon me
and in my bones, so that I shivered violently even as I attempted
to steady my hand for the brushing. I halted and looked about as
I tested the wind, knowing full well that I had not been able to
secure a weapon for the long journey back to the south. This lack
might well mean my life should I come upon the lenga or falth
before I had been able to make a spear, yet the matter was far
beyond my ability to alter. First I must put many forest lengths
between me and the males behind, then I might think upon
arming myself against the children of the wild. My stiffened
fingers fumbled with the leather garment before I was able to
draw it on, my difficulty with it even greater than usual. Much
had I grown to hate the confinement of the garment, yet it was
clear that one might not survive without it in these lands. I freed
my hair of it and drew the bindings tight, securing also the
copper belt about my middle. I had held the belt with the
covering, not wishing to cast it aside where it might be found,
and now retained it for another reason. Soon would I find the
need to hunt, and the metal of the belt might well be used in the
fashioning of a spear or in the setting of traps. I felt no regret at
having left the vellin Tarla had prepared, though its loss would
be felt most keenly upon my journey. The empty woods about
proclaimed the scarcity of game, and my former gauntness was

most likely to come again and this time stay awhile. I paused only long enough to watch the bright-colored leaves fly about over the ground I had brushed, then I turned once more in the direction of my homeland.

Darkness was not far from descending when I paused again to consider my position. The trees waved less now that the wind had quieted, but the cold had advanced to the point where it had become a gnawing thing, turning my hands and face red with its caress. I shivered in the near darkness, standing close beside a tree as though warmth might be drawn from the cold, dead bark, feeling the throb of my wounds from the constant clenching of my muscles as they attempted to fend off the cold. I had not come as far as I had wished, and darkness would not bring a halt to the march. I could ill afford to sleep through the darkness, buried in some hollow tree trunk, for my pursuers could well discover me through accident so close to the village. It would be necessary to continue the travel, though I knew not whether I might find the strength to continue. For some time my breathing had been coming in gasps, as though through lack of air, and I was forced to lean upon the tree I stood near for support. No longer was I concerned with hunting for I felt no hunger, and the rough, ridged bark of the tree against my cheek caused the burning on my skin to increase before it subsided. My hair stirred slightly where it lay against my thigh, and I, myself, was the only cause of movement I had seen since I had left the village. The bare trees were dark shadows against the dimming gray of the skies, and much did I yearn to build a fire in that cold, empty land.

At last I forced myself from the tree and walked on, knowing an easy trot would be best for the distance I must cover, knowing also that even the easiest of trots was beyond me. When the darkness grew too cold and tiring to bear, I would choose a long branch and trim it, then use a stone or tree to sharpen it, thereby giving my mind and hands something to do that would keep sleep from them. Sleep was now my enemy, and enemies must be conquered if one is to survive. I blew upon my hands and rubbed them, causing them to tingle, then held them to my face till the burning in my cheeks had eased. My eyes had found my fur leg wrappings, and I stumbled through the forest watching each step as I took it.

There had been no sound save the crackling of my feet upon the dry, dying leaves and the occasional flap of wings of a feathered child of the wild, yet suddenly there was a great crackling all about among the trees, and lanthay appeared as though from nowhere, their riders guiding them to circle around me. I whirled about, seeking a means through their ranks yet finding none, my heart beating wildly, and then my gaze fell upon him who led the riders. Ceralt sat his lanthay almost negligently, his eyes looking down upon me where I stood, my feet spread wide, my hand groping for a sword which was not to be found. No word was spoken by any of the males, and I felt their eyes upon me as well. I knew not how they had found me so quickly, yet it mattered not. Had I been beneath the protection of Mida, they would not have found me at all. Once again I had erred in thinking Mida at last pleased with her warrior, and once again would Mida show her anger at my foolishness. I kept my eyes from moving longingly to the south and merely folded my arms beneath my life sign, the bitterness of my failure held well within my soul. Ceralt had once more captured me, and he would be the instrument of Mida's displeasure.

Ceralt did not pause long enough in his study of me for the cold to become unbearable. He stirred upon his lanthay, his face difficult to see in the gathering darkness, and then he urged his mount forward till he stood beside me to the right. Again he looked down upon me where I stood, my hair blowing slightly in the nearly still wind, and he shook his head, as though in wonder.

"Truly had I begun to doubt," said he, though more to himself than aloud. "The Snows, through Lialt, directed me to be here this fey, awaiting we knew not what. Now do I see the importance of the matter, and give thanks to the Serene Oneness that I obeyed without reluctance." Then he straightened upon his lanthay, and his voice no longer held the odd, musing quality it had had. It sharpened, and a frown took seat upon his features. "What do you do so far from the village, wench?" he demanded in a growl. "By whose permission do you walk these woods alone?"

His anger had begun to grow, yet I made no answer to his questions for his previous words had startled me. The males had lain in wait in the woods at the direction of—something—from the white land, serving a presence they knew naught of. Well did I remember the feel of the presence in the white land, and well did I know that the presence was not Mida. It had not, then, been by Mida's will that I was once more captured, and therefore was I free to attempt resistance. Ceralt's lanthay stood beside me, dancing about in the manner of a high-strung beast, filled with much restlessness and the urge to do. No sooner had I come to the knowledge that it was not Mida's hand which was before my path, than I raised my voice in the Hosta war cry, jumping toward the lanthay and clapping my hands sharply. The beast exploded from me in great confusion, a scream of its own filling the air as it nearly unseated Ceralt, yet I waited no longer to see more. With my blood racing about inside me, I circled Ceralt's lanthay and made for the gap in the ring his coming forward had produced, and was through and running before the other males knew aught was about. The fur leg-wrappings dragged at my feet, slowing my pace, my breath came in great gasps which threatened to open my chest, leafless branches slapped and flew at me trying to take my sight, yet I ran on through the gloom of coming darkness, determined to win my freedom. A vast ache had begun in my body, attempting to take the strength from my limbs, causing sweat to form upon my forehead, beneath my breasts, in my armpits. Ahead of me was thicker woods, no trail however small, no more than bare trees standing one upon the other. Could I but reach the tangle of their presence, no lanthay might take its great bulk through behind me. I pounded for it, taking no note of the branches which tore at the leather of my covering and plucked at my flying hair, stumbling in my haste, yet where I might once have outrun a lanthay, I could no longer do so. A great toll had been taken by the Silla spears, and Ceralt, upon his lanthay, thundered up beside me, his left arm reaching down to circle my waist. Though I struggled and struck out at him, I was nevertheless drawn to the lanthay's back before him, thrown belly down across the leather band which girded the beast, and held in such a position by Ceralt's right fist in my hair. Cold, hard earth was thrown in my face by the lanthay's slowing, and then we turned about and rejoined the others of the males.

The return ride to the village was a great humiliation. The males had laughed to see me belly down before Ceralt, my hair falling against his lanthay's leg, a fistful of it still in Ceralt's possession. The mount's fur caressed my cheek where it lay, yet sight of Ceralt's leg, so near to my face, diminished whatever pleasure might have come from the touch. I fought the grip which kept me prisoner before a male; however success was not meant to be mine. Ceralt's fist closed tighter still, nearly pulling the hair from my head, and my struggle did no more than take whatever strength remained to me. Still was I held as I had been, the cold blowing down the back of my covering, the sweat turning chill upon my body, the smell of lanthay and male strong in my nostrils. The ground moved past in a blur below me, easily covered by the lanthay's rapid, relaxed pace, and I buried my own fists in the lanthay's fur, for the first time fearful upon a beast. No more than Ceralt's hand kept me from sliding from the beast to the ground, and never before had I been done so, placed before a male as his possession and prize. The head of the lanthay turned to sniff my arm in curiosity, and miserably I buried my face in its side, hearing the laughter and banter of the males all about, yet unable to face it.

All too soon was the village again before us, the lighted squares of its dwellings' windows floating in the darkness. Ceralt and the others rode to my dwelling and halted, the form of Lialt appearing out of the darkness as the lanthay came to a stop. Ceralt released my hair and slid from the lanthay with ease, then reached up and, taking me by the waist, placed me upon the ground beside him. No sooner had my feet been firmly placed upon the ground, than Ceralt's fist was again in my hair. In such a manner was I taken before Lialt, who frowned down upon me in great anger.

"I know not how you found her, brother," said he to Ceralt, "yet surely must the Serene Oneness have intervened. Upon finding her gone, I searched for her trail, yet it disappeared from before my eyes as though she had grown wings and flown."

"All would have had little success in following her," said Ceralt, giving my head a sharp shake by the hair. His anger was cold and his voice displeased, and nearly did I cry out from the shake. "The wench knows the forests and the means to hide her track better than most hunters," said he to an even more deeply frowning Lialt. "She would have been lost to me if not for your timely reading of the Snows."

"Ah!" breathed Lialt, pleasure replacing the frown upon his features. "Her flight was then meant to be, and her recapture as well. Perhaps the episode was meant as a lesson for her, to show her the folly of disobedience."

"Perhaps," agreed Ceralt, turning my head so that I must look up at him. "Has a lesson in obedience been taught you, wench?"

"I have been taught the folly of failing to remain alert," said I, the pain of his grip turning my voice husky. "Had I had my wits about me, the presence of males in the forest would have been easily detected."

Lialt growled in anger, yet Ceralt showed a grin of amusement.

"Still she remains untamed," said he, his eyes never leaving my face. "She has much to learn, and the time is long past for the teaching of it. Let us, in some small measure, begin."

Lialt stepped aside as Ceralt guided me to the door of my dwelling and within, and then followed to close the door behind the three of us. The warmth of the dwelling was so welcome that I began trembling, and Ceralt released my hair to walk from me to the fire.

"Soon deep winter shall be upon us, brother," said he as he stretched his palms toward the flames. "How much longer before we may begin the journey?"

"Matters move more swiftly toward the moment," replied Lialt, walking to join Ceralt at the fire. "The sednet is not yet among us, though the flame approaches with good speed. Once most have been brought together, the journey may begin."

"Good," nodded Ceralt, looking upon his brother. "Read the Snows as often as is safe for you, and name the time when it has become clear."

The two males warmed themselves by the fire, a thing I, myself, would have wished to do had they not been present. Much had the cold gone deeply in my bones, yet sooner would I remain as I was than join them where they stood. I wrapped my arms about me to still the shivering and crouched down where I had been left, ranting silently over the presence of the other males without the dwelling. My hand stole to my hair where Ceralt had gripped it, yet naught was amiss save a sore scalp. The male had previously taken me by the hair so, yet never had his grip been so tight and demanding. Changes had occurred in the male Ceralt, yet none which would find approval in the eyes of a warrior.

"It is my place to read the Snows," agreed Lialt near the fire, "yet the place is one I prefer keeping alone. I have no need of unskilled assistance to hamper my searches."

"Of what do you speak?" frowned Ceralt, searching Lialt's face for a hint of meaning. "There are none within the village who are potential Pathfinders."

"We are now blessed with one," returned Lialt with dryness, moving his gaze to me. "She helped herself to my pipe and sack, and went happily adancing through the Snows of tomorrow with girlish glee and enthusiasm. When I attempted to retrieve her, she refused my will, and I was forced to blend our spirits in order to return." Here Lialt paused, and though he took no notice of my bristling anger, he looked upon a furious Ceralt

shamefacedly. "It is also my place to know one who has the
ability to walk the Snows," said he in a quiet manner. "In this I
have failed you, Ceralt, and nearly was the girl lost."

"My disappointment in your failure is deep, Lialt," said the
larger male, causing Lialt's face to darken and his head to lower.
"There are few a High Rider may depend upon, and surely his
Pathfinder should be one and his brother a second. When the two
are one, disappointment is sharper, stronger, more painful. That
the wench is willful and ever angering you should not have kept
you from knowing her abilities."

Ceralt's voice had been uncompromisingly grim, and Lialt had
made no answer, nor had he again met Ceralt's eyes. The larger
male turned to gaze into the fire, yet abruptly he looked again
upon Lialt with a frown.

"The point had nearly passed me by," said Ceralt to a brother
who gazed upon the wood of the floor. "Early this fey, you
walked the Snows to bring me the message I was meant to have,
yet you were forced to walk them again to retrieve the wench.
How close did you come to being unable to return yourself?"

Lialt, in discomfort, raised his eyes and moved a hand in
negation. "There was very little resistance," said he, his tone
dismissing the thought. "Although Pathfinders have been known
to be forever lost if they walk the Snows more often than once
each fey, the need to bring the girl to safety overrode the will of
my spirit to remain. The Clouds of Seeing did not blind me to
the passage of time, for I knew not how long she had been upon
the Snows."

"Purely a matter of good fortune all the way about," growled
Ceralt, and his gaze came to me where I crouched with my arms
about me. The flames danced in the silver of his belt, yet the
coldness of the dark had entered his eyes. "Remove your boots,"
said Ceralt to me. "Your willfulness has nearly caused disaster
to all, and this time punishment shall not be kept from you."

Beneath his stare, I could do naught save remain in my
crouch. So large was the male, so uncaring in his anger, and no
weapon was there for Jalav to put hand to. A scant moment did
he wait, and then he strode to me and pushed me to the floor.

"You shall learn obedience," he glared, "Sigurr take me if
you do not!" His hands, as he spoke, pulled the fur leg-wrappings
from me, and Lialt's eyes did not leave us. With the leg wrappings removed, Ceralt's large hands took hold of my arms, and
once again I stood upon the worn, gritty wood of the floor. Great
was the anger of the male before me, yet the turning of my

insides shamed me more than had he. In fury at myself and at the male who had caused me to feel so, I struggled in his grip and met his light, blazing eyes.

"Jalav obeys no male!" I hissed, feeling the pain of the strands of my hair caught beneath his hands. "Thrice have I felt the touch of a lash, and should it be Mida's will, I shall bear it a fourth time! Go and fetch your lash, male! No more than my blood shall it take from me!"

The fury rose high in me, memory strong of the pain I had had at the hands of males. No more than pain do males seek to give, for pleasure is to be kept for them alone. Ceralt's eyes had narrowed, disturbance showing clearly within them, and Lialt left the fire to come and place a hand on his brother's shoulder.

"Ceralt, she does not feign her hatred," said Lialt, his tone uneven. "It sickens me to think of that which must have been done to her to make her so. That the hatred shows only with her fear disturbs me even more, for that indicates how deeply it is buried. Though I have often counseled her punishment, I now feel that gentleness may be the only path to the healing of her soul."

Lialt's light eyes were deeply saddened, yet Ceralt stood before me, his head ashake. "She has not yet learned to accept gentleness from men," said he, his voice heavy as his eyes searched deep within me. "Should she be given gentleness, she will see it as no more than weakness, something to be scorned. Once I gave her gentleness and love, and she pushed me aside in her thoughts and went about seeing to her own will. Not again will I be pushed aside so, looked upon fondly but without respect. I will have the respect of the woman who is mine, and I will have her obedience as well. She will not be lashed, but she will be punished."

So firmly had Ceralt spoken that Lialt removed his hand from his brother's shoulder and returned to the fire, standing and staring into its depths, his back to us. Ceralt yet had his gaze upon me, the unruly lock of dark hair again upon his forehead, desire and determination strong in his eyes. His tone had held bitterness when he had spoken of gentleness and respect, as though there were memories within him which had given pain. I had no understanding of what pain he felt, and he did not speak of it again. He merely seated himself cross-legged upon the floor, and pulled me to his lap and arms.

"Jalav, listen carefully," said he, his arms about me holding me to his chest. "You know well enough that I have never lashed you, nor will I ever do so. You, however, must learn that a man's word is not to be refused, else shall punishment be brought to you. You have refused the will of Lialt, and you have refused my will. Now shall punishment come to you through your own actions.''

Gentle indeed had been the tone of Ceralt, yet his hand then went to his belt and withdrew a length of leather. As I had sat in his arms and against his chest, the smell of him strong, the strength of him compelling, a weakness had stolen over me, one that I had felt before when beside the male. Much had his close presence stirred my blood, flashing through the center of my being with desire for him, smothering the anger and the fury and the will to depart. Well did I remember the gentleness he had spoken of, yet gentleness was a thing no warrior might remember when about the business of Mida. Surely Ceralt knew that! I raised my eyes to his face and regarded him, he who was so strong and broad and appealing to a warrior. His eyes were again upon me, and when our eyes met, his lips lowered to mine in a touch which was both strong and gentle at one time. He crushed me to him, taking my lips fiercely, and then was I turned about and held for the leather. My flesh had been bared for its coming, and come it did, the strength of Ceralt's arm well behind each stroke. I writhed and struggled in humiliation, knowing the leather harder than the lash on a warrior's pride, yet there was no escape from that which Ceralt wished for me. When he felt the matter well done, I was released and placed upon my lenga pelt, and I clung to the hairs of the pelt with my fists, burying my face deep, so that none might see me in my humiliation. Ceralt went to the fire and spoke softly to Lialt, and the second male left, only to return long reckid later. Still was I unable to look upon him, for the ache and sting of the leather had not eased much, yet the choice was taken from me. Ceralt pulled me from the fur and held me for the pot Lialt had, and once more the potion took all consciousness from me.

# 8.

## *The circle of choice—*
## *and a vow is stolen*

Thought returned with the opening of my eyes, yet I lay still
for many reckid, unwilling to move. Clearly, in my mind's eye,
lay the memory of the previous darkness, and my bitterness and
humiliation were great. I turned my head in the lenga fur to gaze
at the fire, feeling no comfort from the softness beneath my
cheek and upon my body. No longer was the leather garment
upon me, yet this, too, was an infuriating cause for shame.
Without doubt, Ceralt and Lialt had removed the garment from
me, perhaps even amusing themselves with my unknowing body.
Some small soreness remained from the touch of Ceralt's leather,
and I closed my eyes, tasting the sourness of confusion unrelieved.
Many times had Ceralt done me so, giving me humiliation and
pain, yet never before had he been so firm in his decision, so
hard with the leather. Most often I had felt that he beat me
reluctantly, wishing the need for it were unnecessary, yet this
time there had been much of willingness in his strokes, and my
flesh twinged in memory of such willingness to give me
punishment. Once before had he beaten me so, with willingness,
using naught save his hand, the occasion being the time I had
lured the hunting hadat to me to keep it from being slain by city
males. At that time he had told me that I was never to do again
as I had done with the hadat, and I had known then that I could
not gainsay him in the matter, that his word had been as the

141

word of Mida. Strange did it seem that the word of a male might
be likened to the word of Mida. I drew my hands below my chin
so that I might lean upon them. Was there ever a time that a
male must be heeded as a warrior would heed the will of Mida?
Would there be a time when I, myself, would find the need to
obey Ceralt as I now obeyed none save Mida? I shook my head
angrily, dismissing the thought, yet it continued to plague me.
How often would I find punishment and humiliation at the hands
of the male? How long before I might ride free of his demands
and disapproval?

A fair amount of time had passed before it came to me that
rain covered the dwelling's windows, yet the rain was of a sort
which I had never seen before. Hard as stones did the rain seem,
clattering upon the wooden frames of the windows and upon the
roof as well. Dim was the dwelling even with the firelight, and
few would be the folk about on such a fey. The thought at first
caused little interest in me, then I cursed myself for a fool. On
such a fey might escape be more than possible, my movements
hidden beneath the tears of Mida. On the instant did I decide to
make the attempt, and quickly sat up to throw the covering lenga
pelt from me—only to find that which I had not earlier felt. A
slim circle of metal held firmly to my left ankle, three links then
leading to a bolt set newly in the floor. In anger, I reached over
and tugged at the bolted links, yet my ankle remained held in the
circle of metal as though there was naught which might free it.
In fury, I pulled harder yet, then beat impotently at that which
sealed my captivity. Ceralt had done this, had again set me in
chains, and I would have gone for the eyes of the male had he
been within reach! Much did I throw myself about in rage,
shouting imprecations down upon Ceralt's head, yet my struggles were to no avail. Chained did Ceralt wish me, and chained
would I remain till he saw fit to free me.

In misery, I sat myself upon the lenga pelt, my knees drawn
up to my chin, my arms wrapped about them, my hair partly
beneath me, partly over my shoulder. I now felt the weight and
inflexibility of the metal, holding me where I least wished to be.
The wind blew the stonelike rain against the walls and windows
of the dwelling, now softly, now with a force like that of
charging warriors, and the warmth of the fire seemed to do little
for the chill of the room. I sat so for no more than a handful of
reckid, and then the door opened and closed quickly, admitting a
dripping wet Tarla. The female wore her usual coverings, yet
another covering had been added as well. Upon her upper body

were furs, much like the leg wrappings, yet these furs covered her body to her waist including her arms, then rose from her collar to cover her head as well. No more than her face showed from the midst of them, and as quickly as the door closed behind her, she drew off the body furs, shook the water from them, then hung them upon a wall peg. The leg wrappings followed the body covering, also shaken and stood by the wall, and then the female turned to me, a pleasant smile of greeting upon her face.

"How do you fare upon this new fey, Jalav?" said she, her tone light as she pushed at her hair with one hand. "Though the fey starts poorly, it is sure to improve with the coming of darkness."

She looked down at me where I sat, her large eyes sparkling merrily, a delighted laugh bubbling in her tone. With the metal fast about my ankle, I saw little reason for such gaiety and less for pretending to pleasantness. I looked upon her with the coldness a war leader showed for an erring warrior, yet this, too, seemed to amuse her.

"Now, now, none of that!" she laughed, waving a finger in mock severity. "You must not frown at all this fey, for frowns put lines in the loveliest of faces. As soon as you have eaten your falum, we shall brush and comb your hair to shining."

She then took herself to the fireplace and began preparing falum, humming softly as she worked. Without doubt she had seen that I was chained, yet she smiled and laughed and hummed as though in the best of spirits. I moved my eyes to follow her actions, frowning at such inexplicable behavior. Perhaps her wits had been taken by Mida, and she no longer knew what she was about. If that were the case, I would be kind to her, for one must always be kind to those who are bereft.

In a short while the falum was heated, and Tarla placed some in a pot, then brought the pot to where I sat. The odor of the cooking falum had caused my appetite to stir, yet captivity had ever proven itself an excellent curb to the urge to feed. I had no wish for the falum, and turned my face from Tarla's offering hands.

"Take the falum, Jalav," said Tarla softly, an odd hint of strength to her tone as she knelt before me. "You ate poorly upon the fey previous, therefore shall I see you well fed this fey."

"Shall you indeed," said I, turning again to regard her. "I had thought I had made it plain that I no longer wished your presence."

The female showed no sign of the flush I had expected. Instead, her chin rose high and a flashing anger came to her eyes.

"Oh, aye!" she nodded shortly. "You did indeed make it plain that my presence was no longer wanted! And I, like a silly fool, ran blubbering from your displeasure, allowing you to make away from the village with none to stop you! Had Ceralt not found you and fetched you back across his lanthay, this fey you would be without shelter and food, alone in the woods, pelted by sleet, and half dead! Had I been Ceralt, the hiding you received would have done far more toward knocking the foolishness from you! Now, take the falum and eat!"

Again was the pot thrust at me, Tarla's anger nearly spilling the falum from over the side of it. I was taken much aback by the female's ranting, for she seemed a different Tarla from the one I had known. No longer did she seem to fear me, no longer were there tears close behind her large-eyed gaze. Now there lay a sternness upon her, as though I were not yet a warrior, and she an attendant grown weary of my disobedience, recalling again her warriorhood. Once, when I was a child, an attendant had grown angry with me in such a way, the warrior blood in her coming again to the fore. I had thereafter taken care not to anger her further, for her dagger had been sharp, and I had not had the skill to wield one. This Tarla, however, knew naught of the ways of a warrior, and once past the initial surprise, my annoyance rose to the fore.

"A warrior shall always escape when she may," said I, looking upon Tarla with less than friendliness. "Had I been in the woods this fey, I would have found shelter and survived till the new light. A warrior does not fear that which Mida sends, for she has learned to deal with it. Jalav is no village slave-woman, to tremble before the thought of the forests and the displeasure of males as others do. Take your offering from me, slave, for I wish none of it!"

This time the flush grew ruddy upon Tarla's cheeks, and her full lips tightened in greater anger. "I am no slave," she hissed, "nor shall I ever be! I am a woman of men, a thing far better than being a woman who knows naught of men save what pleasure their bodies may bring! It was not I who smarted beneath the touch of leather last darkness, nor is it I who now sits chained in place as a further punishment!" Her words ceased, and she straightened her shoulders before regarding me levelly once again. "The High Rider has told me that should you fail to take nourishment, I am to send for him so that he may come with his leather and thereafter feed you himself. Should this be your wish, you have only to leave the falum uneaten.''

She then placed the pot upon the floor, beside the furs, and returned herself to the fire where she busied her hands with the clearing away of the pot in which the falum had been made. I sat a moment longer, my arms still about my legs, my thoughts going to the time when Ceralt had indeed fed me. The shame of the memory was so great that I closed my eyes and hid my face against my thighs, but then I saw that I had sought to hide myself too often of late. No more than shame might a warrior expect from a male, a shame which must be borne for Mida's sake. Sooner would I have faced a slow death at the hands of enemies, yet such cleansing in honorable death was not for Jalav. Well did I know that Mida's work was not yet done, and much shame would come to me before its completion. Heavily, I reached for the pot which Tarla had left, wishing to hurl it from me, yet knowing that such an action would bring Ceralt. Already had I been shamed before Lialt; to be shamed before Tarla as well was not to be borne.

The falum had gone down my gullet untasted and I had returned the emptied pot to the floor, when suddenly Tarla was again beside me, her arms reaching out to hold me around. For many reckid did she hold me so, I unmoving in my lack of understanding, and then she leaned from me to look me in the eye, her hand gently astroke upon my cheek.

''Ah, Jalav, I know not what might be done with you,'' she sighed, a sadness now upon her. ''Truly have I come to feel as a mother to you, so innocent and vulnerable are you in your savagery. When I learned that you took kindness for weakness, I grew angry at the thought, and vowed to show you no more affection that you might turn your back upon, yet how may a mother forsake her child? So hopeless did you seem at thought of Ceralt's punishment that I could not bear it. Do not fear, I shall not send for him.''

Her words were a now-familiar jumble of confusion, yet there was that which I was able to comprehend. I pushed her arms from me and held my head high.

''I do not fear Ceralt nor his punishments,'' said I, seeing surprise upon her face. ''Do as you will.''

Many expressions crossed Tarla's features, she seemingly unable to settle upon any of them. Twice her mouth opened as though she would speak, yet no words emerged to fill the silence. At last a sound escaped from her, a sound of annoyance and anger and vexation, and her fists closed tight where they lay upon her thighs.

"Never, Jalav, never have I been so sorely tempted!" said she through clenched teeth, her eyes narrowed. "Were you truly my child, I would take a harness strap to you! Will you never learn to accept the concern of others? I do not *wish* to call Ceralt! I wished only to reassure you in your need!"

"I have no need," said I, understanding neither her words nor her anger. "I am a war leader, and the needs of my warriors are my only concern."

The girl stared at me a moment, then slowly nodded her head. "I believe I begin to see," she murmured, a thoughtful look about her. "You concern yourself only with your warriors. And what do you receive from them?"

"Obedience," I replied, knowing not where her questions would lead. "Unquestioning obedience and loyalty to our clan, or the demand to stand with naked sword. In all things must my word be obeyed, else she who will not follow must try her skill with mine."

"Therefore you must never know doubt or fear," she whispered, a shudder running through her. "You must always be strong and courageous no matter the opposition you meet. And who is there who sees to *your* needs and frailties? Is there no one before whom you may cry out your hurt? Is there no place you may lie safe and protected?"

"A war leader has no need for these things," I replied, again seeing tears in the large, dark eyes before me. The Tarla of old had returned, and I regretted my harshness with her.

Her head bowed low so her face might be covered by her hands, and her shoulders shook to the sobs which possessed her. I placed my arm about her shoulders, attempting to give her comfort from I knew not what. Had I erred in speaking of the duties of a war leader? I had once thought the child Tarla too young to be given such knowledge, and perhaps I had been right. To place such burdens upon one unready for them is a cruelty Midanna do not care for. Tarla cried for many reckid, clinging to me as no Midanna had ever clung to any other, and then her head raised to show me a tear-stained face.

"The pain is too great," she sobbed, attempting to quiet herself. "I cannot bear the thought of such loneliness, such lack of—of—human feeling! Your life is ever in jeopardy, and not only from your enemies! Your own sisters stand ready to spill your blood! To never be able to show fear or hesitation—!'' She shook her head violently, her eyes still upon me. "You are barely older than I, barely more than a child! It is too much to ask of a mere girl!''

"I am neither girl nor child," I explained with a sigh, knowing my words would not soothe the girl before me. "I am Jalav, war leader of the Hosta, foremost of all the clans of Midanna. The position of war leader is not thrust upon one, it is eagerly sought by those who wish it. With my own hand did I slay she who was war leader before me, and with my own hand have I kept the honor mine alone. Do not weep for me, Tarla child. My prayers to Mida have till now been answered."

"Till now," she echoed, her eyes going to the chain about my ankle. "Truly do I believe that you have prayed for escape from Ceralt." Her eyes returned to mine, and a deep pleading had filled them. "Jalav, do not seek escape from him! His love for you is deep, and he shall aid you in freeing yourself from the barren existence you now have! To rest secure in the arms of a man, to have his love as you give him yours, to have his presence banish any hurt that might ever come to you—it is your right as a woman to know these things!''

"Tarla, do not upset yourself," I soothed, wishing I might speak to her of males and hurt. "My life and sword are pledged to Mida, a thing none may change. Ceralt knows of this, yet still he attempts to retain his hold on me, causing misery and pain all about. I am Mida's, and may never be his."

"Ceralt battles the gods for you?" she gasped, her mouth dropping open. "Never have I heard of so magnificent a thing! What mortal man has ever before battled the gods?''

"The matter involves but one god," said I, "and there is hardly what one would call battle. Ceralt ignores Mida as she ignores Ceralt, and—''

"To battle the gods!" breathed Tarla, hearing naught of what I had said. "Ceralt does battle with scores of gods, and shall carry you from them in triumph! Ah, Jalav, how magnificent!''

"Scores of gods?" I queried, feeling the confusion surround me again. What scores of gods might she be speaking of? So quickly did her moods change that my head spun from the effort to follow. Now the look in her eye seemed far distant and dreaming, and no longer did sadness and tears command her. She knelt before me, in some manner enthralled, yet I knew not what she was about. Clearly, my first thought had been truest, and Tarla had, by some means, been bereft of her senses. Abruptly, her mind returned from whence it had journeyed, and again shining-bright eyes were upon me.

"Now must we truly see to your appearance," said she in a firm tone, rising with the pot which had contained falum. "Should a man battle the gods for his woman, it is unthinkable that the woman be dirty and unkempt before him."

Brusquely, she took the pot to cleanse it in a bucket of water which stood not far from the fire, never seeing the manner in which I gazed upon her. I had met few city females in the lands of males, yet somehow they all seemed odd in some manner. Even Inala, in her anxiety to belong to Galiose, the High Seat of Ranistard, was not like warriors of the Midanna. In no manner was I able to fathom their actions, yet they seemed well made as companions to males. It is said among Midanna that like cleaves unto like; city males and females prove the saying sound.

With the pot returned to its place, Tarla came to stand before me again, her gaze thoughtful. I leaned back upon the lenga pelt, showing no concern, yet I felt a wariness as to what would next come to mind with her. Those who are bereft are not like other folk, and one does well to be on one's guard with them. The coolness of the air made the thought of the covering pelt a welcome one, yet the chain about my ankle was hobble enough. Should the need for rapid movement arise, I would not care to have the added restraint of the pelt to overcome.

"Your hair we may brush," murmured Tarla, a finger to her lips, "yet what may be done about bathing? The cleansing halyar is even now being readied, yet the chain remains fast about your ankle. The baths may not be brought here, and we may not go to them. I shall have to speak to Lialt, and obtain the key to your fetters. There is no other course of action possible."

The rapid decision was accompanied by a firm nod, and then the female fetched the brush and comb with which to see to my hair. I had not thought that obtaining the key to my fetters from Lialt was at all possible, yet there are indeed some matters which the bereft may see to more easily than those of sound mind. Should my release be one of these matters, I would seek no basis for disagreeing with the outcome. At Tarla's direction, I again sat straight, and we two worked at freeing the snarls and tangles which had settled in my hair.

The matter of my hair combing was nearly done when the door flew open with a rush of wind, admitting Lialt. He hastened within and shut the door, yet the wet and cold which accompa-

nied him caused a shiver all through me. Tarla quickly took up
the lenga pelt and threw it about me, yet the reason for her action
was not clear. Her eyes had been upon Lialt's entrance rather
than my shivering, and the closing of the door left the dwelling
no colder than it had been before the male's arrival. I pulled the
pelt somewhat down from my face as I spat out lenga hairs, and
judiciously chose not to pursue the matter.

Lialt, too, wore furs about his upper body, and he, too, shook
the wetness from them before placing them beside Tarla's upon
the wall. He then strode to the fire, leaving large, wet tracks
behind him on the floor, and held his hands to the warmth with a
contented sigh.

"This fire would be worth the fighting for," said he, his back
to us. "Winter comes too rapidly upon us, yet we may give
thanks that sleet falls rather than snow."

Tarla, who had again put the wooden comb to my hair, made
a vague sound of agreement, then moved a bit where she knelt.

"Lialt, I shall soon require the key to Jalav's fetter," said she
from behind me, the comb not ceasing in its movement. "I find
it necessary to free her."

Lialt snorted where he stood, and turned to face us. "The
necessity for such an action escapes me," said he, his tone dry.
"The fetter shall stay as it is so that Jalav does not do the
same."

The comb was abruptly gone from my hair, and Tarla rose to
her feet to approach Lialt. The male stood within the glow of the
fire, his arms folded upon his chest, tall and broad in his leathers
and fur leg wrappings, the silver of his belt atwinkle in the
dimness, the dark shape of a sheathed dagger at his right hip.
Tarla, barefoot, in her knee-length leather garment, seemed tiny
before him, yet there was no fear in the hand which reached out
to touch his folded arms.

"Lialt, she must be freed," said Tarla softly, her face raised
to the male. "I know not how long it has been since her last
bathing; in truth it matters not. Is Ceralt to throw his claiming
leather about a woman who has not been properly prepared for
him? The lowliest of his riders would not accept such a thing.
Must he?"

Lialt made no immediate answer, but stood looking down
upon the female before him, her hand yet upon his arm. The fire
crackled in the silence, going about its business of consuming
the wood in its embrace, and the rock-hard rain threw itself
against the walls of the dwelling, mindlessly attempting entry.

At last Lialt stirred, and a tender smile touched his lips as his hand reached out to stroke Tarla's hair.

"Tarla mine," said he, most gently, "your constant concern for those about you has never failed to touch me. My brother shall not lack that which is due him, for this you have my word. When the other wenches have quitted the cleansing halyar, Jalav may then visit there. Ceralt would wish to give her no opportunity to lose herself amid the confusion of many wenches beautifying themselves."

"But, Lialt, that will leave no time for all of the small things which should be done!" Tarla protested, stepping closer to the male. "The rain of flower essence, the mists of softening, the dance of desire . . .!"

"There will be desire aplenty on the part of Ceralt," laughed Lialt, interrupting Tarla's words. "Jalav is hardly a village wench whose fear of a man must be lessened. It will do her no harm to know a man's full strength with undulled senses, and it may do her good. Now, heat a pot of rangi for me, so the chill may be chased from my bones."

"Yes, Lialt," said Tarla, a heaviness in her voice as she moved past the male to the fire. She, a village slave-woman, would not object further, for a male had put his will upon her. I made a sound of disgust and turned from them, seeking the comb so that I might see to my own hair. Tarla dared not be other than slave-woman to Lialt, and I, myself, had been bereft to believe that I might be unchained through her efforts. I remained a prisoner to males who must free herself, for my warriors were far behind me in their own imprisonment.

The fey was long and chafing, nearly driving me mad with triple confinement. The linked chain upon my ankle allowed no movement from the lenga pelt, and even had I been free of the chain, the frenzied rain beat ceaselessly from without, warning all who heard it of its savagery. Again, had I been free of the chain and uncaring of the strength of the cold, unnatural rain, still would I have been unable to leave the confines of the dwelling. Tarla had questioned Lialt upon the whereabouts of my covering and leg-furs—she, unlike me, having noticed their disappearance—and Lialt had replied that they lay in Ceralt's possession, a further assurance that the cold, if not the chain, would keep Jalav from the woods of freedom. Hearing such a thing had caused me to hurl the wooden comb from me in fury, wishing Ceralt's head might be that which was struck rather than the wall. Lialt laughed at my fury, he having taken seat

upon a lenga pelt which had been spread not far from the fire,
yet Tarla had lowered her head in upset, keeping her eyes from me.
She had not again approached me since Lialt's entrance, a thing
which surprised me not at all. The male, helpless, like all males,
required her service, and she, true slave, could not refuse.

Through most of the fey, Lialt drank pot after pot of that
which he had called rangi. Deep black was the liquid, served
with steam curling from the heated body of it, its aroma filling
the dwelling with a strength difficult to conceive of. My nose
wrinkled with the first onslaught of its presence, yet Lialt took it
eagerly to him, sipping with a great deal of pleasure. At first, I
had thought the drink somewhat like daru or renth, yet there was
no hint of fermentation in its smell, and Tarla, too, sipped at a
pot of the liquid, her pursed lips blowing cooling breath on the
roiling steam. None of the liquid was offered me till Lialt saw
my eyes upon him, then he rose from his place and came to hold
his pot out before me. I wished none of the offerings of males,
yet curiosity held me too firmly in its grip for me to spurn the
offer. The aroma coming from the pot seemed to beckon to those
it reached, and I wished to know the taste of the thing which
drew one so. I took the pot from Lialt's hands and put it to my
lips, drawing a swallow from it into my mouth, yet nearly was I
unable to down the stuff! So strong and bitter that my tongue
nearly curled, the liquid burned its way to my throat and stomach,
leaving no doubt as to its previous presence. I drew in a gasp of
air as I coughed, and Lialt took the pot from my unresisting
hands.

"What do you think of the rangi?" he asked, crouching before
me so that he might peer into my face. I saw him drink from the
pot as he awaited an answer, and did not allow my revulsion to
show.

"The liquid is clearly made for city males," I husked, wiping
the sweat from my forehead. "A warrior does better with daru."

"I do not know the drink," he said, rising from his crouch,
"yet it is undoubtedly more suitable for wenches. Not many
women other than Tarla are able to drink rangi unless it is
sweetened with wild honey. Does this daru of yours require
sweetening?"

"Daru requires no sweetening," said I, moving the lenga fur
lower. The single swallow I had taken seemed to have brought
the heat of the fire to all of my insides, causing the dwelling
itself to seem warmer. Lialt stood before me, sipping from
the pot of rangi, his gaze, for some reason, caught upon me. The

dimness disallowed the clear seeing of his light eyes, yet the
gaze brought me discomfort without bringing a reason for the
feeling. No more than a moment did Lialt stand so, and then he
shook himself and turned from me to return to his seat by the
fire. Once he again sat cross-legged upon the pelt, Tarla crept to
him so that he might put his arm about her. The male did so, yet
there was a distraction about him which lasted for more than a
hin. I cared little for Lialt's distraction, and stretched myself out
upon the lenga pelt to think about daru. I would have given
much for the taste of it, yet it was not to be found in the land of
males. Such a thing was wise of daru, a wisdom I would gladly
have shared.

The mid meal brought a cut of meat cooked by Tarla, and also
brought the attention of Lialt when I left the cut where Tarla had
placed it, upon its wooden board, beside my lenga pelt. The
passing hind had succeeded in forcing me deep within the caves
of despair, a place even Mida's light has no power to warm. I
lay upon my back, the lenga pelt covering me from waist to
thighs, my right leg bent, my left leg held fast by the links of
metal. It had become impossible not to feel the clasp of the
metal, not to know that free movement had been denied me, not
to feel a frantic, unreasoning urge to escape. I clenched my fists
where they lay by my sides, fighting to keep from showing
weakness before my enemies. I wished to scream and pull madly
at the chain, I wished to bite and tear at any who came within
reach. Almost did I also wish to bite at my own leg in order to
free myself, and the taste of this need was sharp and sour in my
throat. The timbers of the dwelling's roof lay far above me, in
dimness, gazing down uncaring on all beneath, and then Lialt
stood above me as well, disapproval strong on his face. He
spoke words to me, words which I refused to hear, and in
anguish I turned from him, burying my desperate need in the pelt
I lay upon. I could no longer see the dwelling, and in the
darkness I had made for myself, there was somewhat of a
lessening of shame for the tremors which shook me. To be free!
To be free! The words rang in my ears without sound, taking all
else from my perception. Even when the furs were drawn more
closely about me, I knew not whose hands had done the deed.
With all my strength, I begged Mida to free me from the metal,
for I could not free myself, yet naught came of the aid I had
begged for. Weariness came then to add weight to the despair
already too heavy upon me, and at last sleep came, to conquer
them all.

I awoke to a knocking upon the door of the dwelling, opening my eyes to see Lialt cross to the door. Without were two males in leather, muffled close in furs which blew with the wind. The strange, hard rain had apparently ceased, and I moved lower in my lenga pelts as Lialt took a pile of leather and fur from one of the males, spoke quiet words to them, then closed the door. Tarla stood not far from me, and it was to her that he brought what had been given him.

"You may now dress her," said he, handing to Tarla the leather and furs. "I will wait with the others."

He then withdrew from his silvered belt a small bit of metal, that which I had learned was a thing called a key. Use of a key releases one from the grasp of chains, and in no more than a moment the metal fell from my ankle, to torture me no more. I sat up quickly in the furs, drawing my leg to me so that I might rub it, and again found Lialt's eyes upon me.

"So much like a hadat released from a trap," he murmured, his dark-shadowed face without expression. He then rose from his crouch and went to the wall where his furs hung, donned them, and left the dwelling. Tarla waited till the door had closed behind him, then she knelt and placed the leather and furs upon the floor.

"There is very little time, Jalav," said she, handing to me my leather covering. "Lialt will see you to the cleansing halyar, and thence to the meeting hall. I would accompany you if it were possible, but I would not be allowed within the hall." Her large, dark eyes, filled with sadness, were upon my face, and then her arms were about me in a brief embrace before she knelt again as she had done previously. "This should be an occasion filled with gladness," she whispered, brushing at her eyes. "Why must I echo your pain rather than you echo my happiness?"

So upset did the female seem that I attempted a smile as I placed my hand upon her shoulder. "There is little use in feeling the pain of others," I informed her, yet gently. "Is it not enough that one must feel the pain? And what occasion for happiness might there be? I could well use a thing to lighten my mood."

Tarla stared at me so long that I was able to don the covering before she spoke.

"You cannot mean you do not know," said she, shaking her head. "It is the time we have so often spoken of, the time Ceralt has so impatiently been awaiting. This darkness you must circle before the elders, where Ceralt may drop his claiming leather upon you."

I halted in the tightening of my garment's ties, my hands' motion frozen in shock. I had not escaped the confines of the village, and now the males would seek to make me as their own females were, mindless and without volition or pride. I shook my head and whispered, "No!" then rose quickly to my feet and shouted, "Never!"

Tarla gasped, the back of her hand to her mouth, but I paid her fear no mind. My eyes darted about, seeking escape from the dwelling, finding no more than the sealed windows and the door. I would not again be placed before males as a slave, a thing to be looked upon and taken. Brushing past Tarla, I made for a window, yet the door opened before I was able to reach it. Lialt and the other two males ran toward me, obviously knowing my intent, giving me no time to rip the maglessa weaving from its frame. Lialt reached me first, and my head whirled with fury and battle lust, sending my clawed hands to his eyes and face. The male shouted hoarsely, fending me off, and Tarla's scream sounded as spur to the actions of the other males. Roughly was I taken by the arms and pulled from Lialt, one of the males treading upon my bare feet in his haste, and then my arms were fast behind me, held in the grip of those with greater strength than I. I struggled uselessly, attempting to reach flesh with my teeth, yet Lialt's hand tangled itself in my hair, pulling my head back so that I must meet his eye.

"The time is written clearly upon the Snows, wench," said he, his chest rising and falling rapidly with his exertions and the heat of his furs. "In order that all may survive, the hadat must bow before the strength of the lanthay. Should Ceralt fail with you, all will know a similar defeat. I do not believe Ceralt will fail. Complete her dressing."

The last was to the males who held me, Lialt then releasing my hair so that they might obey his word. I continued to struggle, still furious, and the males cursed as they tightened the ties to my covering, forced the leg-furs upon me, and lastly put the furs about my upper body. The sweat covered me strongly as Lialt stepped forward to clasp the copper belt about my waist, and he studied me briefly before turning to a Tarla who was sunk in misery. The female wept softly as his arms circled her, and his lips touched her hair in a gesture of comfort.

"All shall soon be well, Tarla," he murmured, stroking her back. "Her destined place is with Ceralt, and happiness shall one fey find her there. There is no longer time for her to visit the cleansing halyar, and we also could not wish the need to force her within clothing a second time. Ceralt himself shall see to her with the new light as he cannot do on the moment. Return now to your father's halyar, and do not distress yourself further."

At Tarla's nod, Lialt released her and gestured to the males who held me. We then moved to leave the dwelling, Lialt going first, I being taken by the arms after him. The darkness without was a great deal colder than it had been, a thing I would not have believed possible had I not felt it in my own flesh. My breath emerged from my mouth as a cloud of white, torn immediately away by the ravening of the dagger-sharp wind. The darkness contained a palpable cold, one which entered one's coverings at any point it might, clutching with a blue-chill hand to freeze the blood, turning the sweat upon my brow to ice. I shuddered and tried to cringe back from the awful feel of it, yet the grip upon my arms disallowed this. Further from the warmth of the dwelling was I taken, beneath the dark upon dark of a storm-cloud-filled sky, past the flicker of wind-blown torches upon the dwellings, over a thin layer of white which covered the ground and crackled as one stepped upon it. The breath was snatched from my lungs, my cheeks felt brittle and cut, my body shook to the onslaught of the elements, yet I was hurried forward by the males, they seemingly uncaring that the death of the world would soon be upon us. It then seemed impossible that warmth would ever be known again, or that anything or anyone would survive to know if it did.

The walk, seemingly a lifetime in length, led across the central ground of the village, to a very large dwelling which stood, across the span of the open place, opposite the dwellings of Ceralt and Lialt. Each dwelling of the village was lighted from within, yet this overlarge dwelling fairly blazed with light through its many windows. Tracks in the white covering upon the ground showed that many feet had approached as we did, and others came even as we reached the door and walked within, still preceeded by Lialt. The dwelling was more than thrice the size of other dwellings, with two fires blazing at either end of the room, and torches set close upon the walls. Some females and many males were about, most speaking with others or walking slowly to greet those who were newly come. The heat of the place was incredible after the cold we had come through, yet I was forced to the far side of the room before the body furs and leg furs were taken from me. I was then released by the males, to stand barefoot as I rubbed life back into my cheeks and hands, while they took my furs to the dwelling's door. They shed their

own fur coverings when they had taken up positions to either
side of the door, and stood with arms folded to gaze about
themselves with some small interest. Had I wished to face the
darkness as I was, I might have sought a window, yet even that
was denied me. Lialt, his fur upon his arm, had gone to speak
with others in the room, yet his words had been brief and he
quickly returned to my side.

"It is soon to begin," said he, gazing about the room. "The
wenches are here, and nearly all of the riders. Ceralt and one or
two others shall presently make their appearance."

I made no response to him, instead looking about at those who
occupied the dwelling. Many lenga pelts covered the floor near
where the greater number of males stood, yet none sat or lay
upon them. The males themselves seemed pleased and unhurried,
speaking and laughing in low tones as they gazed upon the
females who stood by the wall, not far from a fire.

The village females stood about together, perhaps four hands in
number, huddled among themselves like herd beasts. Some seemed
unconcerned over the coming ceremony, yet most appeared both
anxious and frightened. They glanced covertly at the young
males who studied them, and their rapid breathing bespoke their
agitation. One female stood somewhat apart from the others, her
hands upon her hips, her head insolently high, anger clear upon
her features. It took no more than a moment to know her as
Famira, the female who had set herself against me when I was
yet unable to stand unaided, and my own head rose high, in
pleasure at this second meeting. Perhaps the sight of Jalav
cause her to give challenge once again, and I would then be
granted the gift of spilling her blood. I stepped away from Lialt,
then stopped where I might be seen and folded my arms beneath
my life sign. To answer a challenge in this place of males would
be pleasure indeed.

To my great disappointment, there was no opportunity to give
or answer a challenge. Before the female Famira grew aware of
my presence, a male approached the females with what appeared
to be a water skin. Gently, he urged a swallow upon most of the
females, then went to offer the same to Famira. My enemy
tossed her head in disdain and refused the skin, whereupon the
male shrugged and took himself off toward me. As he neared,
Lialt stepped out before him with a hand raised and slowly shook
his head. The male halted with raised brows, glanced curiously
toward me, then shrugged once more and returned to the other
males, from whence he had come. An elder male stepped forward,

arms raised high. At sight of this male all speaking ceased, and the male looked slowly about himself.

"We have come to another occasion for choosing," said he, his eyes first upon the females and then upon the males. "Choose gladly, young riders, for there be many desirable wenches to choose from, yet I also caution you to choose wisely. The wench you take to frolic with will one fey bear your sons and daughters. Should you be unsure, give thought to it and await the next choosing. Now, we will see the beauties who await your pleasure."

With these words, he gestured toward the young females, near whom were now a number of males. These males gently but firmly urged the females forward, sending them toward the center of the room where they began to move in a slow circle, looking out toward the young males who also moved to surround them. The female Famira, in fury, had been forced to join the others, and then Lialt's hand was at my back. With a great shove, I was thrust forward into the midst of the circlers, and the males laughed as the outer circle of those surrounding us closed tight. I stood angrily amidst the moving females, forcing them to walk around me, refusing to give heed to the shouts of, "Circle with the others, wench!" and, "Let us see you move!" Again I folded my arms beneath my life sign and held my head high, showing that a war leader of the Hosta feared none of them. The small village females stumbled about me in their circling, urged on by the calls of the males, and even the haughty Famira moved so, obviously fearing what would come to her should she halt without permission. Her gaze touched mine and hatred flashed in those large, dark eyes, yet the hatred was not meant as mine alone. The female felt hatred for all those about her, and well was I able to share the feeling. I, too, stared about at the laughing, shouting males, seeing hunger in the eyes of many, also seeing great hatred upon the face of him called uncle, who stood behind the ring of younger males. His gaze went from Famira to me, bitterness filling his eyes and clenching his jaw muscles, yet no word of objection or intervention came from him. I knew not what ailed the male, yet it was of little moment beside my own towering anger.

The bright-lit room was close despite its size, filled with smells one might easily identify. The smell of fear clung thickly to the females, each as barefoot as I, each, perhaps, receiving the need-smell of the males, for they circled more and more tightly, attempting to take themselves from the watching, laughing males. The torches burned the air acrid from pitch, the fires

added a pungent crackling, my own body added the odor of
sweat, and behind all, very faint, was a sharp, spicy odor I
thought I knew. My nostrils flared wide, attempting to catch
more of the elusive odor, yet the body smells of male and female
grew too heavy to penetrate. A number of the females now
moved strangely in their circling, their bodies relaxed and free
from fear. They slowly stepped wide and whirled about, their
arms moving up and out, then toward the males, and murmurs of
appreciation arose from the watchers. Much did this movement
seem to bring pleasure, and more and more of the females joined
those who had already begun. A sound, high and wild, had
begun somewhere behind the standing males, a thumping accompanying it, and the females seemed to catch the sounds and move
with them, each moving in her own way, yet also moving with
the sounds.

Then all whirled around and about save Famira and myself, I
standing as I had been, she stopped on the far side of the circle,
her fists clenched, her body bent forward. Sweat shone on the
face of her, and she searched the features of those males who
stood about as though desperately seeking a particular one. More
and more tightly was her body held as she searched from face to
face, and then that occurred which took my attention from her.
From the corner of my eye, I saw a leather rope flash out, falling
about the body of a female who whirled with her arms high
above her head. The rope tightened, halting the female in her
whirling, and then was she drawn toward the male who had
thrown the rope. Rapidly, her chest rose and fell, her eyes
unstraying from the face of the male before her, he grinning
slightly, then slowly laughing aloud as she attempted to resist the
pull of the leather. Hand over hand, with little or no effort, the
male drew her toward him, and when she was within his arms,
he lifted her from the floor and carried her away, her own arms
tight about the neck of him. The circle closed about the place he
had left, and other ropes flashed out to fall about others of the
whirling females.

Nearly two hands of females had been taken from the circling,
moving throng, when a scream rang out, stopping laughter and
movement alike. My hand aching for the presence of a sword, I
sent my eyes about, searching for the source of the scream, and
found that the female Famira had gotten herself well within the
confines of a rope. The leather lay tight about her arms and
body, yet she struggled wildly, attempting to free herself. The
male who had thrown the leather laughed at her struggles and

slowly, slowly, drew her to him, causing her to throw back her head and scream again and again. The screams continued till she was no more than three paces from the male, then she frantically raised her arms as best she could, and held to the leather which drew her forward.

"No, Cimilan, no!" she begged, her face drawn with fear. "Choose another from the circle as your woman, not I!"

The male, as large and as broad as Ceralt, laughed well at the pleading female. "But it is you I have always wanted, Famira," he said, strong teeth showing in his dark face. "It was you, was it not, who laughed in ridicule when I first attempted to smile upon you? It was you, was it not, who boasted that a better man than I would draw you from the circle? Did you not scorn my very presence, saying that you were far too good for one such as I? Where is your superior suitor now, Famira? Why does he not come forward to challenge my claim?"

The frightened female did no more than shake her head, attempting to deny, not his words, but his intent. Surely she knew that the male would soon take his vengeance upon her, yet still she attempted to deny the consequences of her past actions. Briefly my thoughts touched Fayan, sister warrior to me in happier feyd, and I wondered how she had fared at the hands of Nidisar. So far away were the Hosta, so far from their war leader and their home lands. The constant ache in me throbbed with the thought, an unhealed wound which seemed destined to fester forever.

And then another rope flew, one which came from my right and settled about me in the same way that Famira had been taken, pinning my arms to my sides. I snapped my head about and saw Balinod, the male of the lanthay enclosure, his fist tight upon the leather, a laugh strong upon his face. Many another male laughed as well, for they saw me as naught save one like Famira, yet I was no empty-headed village slave-woman. Jalav herself had taken many wild mounts with tightened leather, and knew well enough that the leather remained tightened only with the pull of resistance. As quickly as thought, I jumped toward the male, bringing my arms out and away from my body, loosening the loop about me, and finally throwing it off. The male Balinod was caught unawares, and his frantic, over-late pull brought him naught save an empty loop. I returned to where I had stood to the sound of much laughter, yet the laughter was not directed toward me. Balinod, red-faced and furious, was the object of the ridicule, a thing his foolish actions had earned him well. With hands upon hips, I tossed my head to rid my face of loose-flying hair, keeping my eyes carefully upon the infuriated male who was then recoiling his leather. Should he be so foolish as to cast at me again, he would learn the true speed of a Hosta.

And then a loop dropped upon me from behind, one that closed tight upon the instant it settled. I twisted about, cursing at my inattention to any save Balinod—and saw Ceralt, his fist hard upon the leather, a wide grin splitting his face. In fury, I fought the hold of the leather, again attempting to move toward the male who had thrown at me, yet Ceralt was not like Balinod. Full alert was he to my movement, stepping back as I stepped forward, and then I saw the knots which had been placed in his leather. The knots were doubled toward their top, allowing the small loop through which the leather passed to draw tight, yet doing much to obstruct backward movement. Ceralt circled right, keeping the small loop tight against the knots, and slowly began to draw the leather through his hands. Against my will was I pulled toward him, a dragging step at a time, the edges of the leather digging into my arms through the garment I wore, my hair pinned behind me as my arms were pinned to my sides. The wood of the floor was smooth and worn, offering no foothold in aid of resistance, and Ceralt loomed closer and closer, his light eyes triumphant and very, very pleased. Another step was forced upon me, and another—and then a second loop flashed past my eyes to settle below my breasts, just above Ceralt's leather. Exclamations came from about the dwelling, male voices rose in a flurry of murmurs then died away, and Ceralt's eyes no longer showed pleasure. Snarling anger flashed there as his gaze went past my shoulder, and he no longer drew me to him. Though I was caught between the two loops and could not turn, I had no doubt that Balinod stood behind me, his leather at last secure about me. I attempted to use the interruption to loosen myself from the loops, yet found the thing impossible as both males held fast to their lines. The warmth of the dwelling had increased tremendously, and the brightness of the torches caused an ache to the eyes.

The males and females all about drew back somewhat, allowing the elder male who had spoken earlier to step forward. This male looked with uncertainty at Ceralt, glanced past me to Balinod, then drew himself up.

"A challenge has been put forward upon the female now being drawn," said he, his voice expressionless as his eyes rested upon me. "Let her be bound in the circle till the dispute has been settled."

Two strange males came forward, each taking the leather from the two males who held it, and Ceralt and Balinod were free to step closer to one another. Ceralt stared at the other male, his gaze seeing naught save him, his fingers toying with the dagger at his silvered belt, his face expressionless save for a tightening of the jaw line. Balinod grinned into the face of Ceralt, insolent and uncaring in his challenge, well prepared to again make a fool of himself. His arms were folded across his chest, well away from his dagger, a stance no Midanna would have taken had she chosen to try her strength with her war leader. Once a challenge is given, the warrior in question is no longer beneath the war leader's authority and protection, and may be struck at with full warning or no warning at all. Had Balinod been Hosta, he would have quickly lain in a pool of his own blood.

The two males who had taken the leather from Ceralt and Balinod were now beside me, the ropes held tightly in their fists, their free hands reaching for me. In anger, I fought them, yet my anger was destined to grow greater, for my strength was no match for theirs. Easily were my wrists put behind me and bound with Balinod's leather, and then I was lowered to the smooth wooden floor so that my crossed ankles might be drawn up behind and bound with Ceralt's leather not far from my wrists. Both loops remained about my body, allowing no freedom of movement to my limbs, and I writhed helplessly in the bonds, staring up at the males who towered over me, feeling the tightened leather cut into my flesh. I lay to the left of Ceralt and Balinod, and the position seemed to suit those who had bound me. They grunted in approval and nodded to one another, then left the emptied circle to stand with those who watched from without.

Strangely, naught had yet occurred between Ceralt and Balinod. They stood as they had, with the elder male beyond them, till all were gone from within the circle, then both looked toward the elder male, who again drew himself up.

"Should either one of you have rethought his position," said he, his eyes upon Balinod, "that one may now end the matter by reclaiming his leather." Neither male made answer to this statement, and the elder male nodded solemnly. "Very well," said he. "As you each feel the need for a test of blades, you may now proceed. I may do no more than urge you to keep the laws of the Belsayah clearly in mind."

The elder male stepped back to the ranks of those without the circle, and I frowned as I watched Ceralt and Balinod draw their daggers. What laws had the elder male meant in his speaking, and why had the two younger males awaited his permission to draw their weapons? When two warriors stand blade to blade, there is naught to concern them save who shall survive the meeting of metal. Even their war leader might deny them personal conflict only if there are enemies about. Straining at the leather, looking up at the males, confusion adding to discomfort and rage, I again wished myself elsewhere than among these males of strangeness, yet Mida either heard not or chose to disregard my plea.

Ceralt and Balinod now circled with drawn daggers, their eyes upon each other, Ceralt remaining expressionless, Balinod still possessed of his insolent grin. A moment longer they circled, then Balinod slashed toward Ceralt, trying for his middle, yet found naught save empty air for his blade to part. Ceralt had quickly moved from where he had been, and just as quickly closed again to catch the other male's right arm with a backswing. Balinod paled as both sleeve and arm were opened, covering the edge of Ceralt's blade with bright red, and the insolent grin was at last gone from him. He staggered briefly as pain touched him, his teeth clenched in his dark-skinned face, then managed to bring his blade up to guard himself as Ceralt tried for his left side. With the blow countered, the males again returned to circling, yet matters were no longer as they had been. Ceralt now showed a grin for the sweat upon Balinod's brow, and Balinod's dagger arm seemed to grow heavier and heavier for him. Much difficulty did the male have in raising it toward Ceralt, and then Ceralt moved again. Through the stream of blood flowing to the wood, Ceralt leapt upon Balinod and drove the other male backward, finally sending him flat to the floor. Balinod's right wrist was in Ceralt's left hand, Ceralt's knee was deep in Balinod's chest, and Balinod's throat lay hard against the point of Ceralt's dagger. Surely, I thought, the male would now pay with his life for his foolishness, yet even so simple an action was far beyond the doing of males.

"I yield!" screamed Balinod, writhing as the dagger bit into his throat. "In the name of the Serene Oneness, I yield!"

Ceralt, as was proper, seemed deaf to this plea, yet the elder male who had spoken earlier hurried from the fringes of the circle to place his hand upon Ceralt's shoulder.

"He has yielded, High Rider," said this male unevenly,

grasping Ceralt's shoulder. "The wench is yours, and you may now release him."

To my great surprise, Ceralt then leaned back from Balinod, wiped his blade upon the wounded male's leather, then sheathed his weapon and rose to his feet. He stood above the weeping Balinod, gazing down upon him, and I felt my lip curl in disgust at the doings of these males who presumed to feel superior to warriors. Never does a Midanna warrior show quarter in battle, whether the battle be one to one or involve many clans. To allow an enemy her life is to invite attack when one's back is turned, and to spare a craven is to weaken the group as a whole. These males seemed not to know such things, else they knew and did not care. Ceralt turned abruptly from his inspection of Balinod, caught sight of my expression, and felt the sharp rebuke therein. His face darkened as he scowled, and he strode purposefully toward where I lay, then crouched down beside me.

"My actions do not have your approval?" he mumured softly, for my ears alone, his light eyes angered. I made no answer to him, for the thing was self-evident, and his anger grew even greater. He shifted quickly to one knee, reached toward me and lifted me from where I had been placed, then stood and carried me past the still-weeping Balinod into the mass of males who had watched the dispute. The male called uncle now knelt beside Balinod, attempting to stop the flow of blood from his arm, and as Ceralt passed, he sent a malicious glance toward his back. There was another one, I thought, who would not long be left among the living had there been Midanna about. To give one such as he the opportunity to do ill was foolishness indeed, yet Ceralt paid the elder male no mind. The group of males parted to allow Ceralt his way, and I was carried toward the side of the dwelling, where lay the lenga pelts I had seen earlier, yet much reduced in number. Ceralt placed me upon one of the remaining pelts, then stepped back to regard me as others of the males came to clap him on the back.

"A fine catch," grinned one, looking down upon me. "I, too, would have taught Balinod his place had he attempted to take her from me."

"Aye," laughed a second, standing to Ceralt's other side. "With one such as she, a man has no need of a fire in his halyar."

I writhed against my bonds in fury as all joined their laughter to that of the second male, and even Ceralt showed a grin, though his anger was still with him.

"Her fire derives too much from willfulness," said he, his eyes yet upon me. "I shall quickly give it a new source, and teach her that which has been too long in the coming."

He then turned from the males and walked a few steps to where a fur covering had been placed upon the wall. He took the covering and donned it, and began to turn back toward me when his eye was caught by the sight of the two drinking skins hanging upon the wall not far from him. Ceralt now gazed briefly upon the drinking skin to the right, then walked to it and took it from the wall. The males who yet stood above me guffawed loudly and elbowed one another at sight of the skin at Ceralt's lips, and some few turned to grin down upon me with secret knowledge in their eyes. I still knew not what the skin might contain, yet it certainly seemed that its contents were not meant for my benefit.

Ceralt replaced the skin upon the wall, wiped his mouth with the back of his hand, then returned to where I lay and drew his dagger. One touch of the blade freed my legs from their cramped position, yet did not remove the leather from about my ankles. Ceralt straightened my body upon the pelt, wrapped me in it, then threw me easily to his shoulder.

"I bid you all a good rest this darkness," he called cheerfully to the other males as he carried me to the door. Bound and wrapped in a lenga pelt was I, upon the shoulder of a male, seeing naught of where I went save the backs of Ceralt's leg furs as he crunched upon the thin white ground covering. Ceralt had me, and what befell me next would be entirely of his choosing.

The fire in my dwelling seemed bright when we entered, so bright that I averted my eyes when Ceralt turned to close the door behind him. He turned again to continue into the room, and I saw that he had pulled the leather through the door hole, leaving it to hang within the dwelling. Now none might enter the dwelling from without save by the actions of one within, although the chill we had left in the darkness entered somehow to touch me deep. I recalled the Ceralt of old, considered what he had come to be, and again attempted futile efforts to free myself. I did not wish to be with him, yet as he had said, my wishes were of no consideration.

Without ceremony, I and the lenga pelt about me were dropped to the pelt I had slept and lain upon so long. Ceralt pulled the covering ends of pelt from me, then removed the copper belt from my waist before turning away. I lay upon my back, my bound wrists beneath me, my ankles crossed and tied as they had been, the crackling fire throwing shadows everywhere I looked.

Never might one feel so helpless as when one is bound tight and weaponless, awaiting that which Mida has seen fit to send. Over and again does Mida test her warriors, and often does she send punishment to those who displease her. Much had I displeased her of late, and if I were not faced with punishment, then testing was to be my lot. I threw my head from side to side, breathing heavily, yet there was no escape from the misery which held me.

Ceralt I found in the midst of removing his coverings, leaving naught save his leather breech. The breech, too, was quickly removed, and when he had tossed it from him, truly did I wish to gasp at sight of him, for never had I seen his manhood so enlarged nor so enraged. The male hungered furiously for the use of Jalav, and nearly did I miss the sight of the dagger in his hand and the strange glint in his eye. When he saw my gaze upon him, he smiled faintly, and moved to stand over me where I lay.

"Your disapproval of my actions is no longer evident," said he from his height, free hand caressing the blade he held. "Have you come to change your opinion, or are you merely concerned with other matters?"

The softness of his tone disturbed me, as did the flashing of the firelight from the blade in his hand. I wet dry lips with an anxious tongue, and made no attempt at response.

"Your sharp tongue seems stilled," he mused, crouching down to stroke my hair. I shivered at the touch and attempted to shake his hand away, but he held my head still. "No, Jalav," he denied, tightening his grip till my neck felt close to snapping and tears stood out in my eyes. "You are now lawfully mine, and may not deny me. So you feel I showed weakness in not slaying Balinod, do you? Had it been you, would your dagger have drunk from his throat?"

He crouched above me, his fist in my hair, his broad, strong body menacing, his eyes demanding a response. My breath came and went quickly, shaking me, and never had I felt so before another living being. It was my will to give him no answer to his demands, yet my voice, of its own volition, whispered, "Yes!"

"So you would have killed him," he nodded, his grip loosening somewhat. "A savage has no mercy within her to bestow upon another, yet a man deals with others as he sees fit. To Balinod, a man, I chose to show mercy, yet you, wench, shall have none of it. You are not a man."

His hand, holding the dagger, moved to my throat, and I felt the cold, sharp edge of it upon my flesh. My hands and feet, bound tightly in leather, were numb, and a similar numbness

touched the rest of me, shocked that Ceralt would act so. I had
never thought the male capable of such a deed, and the light
touch of his breath upon my face cooled the sweat which covered
my brow. A long moment he remained unmoving, during which
time I held firmly to the memory that my life sign still hung
about my neck, and then he grinned and moved downward with
the blade, severing the leather tie at the top of my garment.

"I had not really expected you to beg for your life as Balinod
did," he said softly, removing his fist from my hair. "Had you
done so, I would have been disappointed, yet there are other
things which touch you more deeply than a threat to your life."

His grin widened as he said this, yet I knew not which things
he meant. A great relief had come with the removal of the blade,
for it is deemed a deep shame for a warrior to die so, bound at
the feet of a male, without the glory of battle. I had been
prepared for the journey to Mida's realm, yet I was greatly
pleased that I need not arrive there in shame. Ceralt moved his
blade first to one side of my garment then to the other, and with
the final passage of the blade, my garment hung loosely upon
me, having been cut at the points where the ties had bound it
closed. Though I knew not what he was about, the grin was
strong upon him, the gleam in his eyes now pleased. Ceralt took
hold of the severed garment still upon me and continued to pull
and tug at it till it was free of my body and he was able to cast it
from him. I then sat up, struggling to remove my hair from
before my face so that I might see what was about me, yet the
seeing was no comfort. The male had placed himself upon the
pelt beside me, the dagger no longer in his grasp, the sword of
his body nearly quivering in its eagerness to plunge deep. It was
my will to have naught further to do with this male Ceralt, yet it
had been so long since I had last taken a male, and my body
recalled the pleasure he was able to give. The moisture flowed
from within me as I smelled the strong smell of a male in need,
the familiar smell of Ceralt, the smell of my own desire, yet I
attempted to deny the urgings thus brought upon me, and began
to move from the side of the male. He, however, liked not such
movement, and quickly grasped my arms to draw me close.

"You seem reluctant," he murmured, pressing me so close to
the hair of his broad chest that I could taste him. Strong was the
taste of Ceralt, full and hard as the manhood which thrust against
my thigh. I moved in his arms to escape the embrace, yet his
strength was, as ever, too great to overcome.

"I do not desire you," I whispered, my hands upon his deeply muscled arms. "Release me at once so that I may complete Mida's work."

He laughed softly and stroked my side from breast to buttocks. "You have already completed all that you shall ever do for your Mida," said he. "You are now in my service, and shall remain there till I release you. And I shall not release you." His hand then darted to my tightly clenched thighs, forced its way between them, and found the moisture I had wished to keep hidden. He laughed at my moan of misery, and touched me deep as he had so often done before. My body writhed well at his touch, and I felt the slickness of sweat on all of my face as the flames rose to roaring within me.

"For one who does not desire me," he murmured, "you seem well prepared for my arrival. Is it possible that you would dare to lie to me?"

I raised tortured eyes to his face, and saw the faint grin upon it, the dark, unruly lock of hair upon his brow, the deep hunger in his light eyes. Again I shuddered to the questing of his touch, and dug my fingers deep within his arms.

"Perhaps you do not lie," he continued, lowering his lips to my shoulder. "Perhaps you are merely unknowing of your desire, and need only be shown."

And then his lips took mine, hungrily crushing the breath from me as he sought my soul. What little resistance had been left to me was then gone, taken by his strength, leaving naught save the weakness which his presence brought. Deeply was I lost to his embrace, my lips responding to his, my thighs clenched about his hand, my breasts pressed into his chest. I felt his nearness with all of my body, the heat within me crying out to be quenched by him, demanding it, begging it. I moved wildly in his arms, no longer in possession of my will, and he, with a laugh, thrust me to my back upon the fur. I opened my thighs wide, welcoming his presence, and when he thrust within me, I cried out in ecstasy, closing my eyes so that I might feel his strength with every part of me. As from a distance, I felt his hands about my wrists, forcing my arms above my head, and then his lips were upon my breast, bringing screams to my throat with the nipping of his teeth. In madness, I threw my hips against his thrusts, seeking to bury him deeper within me, and knew not that one of his hands had left my wrists till that hand held to my hips, stilling my movement. I screamed in fury, trying to wrench loose, and then his manhood withdrew from me, poised at the entrance to my inner being, no more than a

finger's width within. My fury turned instantly to deep fear, and
I whimpered and trembled, unwilling to face the possibility that
he might leave me so, aflame in every fiber of my being, my
need rising up to choke the breath from me. My eyes opened to
the sight of his shadowy form above me, he crouched unmoving
as he gazed down upon me, my wrists yet held by one of his
hands, his other hand firmly at my hip. Again I whimpered and
moved in his grip, and his light eyes, catching the flicker of the
fire, glowed strangely in the darkness of his face.

"Jalav," he whispered, leaning forward slightly, "tell me
now whether or not you desire my use. I would hear the words
from you."

My mouth no longer had spittle to wet it, yet I could not have
held back the words to save my soul. "I desire your use,
Ceralt," I whimpered, looking up at him entreatingly. "I ask
your use. I beg it!"

He laughed softly, and moved against me enough to set me
moaning. "Poor Jalav," he whispered, leaning down farther to
blow upon the spears my breasts had become. "Again does
Ceralt force her to beg her use, as though she were no more than
a wench beneath a man. Tell me what you are, Jalav."

I attempted to swallow dryness as my body shook to his breath
upon it, knowing what answer he sought. Within me a scream of
rage began, yet I blurted out, "I am a wench beneath a—a man,
Ceralt! Do not leave me unused!"

"Calm yourself, Jalav," he chuckled, attempting to sound
soothing. "You have now learned what your place in this world
is, but you do not yet believe it. Should I continue to use you,
the end of your use will again bring you to your former state.
Perhaps it would be best if I made no use of you at all."

"No!" I screamed as he withdrew even farther from me. My
limbs trembled uncontrollably, my head flew from side to side,
and my need was a crippling, demanding thing, impossible to
refuse. "Ceralt, do not leave me so!" I begged, tears coming to
my eyes. "The agony is unbearable! I will be anything you
wish!"

"You will be no more than a wench beneath me?" he
demanded, his hand tightening about my wrists.

"Yes!" I wept, throwing myself about. "I will be that to
you!"

"You will be a full woman to me?" he demanded, presenting
himself again to my desire and thrusting a short way within.

"Yes!" I screamed, the ache in my thighs too great to think

upon. I babbled then, caring naught for what I said so long as he returned to ease me.

"You will obey my every command?" he demanded, withdrawing again. "Swear that you will obey me!"

"I swear!" I screamed, demented beyond knowing ought save my need. "By Mida do I so swear!" I wept. "Return to me, Ceralt! Do not leave me so!"

"You shall not be left so!" his laughter boomed out, pleasure and triumph strong in its sound. "My own hunger need no longer be contained, and now that I have what I wish from you, I shall also have your body. I, too, swear, Jalav, that you shall always recall the use you so ardently begged for."

And then he thrust deeply within me, so deep that I screamed again to the feel of it. Never before had he used me so fiercely as he did that darkness, and as I was swept away before his hunger, I knew I would truly never forget it.

# 9.

## *The sharing of falum— and a place is found*

The dwelling was chilled and dark in the gray of the new light, and I found that I had no desire to move from the warmth of the place I had been given in Ceralt's arms. No fire leapt in the hearth to send forth its warmth, and briefly I thought upon the fact that a fire had ever before greeted me upon awakening in that village. Then I recalled that none could have entered to build such a fire, for Ceralt had seen to our solitude the darkness

before. I lay wrapped in his arms, my cheek against the coarse
hairs of his chest, my body pressed to his, the slow rhythm of his
breathing attempting to force itself upon my own. I did not move
where I lay, for an unaccustomed soreness was upon me, a result
of the fierceness of Ceralt's use. Over and again had he used me
through the darkness, at times upon my back, his lips to my
throat, at times upon my belly, my hips raised to the fury of his
thrusts. At no time had his manhood flagged, a thing most
astonishing, and not till the new light lay no more than a few
hind away did he allow me rest from the pummeling. I had then
been taken by an exhausted sleep, knowing no more till my eyes
had opened a scant few reckid earlier. I sighed softly and moved
my tongue to the dark hairs that lay beside my cheek, licking at
them lightly so as not to awaken Ceralt. Never before had a male
used me so, giving such pleasure through uncompromising
demands. Solely at his bidding had I been allowed to move, no
actions of my own devising being permitted. At first I had raged
and attempted to defy him, yet his presence within me had
brooked no defiance. He made his demands and saw them
obeyed, and I had wept and cried out with the depth of my
pleasure. Such thoughts of his doings awakened my body, the
moisture again beginning to flow, soothing the soreness his
actions had caused. I little regretted the soreness, deeming it a
small inconvenience for the glories of the darkness, and found
that my belly rubbed against Ceralt's without my volition. I stilled
my hips, thinking it possible that I might be clad and away
before his awakening, yet such proved impossible. Ceralt's hand
moved upon my back as his breathing altered, and I then knew
him to be awake. His other hand came to my face and raised it,
and his lips met mine with a softness which had not been present
during the darkness. I drank in the softness with a different sort
of pleasure, one that contained neither heat nor excitement,
merely a soothing pleasure stemming from I knew not what. His
lips remained upon mine some few reckid, and then his head
raised so that he might look upon me.

"The darkness has ended, little savage," he said softly. "How
did you find it?"

"Like no other," I replied, running my hand down his firm,
hard belly to what lay beneath. "Ceralt is a male without equal,
fit for none save a warrior."

The laughter of his pleasure sounded even as his manhood
stirred beneath my fingers. "Such is not the reply of a well-bred
village wench," he chuckled, striking me smartly upon the

bottom. "Such a wench would bewail the tortures she had gone through, begging the Serene Oneness to spare her from such use again. You do not see the matter in such a light?"

I stiffened in anger at being struck so, and also at the mockery in his tone. "Tortures are to be avenged, not bewailed," I informed him, drawing away as far as possible. "And your words hold no meaning for me, as it was pleasure I felt, not torture."

"There, you have done it again," he laughed, paying no heed to my stiffness. "Such immodesty is unbecoming in a good wench, and we must school you in the matter. Do you wish my riders and their wenches to think you a pavilion-she—a mere varaina?"

His humor grated as did the term varaina, which was unfamiliar to me. "I do not know the word!" I snapped, truly annoyed. "Nor do I comprehend the nature of a—a pavilion-she! I am a warrior of Mida, a war leader, not a denizen of villages and cities!"

My opinion of the places of males came through clearly in my tone, and Ceralt grinned faintly as his hand went again to my face.

"You are a what?" he asked, his voice soft yet filled with that which I could not define. "Surely I could not have heard what I thought I heard."

His face was mainly in shadow, his voice was not menacing, yet the words he spoke were somehow disturbing. With uneasy awareness of his hand upon my face and his arm about me, I replied, "I am a warrior of Mida. Ceralt has known this since first we met."

"Since first we met," he echoed, the strangeness yet within his voice. "And from the moment I first laid eyes upon you, I vowed that one fey you would be mine, not as a warrior, but as a woman. My woman. That fey has now come to pass."

No further trace of the grin was upon him, and his hand had tightened where it held my face. I moved in discomfort against his grip, finding instead that his reawakened manhood sought me also where I lay against his body. So large was this Ceralt, and lately so strange, that Mida herself might have hesitated before him. I knew not what his intent might be, yet it seemed one with the chill of the air and the gray of the fire's ashes.

"Ceralt has ever known that Jalav is Mida's," I whispered, my hands to his broad, bare chest. "Though once I might have wished it otherwise, I can never be yours. Do not fault me for

that which is beyond my power to alter, Ceralt. I am chosen by
Mida to serve her, and must do so till the sweet earth drinks of
my blood. Such are the ways of Midanna."

"No longer are you of the Midanna!" he snarled, so like a
child of the wild that my hand grasped frantically for a weapon.
No weapon came to me, and I shivered, held there so near to
him. "Now have you been chosen by me," he rasped. "Your
service mine alone! By Mida you vowed that you would be full
woman to me, that you would obey me in all things, and so it
shall be! Do you recall the vow, woman? Do you?"

He shook me now, by the face and the arm, so savagely that
my neck and shoulder ached to the clenching of his fingers.
Wildly, I pulled at his hand, attempting to free myself from it,
all the while refusing to hear the import of his words.

"No," I moaned, unable to counter his strength, a vast emptiness spreading within me. "I could not have vowed such a thing!
You lie! You lie!"

"Do I?" he demanded, the lightening of the fey spreading
within the windows to show me the coldness in his eyes. "Do I
lie, Jalav? Are you to be forsworn?"

"Never!" I screamed, throwing myself at him in a frenzy.
"Sooner the final death than to be forsworn!" Madly I clawed at
him, raking furrows in his arms and chest, my body twisting
upon the furs so that I might have greater purchase in my attack.
I wished to destroy him then, to send him to Mida's chains or
the great darkness, to still his tongue so that it might never speak
again. My chest heaved and ached with the madness of my
efforts, yet his strength kept my claws from his eyes, my teeth
from his throat. His hands captured mine and his body fell upon
me, forcing away what little air I had. I threw my head to one
side, away from him, squeezing my eyes shut so that I need not
look upon him. Deeply I gasped for air that would not come, my
wrists held prisoner between his hands, my body caught beneath
the weight of his, my agony too horrible to bear. I had made the
vows he had said I had made, faintly yet clearly I recalled the
act, yet I could not accept the results of the vows upon my
lifeshadow. When a warrior stood in her true self before the
Midanna who had gone before, all actions of her lifeshadow lay
open to their view. To think how such vows would be seen by
them! Rightly would they condemn such a one to eternal solitude,
never to join Mida's everlasting legions! I screamed then, feeling
the tortures of my loss from the self-imposed darkness of a
withered soul, cursing my body for the consequences its hungers

had brought upon me. I, once a war leader of the Hosta of the Midanna, was now no longer fit to stand in the company of the lowliest of warriors, was now to be thought of as less than the least of city slave-women. My screaming grew higher and wilder, rising in waves to the dwelling's rafters, then Ceralt's hand struck my face hard, and again, driving the screams from my throat. I lay shaking beneath him, shattered by the enormity of what I had done, yet even so his annoyance came to me clearly.

"Jalav, cease this caterwauling," he commanded. "I shall not allow you female hysterics over the simple fact that you have been mastered. You are mine now, and shall remain so forever. Accept it."

Accept it. So easily did he command me, he who knew naught of honor. Bitterly I looked upon him, seeing the deep scratches upon his chest and arms which his light eyes refused to acknowledge. As ever, a lock of his dark hair fell over his brow, a clear symbol of the unruliness he demanded for himself, yet would never allow to me.

"Release me from the vows!" I rasped, breath still coming hard to me. My cheek burned where he had struck me, and my hands and wrists no longer had feeling.

"Such is not my conception of acceptance," said he with a dryness in his tone, and then he grinned. "Know yourself defeated, my varaina, bested as surely as though you stood among your own, and nearly as savagely. Your life has not been lost to you in the living, merely in the directing, and though your restrictions shall be great, the living of it shall prove sweeter. You are now no more than a wench beneath a man, a position you will often be required to take. How stand your views upon the matter now?"

Well amused was he, this male who spoke of besting a war leader without sword in hand, he who sought vows when others sought pleasure. I moved my wrists within his hand, seeking to regain use of my fingers, recalling the time I had thought myself bested by him. Mida had appeared to me then, in a dream, and had assured me that the strength of males might never best a warrior. Only upon the point of a blade might a warrior be bested, her lifeblood sole proof of her loss of position. I had often questioned my ability to raise sword to Ceralt for the male affected me strangely, yet now, with the possibility of an eternity of solitude before me, I saw that the thing must be done.

"Jalav has never been bested," said I, foolishly seeking to hold my head high. How might a warrior hold her head high beneath the immobilizing bulk of a Mida-forsaken male? Abandoning the attempt, I merely met Ceralt's gaze. "Jalav has considered the matter," I continued, "and agrees to meet the male Ceralt with swords. Should the male overcome her, she shall then be bested. Let the matter be done now."

"So you would agree to meet me with swords," he mused. "And from whom would you receive permission to touch a sword?"

My mouth opened to reply, yet no reply came forth. I had been about to say that a warrior needed no permission to defend her honor, yet he had not released me from my vows, and his feelings upon weapons and myself were well known to me. That his permission was necessary before I might face him with a blade was infuriating, and I writhed in frustration beneath him as he laughed.

"I see you understand the point," he grinned, his hand moving to pat the top of my head. "Jalav must now be an obedient wench, asking Ceralt for his leave before she undertakes an action. Should Jalav truly wish a thing, she must ask politely."

Fury rose up to tangle my tongue in its curling, blazing vapors, yet I forced myself to hiss, "Indeed, I shall ask for that which I wish! I wish to see your blood upon my blade, Ceralt! I wish to send you to Mida's chains and an eternity of sthuvad use! Allow me but a few short reckid with sword in hand, and the matter shall be quickly seen to!"

Again my breathing had grown heavy with the heat of emotion, yet a gasp was forced from me as Ceralt's grip tightened upon my wrists. No longer was he amused, and that strange glint shined coldly from his eyes as he leaned nearer to me.

"A man cares little for being threatened by another man," he rasped, his voice grating with anger. "Should the one who threatens him be female, he may choose between amusement at such foolishness, and punishment for such insolence. I am not amused."

His hand went again to my hair, and nearly did I cry out as his fist took strong purchase therein. "Perhaps, by cause of what has previously occurred between us, you feel I fear to face you with sword in hand." His voice, laced with contained anger, had grown very soft, so soft that my fury cooled quickly in the face of it. "Such is not the truth of the matter, yet I feel no need to present you with proof you would accept. Suffice it to say that you shall not again touch hand to sword, dagger, bow or spear for any reason, save with my express permission. You are to banish all thoughts of flight from your mind, for you travel to no place lest it be by my side. Should the fey ever come that I raise sword to a female, that female will not be you. I do not fear you, varaina, yet you may perhaps learn to fear me. Some wenches require such fear to keep them where they belong."

That disturbing coldness did not leave his eyes as his maleness sought and found its place within me. I no longer wished the vigor of his use, yet he took me as he willed, knowing he increased the soreness he had caused and caring not. My femaleness flinched from him in vain till my body acknowledged its helpless response to his presence, and then was I soothed and lifted in his wake, to follow slave-like the demands he put to me. Well used was I by this Ceralt who ruled me, yet his anger increased with each of his thrusts till I thought he would end me with such fury. I cried out in protest, half with pleasure, half with pain, yet he chose to ignore my protest though his eyes had not left my face. He used me to the full, at last sending his seed within me, an action which seemed to drain his anger as well. When he left me to lie beside me, his breathing had already begun to quiet, and with great difficulty I moved my arms to where I might see my wrists. An angry redness circled them from his unrelenting grip, and the daggertips in my fingers tingled then blazed with pain. A moment I flexed my fingers, regaining some sense of feel, and then I clumsily touched myself, wondering if Ceralt had caused me damage. Was this male ever to do me as none had before him? In the past, it had ever been a warrior who took an unwilling sthuvad, never the warrior who was taken herself. I cared little for the manner of turn about; however I saw no way the distortion might be corrected. Males are strange in their doings and thoughts, and seem ever to wish the rights and privileges of warriors.

"Do you at last begin to learn the meaning of your place?" asked Ceralt from beside me. I turned my head toward him, and saw that he lay stretched upon his side, leaning upon one arm. Those light eyes noted where my fingers had gone, and my cheeks filled with heat at the grim satisfaction he showed. Surely he now thought me bested, for he had taken his pleasure with me above my protests. I had no wish to see the matter so, yet his gaze was difficult to meet. I turned to my left, away from him, bringing my hands to my middle and drawing my knees up, suddenly feeling the lack of the lenga pelt upon me. The dwelling was cold in the gray of the new light, and the dampness of my flesh drew the cold as an unprotected infant kan would draw

a hungry zaran. Ceralt watched me turn from him, yet he would
not allow me to take my shame from his sight. His hand grasped
my arm and returned me to my back, then placed itself upon my
breast.

"This is the sign of a woman," said he, stroking the breast
then cupping it in his palm. "Women are smaller than men and
weaker, not nearly as swift, and easy prey to men. Such things
are necessary, for women are also the bearers of children, and if
it were impossible for men to take the women of their choosing,
our race would not survive. The lives of your clanswomen are
perversions, Jalav, for they do not acknowledge this necessary
difference, and waste untold numbers of precious child-bearers
in bloody and senseless battle. I may not know how such a thing
began, but I need not allow it to continue. I shall show you the
vulnerability of a woman again and again, till the truth of the
matter is known in the very bones of you. Then, perhaps, we
may seek another manner of living with one another, yet the
choice will be yours. I shall not change my treatment of you till
you request it."

So seriously did he gaze upon me as he spoke, and so quietly,
that I knew he felt the matter one of importance, yet I could not
fathom his meaning. All knew of the physical differences between male and warrior, and all knew as well that males could
not bear children, yet when he spoke of waste, I could not follow
his reasoning.

"Those warriors who are with child are never wasted," I
informed him, ignoring the discomfort his fingers brought.
"Though some might wish to hide the presence of the quickened
seed within them so as not to be denied the glories of battle, all
Midanna know it their duty to bear new young warriors into the
world. They then give over battle till the child is born, returning
to a warrior's life only upon placing the child with Keeper's
Attendants to raise."

"So they then give over battle," Ceralt snorted, removing his
hand from me as he sat up and crossed his legs before him. His
eyes were angry now, and he tossed his head impatiently. "And
if they do not survive the last battle they have allowed
themselves?" he demanded. "The child within then dies as they
do! And to go even further, how many are slain before there is
aught within them? There are few men to see to the women in
your lands, and rarer yet is the man who is allowed to decide
which of the women will bear his seed. Should a warrior woman
love battle too greatly, she need only refrain from using a man to

remain childless. In our lands, such a woman's foolishness is not tolerated. If she possesses qualities which men desire, she is bred whether she wishes to be or not. Upon such a thing does survival of the race depend, and women cannot be trusted with the decision. Too many fear to bear the children of men, so the decision must be made for them.''

"Warriors do not fear males!" I hissed, beginning to sit up. "It is a warrior's decision whether or not she will use a particular male, and there is no fear involved!"

"So say *you!*" he retorted, pushing me flat again. "And I say that there is deep fear within the woman who refuses to bear a man's child! Do you fear that you will not survive, Jalav, or is the fear an entirely different one? A woman who is given a man's child is one who has been possessed by him in her entirety, one who has been made to bow to his mastery. Should she have mastered him, he would bear her child. I think the root of your problem lies in the fact that you have never been bested in battle. You have never been taught the value of submission to those stronger than you, and such is not the way of survival.''

"I *have* survived!" I snapped, struggling against the hand at my throat which now held me down. "Many have come forward upon the field of battle, claiming to be stronger, yet none have been able to stand against me! Submission is for slaves, not for those who would lead!"

"And you wish to lead," he murmured, calmly taking in my struggles beneath the strength of his hand. "There is no shame to be found in wishing to lead, yet one must first know where he is leading, else all those who follow are as doomed as the leader. You now lead blindly and to no purpose, yet perhaps the matter may be rectified." Till then he had spoken as though to himself, yet with the final words he straightened himself and hardened his gaze upon me.

"Cease this useless motion!" he commanded, tightening his grip upon my throat. "Will you never learn the futility of testing your strength with me? I am now going to dress, but you must first be punished for your earlier insolence. Sit up and obey me as though I possessed your sworn word.''

At reminder of my vows I ceased struggling, and his hand came away from my throat. Bitterly, I raised myself to sitting upon the lenga pelt, knowing not what he would do, yet knowing that my body deserved whatever pain he brought to it. Come the leather or the lash, an unwarrior-like hunger had invited the thing, and Jalav must now face what her weakness had wrought.

Truly were the ways of the Midanna wise, to allow no males among them, save through sthuvad use.

"I do not care for the manner in which you sit," said Ceralt, studying the cross-legged position I had taken. "The posture is ungraceful, hiding the lines of a woman's body. Place yourself upon your knees, varaina."

I bristled at the name he again called me by, yet there was little I might do other than obey him. Brushing my hair well back from my arms, I knelt where I had formerly sat, and Ceralt nodded thoughtfully.

"Better," he conceded, still unsatisfied. "Yet you still seem too well prepared to defend yourself. A woman must know her vulnerability before men before she may learn submission. Reach back and grasp your ankles, and do not release them."

I wished to snarl at such direction, yet the doing would have been idle. I reached back beneath my hair which now fell about my feet, and grasped my ankles from within as I had been bidden. My hands now rested between thighs and ankles, held easily in place by my body weight as I sat upon my heels. Ceralt rose from his place to crouch before me, and his hands took my thighs and moved them widely apart.

"This position is more to my liking," said he, a grin beginning as he gazed upon me. His body, so broad and hard, rose before me even in a crouch, and suddenly the knowledge struck me more fully than it had before. This wide-chested male, whose arms were nearly the size of my thighs, might use me whenever he wished, his former concern for my comfort no longer present. How might I, weaponless and alone, aid myself against his will? I knelt before him, my breasts thrust forward, my thighs invitingly open to his sight and touch, and a trembling prepared to claim me that I might not even draw away. In misery, my eyes sought his face, and he chuckled when our gaze met.

"You do not care for being placed so?" he asked, his hand moving to my face. "Such is a great pity, for this is the position you will take whenever I require it of you. Your insolence brought this upon you, little savage, and I would have you consider a thing: should we ever face one another with swords as you so earnestly requested, I will not take your life. I will rather take your sword from you and kneel you so before all of your wenches, and make you beg your use. They are sure to find the sight most entertaining."

I looked upon him with great horror, my mouth falling open, yet he did no more than laugh at my plight. Those without souls have no concept of honor, yet would even a male do such a thing? Many lives had I taken in my kalod as a warrior, yet never had I so shamed another, nor even conceived of the possibility. Vile and dishonorable are the males of the cities, and I vowed within that I would never so lose myself to the touch of a male. Sooner the touch of an edge to one's throat, and a slow beginning upon the journey to Mida's realm.

"You now seem determined," mused Ceralt, a grin still upon him though his light eyes glinted. "Perhaps you feel yourself able to resist me. If such is the case, look here."

Without volition, my eyes followed his hand as it left my face and moved lower, his second hand joining the first at my breasts. He did no more than brush at them before taking my life sign into his hands, yet my skin burned hot where he had touched, as though I had been struck. He held my life sign for a moment, his thumbs rubbing at the texture of it, and then he placed it against my skin, his fingers tracing the shape of the hadat upon me. My breathing had begun to grow rapid and uneven, and I was unable to move my eyes from his hands even as my limbs began to tremble. I heard his chuckle as though from a great distance, yet watched with unusual clarity as his fingers traced a slow path from my life sign, down my belly to my thighs. My breathing now grew wilder still, yet his hands did not remain upon the tops of my thighs. To the sides they went, beginning at my knees, and then singly, slowly, began the ascent. I writhed where I knelt, unable to free my hands to stop him, knowing that even had my hands been freed, I could not have stopped him. My body cried out for him to hurry, my mind cried out for him to leave me be, yet both were overcome when my voice cried out at his touch upon my heat. My need was great then, yet the soreness he had brought upon me caused my eyes to close and my head to throw itself back in misery, wishing his touch with every fiber of my being, shrinking from his touch lest further pain attend me. I moaned and tossed my head about, shamed through the needs of my own body, then gasped as his fingers entered me to probe gently at my pain.

"Have I used you too far, little savage?" came Ceralt's voice as I sobbed without tears at his testing. "Though it was my intention to impress you, I had not thought it possible to accomplish this. I now find myself pleased."

I forced my eyes to look upon him, and he regarded me in turn, the glint strong in his eyes. His fingers had not left me, and I knelt before him in great need and much pain, biting back the plea that he use me and ease some part of my suffering. His fingers moved again and I stiffened with a moan, yet no more than satisfaction showed itself upon his face.

"Do you recall our first meeting, wench?" he asked, his voice so soft that I shivered. "The first fey you kept me for yourself alone, yet after that I was given over to your—warriors. Do you know the fate of a man at their hands?"

His eyes had grown so hard with memory that I knew not what he might be about. No longer could I bear his touch, and wished no more than to thrust his hand from me. I began to rise from my heels to free my hands, yet the sharpness of his tone froze me in place.

"Be still!" he snapped, an icy wildness having entered his eyes. "You may not move till I release you! I asked you, wench, do you know the fate of a man bound before savage females?"

His fingers probed so deeply now that I closed my eyes again, nearly lost between screaming need and shrieking pain. Sweat stood out all over me, causing my body to shine in his sight, yet I suddenly knew that his eyes saw another sight, one which came to me in the darkness 'neath my lids.

"I was bound wrist and ankle to stakes in the ground," said Ceralt, bitterness causing his voice to choke. "My severed clothing was then brushed aside, and I lay bare to the laughter of the females who stood about me. I fought the leather they had bound me with till my wrists and ankles were near to bleeding, yet I could not free myself, nor could I keep from swallowing too much of that Sigurr's brew which my men had also had forced upon them. Then the females put their swords aside and crouched about me, waiting for the brew to do its evil work."

I felt his body move upon the lenga pelt, and then his fist was tight within my hair, forcing my head even farther back, his other hand as deep within my body. I moaned aloud as he did this, not only from the pain he gave, but also from the fury of his memories. Harsh was his breathing not far from my ear, and I kept my eyes tight closed lest I look upon what welled within him and cry out from the sight.

"In no more than a matter of reckid, my body was no longer mine," growled Ceralt, far too close to where I knelt. "I looked upon the females about me, saw their bare, impudent breasts, the softness of their bodies, and fought to reach them with my manhood. I burned, Jalav, burned as I never had before, aching with my need and nearly splitting asunder. The females laughed again, that sneering, insulting laughter piercing to my very pride, and then one of them rose from her crouch and approached me. No more than a child was she, barely nubile and with breasts too large for her frame, yet she placed her hand upon me and laughed at my efforts to reach her. I would have torn her apart in the depths of my need, yet I was unable to reach her! And then she lifted up that bit of skirting done in Hosta green and straddled me, allowing no more of my manhood within her than suited her pleasure. Slowly did she take her pleasure, slowly driving me insane, and when my stream burst forth to fill her well, she moved from it, and laughed again to see me cover myself and the ground. No release had I found in spilling my seed, instead the fire burned higher, and then another took the place of the first, and then another and another till I could do no more than shout and curse and demand the surcease of death! No surcease did I find till all had used me to their will, and with the waning of the drug came a pain the likes of which I had never known. My manhood seemed a thing apart and truly aflame, and I heard the moans of my men even above my own. That, Jalav, was what I found at the hands of your females. I had thought to forgive you your savagery, excuse the necessity of that which you did, yet I now find myself unable to do so. Do you ache from my use, Jalav? Shall I tell you how pleased I am? I took no more than a single swallow of that which aids a man in impressing a stubborn woman, yet I now wish I had had access to that brew once given me at your orders. Your ache would be considerably greater.''

He released my hair with a final shake, and sharply pulled his fingers from me, leaving me to kneel untouched by anything other than what had just transpired. I shook from the venom of his narrative, from the heat risen within me, from the pain of many things, and knew naught of what occurred about me save an occasional scrape till the sound of footsteps came, approaching the door. Once there, the voice of Ceralt came again.

''Remain exactly as you are till I return, Jalav,'' said he, his voice no longer uncontrolled. ''When I return, you shall follow me to my halyar.''

No more than those few words did he speak, and then he was gone, the sound of the closing door preceded by a gust of colder air. I shivered more deeply at the touch of it upon my skin. My eyes remained closed to the sights of the world, yet my inner eye insisted upon viewing sights which were long past, sights which brought even greater pain upon me. Ceralt, he upon whom I could not look without a strange weakness taking me, was no

longer the Ceralt I had known. That Ceralt had been strong and
fine, humor warming his light eyes, concern creasing his brow
beneath the lock of dark hair, a gentleness often to be found in
the touch of his hand. This Ceralt had been taken by—I knew
not what—and the gentleness was gone as though it had never
been. Again I threw my head about and cried out in the emptiness of the dwelling. I had not known how sthuvad use would
touch him, by Mida do I swear this! Why, in the name of the
final glory, had it not been so before?

My head fell forward upon my chest, and my hair came about
my arms to cloak before me. I shifted very slightly where I
knelt, yet little ease came to feet, hands or legs. I knelt as Ceralt
had left me, open and bare to the sight of any who might come,
and again my heat surged so high that my head tossed about and
I moaned. Why had he not used me? Why had he left me
kneeling so—and why did the memory of his sthuvad use burn
so within him? He was male, and what else might a male expect
save sthuvad use?

No longer was I able to bear shutting out sight of the world,
therefore I opened my eyes to look miserably about. The dwelling was empty save for myself upon the lenga pelt, empty and
dim despite the strengthening gray light from beyond the windows.
My breathing was much too rapid, yet I could not calm it. His
fingers had touched me, upon belly and thighs—I screamed
madly, needing to tear at myself, unable to tear at myself even
though neither chain nor leather touched me. *He* had touched
me! *Ceralt, I did not know!* Ceralt, do not leave me so! Ceralt! I
wept and moaned, writhing as I knelt, demanding answers from
untenanted air. He had not been so changed when first he had
found me, when I lay near dead from Silla spears. His gentleness
had then been with him, yet now it was gone and bitterness and
hatred had taken its place. What other purpose might males be
put to if not sthuvad use? Did all males see it as he did, was this
why they fought the leather and the drug? I gazed down at my
opened thighs and shook, recalling the sight of his hand there.
Why had he knelt me so, commanded to remain unmoving?
What else is a warrior to do with a male? *Ceralt!*

I know not how long I knelt there in the dwelling, yet the time
then seemed to be measured in feyd. Brighter and brighter grew
Mida's light, more and more numb grew my hands and legs and
feet. I shivered from the lack of a fire, yet a constant moisture
crept from between my thighs. My body ached as though I had
been hind upon a hard, fast trail, and my head hung down,

bringing my hair forward to gather about my face. A throbbing had begun within me, and I knew not how it might be made to cease. A sound at the door brought my head up sharply, for it might have been any who entered, yet my eyes met Ceralt alone, upon his return. He gazed at me closely as he closed the door, then came to stand over me where I knelt. I sent my own gaze to the stained and well-worn lenga pelt beneath my knees, to see no more of him than the tops of his fur leg-wrappings.

"It seems I have been obeyed," said he, a satisfaction to his tone. "How has the time passed for you, varaina?"

"Slowly," said I, attempting to recall that I had once been a war leader of the Hosta. I keenly felt the humiliation of my posture, yet even as I strove for a dignity that had been lost to me, my body felt the nearness of Ceralt and gave him his slave due. The heat he had left me with had quieted only a little, and he chuckled his amusement with renewed good humor.

"Never had I thought to see you so completely within my power," said he, and a pile of furs and other things fell to the floor beside me with a thud as he released them. "It makes a man feel—odd to have it so, yet greatly pleased. Do you yet know why you have come to such a pass, Jalav? Are you now able to see your vulnerability?"

He stood above me, awaiting an answer, and I saw little reason to withhold it from him. "Long have I known of Mida's displeasure," said I, refraining from raising my head. "I am either to be punished or tested, yet in any event, my trials are yours to mete out. I am abandoned by Mida's love and helpless before you, male. Why do you not end me and have done with it?"

A moment of silence followed these words, then Ceralt crouched before me to once again take my hair in his fist. More gently than previous was my head raised so, and sight of his eyes showed a great annoyance aflicker there. The dwelling was cold without a fire to warm it, yet much warmth was brought by the mere presence of his hand upon my hair. Surely Mida's judgment had been harsh upon me, to so enslave my body to a male. Much harm had already been caused by it; could there yet be more?

"You are the stubbornnest, most ridiculous female I have ever met!" said Ceralt, his annoyance evident in his sharpened tone. "Have I not told you that you are no longer to be concerned with this Mida nonsense? How might a fiction be displeased with you? It is *my* displeasure which must concern you, for it is I, and

I alone, who has put you upon your knees! And what idiocy do you speak, asking why I do not end you! Would a man draw a woman from the circle of choice merely to end her? Have you no sense within this great, empty head?''

His fist shook my head by the hair, emphasizing his words, yet it was *his* question which was senseless, and then I recalled that it was a male with whom I dealt. The weariness returned to me, and I much regretted ever having ventured forth from Hosta lands.

"Truly, I had forgotten," I sighed, looking past his shoulder to the darkened wood of the walls. "That males have no knowledge of Mida and her doings is understood, yet I had forgotten that through this lack of knowledge, honor is also unknown to them. Even those who had stolen Mida's Crystals and the lives of my warriors were allowed death after their punishment. Males take captives whom they might torture forever."

"Torture!" he snorted in derision, releasing my hair to hang his arm across his thigh. "The sole torture you feel, wench, is the pinching of your pride! Your body has been taught to know mine as its master, and this is what disturbs you. Sooner would that overweening pride of yours face death than see you knelt at a man's feet. You battle with a woman's needs and yearnings, attempting to deny them, yet this shall not be allowed you. You will learn to kiss your place at my feet, and also learn to beg the privilege of being placed there. This I shall see to during our journey.''

Much anger had come to me at the smugness of his insistences, yet his final words gave me pause. I watched as he stood erect and removed the fur covering of his upper body, considering where this oft-mentioned journey might take us. Danger had been spoken of by Lialt, a danger which might, perhaps, free me from the hold of this male. There was no battle within me of the sort he spoke of, no yearnings save the wish to ride free. That my body was in bondage to his was no more than the wrath of Mida, a thing to be ended should she once again allow me her work. Much did I believe this, and even the strain of my hardened nipples did not dissuade me from the view.

Ceralt put his body fur aside, then crouched again to sort among the pile of things he had but recently fetched. Within the bulk of that which seemed to be another body fur were two long leather strings, one short string, and a small, leather-covered pot which he removed, leaving the strings where they were. His uncovering of the pot showed a light pink liquid, thicker even

than sword oil, yet thin enough to run slowly down the side of
the pot when the male held it out toward me.

"Here," said he, gesturing with the pot. "This will ease what
soreness is upon you—till I choose to return it to you. Take the
jar and see to yourself."

I had no need to attempt movement to know the struggle
which lay ahead, for my body's numbness spoke eloquently of it.
Slowly, carefully, I sought to raise myself from my heels, to
release my ankles and free my hands, yet it seemed as though I
was bound in place, my limbs of a weight too massive for
movement. Deeply I breathed, feeling the greasy pads of sweat
upon my forehead, knowing I must bring the pain to my flesh
before freedom would be granted from where I knelt. Ceralt
looked narrow-eyed upon my efforts, then shook his head with a
sound of annoyance.

"Stubborn!" he muttered, once again displeased, then raised
his hands to brush my hair back. "You know full well that you
have knelt there too long to move without assistance," he accused,
"yet I hear no words from you asking my aid. Had you asked,
you would have received it, just as you would have received my
protection from those minions of Vistren who set upon you with
daggers. Then, as now, you spoke not, and I do not care for the
practice. Heed my words, woman, and mend your ways."

I looked upon him in confusion, seeing his light-eyed annoyance and understanding none of it, yet he made no further
explanations. Silently, he placed two fingers within the pot he
had opened, withdrew them covered with the thick pink liquid,
placed the pot upon the floor boards beside him, then held my
neck with his free hand.

"We will see to one pain at a time," said he, his voice now
softened. "This must be done before your limbs are stretched.
Brace yourself."

His hand upon my neck brought further confusion, yet all was
swept away when he reached toward me with the liquid. The
touch of it was icy silk upon my irritated parts, an iciness I
wished to draw away from, yet found myself unable to do so. He
spread the liquid well about, returning his fingers to the pot from
time to time, and in no more than a hand of reckid, I again
writhed where I knelt, having been freed of the lesser pain and
thrown completely to the mercy of the greater. Ah, Mida! How
the touch of him upon my heat was agony! I moaned at the
circular movement of his fingers and a grin appeared upon his
face, shortly to be joined by gentle laughter. My thighs were

opened to him as he had demanded, and he pleasured himself
with that which was unshielded from his touch. Then his fingers
left the victim of his probings, and the pot of liquid was removed
to a greater distance.

"That seems sufficient for the moment," he murmured, putting his hands upon my arms. "Now let us see to your unwinding."

A sudden reluctance was upon me to move, yet this reluctance
did naught to keep him from placing me upon my belly in the
furs. One by one he lowered my legs, releasing my hands, and I
forced my face within the furs to keep from voicing the pain. It
began heavy and dull, a mutter within muscles, rising from there
to a flaming of the limbs, worsened by Ceralt's briskly rubbing
hands. Daggers of fire pierced me all about, bringing to mind the
agony produced by use of two of Mida's Crystals. I thrust the
thought from me and clenched my teeth, at the same time
drawing my arms forward. The effort needed was great, yet I
could not remain unmoving, knowing naught save Ceralt's
ministrations. The male was heartless, rubbing my legs to screaming life, and I had no wish for the same to be done to my hands
and arms. At last my hands were before my face, and I leaned
upon my elbows so that I might flex the fingers and reaccustom
them to movement. My life sign swung between my breasts in
rhythm to the flexing, and I knew that I must rid myself of it,
should it prove impossible to find freedom from the vows Ceralt
had stolen. My life sign was the guardian of my soul, its
presence an assurance that should my life be lost, my soul would
find its way to Mida's realm. With the prospect of an eternity of
isolation before me, I had no wish to enter Mida's realm. Far
better that my soul seek the endless darkness, there to thin and
spread till it was no more. A coldness touched me briefly,
bringing a shudder, for I greatly feared the final darkness, yet
fear was not to be acknowledged by a war leader. Though I was
war leader no more, there was little to be gained by falling prey
to fears and weaknesses. Though my soul would find no more
than the final darkness, it was yet possible for my body to give
up the breath of life with some modicum of dignity. Even should
Mida wish no more of me, she would still expect my end to be
worthy of a Midanna.

"Let me see you move your legs," said Ceralt from behind
me, leaving off the rubbing. My legs now tingled hotly, yet I
knew their control was again mine. Long hind had I knelt upon
the lenga pelt, yet not so long that recovery would be as long or
longer. I rolled to my side and drew my legs up, reaching down

to knead the back of my left thigh. Ceralt's eyes were upon me, yet his gaze had found the spear scar upon my thigh, and his hand reached out to touch it gently, a strange tightening of his lips in evidence at sight of the ridged, pinkish flesh against the darker skin of me. His fingers barely touched the scar then pulled away, and his eyes rose from my thigh to my face.

"Never again shall such a thing happen," said he, the soft menace fully within his voice and eyes. "Above all things, heed me in this, Jalav, for if ever I find a weapon within reach of your hand, your punishment will be feyd in the doing. See if you are able to stand."

He rose from his crouch to await my efforts, and I, with very little difficulty, also gained my feet. I wished to remind him that the wounds had come about by cause of the absence of weapons in my hand, not their presence, yet the glint in his eyes dissuaded the attempt. He wished naught of the truth, this male who looked down upon me narrow-eyed, issuing his commands as suited him, and would not hear it being spoken. I stretched myself as I stood before him, keeping the truth in my own heart, and he in his blindness seemed satisfied.

"Now that you are restored," said he, reaching about himself to pull his leather chest covering over his head and from his arms, "you may see to repairing the damage you have done. Fetch the jar, and salve these scratches you put upon me."

He indicated the pot of pink liquid as he tossed his leather covering aside, therefore I bent to retrieve the pot, then turned to inspect him. The tracks of clawing were deep and inflamed upon his chest and arms, also showing signs, here and there, of having bled. I glanced at his face as he stood waiting, and saw no sign of anger at my having marked him so. Indeed, he seemed serene and complacent, as though such markings were acceptable to him. Confusion, my constant companion, stirred within me, yet I quieted it with a surmise. Perhaps, to the male, the clawings were a symbol of his victory, no more than a small cost for having had his way with me. I now stood before him, having been commanded to tend to his needs, and such victory must be sweet indeed. Midanna warriors tended their own wounds when possible, or were aided by other warriors when such aid was needed. Never would a sthuvad be allowed to perform such a function, for even with males who chose to remain with Midanna after the time of their sthuvad use, the thought of vengeance for their initial capture might come. Ceralt feared no such vengeance, and my lips tightened in fury at the thought. He possessed my word to chain me to him, and knew me helpless before the male strength of him. So close was the dagger at his silvered belt, so close and tempting, yet I had been forbidden the welcome presence of its hilt within my grasp, forbidden its very nearness to me. Angrily, I reached two fingers within the pot I held, coming away with a thick coating of the liquid, yet my wrist was suddenly grasped by his hand before I might touch him.

"Gently," he cautioned, an amusement now clear in his eyes. "I wish the scratches salved, not savaged. Let us see how near you may come to a woman's touch."

He released my wrist and watched closely as I spread the liquid upon the first of the clawings of his chest. It lay among the dark hairs which covered him, much like a sednet in grass, and as I spread the liquid about, I became aware of the rise and fall of the chest I tended. The wounds lay before my eyes, for Ceralt stood a full head taller than I, and I felt that he now looked down upon me rather than the doings of my fingers. I renewed the liquid and moved to another of the wounds, recalling this chest before me, and how often I had pressed my face to it, lost in the pleasures of Ceralt's manhood. My hand trembled in the spreading, and I quickly turned to the markings of his arms, yet the Mida-forsaken remembrances would not give me peace. How often had those well-thewed arms been about me, holding me for his lips and caresses? How often had I clung to them in the throes of his body's delights? Even through the liquid, I was able to feel the warmth and strength of his flesh, and I squeezed my thighs together to halt the flow of the moisture which ran from me, mute evidence of the male's near presence, helpless response to the thought of him. Quickly, I finished the task he had given me, placing the pot once more upon the floor, yet when I stood straight again, I found I was not done with him. His arms went about me, pulling me to the chest I had tended, and then his lips were upon mine, taking the kiss he sought, and more as well. His silvered belt pressed into my body as his hands moved about my bare back, beneath my hair, stroking my skin and bringing forth a moan from my throat. Again was I slave to his demands, held in his arms and to his lips as though the thing were proper, as though his body had the right to own mine so. I shivered in my need and pressed against his hardness, and his lips left mine so that he might laugh.

"Is there aught you desire, varaina?" he asked, laughter in his eyes. I knew he mocked me in my weakness, yet I was unable to free myself of his chains. A warrior often has deep needs, and never before had I been so powerless to satisfy them. The strength of his arms about me, the warmth of his body—I was unable to keep the words from stumbling from me.

"Use me, Ceralt," I whispered, my eyes begging the laughter in his. My body, uncontrollable, forced itself against his manhood, demanding release, piteously pleading for it. His arms tightened about me, holding me still against him, his amusement increasing.

"Think you I have naught to do this fey than put you to your back?" he chuckled, his hand moving to my bottom to halt the swaying of my hips. "It is nearly the time for one's mid-fey meal, and we have not even shared falum as yet. We must now see you clad, varaina, so you may follow me to my halyar. Should your conduct of the fey please me, I shall use you for further pleasure in the darkness. Fetch your garment, Jalav, and do not speak again."

I had been about to plead with him, debasing myself as he had previously demanded, yet his command cut short the flow of words. He released me and turned away, dismissing his own need, and I crouched where I stood, hugging my knees against the pulsing flames within me. My cheek felt the bones within my knee, my feet felt the wood of the floor beneath me, my crumbled pride felt the agony and humiliation of having been denied after lowering myself to begging. That he would do me so, I, once a war leader of the Hosta of the Midanna! Now that he had possession of me, soon there would be naught left save an endless shame, one never to be cleansed. My eyes closed tight, I moved my face against my knees, unexpectedly feeling the touch of the silver ring of a blood warrior, that which was matched upon the other side by the second silver ring of a war leader. A great fury rose up in me, fury at all things which now surrounded me, fury at that which had once meant so much to me. I put my hands to the rings, intending to tear them from my ears, and again Ceralt's hands closed about my wrists.

"The decorations please me," he said, forcing my hands from their grip upon the rings. "Do not touch them again, nor attempt to remove them. And you will be punished for failing to obey me. Now, fetch your garment!"

Miserably, I opened my eyes to see the anger upon him, an anger which shone from his light eyes. Decorations, he had called the rings of a warrior, demeaning them to the point of meaningless trifles, lowering them to the place he had lowered me. Never would a male end the life of a captive, for that would be savagery. Sooner would he show mercy and spare that life, preserving it so that he might make it not worth the living. Truly was mercy a thing of males, a thing far beyond the simple savageries of warriors.

Ceralt pulled me straight again, and despite my pain, I went to fetch my covering. Ceralt knew what pain I felt, long ago had he learned of my body's demands, yet the thought no longer concerned him. Much changed had Ceralt become, and I knew not why this was so. My covering was easily straightened, yet it seemed beyond repair with the ties having been slit by Ceralt's dagger. Ceralt directed the removal of the cut ties, then produced the strings which had lain with the pot of liquid. These strings once within the garment, made it whole once more, yet their color was somewhat lighter than the color of the old strings. Sight of them restored Ceralt's good humor, and though I had no understanding of the significance of such a thing, it mattered not. Walking had become a difficulty, and a further annoyance plagued me. The pink liquid Ceralt had placed within me gave too greasy a feel, yet I was forbidden to touch the place in an attempt to remove it. With the covering upon me, the copper-colored belt once more around my middle, my leg and body furs, fetched from the large dwelling, again in their proper places, I miserably followed Ceralt from the dwelling. The last I saw of it was a cold and finished sight, the fireplace bereft of fire, the lenga pelts soiled and abandoned, the severed strings of my garment scattered about, all in a chill dimness of that which is not to be returned to. Now, I would dwell elsewhere, in a captivity more complete than I had yet known. Ah, Mida! How great my sins must be to have brought this about!

The fey was cold even though a thin remembrance of Mida's warming light shone down in an attempt to scatter the chill. A small wind blew, rifling the leaves which remained upon the trees, and no longer was there a white, frozen covering upon the ground. Males and females moved about the village as I hurried to match the pace of Ceralt, who had decreed that I follow behind him, yet no further than two paces from his broad, fur-covered back. He strode across the hardened ground, not once looking to see if indeed I followed, knowing full well the manner in which I was bound to him. I looked toward the forests as I hastened in his track, feeling their call, longing desperately to flee in the direction which would return me to Hosta lands, yet I could not leave my word unreclaimed, nor could I ignore the whimperings of my body. Well bound was I to Ceralt, and only Mida might free me of his hold.

Well amused were the males of the village who saw us, and I entered Ceralt's dwelling covered by the red of humiliation. Ceralt, who stood to one side of the door to hurry me within, showed a fine grin of amusement, knowing precisely the cause of the color in my cheeks. Much hate did I feel for the male then, he who so gloried in my debasement, he who flaunted it for the world to see. Vile were males in their multitude of ways, and I hated them all for the many things they had done to me. Mida teaches that hate is a useless emotion, for one may challenge she who would normally evoke such a feeling and end the need to feel hatred, yet was I unable to do such a thing among males. My hate of all things male grew higher the longer I moved among them, and I knew not where the thing might end. Perhaps madness awaited me in place of honorable death, yet as I drew my body fur over my head, I knew I cared not. One end now seemed as welcome as another.

"Remove your boots as well," remarked Ceralt, taking his fur body covering to hang upon the wall. With the door closed and a fire blazing in the hearth, the dwelling was overwarm, yet he did not attempt to remove his own leg furs. I sat upon the floor to pull the furs from me, and Ceralt turned to regard me with a faint smile.

"I find great pleasure in seeing you obey without explanation," said he, "yet this matter requires your understanding. Wenches of this village are not permitted footwear within a halyar, therefore you will remove your boots no matter whose halyar you enter. Is this clear to you?"

His eyes awaited an acknowledgment, therefore I nodded, which seemed to be sufficient. He turned from me with a grunt and walked toward the hearth, and my fists closed with impotent fury upon the leg furs I had removed. Stroke and stroke again with the lash of shame, and care naught for the miserable female beneath the lash. I began to feel pity and compassion for those females raised trapped among males, and also began to understand somewhat the why of their lack of escape attempts. Their treatment at the hands of males left little pride to which they might cling, yet Ceralt erred in thinking me of their ilk. The memories of a warrior yet stirred within me, and never would they be excised from my thoughts.

Ceralt's dwelling was much like Lialt's, with lenga pelts scattered about, piles of garments to one side, small platforms here and there, and thick leather strung tied across one corner, yet as I placed my fur body covering upon the wall beside

Ceralt's, I saw the weapons hung to the right of the body
coverings. A large, well curved bow hung beside a sheaf of
arrows, the dark, polished wood grain of it catching the light of
the fire. The string was slack between the curves of its body, yet
I knew a good deal of strength would be required to bend it.
Beside the bow hung a sheathed sword, somewhat longer and
broader than those used by Midanna and city males. The hilt of
the sword was two hands in length, cast in metal and aglow with
the presence of shiny stones, those which males seemed to care
so greatly for. Use of the stones within the hilt seemed improper,
for shiny stones had no value other than to soothe the upset of
males when sthuvad use was done, yet the hilt glowed brightly
above the plain, worn leather of the scabbard which held the
blade. I wished to know the feel of that blade within my grasp,
and put my hand out to draw it from its sheath, yet my hand
halted short of the hilt, bitter memory recalling my new lot. I
drew my hand away again, pain from the stolen vows twisting
within me, and turned to see Ceralt's eyes upon me, a tenseness
to his stance as he watched me from the hearth. No word had he
spoken as my hand had approached the sword, yet surely he had
seen my intent. Would he now pronounce a punishment? Would
he use the twisted leather lash hung at his belt? My body wished
to tremble at thought of that lash, memory of Galiose's doing
suddenly before my eyes, yet I would not allow the trembling. I
took my eyes from Ceralt's gaze and studied the fire, contemplat-
ing its serenity and seeking to share it.

"You may now prepare the falum," said Ceralt, a softness
to his tone, yet not of menace. He stood with a small sack in his
hand, his eyes unaccusing, his stance now relaxed. He made no
mention of what had just occurred, and I saw at last that there
was little cause for mention. Completely had I obeyed him, just
as he demanded, refraining even from touching fingertips to the
weapon. There would be no punishment for complete obedience,
no lash to fall for obeying his word, no more than the sickness
deep within me, of shame and hate and freedom lost forever. I
moved toward him without comment, and took the sack of dried
grain.

The falum was not difficult to prepare, yet when it lay ready
in its pot upon the hearth, I looked upon it with loathing. Never
before had I prepared sustenance for a male, indeed, it was often
that a male prepared sustenance for me, yet Ceralt sat upon a pelt
not far from the fire and awaited his portion to be given him. I
tossed my tangled hair free of my arms, then filled a wooden

bowl for the male who had commanded slave-duty from me. The odor of the falum had returned the pangs of hunger to me, yet I would not ask to partake of the male's provender. Perhaps Mida would smile a final time, and starvation would halt my trials.

"Fill another bowl," said Ceralt, looking up at me as I handed the pot to him. "And fill it as full as possible."

I knew not what the male wished to do with a second portion, yet it was possible that his hunger was great. Males have unreasonable appetites in many things, and a warrior does well to dismiss the point. I filled a second wooden pot with the cooked grain and returned to the male, yet instead of taking the pot, he gestured to the floor before him.

"Kneel there with it," said he, sitting straighter with the pot he held. "I do not care for an unfleshed woman, and you have too long followed your own inclinations. I shall see the roundness returned to your bones, for I am not Lialt."

I knelt as he bid me, frowning at the words he spoke. Still Mida failed to smile upon her warrior, and my frustration was great. Would naught pass the notice of this male before me? Would he leave me no means by which I might escape him? He sat cross-legged upon a lenga pelt, yet the wooden boards of the floor were my lot, immediately bringing an ache to my knees and feet. Again, I had been knelt before a male, and I cared less for it than the instance previous.

"Take this spoon," directed Ceralt, handing to me a stick of wood which was wider at one end, and somewhat hollowed in the wideness. "With the spoon, you are to bring some falum to my lips and say, 'As we share the grain of life together, so may we share our lives forever.' Are you able to recall the words?"

I gazed upon him, the seriousness in his light eyes a palpable thing, and could do no more than nod my head. I knelt before him, a slave to his bidding, the heat within me scarcely bearable, and this was to be my chosen state forever? Perhaps the custom had meaning between others, yet I, from my knees, could not envision such a thing. Stiffly, and with great reluctance, I raised the falum to his lips, speaking the words without tone or inflection, wishing I might hurl the entire thing from me and run to the forests and from the sight of him. He took the falum from the bit of wood, his gaze unmoving from my face, and the taste of the grain seemed more than sweet to him. He swallowed it with great and solemn joy, then took the bit of wood from my hand.

" 'As we share the grain of life together,' " said he, dipping the wood in the pot I held, then bringing it full to my lips, " 'so may we share our lives forever.' "

I swallowed the falum, as was expected, yet the taste of it brought no sweetness to me as it had to Ceralt. The male, however, laughed softly in pleasure, and put his hand to my face.

"Now that I have made you truly mine," said he, "we must remove the sourness from your disposition. That you do not wish to be mine is evident, yet you may not deny me. Perhaps with a hot meal within you, the sourness may be lessened."

He then removed his hand and proceeded to offer me more of the falum, refusing to hear my demurrals. The grain in the pot was fed to me, a bit at a time, till I felt ill and near to bursting, yet the male continued on till the last of the falum had been swallowed. My mouth burned from the heat of it, and my teeth ached as well, yet every drop slid down my gullet till the pot contained no more. I was then given the bit of wood and instructed to see to Ceralt's hunger, and the male leaned back at ease as I fed him from his own pot, his body relaxed upon the pelt, his eyes unmoving from my face. When I was finally done and the falum was no more, Ceralt stretched wide upon the pelt and grinned at me.

"It is truly pleasing having you tend to me so," he said, then placed his hand upon my thigh beneath my garment. "Women bring greater interest to a man's life, and the softness of their bodies is but a part of that. See to the cleansing of the bowls and cooking pot, for I would have you visit the bathing halyar this fey. Tarla shall soon arrive to show you there."

I could not have moved from his hand of my own accord, yet when he withdrew it, I rose unsteadily to my feet and returned the bowls to the hearth. His continued satisfaction was a constant grating upon the sharp edges of my shattered former self, yet I longed for his touch even as I bitterly berated myself for such weakness. Cook this and clean that said the male to a Midanna warrior, and the witless warrior poured forth the juices of her slave-need even as she bent to his commands. There was little wonder that Mida had abandoned me, little question now as to the nature of my sins. Mida had not made my body slave to the male, but had condemned me for the stupidity of my needs, giving me over into his hands so that I might know the suffering I had brought upon myself. How such a thing had come to be I knew not, no more than how such a thing might be ended.

Tarla appeared not long after the pots had been seen to, a gentle knock announcing her presence beyond the door. Ceralt looked up from the sharpening stone he had been using upon his dagger and bid her enter, and I turned from the window through which I had been gazing. The chill of the land was no longer able to touch me, for I had covered myself with a shame which was unending. I had been taken by a male, and had not proved strong enough to withstand him.

"May Jalav now accompany me?" asked Tarla of Ceralt, a shy smile upon the prettiness of her face. She had taken no more than two steps within the dwelling, seemingly fearful to enter farther, for she had not removed her leg coverings. Ceralt looked to the edge of his dagger with a thumb, then nodded to Tarla.

"Show her the whereabouts of the bathing halyar," said he, "and see that she makes full use of its facilities. I wish to see her hair shining again, but do not allow it to be bound."

Tarla acknowledged Ceralt's instructions, then waited as I replaced the needed furs. Ceralt had interest only in his dagger, and looked not once upon me as I left his dwelling. Tarla closed the door behind us, then hurried to match my stride as I walked from my new abode.

"Jalav, I am indescribably thrilled," said she, a breathlessness to her voice. "I heard how Ceralt fought for you, then carried you away with him! How pleased I am that happiness has come to you at last!"

She sighed again as she redirected my steps to the right, and nearly did I speak to her of how I felt, yet she was so much a child and so covered with gladness, that the words hung back and could not be spoken. There were few to whom a war leader might speak, Rilas, Keeper to the sister clans of Midanna having been the sole exception I had found, yet even Rilas would spit and turn away were she to hear what I had done. Forever alone I was destined to be, and that loneliness had begun even before my final breath.

We walked to the far end of the village, away from where my dwelling had stood, till we came to a dwelling which seemed odd to the eye. Upon short legs of wood the dwelling stood, something of a pit to be seen below, and steps had been placed before it, so that the door might be reached more easily. As we climbed the steps together, I saw the crackling of a great fire beneath the dwelling, yet Tarla seemed undisturbed by it. She went directly to the door and then within, and as I entered behind her, I saw the reason for the haste with which she began removing her coverings. The tiny windowless room we stood in, no more than three paces by four, held a greater heat than Midanna lands at the height of Mida's blessing. The walls held flames within boxes, many covering and furs lay about, and as soon as I had closed the door upon the cold without, I, too, began removing my coverings.

"The water should be well heated," said Tarla, removing the twistings of her hair as I placed my coverings beside hers. Tarla had the body of a young girl, sweet in its budding promise, yet she colored in embarrassment when I looked upon her, and averted her gaze. "I know," she sighed, finishing with her hair and placing her hands before her. "I am naught when compared with you, and Lialt will find great disappointment when he brings me to his furs. I have seen him looking at your body, Jalav, and for some time he has not looked only upon your wounds, yet there is little I may do. The Serene Oneness has not seen fit to grant me your largesse."

So miserable did the child suddenly seem, that I could not bear her sorrow. Finding pleasure in the sight of males was a curse to a warrior, yet Tarla was no warrior and never would be. Deliberately I approached her, and placed my hand upon her shoulder.

"Much would I be pleased to see your face when you find yourself mistaken," said I with something of a laugh. "The bounty you speak of has not been withheld from you, it is merely slow in the coming, and even were it to fail to come at all, there is no accounting for the tastes of males. I recall a warrior of mine, made more in the image of male than female, who yet found herself greatly surprised when a sthuvad begged to remain with her. To him, her form was more pleasing than mine, though he often looked upon me with hunger. How may one know the thoughts of a male?"

Tarla once more lifted her large, dark eyes to mine, and great hope shone clearly therein. "Do you speak truly?" she asked, her hands yet held before her. "You do not seek to give false comfort?"

"I do indeed speak truly," I answered, refraining from saying that among Midanna, one doubted the word of another only at swordpoint. The female meant no insult, and sought only to believe that which was so difficult for her to believe. Her face again took on the glow of happiness, and her hands fell from their shielding position.

"Oh, Jalav, I do so hope you are not mistaken." She laughed. "I wish to give Lialt naught save happiness, and now it is possible that I may do so. Let us hurry now to the bathing water, for there is much to be done with you."

Having spoken so, she then turned to a door which led farther within the dwelling. Beyond the door lay the balance of the dwelling, yet it was floored no more than halfway across. Beyond the wood of the floor was water, held within the metal of a container fully half the size of the dwelling. Flames within boxes lit the room to sufficiency, replacing the light which was not permitted through the curtained windows, and many variously colored lengths of cloth lay about upon low wooden platforms and the floor itself. The inner room contained even greater heat than the outer room, yet the numbers of females who sat about upon the platforms or wet themselves within the water, seemed to feel naught of the closeness. Many of them looked about as we entered, and some called greetings to Tarla. Tarla, in turn, returned the greetings, then led me to the edge of the flooring.

"Into the water and soak, Jalav," said she, placing her toes so that she might test the warmth of the water. "Ceralt wishes to see you softened for his arms, and he may no longer be denied. Your softness shall surely please him more this darkness than the last once we are done with you."

"Softness has little to do with pleasing a male," I murmured, yet Tarla heard not for I had spoken very softly. I, too, placed my toes within the water, and was not surprised to find that it had been heated in the manner of the city folk. Often had I bathed in chill forest streams, yet such a practice seemed beyond the ken of those of cities and villages. I sighed in resignation and slid within the water, finding that it rose to my breasts when I stood erect. The water moved somewhat to the motions of the others within it, yet I stood quietly by the edge of the flooring, once more obedient to Ceralt's will.

Tarla moved about among the females on the flooring, and following her, my eyes fell upon a female who was beginning to be heavy with child. As pleased as a warrior did the female seem to be, speaking and laughing with those who sat and stood about, and the sight of her recalled Ceralt's words to me. The male had spoken of my fear of being with child, and had also said other things equally as foolish. To a male, it might seem that the getting of a child was a sign of his mastery, yet the simple truth was that a warrior might take the seed of a male without his let, and still bear the child he had no wish to plant. In such a way did the numbers of Midanna increase, and all warriors knew that it was expected by Mida that she bear her young for the greater glory of her clan. All warriors knew this—and knew as well that a war leader was denied such glory, for she had been chosen by Mida to lead the Midanna to war. One glory replaces another, yet I had once stood above a warrior who held her new-born daughter in her arms, seeing the love my warrior had felt for the tiny life at her breast. This, knowing the fruits of my own body, had been forbidden to me with the placing of the second silver ring, and no male could know the depth of my loss. In obedience to Mida, I had forsaken the life of my life, and Ceralt had mindlessly pratted on about fear and mastery. A warrior feared only the displeasure of Mida, and that I had already found in plentitude.

It seemed more than a hin that I stood within the water, my hair growing wetter and heavier, my skin beginning to grow wrinkled and ill-fitting. I had spoken often to Tarla, explaining my discomfort and my wish to leave the water, yet the young female had maintained that Ceralt wished me to remain as I was, heeding her advice. I knew not whether that was the truth of the matter, yet were it so, Ceralt might find himself regretting the decision. I wiped the sweat from my brow and face, and thought that when Ceralt next put his arms about me, I would likely fall to pieces from so long a submersion in water.

At last Tarla entered the water as well, and moved her shoulders about to wet them before approaching me. In her hand, she carried that which appeared to be congealed fat, lumpy and thick-looking, and of a yellowish color. As she approached me, she gestured toward my hair.

"Lean your head back so that all of it may be wet, Jalav," she directed. "I shall use this soap upon it, and then you may emerge."

I knew not what the term "soap" might be, yet it seemed the thing city folk used in place of cleansing sand. I had little wish to become further involved with city ways, but a protest seemed not worth the effort. I wet my hair further to the satisfaction of Tarla, then allowed the placing of this soap within it. Much did the substance foam like water at the foot of a falls, yet its presence burned one's eyes and filled one's ears so greatly that I gave thanks to Mida when I was at last able to rinse it from me. Tarla put a cloth within reach of my hands so that I might dry my burning eyes, and the first sight which met my gaze was the departure of two of the females who had been there since before my arrival. Those two females had much and lengthily looked upon me and whispered to one another, yet neither one had approached me as I had hoped they would. They two had been

with the female Famira upon the fey she had chosen to confront
me, the first fey I had attempted to move about the village
unaided. Much had I wished them to repeat their challenge, for I
was no longer wound-weakened and strengthless, yet they had
not seen fit to do so. Undoubtedly Ceralt would have been
angered if I had harmed them, yet I had not been forbidden by
him to do such a thing, and no longer had I patience for the
failings of city slave-women. Should they wish to approach me
as Tarla did, all well and good. Should they wish to approach me
in challenge, however, they would find to their sorrow that
chained though I was, their safety was not thereby assured.

When once the door had closed behind the two, the hum of
voices rose to be tinged with low laughter, and another young
female hurried over to lean down to Tarla.

"At last I may tell you of it!" said the female to Tarla,
excitement and amusement both in her voice. "I wished to speak
to you sooner, and came finally to believe that they would never
leave!"

"Calmly, Resta, calmly," soothed Tarla with a laugh as she
squeezed the water from my hair. "What is this most important
thing which you wished to tell me?"

The female Resta sat herself at the edge of the flooring, and
with a hasty glance toward the newly closed door, leaned even
farther toward Tarla.

"Famira was drawn from the circle last darkness!" Resta
breathed, her eyes filled with laughter. "The rider who claimed
her was none other than Cimilan!"

"Cimilan!" Tarla repeated in a gasp, and then she, too, was
touched by faint laughter. "Of all the riders there are, he was the
one she least wished to be chosen by. I believe I begin to pity
her."

"Famira reaps no more than what she has sown," said Resta,
showing none of the pity Tarla had spoken of. "Had she been
less sure that she would go to Ceralt, she would not have given
Cimilan insult so often. She enjoyed parading herself before
him, raising his desire as she spat upon his pride, knowing he
would not give challenge to Ceralt's claim of her. Now she
wears his strings and follows him about, and continues to weep
from his use of her last darkness. Challa says that Cimilan found
it necessary to carry Famira here not long past the new light, so
that the blood might be washed from her thighs and her pain
lessened enough to allow her to walk. I have also heard it
whispered that Cimilan drank of the second skin before carrying

her to her father's halyar, and her screams kept sleep from all those within hearing for the entire darkness. The high and mighty Famira is now no more than a rider's wench, and shall strut no more among us! Cimilan's leather shall teach her silence, and I, for one, have long awaited such silence!''

Murmurs of agreement came from all about the room, and she called Resta looked about in fierce search for such agreement. Her eyes had blazed hot when she had spoken, and the heat of her words was clearly felt. Even Tarla had agreed with a sigh, and I took my hair from her hands and threw it upon the flooring, then vaulted out of the water before the great mass of hair might tumble back and wet itself further. I stood straight upon the wooden boards and shook my hair free so it might drip its wetness more easily, and she called Resta rose from the edge of the flooring to face me.

''I do not know you,'' said she, looking up into my eyes, ''yet it seems that you should find as much pleasure in Famira's fate as we. Was it not she who threw you to the ground not long after Ceralt first brought you here? Her hate for you was deep, and surely you return that hate in some measure?''

No other voices were to be heard in the dwelling, no more than the ripple and splash of water as Tarla drew herself to the flooring. All seemed to await my reply, yet I chose my words with difficulty.

''It is true I have no liking for she called Famira,'' I groped, ''yet I cannot bring meaning to the feelings you have shown. You glory in the pain and shame given her by another, but I heard no words of the times you yourself faced her. Is there none among you who might have faced this female and spoken of your dislike, then offerred her the opportunity to defend her ways or stand in jeopardy of her safety? To find glee in deeds done by others that should have been done by you is not a thing Midanna care for.''

She called Resta seemed touched by confusion, and her hand gestured vaguely as she searched my face. ''But *we* could not face Famira in such a manner!'' she denied. ''She stands taller than any here save yourself, and even had it been possible to match her, her father would have been furious if she had come to harm! Were we to find our own selves in jeopardy, merely to indicate dislike?''

''One must choose between possibilities.'' I shrugged, seeing no confusion in the concept. ''Either one lives silently beneath the yoke of others, or one asserts her right to an undisturbed life.

Having failed to assert yourself—through your own choosing—to now speak gleefully of your enemy's downfall damages with dignity you possess. To feel pleasure at the thing is understandable. To gloat aloud is demeaning.''

The female Resta gazed down at her hands in upset, echoing the silence to be heard from the others. Thinking the matter ended, I began to turn away, yet Resta's hand came to touch my arm.

"You say we should have faced her," said the small, dark female. "Would *you* have faced her? Knowing that Ceralt might well have beaten you for causing her harm? It is whispered that Ceralt's leather has not been idle, and the High Rider is not a man weakened by infirmity. Would you face his wrath merely to assert yourself?"

It seemed the female sought to find a point I would not contest, a point which showed that I, too, lived as she. The thought of Ceralt was not a pleasant one, yet I strove to keep the bleakness from my eyes.

"The matter is not one of merely," I sighed, knowing my thoughts would not come through in my words. "Were Famira a warrior such as I, I would face her even though my blood might well adorn her blade. The importance is in the doing, not in what follows the doing. Should the importance of the doing be great enough, that which follows will be fit, no matter its nature." And then I shrugged, adding, "I know of no other way it might be said."

Resta fought to make sense of my words, and the crease of her brow remained even after she had gone to sit with others of the females. All spoke quietly among themselves, some argued just as quietly, and Tarla seemed deeply immersed in thought. She brought to me a heavy cloth with which to take some of the moisture from my hair, then aided me in combing the tangles from it, yet in all that time, no word was spoken between us. At last we availed ourselves of body clothes and were about to leave, when Tarla seemed to return to herself from a long distance off.

"Nearly have I forgotten the skin lotion," said she in annoyance, walking not to the door of the dwelling, but to a wall which contained shelves. Upon one shelf stood many small pots, and Tarla chose one from among them. "Here, Jalav," said she, turning to hold the pot out. "Do you not believe Ceralt would enjoy this scent?"

I walked toward her slowly, yet found it unnecessary to traverse the entire distance. The odor from the pot she had uncovered reached my nostrils easily, and I knew I wished none of it. Undoubtedly my expression spoke more clearly than words, for Tarla laughed and shook her head.

"Do not wrinkle your nose so," she chided in amusement. "To see you, one would think this were the essence of long-dead falth. Come and let me spread it upon you, so Ceralt will be pleased."

"Such a scent would carry throughout an entire forest!" I protested, unwilling to approach her. "Game would flee instantly and enemies would happily surround it! No one who has ever hunted could wear such a scent, and even Ceralt would know this. He could not intend for me to be done so!"

Pity entered the large eyes of Tarla, and she approached to touch my arm. "Jalav, Ceralt shall not allow you to hunt," said she, her voice very soft. "He wishes a woman with sweet scents upon her skin, not a hunter who is concerned with game. Let me put the lotion upon you, so his wrath may be avoided."

I looked silently upon Tarla, then looked away, for Ceralt's words had again returned to me. No bow, nor spear, nor sword, nor dagger shall Jalav again touch, he had said. I would not again hunt the forests, and Tarla spoke truly. Ceralt wished me made a slave-woman for his pleasure, not a warrior for a hunt. This I had not completely understood, and I slowly sat myself upon the flooring, feeling the emptiness my life had become. The dim, warm room surrounded me, yet I saw it not. I saw instead the many greens and browns of a forest, at times erupting in the splendor of flowers, the golden light falling lazily through thick leafy branches, the flash or stir of children of the wild, the pure, clean air, the blessed ground beneath one's feet. Never again might I partake of this, and I grieved for my loss in silence, barely noticing Tarla's hands upon me. The thick, heady scent given my skin made my insides turn, and I knew not how one was expected to breathe when enfolded in its mists. Some of the other females, Resta among them, came forth from their platforms to sit beside me upon the flooring, and all eagerly assured me that the odor was most appealing and that Ceralt would certainly be pleased. I knew not why they should speak to me so, yet I gave them courteous response, as befitted one who had once been a war leader. I knew not what words I spoke, yet I gave them courtesy for their courtesy to me.

When Tarla at last returned the pot to the shelf, we left the inner room for the outer. What had begun as extreme heat was now a good deal cooler, and I hurriedly donned my garments to

keep the chill from me. My hair remained damp, yet its dampness did not penetrate the leather of my full body garment even
though it hung between that and the fur outer garment. When
Tarla and I were completely clad, we left the dwelling and
returned toward Ceralt's dwelling. I saw little of the waning fey,
for my eyes found the hardened ground beneath my feet, and
took great interest in the steps I took. In such a manner was I able
to refrain from thinking upon the sharp cold which slapped at my
face and hands, and also of what I might eventually become at the
hands of Ceralt.

Upon reaching Ceralt's dwelling, I was prepared to enter the
door, yet Tarla's hand reached before me to take a small, white
square which was held in place by the door. The square contained black strokes, much like that which Ceralt had once called
"writing," and Tarla looked upon it as though the strokes had
meaning for her, then her eyes found mine.

"Ceralt wishes you to await him within," said she, a small
frown at her brow. "I am not to remain with you, though I know
not why this is. You are also to prepare the meat which is left for
you upon the table by the window, for Ceralt shall wish to eat
when he returns. Had I been allowed within, I would have
assisted you with the meat, yet I am not allowed within." She
shook her head, the frown deepening, then dismissed the matter
with a sigh. "Ah well, perhaps I shall be allowed to visit with
you upon the new fey. I shall certainly attempt it. Do not
despair, Jalav. All shall prove to be for the best."

Her hand had come to my shoulder in support of the look of
sympathy upon her face, yet I found myself unable to share her
beliefs. That all would prove for the best seemed highly doubtful,
for Mida had turned her back upon her warrior. I found something of a smile of encouragement to give the child, then entered
the dwelling alone, closing the sight of the lifeless land without
as I closed the door.

A large cut of meat indeed awaited me upon the platform by
the window, and once I had rid myself of body and leg furs, I
unwrapped it from its sacking and carried it to the fire. Cut wood
lay neatly piled to the right of the stone hearth, and it took no
more than a few lengths to see the fire grow stronger and
brighter. When once the blaze had settled itself, I placed the
meat upon the metal spit and suspended it above the fire, high
enough to need no more than occasional turning. With this done,
I sat upon the wooden floor with my back to the fire, seeking to
dry the dampness from my hair with the warmth of the blaze. I

disliked having damp hair in that lifeless land, for dampness seemed to draw the very chill of the air, the gray of the skies, the hardness of the ground. It was a thing one did well to avoid, if one were able.

I stretched out upon my side upon the wood of the floor, seeing the emptiness of the dwelling before me. The dwelling was not as mine had been, unadorned and untenanted save for the prisoner it held, yet it was empty of all life save mine, which was not the life which was meant to fill it. The dwelling was Ceralt's, its walls and floors bedecked according to his preferences, and I merely another adornment, to await his return with the rest, unable to bring true life to the dwelling by my presence alone. It is thought by Midanna that a dwelling takes on a good deal of the likeness of the person inhabiting it, which would account for the uneasiness one feels when entering the dwelling of another. It is much like attempting to enter the body of another, a body which was not meant to be yours. Ceralt's dwelling discounted me as a stranger, allowing me entrance only by cause of the fact that Ceralt wished it so. It did not welcome me as my Hosta home tent had ever done, and I rested my cheek upon the leather which covered my arm, seeking to bring to mind memory of my home tent. I sought for the memories a long time, yet found my home tent too far behind me to be easily brought forth.

Full dark had descended before Ceralt's return, and he did not return alone. I had just swung the spitted meat away from the fire, deeming it overdone enough to suit even the taste of a city male, when the door opened to admit Ceralt and Lialt. The two males entered quickly, a blast of icy wind showing cause for their haste, and just as quickly removed their fur body coverings, hanging them upon the wall before coming toward the fire. I stood with a metal prong in my hand, having just used it to move the spit, and felt the despair welling within me at my body's greeting to Ceralt's presence. Truly had I become enslaved to him, to the dark-haired, light-eyed broadness of him, and I turned away so that he might not see the hunger for him in my eyes.

"It seems we have returned precisely on time, Lialt," said he as he reached the fire. "The terlim is done and awaiting our teeth, therefore let us make haste to partake of it."

"It seems a trifle rare," judged Lialt, halting beside Ceralt to examine the meat, "yet I find myself hungry enough to eat an entire terlim, well done or entirely raw. At that, it is more than I had expected. Have you resorted to sorcery, brother, to elicit such obedience from her?"

"Not at all, brother," Ceralt laughed, turning from the meat to gaze upon me. "Jalav is no more than a wench, and I am the man who was meant to tame her. She will obey me now without question, for she is beginning to learn her vulnerability before men. Is this not so, Jalav?"

The heavy enjoyment in his tone and words caused me to close my eyes, yet I knew that my hand was white about the prong of metal I held. That he would give me such shame before another should not have been unexpected, yet even so, I found that I could not reply to him.

"She does not deny it," Lialt observed in amusement, "yet I would sooner deal with the terlim and save discussion for later. Are we to be served, brother?"

"Indeed," said Ceralt, and his hand came to my face. When I opened my eyes to regard him, he took two squares of wood from above the hearth. "Place the meat upon the platters, Jalav," he directed, handing the wooden squares to me, "and bring the entire thing to me with two forks as well. I shall then direct you further."

He and Lialt then moved away from the fire, giving me free access to the spitted meat. I used the prong of metal I held to force the meat from the spit onto the top square of wood, all the while refusing to feel the tingling which his hand upon my face had caused. Again I recalled the many times males had served me in the Hosta home tents, and a seething anger began that Ceralt would demand the same service of me. My now-dry hair blew about my arms from the sharpness of my movements, yet I nevertheless found myself beside Ceralt, the meat and wooden squares and metal prongs all fetched as he had ordered. He and Lialt had taken seat opposite one another upon lenga pelts, no more than a pace apart, and they shared a skin of near-renth between them. They sat near to the fire and had not lit any of the flames within boxes upon the walls, and Ceralt looked up at me as I offered the meat and such.

"There are vegetables in storage within the dwelling," said he, taking all from my hands to set it before him. "When next you prepare my provender, prepare vegetables as well, for I dislike eating meat alone. In a moment, you may bring Lialt his portion."

No reply seemed called for, therefore I merely stood and awaited the cutting of the meat. Ceralt divided the meat in twain with his dagger, then moved the smaller portion to the second wooden square and returned it to me, along with a metal prong. I took two short steps to my right where Lialt leaned at ease upon his pelt, and placed his provender before him. Despite his comments upon great hunger, he made no move to touch the offering, instead keeping his eyes directly upon me. I disliked the amusement in the look and began to return to the fire behind me, yet his words caused my step to slow and my annoyance to grow higher.

"How do her wounds fare, Ceralt?" said he, little true concern in the sound of him. "I have not had the opportunity to examine them in some time."

"She is well scarred," replied Ceralt about a mouthful of meat, "though the scars appear to be healing properly. Would you care to inspect them yourself?"

I whirled about in anger, thinking Ceralt truly made sport of me, yet his eyes were upon his provender, his body bent over his crossed legs as he cut at the meat. Lialt, however, continued to regard me as he had earlier, and a grin took him at sight of my anger.

"I think it my duty to inspect them," said he with a chuckle, his hands clasped easily upon the pelt. "I should not like to see complications arise due to negligence."

"Very well," agreed Ceralt with a brief glance for me. "Jalav, remove your garment and stand before Lialt so that he may examine you."

Lialt lay in his place wrapped in true amusement, but it was a long moment before I was able to move my hands to the copper belt at my waist. Though Mida had abandoned me, though Ceralt had possession of my life, still was I unable to forget that once I had been a war leader, and such humiliation was difficult to bear. With short, sharp movements, I divested myself of belt and garment, dropping them to the floor where I stood, all the while beneath the eye of Lialt. When at last I stood before him, stiffly and with fists clenched, his amusement waned somewhat as he leaned closer to put a hand upon my calf.

"Surely the Serene Oneness guarded her," he muttered, his thumb moving upon the spear track. "That she lived is astonishing enough, but that she remains uncrippled is a true wonder. I would not have considered it possible upon first sight of her. Kneel down here, Jalav, so that I might see the rest of you."

I stood as I was, unmoving save for the breath of anger within me. That I had lived was no blessing, and any save a foolish male would see the truth in the matter. Lialt looked up in annoyance from my calf, yet I would have stood there to this very fey had Ceralt not said sharply, "Obey him!" If only the male had not possessed my sworn word; if only the Silla had been as thorough as Hosta would have been in their place! I knelt before Lialt, feeling the shame burn deep upon my face, and the male reached forth to run his hand over me.

"The other wounds seem equally well healed," said he, his eyes partially lidded. "I had not noticed sooner, but her skin is much softer than it was. And what is that delightful scent she has been covered with?"

"Women things," said Ceralt, a chuckle in his voice. "I had Tarla take her to the bathing halyar earlier. The choice in lotion was a good one, for I felt its power as soon as I entered. I must remember to thank Tarla, and praise her wisdom."

"The wench is clever," agreed Lialt with a grin. "Jalav has been much improved. Rise again to your feet, Jalav, and turn about so that I may see all of you. If I recall correctly, you are the one who sees no harm in looking upon another with pleasure. Stand again and give me pleasure."

The laughter was muchly with him, and the presence of it caused my teeth to clench. "One fey there shall be a reckoning between us, Lialt." I choked, fury softening my voice to no more than a whisper. "Upon that fey, all pleasure will be recalled, and I shall surely find pleasure of my own."

An angry gleam came to the male's eyes as I stood, yet I cared naught for his anger. My hand ached for the touch of a sword hilt, and the kill-lust screamed within me to be loosed upon all within reach. In all my kalod as a warrior, never had I found the need to deny the kill-lust when it rose, and I cared little for the present need to deny it. Lialt looked up at me where I stood, my arms folded beneath my life sign, my head held high, and he leaned from his arm to sit straighter.

"Apparently the wench has not learned as much as she should have," Lialt rasped, the anger yet with him. "As you are to obey me, woman, you may now turn slowly in my view. And remove your arms from before you! Such is not the stance of a village woman!"

Truly, my stance was not that of the females of the village, and it pleased me that Lialt found it offensive. Should he ever become sthuvad to Midanna warriors, he would find it more offensive yet. Slowly, I unfolded my arms and began to turn, yet Lialt was not done with his bidding.

"Raise your hair away from your body," he directed, at last drawing his dagger to cut the terlim. "I would see all sides of the wench before me."

Angrily, I reached behind and held my hair up with both hands, finding it difficult to keep the mass of it away from my body. Lialt, however, grunted in approval, then waved his dagger indicating that I was to turn farther. As I did so, my eyes fell upon Ceralt where he sat, a large portion of his meat already gone. His light eyes moved slowly about me, appraising that which he saw, enjoying my humiliation before another male. The hatred touched me again even as I longed to throw myself to my knees before him, and I turned more rapidly to take him from my sight.

"Excellent," Lialt pronounced as I faced him once more, his eyes amove upon me as he chewed his provender. "She is truly a tempting and well-made wench, Ceralt, and should provide you with much use. No, Jalav, do not lower your hair. I find the sight of you more pleasing as you are."

I raised my arms again to the position they had been in, and stood so for a number of reckid with Lialt's eyes upon me, the amusement having returned to him in great measure. I disliked such inspection by a male, disliked having to stand so before him, yet I had not been given leave to move. The shame of it! That a Hosta warrior was required to stand so, as though she were a city slave-woman—! Fury burned so within me that I trembled, and I could not take my eyes from the sword which hung upon Ceralt's wall.

"You are mistaken, Lialt," Ceralt said of a sudden, as though there had been no lapse in conversation. "Her appearance is not excellent, it is barely adequate. Such thinness is not acceptable to me, and I will not allow it to continue. Jalav, come here."

I released my hair and reluctantly turned to him, seeing that a good portion of the meat had been left upon his square. I had hoped to find it unnecessary to partake of the meat, yet Ceralt continued to keep escape from me. He gestured to the lenga pelt beside him, indicating that I was to kneel there, and I went and did so, silently cursing his preferences. Lialt preferred slender females, much like Tarla, yet Ceralt knew that my slimness was from lack of sustenance rather than from Mida's will. Had it been Lialt in possession of me, my escape would have been much the easier. I pushed my hair back so that I might not kneel upon it, and watched as Ceralt cut a piece of the terlim with his dagger, finally allowing myself to become aware of the hunger which gripped me. Despite the falum which had been given me earlier, my insides curled with the need for meat, a need I would have much preferred ignoring. Ceralt cut the terlim smaller, and smaller again, and at last raised a piece toward me in his fingers, yet when I attempted to take it from him, he would not allow it.

"No, Jalav," said he, holding the piece away. "You kneel beside me as a proper wench, yet you have still not learned to obey properly. To continue with your lessons, you shall now eat from my hand."

I drew my hand back and stared at him, recalling the time I had refused to feed from his hand, knowing that he, too, recalled the time. Sooner would I starve than feed from the hand of a male, and this Ceralt knew, else he would not have smiled as he did. I could not refuse his bidding, would not be allowed to refuse his bidding, and the hatred rose up so high that it touched all sides of the humiliation he forced upon me. This was the reaping of my body's needs, to be constantly shamed at the hands of a male. Vile were the curses I heaped upon myself as his hand rose toward my lips, yet I was not able to refuse the terlim he placed in my mouth. The taste of him was also somehow upon the meat, yet I chewed without thought of what I did, for the shame was too great to consider. Slowly I chewed, tasting only bitterness, and Lialt's amusement added much to my misery.

Ceralt saw that I fed upon each of the pieces he cut, no matter that the amount was greater than my hunger. He began by placing the meat within my mouth, yet soon he tired of raising his arm so high and bid me bend to where he held the bite. Shame upon shame and misery upon misery, I bent to his hand so that he might place the meat between my teeth, and soon it was necessary to put my hands upon his thigh so that I might reach his hand. I touched no more than his leather leg covering, yet his flesh burned my palms even through the leather, and the inadvertent touch of his arm to my breasts turned them hard and pointed as though the chill without had me in its grip. Again the moisture flowed from me, recalling to my body how it had been denied, and I choked upon the meat thrust into my mouth, consumed by a different hunger of the flesh. Ceralt kept his eyes upon me all the while, knowing the agony of the need he put upon me, grinning at the sight of my arousal as he fed me. His finger deliberately moved to touch the point of my breast, and I gagged upon the meat I chewed, attempting to swallow it and a groan as well. Lialt laughed as Ceralt chuckled, and my face burned red at their amusement, yet I could not halt the heat of my body, a heat which was Ceralt's alone.

At last the meat was done, and the males shared the skin of near-renth to wash down the taste of their own meals. I knelt in the dimness beside Ceralt, wishing even the fire were not lit so that I might not be seen by the males. They had both much enjoyed the sight of me bending to be fed by Ceralt, my thighs locked together, my body quivering at the slightest touch of the male. I felt afire where I knelt, longing to moan aloud, yet kept this final shame from touching me. It was shame enough that I could not withstand the feel of Ceralt's hands upon me; to show my enslavement to him without being touched would be far worse.

"What word have you had from Hannil, Ceralt?" asked Lialt, taking the skin which was passed to him. "Will he join us on the journey, or must we continue without his support?"

"He will join us," replied Ceralt, reaching to where I knelt to stroke my arm. I shivered at the caress and longed to move away, yet his arm came about me and drew me face down upon his lap. He threw my hair from me and stroked my back next, and I closed my eyes and clung to the leg of him, lost in the touch of the male who had captured my soul. As his hand moved over the roundness of my bottom, I could no longer hold the moan within, and Ceralt and Lialt laughed at my torture and helplessness.

"She is a true varaina," Ceralt murmured, both hands upon my thighs as his thumbs worked deeply within me. "See how she writhes to the mere touch of a hand, Lialt. See how she whimpers and quivers. Can there be any question as to what she is?"

"She is female," Lialt replied, a shrug clear in his tone. "When a female is made to feel her heat, she is helpless to the touch of a man. Any female may be done so, should she fall to a man who will use her as she should be used. I have seen many a man come begging a woman's favor, who, when rejected, declared the woman cold. Yet this same cold woman will writhe at another man's feet, begging to be used, for this second man had not himself come begging, but demanding. Women seek for strength in a man, and bow to him eagerly when such strength is shown. This one requires more strength than others, yet she, too, is no more than a woman."

"A woman with the needs of a lanthay mare," Ceralt chuckled, pleased that he had reduced me to sobbing. I clung tightly to the leg of him, my eyes well shut, my hands aclutch upon his leather leg covering. So deeply did he touch me that I felt I must cry out, and when I did so, his laughter joined that of Lialt. No longer was I warrior before them, no longer was I able to defy them, yet so deep was my need that I cared not. I wished no more than use from Ceralt, yet I dared not speak of it lest he refuse me and increase my agony.

"Hannil has sent word that he and ten of his riders will join us," Ceralt continued to the other male as I wept quietly. "He and his riders will bring their women, for he deems it unwise that there be only one woman among us. I have decided to follow his example and allow our riders to bring their wenches as well, for there will be ample time to leave them tented with two riders as guards before we enter the area of danger. Once our mission is complete, they may be taken up again upon the return journey."

"I shall seek among the Snows for an indication of the wisdom of such a course of action," Lialt remarked, obviously disapproving. "I do not care for the thought of so many wenches so near to our goal, and even had I already drawn Tarla from the circle, she would not accompany us."

"There is little else we may do," Ceralt replied, somewhat disturbed. "Hannil must accompany us to give us the support of the villages beneath his sway. The Belsayah and the Neelarhi must be one in the crisis, and I may direct the doing of the Belsayah alone. My village chiefs all stand prepared to move against the coming strangers, yet we alone are not enough. Hannil's Neelarhi must join us, yet they will not join us without the word of Hannil. Hannil has agreed to ride upon the journey, yet he desires the presence of his woman. It is not a question of allowing it, Lialt. It is only a question of seeing it made as safe as possible."

"Lack of choice," Lialt growled, moving upon his lenga pelt. "Always there is lack of choice! How may we succeed with so little choice of action left to us? Are we merely to be pawns of the Snows, doing its bidding? Never before has such a thing happened."

"Never before have we been faced with such danger," Ceralt replied, his deep concern reaching even through my misery. "The Snows have shown the strong possibility of our falling before the will of the strangers, and should such occur, our lives as we know them will cease to be. We must rejoice that there is choice of any sort, even so slender a choice as that before us, else we would be lost before battle was joined. Should we find the ally we seek, even those of the cities must stand with us. The catch is worth the hunt, Lialt, no matter the dangers we travel through.''

"And no matter the losses we face?" asked Lialt, so quietly that the words nearly eluded me. I knew little other than the presence of Ceralt's hand upon me, and cared naught for the sadness within the other male's voice.

"One cannot grieve for the small loss when the greater is thereby averted," said Ceralt, no sadness within his own voice. A dismissal of the unimportant rang therein, and then he laughed. "I would have you remember, brother, that we have as yet sustained no losses. Should the Serene Oneness guard our cause, perhaps there will be no losses."

"Aye, perhaps," Lialt sighed, and then there was a silence, broken only by my moans. I had attempted to turn toward the male who held me, yet he had not allowed it. His fingers upon my flesh had made it plain that I was not to move about other than by his will. Much did I yearn to take Ceralt and use him, yet the accursed strength of males made such a thing impossible, allowing Ceralt, instead, to impose his will upon me. In misery, I cried out to Mida in my heart, bowing to her rejection of me, yet begging for an end to the agony of life. I lay with my cheek upon Ceralt's leg furs, tears of weakness in my eyes, arms about the leg I lay upon, my body writhing to the touch of the one who owned me, who had made me slave to his desire. My need was all consuming, yet he chose to increase it rather than ease it. I no longer knew the male to whom I was chained, yet he had grown to know me well.

"The wench is much taken by her need," came Lialt's voice from where he sat. "Have you no intentions of seeing to her, brother?"

Ceralt's hands left my body to grasp my arms, and I was lifted from his legs as he withdrew them, and thrown to my back upon the hard, cold wood of the floor. I thought surely he would use me then, yet only his hand came to hold me as I was by the hair. My eyes opened to see Ceralt and Lialt to either side of me, Ceralt again sitting cross-legged with no apparent movement imminent. I struggled against the restraint of my hair in his grip, attempting to reach him, yet his head shook slowly back and forth.

"She shall be seen to when the desire is mine," said he to Lialt, his light eyes resting upon me. "Too long have her own desires been catered to, and it has done her little good. She must learn she now belongs to men.''

"I feel she learns only of your ways, Ceralt," said Lialt as the hatred coursed through me again. So broad and sure was the male Ceralt, and so uncaring of the pain he gave me. A growl rose in my throat as I continued to struggle against being held flat upon the floor, and the sudden presence of Lialt's hand upon my thigh startled me.

"She has learned naught of the proper manner before other men," continued Lialt, his light eyes, so much like Ceralt's, filled with a strangeness I could not define. I moved to brush his hand from my thigh, yet his grip tightened. "You see?" he demanded of Ceralt. "She thinks no more of other men than she did when first we found her. In what way do you expect to alter this foolishness?"

"There is but one way to shatter false pride," replied Ceralt, his gaze and tone having hardened. "As you are guest within my halyar, Lialt, I offer you the use of my woman."

Lialt's broad face took on a look of satisfaction, yet I could not credit what I had heard. That Ceralt had once shared me with Telion was well remembered by me, yet Telion, though male, was a warrior, and even Telion's use had been denied by Ceralt after a time. To be offered to one such as Lialt was a great insult, as though I were no more than a sthuvad among warriors. Lialt would have been accepted by many Midanna warriors, yet I, having known him, wished no part of him. Ceralt's hand left my hair, and with anger I sought to free myself from Lialt's fingers, yet Lialt's other hand gripped my arm, and I was drawn to the furs he sat upon.

"It is ever a pleasure to have a desirable wench in one's arms," murmured Lialt, my struggles meaningless against his strength. "You seemed much in the grip of a great need, Jalav. Have you no desire for me?"

I had desire for none save Ceralt, and would have pronounced the matter so had Lialt not touched me just then. My body, so long denied, leaped to his touch, and I cried out in misery as I was held to his broad, leather-covered chest. Again and again did Lialt cause me to cry out, and my shame was so great that I knew naught of his having thrown his breech aside till my legs were thrust apart and he entered me. The sudden presence of his manhood forced a scream from my throat, a scream of denial that I might be used so by one who was not Ceralt. Even as my body delighted in his presence, even as it gave him slave-due, I fought the humiliation of his grinning, jarring use, yet to no avail. He thrust again and again deeply within me, his hands on my arms so that I might not move from him, and slowly, surely, my struggles became less till I could no longer deny what he gave me. Again I cried out, this time with a sob, and I sought to seize him and draw him closer, yet he would have none of it. My use had been given to him, not his use to me, and much did I writhe beneath him, helpless in his arms, helpless before his might, helpless in the demands of his manhood. Much pleasure did he take from my body in the time of his use, and when he found release from his own needs, he held me to him so that I might shiver with the delight of it against his chest. He had not withdrawn from me, and I savored his presence as one would savor the presence of dry ground after nearly drowning. His leather carried much of the smell of him, and I breathed deeply of the leather to sustain the pleasure he had given me.

"Never have I had a wench so eager to serve," he murmured with a chuckle, his lips to my forehead. "Had I had any doubts as to your womanhood, I have them no longer."

My cheek to his leather, I closed my eyes in shame, yet what he had said could not be denied. I had not wished to serve him, had not wished to give him pleasure, and yet he had caused me to do both. The male whom I had scorned had put me beneath him and had caused me to writhe as he desired, leaving me naught of dignity to which I might cling. His manhood stirred within me, chasing all thoughts of the fur beneath my bare back, the leather against my breasts, the silvered belt high against my middle. There was suddenly no awareness of the male save his presence within me, and to my helpless shame, my hips moved against him, acknowledging my desire to be used by him again. I knew not what had brought me to such degradation, yet its existence could not be denied. Hopelessness welled within me even as my heat began to rise, and I knew not what I might do to free myself from the slavery of my needs.

"You were correct in likening her to a lanthay mare," Lialt laughed to Ceralt, his hand to my bottom. "Again she offers eager service to a rider, and the softness of her is most compelling. However," and his hand left my bottom to raise my chin till I might look him in the eye, "it is considered ill-mannered to fail to return a woman in the same state in which she was given you. I feel that your need has now been returned to you, little varaina, therefore I shall also return you to Ceralt. Should you please him sufficiently, he will see to you."

He left me then and rose to retrieve his breech, and I turned quickly in the furs to bury my face in them. What had I done which was so terrible in Mida's eyes that she had abandoned me in such a place? Bound to one male, given to another, enslaved to the manhood of both, finding no relief even in the shame brought upon me, forced to writhe in perpetual need? Nearly had I begged Lialt not to leave me without first using me, and he had smiled at the anguish upon my face and in my eyes. Ceralt had watched my use with no expression, yet his body had been stretched relaxed upon his furs as though he had no more than small interest in what was done to me. That males had no honor and no feeling for others, I already knew, yet somehow I had come to believe Ceralt different. Now he seemed no more than other males and gladly would I have left him, yet I remained bound to him more tightly than the ropes of Nolthis had bound me in his chamber. This time there was no escape for Jalav, no escape, no hope, no honor and no dignity. I shuddered in the warmth of the furs, and sought to still the desire which continued to mount within me.

Lialt and Ceralt spoke warmly a moment or two, and then Lialt donned his body furs and left the dwelling. I heard the door close as a prelude to deep silence, and though my face remained well within the lenga fur, I knew Ceralt gazed upon me. Long did he gaze upon me in silence, and then, at last, his voice came.

"See to cleaning and replacing the platters, woman," said he, his tone empty of all save a slight weariness. "It is time I sought my furs in sleep, for there is much to be done with the new light."

Aye, I thought as I forced myself from the furs and to my feet, there is much yet which might be done to show Jalav her helplessness. It is unfitting to males that a warrior be left to ride free and live as she would. Take her and chain her, beat her and use her, bind her and shame her, and then speak proudly of how she has been saved from the cruelty of her former life. I kept my eyes from Ceralt's as I gathered the wooden squares and carried them to the fire, yet I knew that he looked upon me as I moved, perhaps again assessing my form. I felt that the spear tracks truly disturbed him, and wished that there had been thrice the number of Silla to form the lines. The Silla were falth, and knew naught of the proper manner of doing things.

Once the wooden squares had been cleaned and returned to their place, I turned from the fire to find that Ceralt had removed his garments and placed a number of lenga pelts together, one lying at an angle atop the others as though to be used as a cover. Ceralt took a final swallow from the skin of near-renth, closed it again against spillage, then glanced toward me as he hung the skin upon a wall.

"Pull the door string within so that we may sleep undisturbed," he directed, and then gestured toward the pelts. "The arrangement of my sleeping place is part of your duties, and in future you are to see to it. I wish it done just as you see it, and you may also remove it come the new light. Perhaps, once the danger is past, my people may be introduced to the concept of beds. In my time in the cities, I grew to enjoy their use and presence."

He went toward the lenga furs then, and I went toward the door to draw the leather string from its hole. My mind had at last ceased searching bitterly for Mida's reasons for what had been done to me, for there was no way I might find those reasons. What was done was done, and likely would not again be undone. I returned from the door, my eyes searching for a lenga pelt upon which I might pass the darkness, and Ceralt rose up on one elbow from his furs to consider me.

"For what do you seek?" he asked, his eyes somewhat puzzled. "There is naught left to be done before you may join me here."

I ceased my search with a good deal of disappointment, and slowly went to join him in his furs. Truly, I should have known better than to think I would be allowed surcease from the near presence of him, yet he had spoken of *his* furs and *his* sleeping place. I had not yet truly learned that all possessions of males are spoken of so, and that I, too, was a possession. It was *his* things which I would use, and only by *his* will. One possession had no say concerning the others.

Ceralt drew me down to the furs beside him, covering me as he had already covered himself, and I felt the warmth of his flesh against the chill which mine had been given as I had moved about away from the fire. His arms encircled me as he held me to him, and my body flowed against the hardness of his. A warrior's body was not so muscular and hard, and fleetingly I thought that I would not care to have such a body. Mine had always pleased me more, and had it not been the cause of my downfall, I would have preferred it above all others.

"You served my brother well, little varaina," Ceralt murmured, his hands moving in my hair as a male does when he wishes pleasure from it. "You had no desire to serve him, yet he taught you that you must serve despite your desires. Do you wish to insist that you will not again serve him so, should he seek it?"

I spoke no words for I knew the futility of them, and Ceralt chuckled. "Perhaps you at last begin to know your place among men," he said, sounding well pleased. "You are no more than a wench beneath them, no more than an object of desire. Jalav the warrior is no more, and only Jalav the woman remains."

He then held me closer and brought his lips to mine, and my body was his without thought. Much did he use me that darkness, nearly as much as the previous darkness, and the fire was long dead when at last his breathing grew even in sleep. Cloaked in darkness, covered with the smell of the use of males, I lay in his arms against his chest, hearing his words ring over and over in my mind. Jalav the warrior is no more. Jalav the warrior is no more. My need had been seen to by the male who possessed me, yet a deep ache remained to throb and stab and tear at the insides of me. How I wished that the words of the male were true and Jalav the warrior indeed was no more. I wished it so fervently that tears ran down my cheeks in streams, yet I felt no shame at such weakness. In the loneliness and darkness my life had become, there were none to see another small shame, none to care that no dignity remained to be damaged. All that I had known was no more, yet I, myself, would remain. My tears ran heavily to the chest of the male who held me, and sobs shook my body beyond controlling, yet he whom I once had known slept on, at peace with himself and the glory of his doings.

# 10.

## A slave to males—
## and another escape lost

When Ceralt awoke with the new light, a warm fire blazed in the hearth, and falum bubbled in the pot upon the metal rod above it. Little sleep had come to me through the darkness, so with the first faint touches of red to the skies, I had arisen and seen to the fire. Once the falum had been set to cook, I had crouched beside the fire and sought to warm myself, yet the chill refused to be chased from my bones. It clung steadily with icy fingertips, and even wrapping my arms about myself had not helped. I shivered in the faint glow cast by the fire in the corner of the hearth, letting my mind follow the grain of the wood floor I crouched upon. Though I wore not even so much as my clan covering, it seemed that a great weight fell all about me, holding me in place and making breathing difficult. I knew not what ailed me and cared not, and the grain of the floor whirled my gaze about and held it.

I heard Ceralt stir in his furs and yawn, yet there was no need to look toward him. He would see me easily where I crouched, and should there be a thing he wished, he had only to speak of it. The slave he had taken would obey his wishes, completely and without refusal. There was little else his slave might do.

"Have you built a fire already, varaina?" his voice asked, heavy with sleep. "And can that be falum I smell, ready to warm my insides and chase the drowsiness from my eyes?

218

Indeed you are quickly becoming a woman among women, giving me pleasure in my circle choice. Bring your lips to me now, so that I may taste their sweetness before I partake of the falum."

Ceralt had spoken, and his slave had no recourse save to obey. Slowly and with effort I rose from my crouch, dropping my hands from my arms, and returned to where he lay in the furs. Upon his back, he looked up toward me and raised his arms, a smile touching him as he awaited obedience. I knelt upon the edge of the furs and he drew me to him, raising my face with one hand so that my lips might be his. As strongly as ever, my lips were taken, and his body, warmed in the furs, felt as though a fire burned beneath his skin. I shivered again from the great contrast between his flesh and mine, and he drew his lips away to frown at me.

"You feel as though you were made of ice," he said, his arms bringing me farther within the covering pelt. "Why did you not don your garment when you arose? Do you seek to fall ill from the cold you have not as yet become used to? Must everything be told you before you will behave properly?"

Again he seemed angered with me, yet I felt no urge to defend my actions. I had been ordered from the covering, and had not been given leave to replace it. A warrior might have overlooked such a thing; a slave did not. I lay quietly in his arms, not meeting his gaze, and his hold about me tightened.

"Ah, Jalav," he sighed, putting his hand to my face so that he might stroke it. "It is indeed fortunate that you have fallen to me, for you have not the sense to see for yourself. After we have warmed the ice from you, you will dress before serving the falum. I will not have you so chilled again."

We lay unspeaking for a number of reckid, the stiffness slowly leaving me, and then Ceralt's hand moved from my face to my body. I attempted to hold to the thought that he had made a slave of me, sought to keep my body as uncaring as my mind, yet the blood of a warrior is not to be denied. In no more than a short while, I again moaned to his caresses and writhed in ecstasy beneath him, taking no more than what he gave, begging for the stroke that went deep within me. Ceralt found himself amused at my writhing, and rested his hands upon my hair in such a manner that my body arched up before him, open and at his mercy. He slowed his thrusts and bent to touch his tongue to my breasts, and my screams rang out loud enough to break the clouds from the skies. When he deemed himself at last done with me, a full two hands of reckid passed before I was able to rise from the furs.

The falum had cooked itself to too great a heat to be eaten at once, therefore Ceralt, too, was able to dress before taking sustenance. He sat upon a single pelt, having knelt me before him, and fed upon his own falum before turning to mine. As upon the fey previous, I was fed the entire potful by him, and the grin he showed as the falum was gulped and swallowed by me taught that shame still had the ability to touch me. The humiliation of a Hosta warrior being fed by a male was great indeed, and Ceralt's amusement over my discomfort sharpened it considerably. Although the male ordered me to see to the cleaning of the dwelling before donning his body fur, I was not displeased to see him go.

In some manner, the fey was endless. I knew naught of seeing to a dwelling such as that, and after having replaced the falum pots and lenga furs, knew not what might next be done. The weapons upon the wall might have been oiled and polished, yet I had been forbidden the touching of them. I walked from one end of the dwelling to the other, from side to side and window to window, yet found naught which might fill the time or raise my spirits. Deeper and deeper I fell beneath a heavy cloud of hopelessness, as heavy as the clouds which covered Mida's skies beyond the windows. The fey was dark and unappealing, the trees unmoving in the windlessness, the cold a waiting, stalking thing hanging just beyond the warmth of the fire. I shivered as I looked out upon the dark, frozen ground and colorless village, and became unusually aware of the bareness of my feet. The wood beneath them held the cold without, yet sure knowledge of the cold seeped between the boards in an attempt to enter. I hurried from the window to crouch by the fire, and freed my mind to wander where it willed.

The return of Ceralt startled me, yet I should not have been surprised. He bore a cut of meat for the mid-fey meal, and voiced his displeasure over my having disobeyed him. No cleaning had been done within the dwelling, he insisted, and his anger grew higher the more he looked about. I remained in my crouch in the corner of the hearth, understanding naught of what he said, and my silence and position seemed to turn his anger to fury. With a long, rapid stride, he fetched a length of leather, and I was coldly informed that he had not forgotten my disobedience of the fey previous. That, together with my current disobedience and the fact that I crouched rather than knelt, convinced him that my punishment had too long been neglected. The strokes of the leather were painful and humiliating, and once the punishment was done, I was ordered to see to the meat. I replaced my covering as Ceralt strode from the dwelling, and then saw to the cooking of the meat. I well knew that Ceralt's light eyes had blazed hot with his anger, yet at no time had I attempted to meet his gaze. I returned to my corner once the meat had been set above the fire, and knelt there with head down and arms folded about myself. There was a longing within me for the Ceralt I had once known, a wish that I might have bid him a final farewell before being taken by the male with his features and name, yet such a thing was no longer possible. I now dwelt among cold possessions in a dark, strange room, and the male I had known was no more. The pain this other male gave throbbed upon my body, and I bent further toward my knees with the knowledge of my loss. No Ceralt, no warriorhood, no honor, no dignity, no freedom, yet I remained enchained through having given my word. With all else lost, was there aught to keep me from being forsworn? I no longer had the honor I strove to preserve, therefore what was to keep me from fleeing to the eternal darkness? Mida cared not, Ceralt cared not, and even I had ceased to care. Why, then, this great reluctance to break a word which had in truth been stolen from me? I had only to walk from the dwelling and take to the woods, and soon the cold and children of the wild would end my pain and humiliation forever. The thought was endlessly tempting, yet in Mida's name, I could not cause myself to rise from where I knelt. All that I had lost had been taken from me, and I found that I could not, of myself, give over the small vestige of honor remaining to me. My head bowed farther and touched my knees, and I moaned with the pain I caused myself, yet I could not, of my own doing, be forsworn.

When Ceralt returned, his provender awaited him upon a wooden square, set beside the fire to keep the warmth from fleeing. I knelt again at the corner of the hearth, my eyes upon the flooring, lacking the interest even to look up. I heard him pause before the hearth where the square rested, and then his steps came again till his fur leg coverings were before me upon the flooring I studied. I made no sound nor movement, and he crouched before me to take my face in his hands.

"You have no knowledge of the cleaning of a halyar, have you?" he asked, a strange softness to his tone as his eyes searched my face. "I should have known this without Lialt's having thought of it, yet it had not occurred to me. I thought you merely disobedient."

There was no call to reply, therefore I remained silent and unmoving in his hands. His eyes continued to search my face, and a kind of pain had entered the light gaze. At last, he shook his head.

"Very well," he sighed, removing his hands. "We shall speak no more about it. After we have eaten, Tarla will show you what needs to be done."

He rose and went to his provender, taking a metal prong with the board, then seated himself upon a lenga pelt to feed. I thought I felt his eyes upon me where I knelt, yet his interest or lack thereof mattered not till he bade me come and kneel before him. Bits of his provender were pushed to the edge of the board, and I was directed to take them and feed upon them. I took them reluctantly and fed as was required, yet even the fact that the bits were more undone than the balance of the meat gave no taste to the feeding. I had no wish to feed and no hunger to quiet, and the meat was like stones being forced upon me.

With the meat consumed, Ceralt again went about his business, leaving me naught to do save clean and replace the square and prong, and then return to my place by the hearth. I knelt there perhaps a hin before the appearance of Tarla, who entered quickly yet shyly, then paused to remove her body and leg furs before approaching me. Her words began warm then grew concerned, her eyes grew large and troubled, yet even when she knelt before me and pleaded for a response of some sort, I found I had no further store of reassurance to tap for her. Though she wept and held me about, asking after what disturbed me, I could not find the words to ease her pain. My own pain was too great to put aside, too deep to overlook, and the child Tarla would have to deal with her fears and lack of understanding herself. She wept a short while, greatly disturbed, then dried her eyes and began to explain the why of her being there. I was to learn that which she had to teach me, and so I did, yet it served only to fill the time of the fey. The doing was useless and demeaning, fit only for the hands of a slave, a far cry from the duties of a war leader. I followed her about with cloth and a thing termed broom, and thought no more about the past than of the present.

Tarla stayed no more than a pair of hind, and when she had gone, I began the last meal of the fey. Further meat had been brought by Ceralt the last time he had come, a thing I had not known till I seen it upon the hearth, and Tarla had lifted a number of boards in the floor to show me the whereabouts of the vegetables Ceralt had mentioned the fey previous. Though the need was painful, I asked Tarla the favor of cutting the meat into smaller pieces for me, a request I instantly regretted. The small female sank to her knees and wept so heartbreakingly that it took many reckid before I was able to quiet her grief. I had not understood what touched her so, yet between her sobs I was given to understand that she knew of the manner in which Ceralt held me, and knew, too, of the restrictions imposed upon me. That I might be bound so tortured and outraged her, and she tearfully demanded to know why I did not refuse his bidding no matter the consequences. That I had withstood the blows of a heavy lash no less than three times was firm in her memory, yet she could not reconcile the memory with the fact that I seemed to fear a mere hiding. I knew of no way to explain how one's sworn word binds one more tightly than the heaviest of chain, yet the need to explain was taken from me. Tarla saw the slight trembling of my hands at my own memory of the lash, and immediately asked my forgiveness thinking, no doubt, that it was Ceralt whom I feared. I saw no reason to deny her thoughts, gave her thanks when the meat was cut, and then saw her upon her way.

Water, vegetables and meat all went upon the fire, accented by the presence of an herb called vemis. The vemis I had found among the dried grass which the vegetables lay upon, and I knew not whether city folk were familiar with it. A pale yellow was the vemis, so pale that it sometimes seemed white, and one usually found it growing wild deep in the forests. Vemis had a sharp, unpleasant taste of its own, yet when combined with other edibles, it enhanced the flavor of all. I had no wish to partake of the stew I prepared, yet knew that Ceralt would have me swallow the stuff whether I wished it or not. Perhaps the vemis would do enough to make the provender palatable, yet somehow I doubted it. I had as little interest in feeding as I had in that which Tarla had taught me.

The darkness lay over all parts of the sky when the door opened again to admit others. I stood by a window despite the chill and gazed out upon the vista of dark trees against a darkening sky. So often I had seen the darkness fall, each fey of my life it had occurred, yet now I felt a kinship to this ending of light, this entering into a new cold and dark. Once, a warrior of mine who lay dying had asked after the darkness which slowly descended upon her. As the light of the fey lay near to its highest, she had had no understanding of why such a darkness should come, yet I had known and I had explained the matter to her. She had reached the dusk of her life among the Midanna, and the next new light which shone for her would illuminate the glory of Mida's blessed realm. She saw how fitting it was to depart in darkness, and happily continued on to the blessed realm with a smile upon her face. I envied that warrior now, her place at Mida's side secure, an eternity of pleasure and battle before her. I, who had once been Mida's chosen war leader, had now no hope of the glory to be had by the lowliest of warriors, and the chill felt through my feet threatened to enter all of me, threatened to send me shuddering to my knees, pleading for understanding and pity. I held to the wall of the dwelling with one hand, clenching the fist of the other hand till blood ran from the palm, demanding silently of my frenzied mind just who I would beg pity from. Who was there who would not laugh with scorn to see the former war leader Jalav upon her knees begging pity? The sight would be laughable indeed, even had there been one to whom I might kneel. No, there was naught Jalav might do, and naught she might say, and no more than the will of Ceralt to lie before her. The warrior Jalav was no more, and the woman Jalav would never be.

The sound of more than one set of footfalls meant little to me, for I thought that Lialt again accompanied Ceralt, yet my thought proved to be wrong. I raised my head and turned from the window, and a bellowing laugh sounded at the surprise which must have shown so clearly upon my face.

"Perhaps you thought never to see me again, eh, wench?" laughed Telion, his hand upon the shoulder of a grinning Ceralt. "I must admit I had my doubts about arriving here, yet here I am and still unfrozen. Or mostly unfrozen, though there is a question about certain of my extremities. Ceralt, my friend, may I have the use of that loveliest of fires?"

"Certainly, Telion," Ceralt replied with a chuckle, striking the large, red-gold maned warrior upon a fur-covered shoulder. Telion, though still clothed in the short covering of a male of the cities, had wrapped about himself a badly cured lenga pelt, yet one which had undoubtedly kept the deep cold from him. Having received Ceralt's approval, Telion strode to the hearth with no further delay, and turned himself back and forth before it, opening the pelt he had put about himself so that the warmth might penetrate to his flesh. Despite the jesting tone he had taken, his skin bore an unhealthy pallor and was peeling, speaking of the sort of journey which had brought him to the village. He had spent no more than a moment by the fire before he moved to inhale more deeply above the pot of stew.

"By the gods, Ceralt," he exclaimed, nearly leaning into the pot, "I have rarely smelled anything to equal that. After so long a time with naught save what little game I could find, I feel absolutely no shame in asking whether I might share your feast." He turned his head then, and grinned at Ceralt where he stood. "However, I must warn you that should you refuse, I shall eat the entire thing myself."

Ceralt laughed and shook his head, then went to stand near the second male at the hearth. "My friend, I shall not refuse you," said he, a seriousness tempering the lightness of his tone. "Truly, I had forgotten the pleasure your company brings, and now am able to realize how great a loss it was. I welcome you to my village, and offer you all that I possess, to share as only brothers do, till the fey the Serene Oneness parts us once more."

The laughter left Telion's broad features, and he straightened to look upon Ceralt with an odd expression. "I came to share your battle, brother," said he, throwing off the pelt so that he might place his hands upon Ceralt's shoulders. "I knew not what battle you might be facing, yet I knew my place to be by your side. I cannot stand beside you against Galiose, for he and I were once brother warriors, yet in all else my sword shall drink beside yours."

"It is a thing I had earnestly wished for," Ceralt replied, placing his own hands upon Telion's shoulders. "I recall speaking to you of the quest which would take me from Ranistard, yet I had no more than a hope that you would follow. Was the trail I prepared adequate to your needs?"

"The trail you prepared?" Telion echoed in outrage, withdrawing his hands. "It seemed more like a trail you destroyed! Do you think me a hunter like you, man? I am a warrior, and above such things! Or, if you prefer, to the left or right of them, a thing I found most often to be the case on my journey here."

"I regret your hardship," Ceralt laughed, "yet perhaps I may make amends. Seat yourself there, Telion, and we may share the meal you find so attractive."

Telion moved toward the pelt Ceralt had gestured to, the pelt upon which Lialt had fed the darkness previous, and Ceralt himself took his own pelt. Ceralt had nodded toward me where I stood, therefore I moved to the hearth and prepared to give the males their provender. Telion's eyes had followed me as he settled himself upon his furs, and he took no more than a moment to voice his thoughts.

"So you have indeed reclaimed her," he said to Ceralt, a deep satisfaction clear in his tone. "When I heard that she had escaped the city, I feared she would return to her own lands, and you all unknowing of her destination. How did you happen upon her after Galiose ejected you? Or did she come seeking you?"

"The wench would not have the sense to come seeking me," snorted Ceralt, moving a bit upon his furs. "I found her in the woods beyond Ranistard, she having first been found by others of those savage wenches, and she seemed so near to death as hardly worth the wondering. Spears had been used upon her in some savage rite, and her blood had marked the ground more clearly than the rains. We may thank no other than the Serene Oneness that she now stands before us, for my brother Lialt, who tended her, had not thought she would live."

"And yet, she does live," mused Telion, his eyes upon me as I turned from the hearth with two full pots of the stew. "And not only does she live, but she serves you without refusal. This is not the Jalav I remember so clearly."

Ceralt, too, had his eyes upon me as I approached him, and a faint smile touched his lips. "She is quickly becoming the Jalav I have always desired," said he, taking the pot which was his. "It is merely a matter of knowing the needs of a woman and using them to train her to obedience."

Ceralt's words had no further power to cause me pain, yet when I moved to Telion and gave him his pot, the male warrior's eyes had narrowed upon the streaks of blood still visible upon my hand, and a frown shadowed within the narrowness of his gaze, to move immediately to my face. I avoided his eyes with what was now practiced ease, and returned to the hearth.

"I see," Telion replied quietly, his amusement at my fate well hidden. I stood before the fire, caught by the jumping of the flames, the dimness of the room and the sounds of feeding a soft frame for the fire's setting. After a moment or two, Ceralt's voice came to draw me from the depth of the flames.

"Jalav, the stew is excellent," said he, a good deal of pleasure in his tone. "I would venture to say that it is nearly the best I have ever tasted. Fill a bowl for yourself now, for you have truly earned the fruits of your labors." He paused till I had reached down a pot and moved toward the stew, and then his voice came again. "How do matters proceed in Ranistard, Telion? Have any decisions been made upon the question of the strangers?"

"I know little more than I knew when last I saw you," Telion replied about a mouthful of stew. "I attended no further meetings after your ejection, yet others informed me that the controversy still raged. Some wished to greet the strangers as deliverers, some wished to attack them on first sight, and others, like Galiose, still refused to commit themselves to a position. Galiose, I know, is deeply concerned over what weapons the strangers may bring to bear upon us, yet I am sure he will stand with us should it come to a battle."

Ceralt was silently considering Telion's words, therefore was I able to give myself no more than a taste of the stew, which I carried to the hearth corner. As I knelt beside the hearth, I saw Ceralt shake his head and sigh.

"I find myself capable of no such beliefs," he said to Telion, his eyes hooded in the dimness. "I have always felt that Galiose must be assured victory before he will commit his forces, and these strangers will allow no such assurance. We may find it necessary to stand without him."

"Then there is sure to be a battle," Telion concluded, his provender momentarily forgotten. "When last we spoke, you thought it possible that a battle might be avoided."

"There is still such a possibility," shrugged Ceralt, "yet the possibility grows fainter with each passing fey. It is for such a reason that the journey must be undertaken as quickly as possible, before the battle becomes totally unavoidable."

"I understand little of this," Telion muttered in annoyance, shaking his head. "This journey you speak of, and the coming battle—how might one depend upon the other? And where does the journey take you?"

Ceralt consumed what provender remained within his pot, then put the pot to one side. Telion's eyes were soberly upon him, and he met the other male's gaze with a soberness of his own.

"Many kalod ago," he began, "our village had a Pathfinder of unusual sensitivity and range. The man was able to read the Snows with uncanny accuracy, giving warning of impending events much further into the future than any before or since him. He prowled the Snows almost constantly, risking the danger of being unable to return, returning with everything he could to be considered and interpreted. And then, one fey, he stayed too long upon the Snows."

Telion had begun feeding again, yet his movements seemed without conscious thought for his full attention was upon Ceralt.

Ceralt sighed and stretched out upon his lenga pelt, and resumed his narrative.

"Others of the village, knowing of the Pathfinder's penchant for courting disaster, looked in upon his halyar, and finding his body untenanted, worked feverishly toward drawing him back. At long last they succeeded, yet his spirit was dangerously low and his body had begun to malfunction due to his mind's long absence. It became clear to all that the Pathfinder would soon be no more, yet before he could be mourned, he regained consciousness enough to speak.

"There was a time of great danger ahead of all people, he informed those about him. Not only the Belsayah, but all upon our world would find their very lives threatened. A journey would have to be undertaken by a Belsayah High Rider and his choice of others, and one whose sign upon the Snows was a hadat must accompany them, else the journey would end in disaster for all. The hadat sign was unarguably female, and the journey's destination was unarguably clear—the black altar beneath Sigurr's Peak."

"The black altar!" Telion breathed, his eyes unusually wide. "It has long been said that any who find the black altar may ask the aid of Sigurr the Terrible—if they dare—yet I had always thought the matter to be a tale to frighten women and children. Could there be truth to such prattle?"

"There is indeed truth to it," Ceralt replied somewhat sourly, "and a good part of the truth lies in the danger awaiting any who attempt to use the altar so. It is no simple matter of approaching the altar and stating your needs, you may be sure of that. Risgar, the Pathfinder who first spoke of the journey, lived long enough to give a good number of details, yet the manner in which the altar may be approached is not one of them."

"So you seek an alliance with Sigurr," Telion said, keeping the eyes upon Ceralt as he finished the last of his stew. "Somehow, the suggestion does not surprise me. And the female hadat spoken of—it can be none other than Jalav. What if she had not lived?"

"Then we soon would have joined her," Ceralt replied, moving his eyes to me. "I have delayed the journey, perhaps too long, yet it was necessary that she regain her health and strength. The spear wounds were not the only things which required healing, and should Galiose and I ever again face one another, he will learn of that which stands between us."

Ceralt's voice had grown so soft and cold that it caused a

shiver in the very air about us, and Telion too, seemed oddly disturbed. Again I recalled the touch of the lash, cutting my flesh amid the fury of Mida's tears, bringing agony and agony again with each new stroke, and the pot I held nearly fell from nerveless fingers. Galiose, aye Galiose. He it was who had given me to Nolthis, to be used and beaten and taught the beginnings of hatred for males, and he it was who might now be counted among those I hated. I had hoped one fey to be able to face Galiose across sharpened metal, yet now my hate must fester and turn my insides rotten with frustration, for never would I find the matter done so. Another male had captured me forever, and never again would Jalav be free.

"Galiose is scarcely in need of further troubles," Telion put in with a clearing of his throat, drawing Ceralt's eyes from me. "He finds difficulty enough in dealing with Ranistard's newest citizens—and their bitter blood enemies, the Hosta. Ranistard seems more like a battleground than a city, and Galiose curses the fey he allowed the wenches within his walls."

"I would have thought the Hosta to be less of a problem with Jalav removed," Ceralt remarked, rising from the furs to fetch the skin of near-renth and offer it first to Telion. Telion took the skin and drank from it as Ceralt reseated himself, then passed the skin back with a grunt.

"It is Jalav's removal which has caused the most difficulties," Telion said, shaking his head. "The wenches were wild with fury when Galiose had her lashed, yet their rage turned insane when Galiose was unable to produce her and prove that she still lived. The men who had claimed them found controlling them impossible short of tying them hand and foot, and such a state tends to make normal life unwieldy. Many of the Hosta were punished without mercy, yet they continued to rage and resist. At last, the men demanded that Galiose produce Jalav to calm the fury of the other females, and Galiose promised to do so. When Jalav escaped over the walls, Galiose raged for feyd, yet it all came to naught. The Hosta believed that Jalav was no more, spat upon the men who swore she had escaped, and turned their fury upon the Silla wenches, whose arrival had begun the entire thing. At the time of my departure, two Hosta and seven Silla were in need of Phanisar's skills in healing, and the rest had been confined without exception to their respective places of dwelling."

"And what of Larid?" Ceralt asked, as he returned the skin to Telion. "She could not have accompanied you, I know, and I thought you might have chosen to remain with her."

"I thought long upon the decision I made," Telion nodded, his eyes sad, "yet I could come to no other conclusion. Larid carries my child within her, and I will not have my child born a slave to strangers. Had I remained with Larid, I would have ultimately lost her, and the child as well. I know not how I know this, yet the conviction is strong within me, too strong to be ignored." He paused to drink deeply from the skin, then regarded Ceralt again. "In any event, Larid now resides in Nidisar's house, furious with me for riding off, and furious with Nidisar for continuing with Fayan's punishment. Fayan now heartily regrets having asked for Nidisar as a slave, and grows wide-eyed if he so much as glances at her. I doubt that it will be much longer before she carries Nidisar's child as Larid carries mine."

"Nidisar was too patient with that golden-haired wench," Ceralt observed, a grinning. "Had he refused to allow her coldness with him, he would not have ended her slave, however briefly. Savage wenches look upon gentleness as weakness, and are quick to do as they please in the face of it."

"Perhaps," Telion agreed with a shrug. "Larid has never had more than a hiding from me, yet she has learned that there are times she must obey me. She raged and screamed when I left her with Nidisar, yet she made no attempt to disobey my wishes, and bid me farewell with a heat I will not soon forget." He, too, grinned well, and moved his eyes to me. "Once a man has tasted a female warrior, other females fade from his memory forever. I enjoy much heat in a woman, and a Midanna's heat is easily aroused and not soon quenched. Do you find it the same, Ceralt?"

"Without a doubt." Ceralt laughed in agreement, his light eyes glinting in the fire's glow. The two males each looked upon me, attempting to humiliate me with their laughter, and I felt my lips tighten with hate even as my blood began to stir. Males cared naught for what was denied a Hosta, so long as their needs were seen to.

"I believe I see traces of the old flames in her lovely eyes," Telion chuckled, enjoying my anger. "She was ever one to blaze up in fury, and likely will continue so forever."

"She will not blaze up in fury," Ceralt said, rising again from the lenga pelt. "She will remain docile and obedient, for she is allowed nothing more. Telion, my friend, there are many things I must see to before the journey may be begun. Rest yourself here, for you are to share my halyar, and make free with whatever you find here. You have been many feyd upon the trail, and your needs cannot have been seen to. I shall not return till very late, therefore Jalav's use is yours through the darkness. Jalav, serve him and obey him. Telion, we shall speak again come the new light.''

In just so casual a manner was I given to Telion, and then Ceralt took his body furs and left, giving me not so much as a single glance. I gazed at the wooden pot in my hands, wishing it were possible to break the thing to bits, hating as I had never hated in my entire life. Because of Ceralt, I knelt a slave in a male's dwelling, bereft of all I had ever earned, no more than a possession to be handed about to others, plagued by a twisted need which turned me helpless to his touch. Once I had wondered at the possibility of one being so cruel as to take another's honor and yet fail to take their life as well, yet I wondered no longer. Males called this cruelty mercy, and termed it an honorable thing. So much for the honor of males.

''Jalav.'' Telion spoke from beside me, so close that my head jerked in surprise over not having heard him approach. He crouched before me, his light eyes fully disturbed, and his large hands forced the wooden pot from my fingers, ending my attempts at its destruction. He threw the pot to one side, and sought to draw me closer to him, yet I could not bear the thought of his hands upon me. He would take me as the others had, shaming me in my weakness, showing me again that I was naught when beneath a male. I snarled and fought his arms as a hadat fights the ropes of a trap, yet he would not free me, nor allow me to free myself. Many reckid I fought him, till I had neither strength nor breath left to call upon, and then he held me still against his chest, stroking my hair while making soothing, meaningless noises. He made no attempt to put me to my back, and I could not understand what thing he sought.

''Jalav, calm yourself,'' he murmured, his hand still astroke of my hair. The cloth of his body covering was now unfamiliar to me, yet it seemed much softer and warmer than the leather I had been held to of late. My cheek sought more of the warmth, my body relaxed with a shudder, and Telion's arms tightened even further, yet I knelt so for no more than a moment before recalling that this was a male who held me. Males were the enemies of warriors, those who sought the destruction of warriors, those who coveted a warrior's freedom. Males were those who took a warrior's pride, but not her life. The recollection stiffened my body once more, and Telion released me so that he might look closely upon me.

''What occurs here, wench?'' he demanded, his fingers hard

upon my arms. "What has come to pass between Ceralt and yourself that you are no longer as you were?"

He gazed upon me soberly, awaiting a reply, his red-gold hair of a male warrior's length disarranged in its leather binding from my struggles. I looked up at him, envying the limitless strength of his large, hard form, hating the knowledge that I might easily be bested by him, and found no reply that might be spoken.

"Answer me!" he snapped, shaking me somewhat. "By what means are you bound so to Ceralt?"

Almost did I sneer at such a question. Was I to inform him of the nature of the chains another male had upon me so that he, too, might attempt their use? Ceralt would inform him soon enough, and there was no need for me to make the time shorter. Telion looked down upon me, and nodded in annoyance.

"So your stubbornness, at least, remains intact," he growled, displeasure strong within him. "If you will not speak to me, there is little I may do other than accept Ceralt's offer. Remove your garment and present yourself to me."

He released my arms then and rose from his crouch, then returned to the lenga pelt upon which he had been sitting. The firelight flickered from the hearth as I slowly rose to my feet, looking away from the male and his anger. Was I to believe that he had had no interest in my use before the anger had touched him? Such was foolishness, for Telion had used me before, glorying in that which he had done to me. Much hate had he shown when, as sthuvad to my clan, he had been refused the honor of use by the war leader, and his desire for me had ever been great. Why he wished such a belief in me I knew not, yet his purposes had not been accomplished. I removed the belt of copper and loosened the garment's ties, then drew the confining thing off over my head and dropped it to the floor to one side of the hearth. My life sign, swinging between my breasts as ever it had done since first I had become a warrior, took my attention, and after a brief hesitation, I grasped it in my fist and tore the leather from about my neck. There was little reason left for its presence, and Midanna do not believe in useless adornments. I dropped the life sign beside the garment which I so despised, and turned then to face the male who awaited me.

Telion lay upon his pelt, propped up by one elbow, drinking from the skin Ceralt had given him, not looking up at me till I halted before him. The back of his hand wiped his mouth as his eyes took me in, a slowly growing gleam belying his earlier words. The sight of my body pleased him, a thing which did not please me, yet I did no more than fold my arms across my breasts and attempt to quiet my anger.

"Kneel," he said abruptly, pointing to the floor before him as he rid himself of the drinking skin. There was little I might do save obey him, and when I was on my knees before him, his hand came to my face.

"Do you still refuse to speak?" he asked, his eyes searching my face. "You are truly a tempting morsel, wench, and there is no need for me to resist the temptation."

When no more than silence greeted his words, his hand left my face so that it might touch my body. I sought to ignore the caressing of my breasts and thighs, yet in no more than a handful of reckid, I writhed about upon my knees before him, unable to escape the touch of his fingers, unable to resist the demands of his desire. I bent over his probing hand with a sob, shamed beyond endurance, and he grasped my arms and drew me to the lenga pelt beside him.

"So Ceralt has rechanneled your desires as I have done with Larid," he murmured, his hand again at my body. I moaned and threw myself about in his arms, and his laughter was stinging for all of its softness. "Such a thing is not easily done, yet the results are well worth it. I shall have some use from you, and then we will find the source of your disturbance."

In no more than a moment he had entered me, and his use was as strong and demanding as Ceralt's. I had long since abandoned all attempts at resisting him, for the affliction which was upon me would not be denied. I cried out again and again with the delights his use afforded me, and only when I had attained release and lay panting in his arms did the shame return to me. His manhood retained possession of my body, and I knew he would use me again and again till the smell of his satisfaction was too heavy to escape, too thick to be easily wiped from me. I lay bare beneath him, my sweat and his covering my body, yet he had retained his covering so that my degradation might be more complete. I recalled the time of his use in the Hosta home tents, recalling as well that the presence of his covering had afforded him little comfort. He alone had felt degradation then, yet the memory did not wipe out his presence from above me, nor the slow, throbbing reawakening of his desire within me. He held me possessively in the strength of his arms, and chuckled as my body tightened about his presence.

"So much lovely heat," he observed in amusement, touching his lips to my hair. "And I had thought Larid quick to respond and ever eager. I will see you well attended to, little hanchuck, but I will first know what has taken the spirit from you. When not in the throes of desire, you seem as lifeless as Sigurr's Peak itself."

His eyes looked down upon me, refusing to be ignored, and his body again making me his slave. I threw my head about in misery, knowing my shame would be increased were he to force me to speak, yet his purpose would not be denied.

"Speak to me!" he demanded, thrusting hard enough to draw a gasp from me. "I will know what thoughts twist about in that black-haired, female head of yours! Why does it seem that you have not slept in feyd? Why does your palm bleed as though your fist has been too tightly clenched? Why do you obey Ceralt with not even a murmur? Why does it seem as though you long for a thing which has been placed beyond your reach? Why?"

The pounding of his questions and his body were quickly growing beyond my control to resist. I sobbed as he used me, clutching his arms as I sought to hold the words within, yet I knew that the words would flow forth as rapidly as Telion claimed his slave-due. His light eyes shone in the firelight, hardness and determination clear even in the dimness of the room, and suddenly it came to me how the unattainable might be attained. Telion, a male, broad and powerful in his strength, had once been sthuvad to Hosta. Were his memories as bitter as Ceralt's, the final freedom would surely be mine. I moaned as his manhood went clear to the center of my inner being, and raised my back a handspan from the lenga pelt.

"Telion, no more!" I cried, clinging to his arms. "Do not force me to speak!"

"You will do as I command," he returned, thrusting me flat to the pelts again. "I will be obeyed by the wench I use."

"Mida take you!" I screamed, struggling in fury. "I ask only to see the fey when you again lie tied in a use tent! I will spit upon you then, and order the drug fed to you without stop!"

"Do not speak so," he growled, his grip tightening upon me as his eyes went strangely cold. His voice was very soft, yet trembled in an unexpected way.

"It was I who first named you sthuvad," I gloated, then laughed in unabandoned delight. "Had I known how pleasing you would be to my warriors, I would have called for the Hitta and Helda as well! When next you taste of the sthuvad drug, I shall not fail to assure their presence!"

"Be silent!" he whispered, a rage growing to fill his mind and choke him. His face twisted from its familiar lines, near insanity outlining over-bright eyes, and it seemed as though I were held in bands of metal. My fingernails dug deeper into those bands of metal, and I laughed again, more mockingly than before.

"Yes, it was I who decreed your use by warriors!" I pursued relentlessly. "It was by my word alone that you were thonged to stakes and made to give pleasure, forced to serve your betters! And I shall see it so again, Mida take me if I do not!"

"Never!" he rasped, the trembling taking all of his body, the madness bright in his eyes. "Never will I be forced to feel such shame again! Never will I forget the shame of the first time! And you! You were indeed the one who caused it!"

His arms left me as his hands went to my throat, the madness completely in possession of him. Though I truly wished for the surcease of everlasting darkness, I could not help but claw at his hands as they tightened about my throat. His fingers pressed against the flesh of my neck, and his voice came strange to my ears.

"You, the savage female who was the source of my debasement," he muttered, his fingers tightening more and more. "You, the she who laughed at my captivity and use, the she who sneeringly refused me her body when the thought of her use was all that kept me from screaming out the agony of body and soul! You laughed then and you laugh now, yet I shall take the laughter from you forever!"

A roaring had filled my ears, and his face swam about in the rippling of my vision. I scratched feebly at his choking hands, all strength having left me, yet even had I been possessed of all my strength, I could not have loosened his metal-thewed grip from my throat. Even in airless, choking pain, I knew my victory, and I exulted as the darkness rose up to swirl me in its midst.

A silence filled with no more than the crackling of a fire came to me first, and I knew not why such disappointment should grip me till I realized where I lay. Again I opened my eyes to the dimness of Ceralt's dwelling, and the bitter knowledge that I still lived forced a moan from my lips. My throat ached from the fingers which had gripped it so tightly, yet the grip had not been tight enough. I was still in possession of the burden of my life, and the darkness of the raftered roof above me was no darker than my hopes of freedom.

"Why did you do such a thing?" Telion's voice came, and then his face was before me as he leaned closer. "I nearly took your life as a result of that taunting, and I fully believe that that was your purpose. Why do you wish to find death?''

I stared at his pained and bewildered face for a moment, then rolled to my side upon the lenga pelt, rose to my feet, and walked to the hearth to gaze down into the fire. Telion had once been the one male upon whom a warrior might look with the least displeasure, yet even he had taken my use with satisfaction, seeing naught amiss in placing me beneath him. His great hatred for his own captivity had not given him insight for my own hatred, for he felt it proper that a female be held by a male. How was one to speak to such a male, how might one describe the torture of imprisonment, when the one spoken to gave full approval to such imprisonment? I crouched before the fire and drew my hair about me, grasping its ends and holding them up before my bowed head. In all things I had been thoroughly shamed, yet even the final death was to be denied me. What more could be done to add to my tortures? What more?

# 11.

## *A thing called snow— and the beginning of freedom*

I woke to the light of the new fey, and found that I lay wrapped before the dying fire in the badly cured lenga pelt which Telion had worn upon his journey to the village. The dwelling was somewhat chilled, yet it seemed clear that someone had put wood upon the fire rather late to assure a continued fire through most of the darkness. I remembered naught of having fallen asleep, nor did I remember having wrapped myself within the pelt. Telion had not spoken to me again after I had left his side, but another had spoken to me as I lay in sleep, and my confusion was now greater than ever.

As had happened once before, Mida had walked my dreams, and had spoken to my sleeping mind. The golden glory of her had not so much awed me as given me pain, and I turned my head from her glowing brilliance, knowing I was not fit to look upon it.

"You have called to me much when I was not able to answer," she said in the sweet tones I knew so well. "Have you no questions for me now that I stand before you?"

"There is only one," I replied, keeping my face turned from her. "I would know my full failure so that I might in part understand my punishment."

"Ah, Jalav," she sighed, and the sadness within her voice dimmed the brilliance I had come to expect. "My warrior has not failed me, nor is it punishment that you now face. As ever, you serve my purposes, and serve them well and ably. Had I been able to speak to you of this sooner, much agony would have been spared you."

"Mida, I do not understand!" I cried, turning again to her golden, glowing form. "I have been made captive to males, shamed and enslaved by them, and this was done by your will? How can it not be punishment?"

The golden glow surrounding her pulsed in agitation, and I saw that complete calm was no longer hers. Her slim, long-fingered hands grasped one another, and gentle pain showed upon her lovely face.

"Jalav, it was necessary that you join these males upon their journey," she said, her voice striving for my understanding. "It is a thing that has long since been decreed by the Snows, and a thing that I, myself, cannot change—nor would I change it even if I were able. If we are to be victorious over the coming strangers, you must make this journey shown so clearly in the Snows."

My head whirled with confusion, yet there was no need to voice my disturbance. Mida stepped closer, and looked down upon me with pity.

"I know well the many shames you have been subjected to," she said, "and know, too, that there is more yet before you. You must bear it all with the strength of a war leader, for there is much left for you to do. There is no other I may call upon save you, Jalav, and you must not fail me.''

"I hear, Mida," I whispered, still finding no understanding. "I will not fail you.''

"I have never doubted the loyalty of my Hosta war leader." She smiled, the calm now returned to her. "That your life has so many times been returned to you should prove my continued love and need. Do not again seek destruction, Jalav, for all shame will eventually be wiped away. If I do not speak to you soon again, do not despair. I cannot reach through when you lie close beside a male or in the grip of a sleeping potion. When next we meet, it will not be in sleep.''

She faded from my sight then, and deep sleep returned to me, yet upon awakening, I could find little sense in what I had learned. There was endless relief in knowing that I had not been abandoned in my need, yet Mida had not said when my captivity would end, nor had she given me leave to resist it. My sworn word still bound me as closely as ever, and somehow I felt that Mida was unable to intercede for me. To my great disappointment, it was now clear that Mida was not all powerful, that there was another whose will superceded her own. I moved in annoyance within the lenga pelt, wondering if I were to assist her in destroying this other. No mention had been made of what was expected of me, save that I was not to seek destruction, and that I was to bear the shame given me without regret. I turned my head to see Telion and Ceralt asleep in their furs, and an anger tinged with hatred filled me. What further shame would be heaped upon me by their doing? What more must I face before freedom was again returned to me? I knew not, yet I had no doubt. Mida had spoken of it, and it would prove to be so.

As I no longer felt the need for sleep, I arose from the fur, donned my leather covering, and began encouraging the fire into new life. My life sign had lain upon the floor where I had dropped it, and after no more than a brief hesitation, I had again knotted it about my throat. I had as yet no real desire for my soul to be preserved, yet Mida had said that there was much I must do for her. Perhaps in that doing, the shame would be washed away from my soul, and I would again be worthy of the Blessed Realm. I had no real hope of such a thing, yet was it possible.

After I had set the falum to cook, I went to a window to look out. It seemed much lighter past the window than it should be, and my curiosity had been aroused. I had no other thing to do than set the falum to heat, for the pots which had been used the darkness previous had already been cleaned and returned to their places. I knew not whose hand had done the deed, yet I was pleased that it need not be my hand which was set to such an undertaking. This cleaning and cooking was fit only for males and slaves, and I, a war leader of the Hosta, need not concern myself with them forever. At some time, with the blessing of Mida, I would again ride free.

When I reached the window, all thoughts of cleaning and cooking and males left me, and I found myself able to do no more than gape and stare. There was much reason for the lightness I had seen there, and I grasped the edges of the window in wonder as I looked out. Everything without was covered by a blanket of whiteness, the ground, the trees, the dwellings— everything! Lightly, lightly, a flaky whiteness fell from the skies, thicker yet more silent than rain, and as the whiteness fell, all beneath it was completely covered. Never had I seen such a thing, and never had I imagined that such a thing might be. The whiteness fell and covered all beneath it, and seemed be going to continue forever. I saw that the ground could no longer be seen, and wondered how one moved about in such a medium.

"That is called snow," came Ceralt's voice from just behind me, a light amusement clearly to be heard. "It is another reason why wenches here wear full garments rather than clan coverings."

"From whence does it come?" I asked, unable to draw my eyes from the silent inundation of whiteness. "And how long will it continue so? Already many things cannot be seen."

"It comes from the skies as rain does," Ceralt replied, his hand gently stroking my hair. "It is far too cold for it to appear as rain, yet it is not cold enough for sleet. I know not how long it will continue this time, but there have been snows which have covered entire halyars, roofs and all."

My first response to a statement such as that would normally have been anger, thinking that I was being made sport of, yet the rapidity with which the whiteness covered all it touched made the statement a not unreasonable one. I stared without in dismay, standing higher on my toes to see the depth it had already reached, and Ceralt laughed in high humor.

"Do not fear, wench, we will not be snowed in this time." He chuckled, putting his hands upon my waist to draw me from the window. "Our journey shall begin with the next new light, and there is naught that Lialt has seen to keep us from it. Though as I think upon it, being snowed in would undoubtedly suit you quite nicely."

"Suit me?" I echoed, not following his reasoning. "I know naught of this snow, and have never experienced it. How, then, might it suit me?"

"In such a way," he grinned, drawing me closer to his bare chest. "When one is snowed in, there is little else to do other than dally and sport, a thing you have great interest in, eh, varaina?"

My cheeks burned red at the memory of my shame, and I sought to push from the circle of his arms, yet he held me to him with a further laugh and took my lips despite my struggles. How I hated the thought of his ridicule, yet when his arms were about me and his lips were upon mine, I was no more than a slave to him, his without question. He held me still and took my lips, and my body burned with the need for him even as I begged Mida to hasten the time I might be freed from him. The crippling need he brought upon me had no place in the life of the war leader, and I wished no more of the slavery of blood heat, the chains of my body's longings. His lips left mine to touch my throat, and I moaned and pressed myself to his bare body, begging his use in all but words. Again he laughed, exulting in my weakness, and then I was lifted in his arms, to be carried to his furs and placed upon my back. My body writhed with desire as his hands went to my copper belt and removed it, and I raised my hips so that he might rid me of the covering I wore, yet I realized too late that he had not loosened the ties of the covering. With the garment up above my head and arms, it became clear that the oversight was no such thing. With the garment and much of my hair in one of his hands, I was forced to my knees upon the pelt, my face and head hooded, and made to writhe and cry out to the urgings of his free hand and lips. I was able to see naught save the leather before and about me, yet the darkness was little comfort in the agony he caused. Ceralt saw, and Telion as well, and my body leaped and rose in a light unshared by my vision. I sobbed and wept and begged for my use, and when at last this was granted me, it was as a slave I was used. Still upon my knees, head and arms forced down to the pelts, I was used by Ceralt from behind, knelt before my master and forced to give him pleasure. Though the use was not the same, the position brought strong, ugly memories of Nolthis, and I cried out in protest over such humiliating use, yet Ceralt took no more note than Nolthis had. I was used completely and well, and then allowed to lie undisturbed a moment before Ceralt announced his wish for the falum. Choking upon a bottomless rage, I raised myself from the fur, fought my garment straight, then retrieved my belt. Telion lay upon his own fur, his hooded eyes upon me, and I burned with shame that he had witnessed such humiliation. I took my gaze from him and went to the hearth, and heard naught of what passed between the two males in conversation.

The fey was too long, giving me overmuch time for thought. Ceralt saw to his own feeding and, as was to be expected, mine, then he and Telion left the dwelling. Ceralt had provided leather and fur garments for Telion, and the male warrior donned them with much relief, afterward buckling on his swordbelt below the silver belt village males wore. The fur leg coverings gave height to his appearance, a thing his massive frame had no need of, and something of good humor had returned to him by his departure. I saw to the falum pots and the doings which Tarla had taught me, then went to kneel in the hearth corner.

The whiteness still fell beyond the window, yet I could no longer find interest in the thing. My eyes insisted upon sliding to the weapons upon the wall, and my hands upon my thighs had turned to fists. When I had thought myself abandoned by Mida, something of acceptance of the slavery had come to me, yet that acceptance was no longer to be found. I now burned to be free and upon my way once more, and no more than the will of males stood before me. My head rose high at the thought of Ceralt, and much hate consumed what inner calm I had managed. For him to treat a warrior so, a war leader of the Hosta! I looked about the dwelling I knelt in, seeing the wood of the floors and walls, the piles of garments, the small platforms, the stone hearth beside me, all things which were possessions of Ceralt, all things which he might use as he willed. I knelt among these things, yet I was no longer one of them, no longer that which Ceralt might own. Soon I would find myself freed from his possession and again about Mida's work, as I had always wished to be. Then, briefly, I recalled how Ceralt had once been, strong yet gentle, difficult to please yet caring, and again a sense of loss came to me which bowed my head, yet I pushed these thoughts aside and straightened once more. Ceralt the male was naught to me, no more than a male should be, and it was foolishness to find disappointment in that which he did. Soon I would be rid of him and all things male, and would again ride beneath the shield of Mida.

Ceralt and Telion returned for their mid-fey meal, then left as soon as it had been consumed. Their words had been much concerned with riders and tentings and lanthays and supplies, and I wondered at the need for such lengthy preparations. When

Hosta rode to hunt or war, little more than mounts and weapons were needed or sought. Should these males find the need to do battle, I thought it likely they would take a hand of feyd and more to find the place of their swords. I disliked the taste of the meat Ceralt had fetched and ate little of it, yet the male took no note of my actions, instead being too occupied with speaking to Telion of the ways which must be traversed to reach Sigurr's Peak. Telion, however, between jocular remarks upon the object of our journey, took full notice of how little I fed upon, yet made no mention of it to Ceralt. I knew not why this should be, yet also cared not, and was pleased to see them go. The actions of males were a warrior's shame, and best kept well away from them.

The whiteness continued to fall most of the fey, yet ceased a hin or so before full darkness. It lay mounded upon the ground between dwellings, surely more than ankle deep, and the great silence surrounding it and the village was somewhat unsettling. The Entry to Mida's Realm, round and golden, rode the skies as darkness fell, and strange shadows chased one another across the unbroken whiteness. I stood by the window and gazed out, finding an odd and chilly beauty in the sight, pleased that I had been able to see the thing called snow, yet anxious to return to lands which were not covered so. It seemed likely that game would now be scarce, and the villagers would find greater need to depend upon the herds they kept to feed upon. A true need for those herds was now evident, yet I liked it not. Far better to feed oneself from the bounty of Mida's forests in warmer climes, and leave the chill of the snows for those who knew no better.

The males returned in good spirits, laughing with one another as they stamped the snow from their foot coverings, and hung their body furs upon the wall. All was now prepared for the journey, it seemed, which would begin with the first, faint touches of the new light, and both males appeared anxious to begin. Ceralt carried rolled up leather which he placed beside him upon his lenga pelt, and did not return his attention to it till we had fed. Again I had been knelt before him to feed, and when he had seen the last of the grilled meat and vegetables within me, he put his board and pot aside.

"Telion and I have brought you a gift," said he with a grin, reaching for the rolled up leather. "Remove your garment, and we shall see how well it becomes you."

I knew not what he was about and cared little for his humor, yet there was naught I might do save obey. When my copper belt and leather garment lay upon the floor, he unrolled the leather and produced a breech, body covering and leg coverings such as those he wore. The garments seemed odd to me, and he chuckled as he held them out.

"Go on, take them," he urged, his eyes measuring my body. "They should be a passable fit, and better than the other wenches will find. They are not as long of leg as you, and few of my riders fail to top them by less than four hands. The poor wenches are sure to be dismayed, yet one cannot ride a lanthay in a skirt."

"At least, not the sort of skirt your village women wear," Telion put in as I took the breech from Ceralt's hand. "The skirting of Jalav's wenches seemed no hindrance at all."

"They would also be no hindrance to freezing solid," Ceralt added with a laugh. "No matter how attractive the style, it becomes highly impractical outside of their own lands." His eyes followed my motions as I first donned breech and body leather, then slipped into the leg coverings, which were secured to the breech at either side of my body at the hips. The leg coverings were somewhat long, yet otherwise fit well, and with all in place, it was easily seen that the fur body covering worn without the dwelling would fall to a place upon my thigh below the junction of breech and leg covering. In such a way would the chill winds be kept from my flesh, while avoiding the confinement of my previous garment. The new leather pleased me, and I smiled a bit realizing that freedom was beginning to return to me. Mida had spoken, and her warrior would soon find release.

"Do not grow too fond of such trappings," Ceralt's voice came, and I looked down to see that his eyes were upon me, a hardness in them even though his face wore an easy smile. "When we return from this journey, you will return to the garments of a woman, for that is what you are. A woman. Clear the plates and prepare my furs, for the new fey brings an early beginning."

I stood no more than a moment before turning to do his bidding, yet it must surely have been with Mida's aid that I controlled my fury. Stiffly, I took the boards and pots to the hearth, yet my mind knew naught of what my hands did. You are a woman, he had said, no more than a lowly female, he had meant, and the thought drove my rage so high that I trembled in an effort to contain it. Aye, Jalav was female enough, yet was she also a warrior of Mida, a war leader of the Hosta. Ceralt knew well enough of the former, yet come the fey my chains were struck away, then, then! he would learn well of the latter! Never had I raised weapon to Ceralt, and much had I believed that I would find myself unable to do so, yet the passing feyd made the thought of such a doing more and more pleasant.

I did as I had been bidden to do, and fumed all the while, and at last all was seen to and my anger somewhat cooled. When I returned from drawing the leather through the door, Telion already lay within his furs, as did Ceralt. I had earlier heard my use being offered once more to Telion, yet the male had refused, saying he had greater need of what sleep he might find, so I was therefore gestured to Ceralt's furs. My mind felt great reluctance when I knelt beside him, yet my body quivered when he drew me close and put his lips upon mine. Such insanity it was, this desire of my body and hate of my mind, the pulling and tugging of each emotion threatening to tear me asunder with its violence. I shivered and fought the conflict within me till I was weak with the effort; then Ceralt's hands stilled the conflict with almost no effort at all. I was his once more, body and mind, and I wept within at the ease with which he claimed me. When his use was done, and I lay in his arms, I prayed to Mida to set matters right, although as I lay against that broad chest and hard male body, I knew not how it might be done.

# 12.

## *A journey is begun— and a secret is learned*

The fey had not yet truly begun when we left Ceralt's dwelling. A deep cold rode the air heavily, but the lack of wind left the cold bearable. Some few light clouds floated upon the still-dark sky, and white breath-streams flew from our noses and mouths as we crunched along upon the mounded snow. So lightly and so gently had the snow fallen, yet it had in some manner hardened upon the ground so that one might walk upon it, yet this hardness was not to be found everywhere. As I moved slowly and carefully between Telion and Ceralt, my hands covered by leather and fur in a device termed "gloves," my fur-clad right foot suddenly penetrated the snow mound to mid-calf depth. Had Ceralt not quickly grasped my arm to steady me, I would surely have sprawled upon the hard, treacherous snow, unknowing victim to its snares. I retrieved my foot and steadied my stance, and we continued across the nearly empty village toward the lanthay enclosure, yet I no longer looked about me at the skies and dwellings. My gaze was solely for where I put my feet, and I no longer found innocence in the whiteness of the snow.

The lanthay enclosure was as well tenanted as the rest of the village was empty, for two hands of males and a like number of females awaited us amid lanthay which were either heavily laden or bridled in preparation to be ridden. Ceralt greeted the males cheerfully then looked about himself, seemingly seeking one who was not there. I knew not who he might be seeking till further crunching sounds came, and all turned to observe the arrival of Lialt, accompanied by a saddened Tarla. Lialt paused a length from the enclosure to give Tarla his lips, then left her to stand alone as he came up to us.

"I am now prepared to depart," he announced as he entered the enclosure. "Why do you all stand about here as though there is time to be wasted?"

Upon hearing this, the males laughed aloud, and Ceralt shook his head with a grin. "We await the arrival of one who has grown too fond of his furs," he informed Lialt and folded his arms. "Should our Pathfinder have become too old and infirm to arrive at an appointed time, perhaps it would be best if he were left behind us."

"All bow to the will of the High Rider," Lialt intoned solemnly, his light eyes in no way embarrassed, "yet without the Pathfinder, the High Rider may well find himself riding in circles. Should this be his wish, who am I to oppose him?"

Lialt's deference was betrayed by the gleam of amusement he showed, and Ceralt laughed aloud and clapped his shoulder.

"The Serene Oneness protect me from those who will not oppose me," he chuckled. "Take yourself to your lanthay, brother, and let us be on our way before the mid-fey meal is upon us."

Lialt returned the grin and the shoulder clap, and all within the enclosure then sought mounts, a doing which proved most interesting. The males, I knew, were well acquainted with the white-furred lanthay, yet the females proved to be much in awe of them. Clad in the leathers of males, they stood about staring nervously at the enormous mounts, obviously filled with little desire for taking seat upon any of them. The males each caught up the rein of a lanthay and gestured their females to them, and then began a battle consisting of calming the lanthay, calming the female, quieting the lanthay to be mounted, and raising the females to their backs. One or two males accomplished this easily, yet most found the need to call down the wrath of Sigurr upon the heads of lanthay and female alike. Males cursed, lanthay squealed and reared, females howled and backed, and I laughed as I had not laughed in many a fey. The males, in imagined superiority, had kept their females from a knowledge of riding, and now reaped what they had sown. Warriors were not well thought of by village males, yet warriors would not have feared the nearness of the beasts.

"Best you quiet that braying and get yourself mounted," Telion said quietly as he handed me the rein of a lanthay. "Ceralt sees no humor in this fiasco, and would not take kindly to your amusement. Though I must admit that I have rarely seen anything funnier."

The male warrior looked down upon me with a grin fixed well upon his face, and we both laughed at the shouting and screaming and churning of snow. All about us was a true bedlam, and Ceralt worked feverishly to quiet all concerned. Of those who stood about, including Lialt, he directed the temporary pairing with a male who could not get his female mounted. The two working together, one to hold the lanthay, one to lift the female, soon saw all of the females upon the backs of mounts, and males at last sought their own mounts, wiping sweat from foreheads with hands which seemed much wearier than previous. I turned to the lanthay I had been given, grasped its fur in both hands, then vaulted to its back with very little effort. The lanthay danced beneath me as I sought and found a proper seat, and Ceralt stalked angrily back to take possession of his own mount.

"Curse Hannil and his insistances!" he muttered darkly as he leapt to the back of his lanthay. "Wenches must be brought, yet they cannot be ridden behind their men lest their presence prove catastrophic should the need to fight arise! Were this journey not so desperately urgent, I would send those wenches straight back to their hearths, damn me if I would not!"

He then jerked upon his rein so hard that his lanthay squealed and reared, yet truthfully, I could not fault him for his anger. The females, now mounted, were no less a problem than they had been. They clung fearfully to the fur of the lanthay, most bent over, some sobbing their fear aloud, and it was easily seen that they would be unable to ride or control the beasts through their own efforts. The males looked about at one another helplessly, then wearily dismounted and began bringing pack lanthay forward. To each female's left a pack lanthay was secured to the neck of the lanthay she rode, and then the males remounted and moved their own lanthay to the right of their females. In such a way were they able to lead both pack lanthay and female's lanthay, and the female was somewhat comforted by the presence of more than the hard, distant ground to either side of her. Lialt rode ahead to open a gate in the far side of the enclosure, and the sky began to show the first touches of pink as the last of us rode through. I rode beside Telion, who sat upon his own lanthay, and had turned to look behind me only long enough to raise an arm in farewell to Tarla, who had climbed the enclosure to watch our departure. Tarla had raised her own arm, shyly and with reluctance, and had wept and left her place when Lialt had touched his palm to his lips to her. Lialt looked longingly after her a moment, then closed the enclosure and rode with Telion and me, and the journey so often spoke of by so many was finally, if not quite easily, begun.

The fey grew clear and bright, the skies pale blue above us, the snow blindingly white beneath the hooves of our lanthay. A good deal of the cold was dispelled by the motions of riding, with some assistance from Mida's light, and the lanthay proved a not unattractive beast. Instantly responsive to the touch of knees and rein, the lanthay was a delight to the experienced rider, as well as a welcome comfort. The beast's thick covering of fur was far superior to the gando's scales and the kan's hide, yet Telion did not seem to share my enjoyment of the lanthay. The male warrior sat his mount surely, yet obviously unaccustomed to the lack of a leather seat such as kand were wont to be provided with, and from time to time muttered a regretful word or two about the kan he had left behind in the village. I spoke no word of my own, being too well pleased with the snow-covered forest about us and the increased feeling of freedom to wish to be drawn away from them, and we continued on through the snow and the trees and the fey, till a halt was called for the mid-fey meal.

The fall of darkness found us already encamped. Though the fey had been a pleasant one for me, few of the others of our party had found it so. The halt for the mid-fey meal had been filled with wailing from the females and attempts at soothing from the males, yet even soothing had not allowed the miserable wenches to ride till Mida's light had gone. Stiff and sore, they wept and begged to have the ride over, and their males, with weary agreement from Ceralt, had chosen a snow-covered clearing and erected strange-shaped tents. The tents of Midanna are circular, with spires rising from the near flatness of their roofs, yet the males used tents which were more triangular than circular, with each section having the ability to stand alone and house two, or be joined with one or more others and house many. The males of Ceralt's party chose to stand their tents singly, only Ceralt and Lialt combining their tents with Telion's to make a larger one, and in very little time, the weeping females had been led within shelter. I was somewhat tempted to feel pity for the females, yet scorn for their weakness and helplessness rose too

far to the fore. These village females wept and moaned and cried
of tortures forced upon them, yet they knew naught of what true
torture meant. That which had set them weeping and groaning
was no more than every-time doing to a Midanna, and this was
not all that set them apart from a warrior. To so easily show
weakness seemed a part of village slave-women, and no shame
appeared to attach itself to them over such humiliating actions.
Shame, I knew, touched all in different ways, yet how was it
possible to cling so tightly to a male and weep so helplessly, and
not be touched by shame? I knew not where to find the answers I
sought, and knew not even if I wished to find them, for somehow the matter seemed more complex than one would expect it
to be.

"You seem quite intolerant of the delicacy of the other
wenches," Ceralt said, looking down upon me with something
of anger in his eyes. "Since you do not share their delicacy and
infirmities, you may now take our lanthay and tie them to the
ramuda string. Later, I shall also allow you to feed them."

My chin rose high at the hateful edge to his voice, and sooner
would I have walked the lines for the Silla a second time than
speak of my own need for warmth and rest. Without comment, I
took Telion's rein and Ceralt's and Lialt's as well, added them to
the rein of my own lanthay, and walked from the males toward
the string of leather which had been hung between two of the
trees. All of the other lanthay had been tied to that string or two
others set about the camp, and they stood where they had been
set with heads down and hooves scratching at the snow, seeking
that which might be fed upon. I, myself, had the habit of seeing
to my mount's comfort before my own, yet the males of the
party had merely tied their mounts and unburdened them before
hurrying to the sides of their females. For a journey of great
importance, the entire thing seemed ill-omened and ill-conceived,
and I could not envision success with so poor a beginning. I tied
the lanthay securely upon the line, giving them leather enough to
lower their heads, then left them to their useless foraging. The
light was low in the skies, and no other appeared to sight about
the camp, therefore I paused some steps before the entrance to
Ceralt's tent to rub at the throbbing in my left thigh. As I stood
close up beside the tent wall, it was then that I heard the voice of
Telion from within.

"Ceralt, I shall say what I must say before she returns," I
heard, no humor to the tone of the male warrior. "I know not
what has occurred between the two of you, but I tell you now

that should you continue to treat her so, she shall soon grow to
hate the very sight of you.''

A brief silence passed after the words of Telion, and then
Ceralt spoke, quietly and with a great weariness. "She has
already grown to hate me," he said quite simply, "and that is
exactly what I wish her to do.''

"But, why, man?'' Telion burst out, with a bewilderment to
match my own. "She had begun to feel love for you, a love I
thought would match yours for her! Why do you now seek her
hate?''

"It is all rather simple,'' Ceralt replied, and I felt that he held
his voice even only through effort. "Lialt has searched the
Snows many times since my return from Ranistard, and each
time he searches, the more convinced he becomes—there is
almost no chance of my living to return from Sigurr's Altar, yet
Jalav will live—and continue to thrive. Had I allowed her love to
grow as I so achingly wished to do, she would have been left to
mourn and grieve for me—and even, perhaps, to seek vengeance
for my death—and that I will not have. I now humiliate and
shame her in every way I might so that pleasure will come to her
at my death, not pain. Such an end is worth the price I pay.''

"This cannot be so!'' Telion protested, and I heard the sound
of movement. "And even should it be true, it makes no sense!
What if you should live after all? And what is to become of the
wench should you die?''

"Both questions have already been seen to,'' Ceralt replied
with a short laugh. "If I live, I will then attempt to make some
sort of reparation for the difficulty I have given her. If reviving
her love proves impossible, I will then do what I have charged
Lialt to do in the event of my death—find a man who is capable
of giving her kindness she can accept, and a life which will be
gentle for her. I will not have her returning to her former life of
blood and battle, and my cruelty will have one beneficial aspect—
she will soon yearn desperately for a kind word or look, and will
cling to any man who gives her that. In such a way will she
accept the man chosen for her.''

I could not believe the words I heard, and I stood numb in the
growing wind, knowing not which way to turn my thoughts. I
had never felt this—"love"—for Ceralt, yet—Ceralt was to die?
And I was not to be allowed to mourn or avenge him? The
shame he had given me was deliberate, his actions to a purpose,
for he was to die?

"Ceralt,'' began Telion slowly, "there are things which you

do not know, and therefore cannot have taken into account. You must change your tactics with the wench, for I now understand why she sought to goad me into destroying her.''

''Destroying her?'' Ceralt barked, and sounds of sharp movement came. ''What do you speak of?''

''Gently,'' Telion soothed, and again there were soft sounds. ''You know well enough that I would not harm her, yet she caused a madness in me that nearly took her life. I shall not speak of that which she used to produce the madness, yet you have my word that the action was deliberate. She desperately sought not the kindness you spoke of, but the death we both know she was pressed to seek once before.''

''Death,'' Ceralt echoed, an illness clear in his voice. ''Why in the name of the Serene Oneness must she seek death rather than kindness?''

''Perhaps because she has been led to believe that kindness does not exist,'' Telion replied heavily. ''You asked me once of the lashing she had at the hands of Galiose, and I turned the talk to other things rather than speak of the matter, yet now I feel the time has come to speak of it. Ceralt, she was given twenty-five strokes of the heavy lash, and then she was given to a Captain of the Palace Guard named Nolthis, a man known to all save Galiose as one who broke women to his will, one who took great delight in shattering them. It was Inala who freed her from Nolthis, and even now it sickens me to recall Inala's words of how he kept our black-haired wench. Should I ever again lay eyes upon this Nolthis, I will speak to him with swords of my feeling for him.''

''Galiose,'' Ceralt choked, and a dull, heavy thud came. ''Galiose and Galiose and Galiose! The thing between us grows larger and larger with each new thing I learn! Twenty-five blows of the heavy lash! Given to a Guardsman who delighted in her torture! Ah, Jalav mine, how did such a thing come to be?''

''And then she became yours,'' Telion continued, remorselessly. ''I know not how she came to obey you; however I do know that she sought death at my hands. She once had trust in me, looked upon me as a brother warrior despite my being—male, yet now, in her eyes, I am no other thing than male, a thing to be hated and distrusted. How well have your plans gone, brother? Once free of you, she will never mourn any male, no matter what kindness he shows her. She will spit upon his kindness and his lifeless corpse as well.''

A sound came from Ceralt, a sound I could not put name to,

yet a sound which most often came with the thrusting of one's
sword into another's belly. I turned from the sound and the tent
and the males, and made my way back to the tree near which the
lanthay were tied, and crouched down beside the tree, resting my
shoulder upon it. No more than a small part of the sky remained
light, and the wind sought to open my garments to the caress of
the cold, yet I crouched in the darkness, huddled into my fur,
and fought to clear my mind.

Ceralt was to die. This, above all things, stood out so clearly,
though I knew not why it should. I hated the male, hated the
very thought of him, so why did I not rejoice at the thought of
his death? He had shamed me and humiliated me many times
over, had stolen the vows which made me his slave, had denied
to me all that had ever had meaning, and yet thought of his death
did not bring me joy. This, then was the loss Lialt had once
spoken of, the loss which Ceralt had laughed at. Ceralt was to
die, and Lialt already mourned, and I was to rejoice at my
coming freedom, then gladly embrace the male of Lialt's choice.
My hands in my fur gloves turned to fists, and I pounded upon
my knees in voiceless fury. How I hated the male Ceralt for
seeking to send me to another, how I hated him for the shame he
had so deliberately heaped upon me—and how deeply I mourned
the loss which was destined to be. My head bowed low as my
arms went about my middle, and I knew not what in the wide
world to do.

Some short while after the fall of full darkness, various of the
males appeared to tend to the feeding of the lanthay, and also to
the setting of guard posts. I remained crouched beside the tree,
seeing the flames within boxes which the males carried to the
lanthay, and still I knew not what there was to be done. Was I to
speak of that which I had learned, or keep silent? If I chose to
speak of it, to whom would I speak? These questions and others
filled all of my mind, and were put aside only upon hearing the
crunch of snow beside me. I looked up from where I crouched to
see Lialt, who gazed down upon me with something of disapproval.

"Has it taken you all this time merely to tie the lanthay?" he
demanded, the wind playing with his words. "Why have you not
come to the tent?"

"I was told I was also to feed the lanthay," I replied, not
wishing to discuss my thoughts with this male who so often
disapproved of me. I stood straight to face him, and the darkness
about us howled with the cold.

"I will feed the lanthay," said he, narrowing his eyes somewhat.

"Ceralt wishes you within the tent before the cold sucks the life from you. Get you there now and do not dawdle."

I met his eyes as he spoke, and though I said no words in return, the knowledge came to him that it was not he who was to be obeyed, for anger touched him as I turned away. He did not call after me as I walked toward the tent, and this seemed strange as I could not walk quickly upon my left leg, yet I dismissed the thought as I reached the tent and entered.

Within the thick, overlapped entrance, a welcome warmth was to be found. The tent, perhaps three paces by four in area, of a height great enough for the males to stand erect across most of it, made of tan leather upon the outside, was white-furred within, both walls and floor, and was lit by a number of small boxes with flames. At the far side of the tent and to the left of the opening flap, stood two κnee-high boxes of thin, light metal, each filled with dull black stones which glowed red with the heat of the fire within them. Some of the black stones had begun turning gray, and the pleasurable warmth came from these two sources. I pushed back the hood of my fur body covering and began removing the devices called gloves so that I might open the body covering, and Ceralt looked up at me from where he sat to the left, back toward the far wall.

"It should not have taken you so long to see to the lanthay," he informed me, something of Lialt's disapproval in his tone as well. "This cold is not the sort one stays out in unnecessarily, and I do not wish to see you fall ill. Remove the furs and your boots, and come here."

Not knowing what reply might be made, I made none, doing no more than glancing toward Telion, who sat cross-legged to the right, oiling his sword, before doing as Ceralt had bid. My body and leg furs I left beside the flap before going to Ceralt, and walking was much the easier without the weight of the leg furs upon my feet. The feel of the fur beneath the hand which had raised me erect spoke of lanthay as its source, showing that those of the villages used more of the beasts than their backs. The thought of doing the same with gandod was amusing, yet the amusement turned quickly to startlement when Ceralt reached up without warning and threw me to the fur beside him.

"You have, as yet, no true knowledge of this cold," said he, taking my right foot in both of his hands and beginning to rub it. Strangely, at first I could not feel the rubbing, and then the feeling returned with a rush of stabbing needles, as though I had knelt upon the foot too long, and I moved uncomfortably in his grip, unable to extricate the foot.

"Even through the boots, your feet will become frost-bitten if you stand in the snow too long," said Ceralt, finishing with the right foot and then taking the left. "In this weather, you are to do what you must as quickly as possible, and return to the warmth as soon as may be. Do you understand?"

As he then had my left foot, I was able to do no more than nod in response to his question. The brisk rubbing not only awakened painful life in my foot, but echoed and reinforced the ache in my thigh. I showed none of the pain I felt, yet it was a near thing. Beads of moisture grew upon my forehead, and I had grasped the lanthay fur in both fists before I was finally released.

"You may now cook and serve our meal," Ceralt allowed, leaning back in the fur to reach to the place where he had put his sword. It was not the same sword which had hung upon the wall of his dwelling, yet his gentle touch upon the weapon clearly showed his fondness for it. He took as well a soft cloth and a small pot of oil, and I raised myself slowly from the furs and went to the packs of gear which had been placed at the back of the tent. With no eyes upon me, I was able to wipe the sweat away, then search for the meat which was to be our provender. Mid-fey meal had been cooked, dry meat, much like leather, and had I had the choice, I would have done better without.

Cooking the meat above the hot, black stones was not like cooking upon a fire, and Lialt had long since returned before the provender was edible to the males. Ceralt divided the meat in three, and I felt the heavy touch of annoyance upon realizing that I was again to share his; the need for obedience was a constantly grating noose about the neck of my dignity and clan position. War leaders of the Midanna were not raised to be slave-women to males.

Telion accepted his provender with no more than a grunt of pleasure, yet Lialt eyed me in a strange manner before I turned from him. I knew not what the strangeness meant, and had taken two steps from him when suddenly he spoke.

"Woman, remove your leggings," said he, a snap of annoyance to his tone. "I have no doubt that you said not a word!"

I halted in the middle of the lanthay fur, making no attempt to turn toward him for I felt I now knew what his look had meant, yet Ceralt raised his head from the meat and sent an inquiring gaze toward his brother. Lialt made a clear sound of annoyance, and shifted where he sat.

"Have you not seen how she favors her left leg?" he demanded of the others, confirming my suspicions. "The foolish
wench has undoubtedly strained the healing wounds, yet stub-
bornly refuses to speak of it! Does she seek to cripple herself
permanently?"

Ceralt had straightened where he sat, anger in his light eyes,
and he threw the hair back from those eyes with a shake of his
head, fastening his gaze upon me.

"It appears that she is again ruled by that misbegotten pride
her kind seem to favor," he replied to Lialt, yet his words were
also for me. "I will see that pride forgotten by her, to be
replaced with common sense, else I shall see to its removal
myself. For this, Jalav, you have my word. Remove the leggings
and return to Lialt."

His anger was familiar, yet my own anger was a full match to
it. I stood in the lanthay fur, my hands turned to fists, and
looked down into the blaze of his eyes.

"The insolence of males!" I hissed, fury growing high within
me. "Is a sense of dignity to be yours alone, jealously denied to
any who cannot also be called male? In what manner are you
harmed when I choose not to speak of what pain I may feel?
That Mida knows of my pain is sufficient, for it is she who
brings healing, not Lialt and his salves and potions! I am a Hosta
warrior, a war leader of Mida, and my pride in such is beyond
your ability to take! You may draw your blade and take my life,
male, yet my dignity is *mine*!"

Ceralt seemed taken by frowning surprise at my outburst, yet
by the time my words were complete, he no longer remained
seated as he had been. He stood before me, tall and strong, and
the feel of his fingers in my arms was much like the grasp of
metal.

"Why must you be so ignorant a savage?" he demanded,
shaking me at the urging of his anger. "Why do you not yet
know that never would I raise a weapon to harm you? Why have
you not yet realized that your precious Mida moved not a single
finger in your defense when you faced those other savage wenches,
yet Lialt strove through light and darkness, forgoing his sleep
and sustenance, straining his abilities to the limit, to coax forth
that tiny spark of life which was all that remained to you?" His
hands ceased their shaking, his eyes filled with pain, and his
voice, which had been so full of anger, became no more than a
hoarse whisper. "And when will you become as other women,
sharing your pain with me so that I may soothe it? When will

you show a need for me, a need beyond that of the furs? Your sense of dignity disallows such things, and I am to accept it?'' His voice choked then, and the desolation in his eyes was swept away by the shaking of his head, as though he shook sleep from him. ''It is idle to discuss such things, idle even to think upon them. Remove your leggings and go to Lialt, and no more backtalk from you.''

He thrust me back toward Lialt then, with little anger, yet his strength was such that I nearly tripped in the lanthay fur from the thrust. He returned to the place he had chosen to sit amid silence from the other males, and I, too, could think of no further words. When speaking with Midanna, it was ever clear that those who spoke all spoke of the same matter, yet speech with males was a time of confusion, for males were wont to speak of things far distant from that which a warrior expected. From pain to pride was an easy step, yet how was one to go from pain to need? As I slowly removed the leg coverings from me, the constant confusion I felt among males swelled greatly, attempting to swirl my mind away with lack of understanding. How was a warrior to deal with males, when their very thoughts were beyond all rational bounds?

''As you are about it,'' said Ceralt, taking my thoughts from a place of spinning, ''remove the balance of your garments as well. A man's leather may be necessary for the journey, yet it has no place here in my tent.''

I looked upon him then and he returned the look, yet there was no further trace of the anger and dismay he had shown but a few moments earlier. He meant no more than to command his slave and see himself obeyed, and would not allow the matter to be discussed. With lips tightened to a line of anger, I turned from him again and commenced the removal of the balance of the leathers, knowing only that the fey of my freedom was inevitably approaching. Upon its arrival, this matter and others would be well seen to.

When all of my garments lay thrown to one side, Lialt put his meat aside and gestured me closer. He had earlier gone to the packs at the rear of the tent, and had returned with a covered pot which seemed familiar. As I stood before him, he uncovered the pot to show a pink liquid, thick yet thin enough to flow slowly, and I knew the why of the pot's familiarity. Ceralt had once used the pot's contents upon me, just as Lialt now placed his fingers within the liquid, then raised them covered to my thigh. The liquid seemed cool to my flesh, yet a moment of gentle rubbing

removed the coolness and also somehow eased the ache in my
thigh. Lialt looked critically upon the other tracks of Silla spears,
added the pink liquid to those he disliked, then took a cloth upon
which he might wipe his hands.

"She should now rest," said he to Ceralt, reclaiming his
provender and biting from it. "With her wounds as recently
healed as they are, the journey will not be easy for her."

Ceralt nodded and looked upon me sourly. "The journey
would be less difficult for any other wench in her place," said
he, his eyes for some reason impatient. "Jalav being Jalav, the
difficulties will surely increase. Place yourself there, wench,
belly down and lying still."

The other males chuckled at Ceralt's words, yet I was able to
see no humor in them, nor was I able to find approval in his
command. The place to which I had been directed was in the
midst of the males, and my reluctance as I lay flat in the lanthay
fur was great indeed. I did not care to be in the midst of the
males, belly down and unclothed before them, no more than a
pace from any of them. The lanthay fur was soft, holding my
breasts and belly and thighs gently; however, the eyes of the
males were not soft. All fed upon the provender I had prepared,
yet none seemed immersed in the business of feeding. Lialt lay
at ease upon his left arm and side, his jaws busily working the
meat he had been given, his eyes moving openly upon me as
they had not done when the pot of liquid had been in his hands.
Telion sat cross-legged to my right, healing his hunger absently,
his eyes deeply involved in following the line of my body where
it lay before him. Ceralt, too, studied me where I lay, the bright
look in his eyes most familiar, and it came to me that each of
these males had had me, that each had made me writhe beneath
him, helpless before his manhood. I lowered my eyes to the
white fur beneath my arms and studied it, allowing no more than
the memory of Telion and Ceralt beneath the hands of my
warriors to come to me. I held to such memories, yet the weight
of the eyes of the males upon me did not lessen.

I lay so before the males for a number of reckid, and my mind
insisted upon returning to the strange words Ceralt had spoken
to me upon the matter of pain. He had voiced a desire to share
and soothe my pain, a thing I did not fully understand, yet
perhaps it was something of an explanation for the actions of city
women. Should other males feel as Ceralt did upon the matter,
city females would be taught to voice their pain rather than
refuse it acknowledgment as Midanna were taught. I saw no

reason for such a thing, for pain is more easily bested in silence, yet city females voiced their pain to their males, perhaps in the foolish hope that the pain would be more quickly lessened. Thus far was I able to struggle toward understanding, yet meaning for the balance of his words eluded me. A warrior often called upon her sisters for aid, for they were Midanna and often of the same clan, yet which Midanna would be foolish enough to seek aid from a male? Males wished use from a Midanna and blind obedience, and I knew not why Ceralt would speak of asking his aid. What aid would a male spare for a warrior? And what need had he meant, a need I might find for him beyond the need of the furs? In what other way does one feel need for a male? Of what good are males, that a warrior would feel need for one? I tugged at the lanthay fur beneath my fingers, rubbed my cheek upon its warmth and softness, and fought inwardly to know the meaning of the thoughts of Ceralt.

"Jalav." Raising my head brought sight again of Ceralt, for it had been he who had spoken, and who now looked more directly into my face. His meat had been consumed, yet a portion of it remained, already cut, and I had no doubt as to the reason for its having been left untouched.

"You have not yet been fed," said he, moving closer to where I lay. He now sat cross-legged just before me, his knee near to my face. As he looked down upon me, a gentleness entered the strange, light eyes of him. "The fey has been long for one so recently healed," he said. "Surely you feel hunger?"

I knew not what he sought with such a question, the answer to which should have been obvious, and therefore remained silent under his gaze. With the wordless passing of time, the gentleness faded from his eyes to be replaced with his usual look of strength.

"Woman, I require an answer," he said, his voice without anger yet tinged with impatience. "Do you feel hunger?"

"Jalav feels some small hunger," I replied cautiously, wishing to give him naught with which he might shame me further. My hunger was indeed great, as it had been for some time, yet I would not show weakness before males.

"Good," said Ceralt, smiling as though pleased with my response. "The female Jalav feels hunger. Why, then has the female Jalav not fed herself?"

A frown came to me upon hearing his question, and I could not rid myself of the feeling that he spoke to a purpose. Too often males speak in dizzying circles, yet Ceralt had a look about him that I had seen before and knew well. The male had set himself to bedevil me, perhaps with that which he termed a lesson, perhaps to idle time away in amusement, yet bedevil me he would, with none to deny him.

"I do not know what answers you seek," I informed him, finding difficulty in raising my head high. I lay upon my belly before him, my neck already stretched so that I might see him, and the position was not one easily described as dignified.

"Allow me then to assist you," he chuckled, his hand reaching forth to brush loose hair from my cheek. "You hunger, yet have not fed yourself, and there is but one reason for this: men have not given you permission to do so. Do you understand my meaning?"

"Indeed." I nodded, certain that he would not care for my reply. "Males fear to set themselves against Jalav in the hunt, therefore has she been kept from it. Were she able to hunt, she would not hunger."

A noise, somewhat similar to strangling, came from Telion, and when I looked toward him, saw that his hand rubbed at his face as he coughed. I thought it likely that he had swallowed wrong and returned my gaze to Ceralt. The light-eyed leader of those called Belsayah also looked upon Telion, though not kindly, and then his annoyance was again directed toward me.

"You are in part correct," said he, lowering his brows to look upon me sternly. "Jalav is female, and females do not hunt. Should a female wish to eat, she must look to a man to provide for her. Each morsel you eat is provided by me, and should I wish to punish you, you will be made to go hungry. I shall not go hungry, nor shall Lialt nor Telion, yet should it be my wish, you will not be fed. Is this now more understandable to you?"

The cut-up meat lay clear to my vision, and Ceralt's words were equally as clear. Should the male be displeased with me, he might easily deny me sustenance, disallow my feeding as easily as he formerly demanded it. My insides churned at the thought, increasing my hunger, yet my anger would not be denied.

"Were Jalav able to hunt, she would feed," said I, moving my eyes from Ceralt's. "Should the need arise, she is well able to do without."

Ceralt's hand came to my chin, and again I was made to look upon him. "Jalav shall not hunt," said he, the words clearly pronounced. "Jalav is female, and shall eat only if it pleases me to feed her. Should I not be pleased to do so, Jalav shall have no choice save to do without. A woman eats only at the pleasure of men. Hear my words and recall them clearly, wench. I shall now feed you for it pleases me to do so.''

He then took a bit of meat and placed it between my teeth, watching closely to see that I chewed and swallowed as he wished. The meat was cold and overdone, slick with fat which had congealed, and surely was the taste of it more bitter than any meat ever given me. I fed by the will of Ceralt, my hunger seen to by that which he had no desire for, given a male's leavings and only because the act gave him pleasure. My fists curled tight as each bit of meat was placed between my teeth, and rage grew higher in me at what the male had done. I, a war leader of the Hosta, had been put to her belly before a male and made to feed from his hand! Not through her will did she feed but through his, and the thought nearly drove me insane! Mida, hear me now! When is my captivity to be at an end?!

Mida heard not, and Ceralt would not see me free from him till the last of the meat was consumed. I was achingly aware of the presence of the other males, and when I was at last allowed to move from beside Ceralt, I could not fail to see how they looked upon me with amusement. I moved just past Lialt and Telion, lying again upon the fur with Lialt to my right, Telion to my left, and Ceralt beyond my feet, and Lialt's chuckle was clear even though I did not look upon him.

"I feel the wench now has a deeper understanding of her place among men," said he to Ceralt, his voice heavy with approval. "Such understanding is necessary for every female."

"Some do not see it so and must be taught," agreed Ceralt, a satisfied sound to him. I grasped the lanthay fur beneath my hands and cheek and ground my teeth in silence.

"A woman's anger is understandable as well," said Telion quietly. "Should the wench be one who has never sought the presence of a man, should she be as wild and as free as the urchins of a city's poorest district, she will undoubtedly be hurt and bewildered when chosen by men to serve them, yet she should not be. A wench who is sweet-bodied and fair of face will ever find herself sought by men, and there is little she may do save learn to serve them well."

"She must learn there is no denying men's desires," said Ceralt, seemingly agreeing with Telion's words. "Rage as she might, men will take her and keep her, using her as they will. Turn upon your back, woman, so that men may look upon you to their pleasure."

I had no will to turn as Ceralt commanded, yet there was

naught I might do other than obey. I turned to my back, sending my eyes to the tent roof so that I need not look upon the males, yet I knew that their eyes were directly upon me.

"See how nicely her hip turns," said Lialt, a thickness to his voice. "Full, firm thighs above rounded calves, heavy breasts to cushion a man, slender arms to hold him close. A woman without doubt, Ceralt. A woman of great desire."

"Aye," said Telion, his voice much like that of Lialt. "Long black hair in which a man may twist his fingers as he takes her. Use of a short-haired woman is not the same."

Their need was as clear in their voices as it was in the smell of them, and I brought my arm to cover my eyes as I choked out, "I am a warrior of Mida, a war leader of the Hosta!" The fierce whisper was to have been for my ears alone, an aid against these males and their insistences, however all heard and all laughed softly.

"She seeks to cling to her former beliefs," said Ceralt, less amusement than satisfaction to his tone. "She has begun to know the falsity of her former position, has begun to feel her vulnerability before men, and desperately strives to regain her former viewpoint. See how tightly her thighs are clasped, a foolish female attempt to keep men from her. We have been told we have a warrior before us, brothers. Who would be the first to show the warrior her womanhood?"

"I would be pleased to do so," breathed Lialt from my left, so close that his hand caressed my calf and moved upward to my thigh. I cried out in misery and attempted to force him from my side, rising half upward from his lanthay fur to grapple with him, yet there was no besting the strength of a male. Gently yet irresistibly I was returned to my back, my arms held above my head with my wrists pinioned in one of Lialt's hands, and then he began to search for my heat. Through my distress, I was determined to give no response to him, sure that my body would feel no desire for one such as he, yet his hand forced its way between my thighs and his lips bent low to taste of my breasts, and I could not deny the demands he put to me. In but a few reckid, sobbing and mewling, I writhed beneath him, aching for the feel of his manhood, begging to be taken with every motion of my body. Lialt, a male, knelt above me, his fingers and tongue and lips taking all he desired, his eyes bright with the knowledge that I could no longer deny him, and I trembled with the memory of how I had taunted him. I was now his to do with as he pleased, and my needs would slay me were he pleased to leave

me unused. I need not have feared. however. for my legs were
suddenly thrust apart and Lialt was deep within me, taking me as
completely as though I were slave to him.

When Lialt's need had been seen to, I lay upon my side in the
dimness of the tent, my knees drawn up to my belly, my face
buried in my arms. Great shame had been given to me that
darkness, yet it was a shame borne of my own failures, my own
crippling needs. To defy Lialt in future would be idle, for it was
easily seen that he need do no more than touch me to bring me
groveling to his feet. I wished desperately to speak with Mida
and ask her what might be done to lift the curse from my body,
yet she had said she would not walk my dreams again, and there
was none else to whom I might speak.

A hand touched my arm, slowly, caressingly, and in my
startlement my head flew up from my arms. Lialt, I knew, sat
and shared near-renth with Ceralt, and this was Telion who now
sat beside me. His light eyes, shadowed, looked down upon me,
yet even shadowed there was no mistaking his intent.

"Telion, no!" I whispered, seeking to back from him in the
fur. His hand moved quickly to grasp my hair, and then he had
taken me in his arms.

"Jalav, this is a woman's purpose," he murmured, his hands
moving about me. "Do you feel no desire for me?"

My breasts were hard against the red-gold hair of his chest, his
manhood was a rock in my thigh, and to my horror, my heat had
again begun to rise.

"Telion, I wish to be left to my misery," I whispered hoarsely,
looking up into his broad, male face. "Release me, for I indeed
have no desire for you."

"A wench would do well to learn not to lie," chuckled Telion,
stroking my hair. "For lying, you must now be punished."

And then his hand went to me, and I gasped and stiffened in
his arms at the touch. The moisture flowed from me as though I
were just emerged from a stream, and I could not keep from crying
out again and again. This the males found highly amusing, for
Telion would not let me rest. Over and again he caused me to
sob and cry out, digging at his arms with my fingernails, my body
a desire-racked, flailing thing whipping about beside him. When I
screamed and threw myself upon him, he grinningly held me still
and demanded to know if I yet felt desire for him. I wept then
and screamed again and the male at last saw fit to ease my agony.
Much pleasure did this Telion bring me, yet he stayed till his own
pleasure had been taken in full measure. When he left me, I knew

well that I had been used, and my mind was too beclouded to think.

I must have slept briefly, for the next I knew, Ceralt's foot nudged me awake. The tent had been dimmed to one, small flame in a box, and the previous warmth was nearly gone, for the two pots of black stones had been quenched with water. Lialt and Telion lay wrapped in lenga pelts to the right, and when Ceralt saw my eyes upon him, he gestured to the left.

"Take yourself to my furs, woman," said he, stretching hugely before beginning to remove his leathers. "The journey begins again with first light, and I wish to sleep."

Miserably, covered with the smell of males' satisfaction, I crept to Ceralt's furs and within them. His dark form moved about briefly till his leathers lay disgarded, then he, too, had slipped within the furs beside me. He moved a bit to find comfort, and then his arms were strongly about me, holding me to his broad chest. There was naught I felt the need to say, yet his hand found my chin and lifted my face toward his.

"This darkness you were punished, little varaina," said he, his voice soft as breathing. "Do you yet understand the reason for your punishment?"

Though I could not see him, I knew his eyes were upon me and that he would feel the shake of my head. I had not known that I had been given punishment, nor was I able to see a reason for such. Ceralt sighed, and his hand moved gently upon my face.

"You were given punishment for having declared yourself a warrior," said he, the gentleness of his touch matched in his tone. "My Jalav is a woman, no longer a warrior, and so long as she insists upon ignoring this truth, so long will she be punished. Lialt and Telion found no warrior beneath their hands, but a woman, one who could not deny men their due. Your body has learned what your mind has not, that you are now bound to men as tightly as any other woman. Soon your mind will know it as your body does, and your anger and misery will be no more. It is that fey which I look forward to."

I made no answer to his words, yet my mind seethed with fury. The male sought to break me to his will, to enslave my mind as he had enslaved my body, yet this I would not allow. I was in possession of Mida's words that I remained a favored warrior, and this, above all else, would keep me from the folly of belief in his words. It shamed me deeply that I was unable to deny Lialt and Telion, yet this, too, must have a purpose in Mida's scheme of things. I would not cease to believe in my warriorhood, nor would I refrain from speaking of it should the occasion arise.

"That stubbornness has taken you again," said Ceralt, annoyance sharpening his tone. "I can feel the stiffness to your body, the refusal of your inner self to obey. If further punishment is what you seek, varaina, so be it. Your use will be free to my brothers till the fey you declare yourself a woman and mine. Upon that fey you may ask that I alone use you, and perhaps the favor will be granted. At this moment, however, I feel a desire to be pleasured. See to pleasing me, woman, and do not be clumsy."

He released me and lay flat upon the furs, and I sat up and stared at the dark shape of him in confusion.

"I know naught of pleasing males," said I, never having heard the demand before. "Are males not pleased through the use of females?"

"They are," agreed the dark Ceralt shape, "yet there are other means by which man may feel pleasure. Do you recall our first meeting, in the woods three feyd from Bellinard? Think back to the time, varaina, and do to me now that which you merely began at that time."

The time of our first meeting was easily recalled, yet the memory brought dismay rather than enlightenment. What I had done to Ceralt was a warrior's way of firing a male without the use of the sthuvad drug, and was not meant to be used upon a male who was unbound. I attempted to explain this to Ceralt, yet he refused to hear my words, demanding instead that I begin to serve him. His fist in my hair disallowed further discussion, and the results of my efforts were far more distasteful than even I had imagined. Ceralt could not resist the touch of my lips and tongue upon him, yet I, too, found the flames lapping high in my belly. The heat of him, the smell of his desire, the feel of his firm, male body beneath my hands—madly I thought myself again in that forest, a bound male before me, my warriors ranged about awaiting their own pleasure. I laughed and told him of how I would take and use him, and then the horror of the true situation was forced upon me. The male I had thought bound was free to throw me beneath him, and then I, not he, was taken and used, a lust not to be denied driving him harder and harder. I cried and sobbed many times during that use, not all deriving from pleasure, and when the storm had passed and I again lay quietly in his arms, his body still in possession of mine, I at last knew the full dangers of arousing a male. Weaponless, a warrior might do naught to deny him, weaponless, she could only endure.

"You need not fear punishment," murmured Ceralt, and his lips touched my hair very gently. "Long had I wished to find myself before you in such a way again, only this time unbound, and my wish has been granted. You have given me great pleasure, and perhaps, in the future, I might again allow you to pretend to warriorhood."

He chuckled then and kissed me a second time, his arms closing more tightly about me so that I might not struggle free. My struggles lasted only a brief time for I had little strength left with which to struggle, yet my anger continued to seethe even till Ceralt had fallen asleep. That he would "allow me to pretend to warriorhood" was the foulest blow of all, for he had made it seem that my actions had been no more than obedience to his desire. I moved angrily in the prison of his arms, then drew my breath in sharply as his manhood throbbed in response to my movement, sending a weakness through me that could not be overcome. Even in his sleep he was able to debilitate me, take my strength and fire my blood so that I could not resist him. I pressed my lips to his chest, tasting the sweat upon the hairs there, then licked at the spot as I moved my hips, gently soothing the desire begun in me. Ceralt slept on, all unknowing, and soon, I too, was able to sleep.

# 13.

## A halt in the journey—
## and a thing termed reading

The new fey brought a strengthening of gold in Mida's light, yet even the gold was unable to ease the clutch of the cold upon all beneath it. Once again the lanthay made their way through white mounds surrounded by bare, leafless trees, a landscape of desolation and emptiness which seemed to demand the reason for life being found in any of us. The village females rode farther ahead with their males, frightened yet, though less than they had been, apparently greatly eased by the rest of the darkness. I, of all in the set save Ceralt, rode alone, I near the end of the formation, Ceralt at its head. No others save Lialt and Telion sat their lanthay behind me.

My solitary position was of my own choosing, for I had much to think upon. The happenings of the darkness before had been disturbing, yet no less so than the happenings of the new light. Upon first awakening, each of the males had paused before donning his leather to press his lips to mine, yet none had sought nor attempted my use. Each had seemed most pleased with the world about him, and each had given me greetings for the new fey with friendliness and lack of anger and disapproval. Never before had males seemed so pleased with a warrior save during her use, and I could not see what end they hoped to accomplish. Full suspicious and wary, I had folded Ceralt's furs and those of the others, then had accepted the bit of dried meat given me. This had been consumed beneath the eye of Ceralt, he who was pleased to allow me to feed, and then was I commanded to don my outer garments so that tent and all within it might be prepared to journey further.

The gold of Mida's light shone blindingly from many places in the snow, bringing an ache and tears to the eyes when one looked upon it. It was not well to ride a forest with eyes closed, yet there was little I might do even should an attack come, for I sat weaponless among males. I closed my eyes, giving the burden of where we rode over to my lanthay, feeling the cold upon my face, the movement of lanthay muscles between my legs, hearing the sounds of our passage and an occasional voice floating back from those before me. Lialt and Telion had spoken to one another earlier, yet now rode in paired, companionable silence. My thoughts continued to touch Ceralt and the other two males as well, again searching for one who might be spoken to of the death seen for Ceralt by Lialt. There seemed to be an acceptance of this on the part of the males, an acceptance foolish where the will of Mida and the demands of honor were not involved, one I did not fully understand. I slitted my eyes to catch a glimpse of where we rode, finding no more than that which had gone before, and struggled to know the workings of the minds of males.

The journey continued through the early part of the fey, and to the surprise of myself alone, a village appeared at the time of the mid-fey meal. It stood much as Ceralt's village had stood, wooden dwellings ranged about an open area, yet it also lay somewhat quieter, gripped in the fist of cold and snow. More than a hand of males came forth to greet us, each bowing deferentially to Ceralt and calling him High Rider, and then we were led to the overlarge dwelling of the village, where village females had prepared provender for those who rode with us. It was easily seen that those of the village had known of our coming, and also easily seen that the females of our traveling set had great need of such comforts as were provided. They crowded round the fire over which meat roasted, happily warming the cold and ache from their bones, chattering in relief to those females who tended the provender. The males had been welcomed with the presence of skins of near-renth, and sat about in a circle of companionship, passing the skins about as they spoke and leaned at ease. Only one female had failed to join those at the fire, one who had instead placed herself to the left of the hearth where she might partake of the warmth yet avoid those others who moved herdlike

near the provender. She called Famira stood apart from the circle
of females, closed from their midst by purposely turned backs,
shut out by ears which would not hear her, eyes which would not
see her need. She had gazed longingly upon the happiness of the
others before placing herself apart from them, for the other
females, seeing her held firmly in place by the hand of the male
Cimilan, had lost their fear of her and had turned their faces
from her, denying her a place among them. This the dark-haired
female had accepted without protest, appearing to my eye as
having been emptied of protest. I took my gaze from her as I
removed my fur body covering, reflecting that the cold of the
land would not be bested by running to warmth at every
opportunity. Better to remain a distance from the fire, the more
easily to reemerge into the cold once the feeding was done. I
crouched beside a far wall, away from those others with whom I
traveled, knowing myself content to be undisturbed by males,
knowing also that the female Famira might no longer be considered an enemy. She knelt in silent misery, her hands clasped
before her, her head bowed, the laughter and speech of the
others in the dwelling a painful prison holding her without. She
had not the inner strength of Midanna to stand firm in the midst
of enemies, nor was she able to think of those about her as
enemies. I felt something of pity for the luckless female, for her
previous arrogance had been caused by the reluctance of others
to teach her differently, and now she alone bore the fruits of
the actions of all. She did not weep in her misery, a thing to her
credit, yet she was no longer fit to be called enemy to a Midanna.

With the provender full roasted, all of the females carried
wooden squares to the males who sat drinking from skins. Those
females of the village vied for the opportunity of serving Ceralt,
and to a lesser extent, Lialt and Telion, and the males laughed at
the manner in which the females pushed one another aside in
their frantic desire to be pleasing. The female Famira fed beside
the fire where she knelt, yet all of the others of the females went
to their males with boards of their own. Ceralt, seemingly taken
with the presence of the new village females, gave his laughter
and looks of approval to them alone, sparing no whit of attention
for the warrior who crouched alone beside a wall. This, then,
was that which Ceralt wished from a female—empty-headed
laughter with no cause, looks of desire which lowered shyly
upon his seeing them, gentle touches to his arm in anxious effort
for his attention, eagerness to serve his needs no matter their
nature. I looked to the well-worn boards beneath my feet, seeing

how clean they were kept, knowing the deed had been done by females. Ceralt wished a female who would be pleased to keep the floor of his own dwelling so, one who knew naught of the use of arms nor the call of Mida. This, he thought, might be had from a warrior of Mida, yet he knew not how foolish such a thought would prove to be. There had been those warriors of Mida who had been taken by males and changed from that which they once had been, yet no war leader had been numbered among them. War leader to Mida was a special state, and I, more than any, was Mida's alone, pledged to serve no more than her will till the last breath had fled from me. I heard again the senseless laughter of the females, and made no effort to look upon them. They and their doings held pleasure for Ceralt, I and my doings giving no more than anger. All those in the dwelling saw happily to their hunger, and I, acrouch beside a wall, had none to see to.

Much time fled in the consuming of the provender, yet the males seemed unconcerned over the loss of trail time. I, deep in my thoughts and far distant from the dwelling, knew naught of their having finished till a presence was felt quite near me. I raised my eyes to see Ceralt above me, standing beside the males of the new village, and all appeared much interested in the look of Jalav. Ceralt rested his hand upon the hilt of the blade he wore, a thoughtful look to him, and one of the males beside him gestured toward me.

"And this, you say, is the wench," said he, uncertainty in his tone. The male stood less than the height of Ceralt, broad yet lacking Ceralt's broadness, dark of hair and eye as were all of the village males save Ceralt and Lialt. Though I knew no reason for it, I cared little for the doubt he showed, and rose to my full height as Ceralt nodded.

"This is she for a certainty," said Ceralt, an unexplained gleam in his eyes. "Are you able to look upon her as she stands before you and continue to doubt?"

"See what she wears about her neck!" exclaimed another, and all eyes went to the carved hadat upon its tie which lay upon my leather body covering. My life sign was meant to be seen, and for this reason I had taken to wearing it above my garment rather than below it. The gathered males made sounds of astonishment and surprise, and he who stood nearest Ceralt locked eyes with me, attempting to cause me to lower my gaze, yet I felt no shame before these strangers. That I had been captured was no matter of pride, yet capture may happen to any.

"She is not a wench of the villages, that is for certain," said the male beside Ceralt, a frown creasing his brow. "The insolence in her eyes seems nearly a match to her size."

"She is wild yet and displeased with her lot," said Ceralt with indulgence, a faint grin pairing with the gleam in his eyes. "It is my intention to make her fully mine before the journey is ended, a thing which she is aware of yet does not care for. She will learn the proper respect for men, for this you have my word."

"A satisfying assurance," grinned the other male, clapping Ceralt upon the shoulder. "Even though she is chosen by the Snows, she is no more than female and must be taught her place. Hannil will not care for such a look of insolence."

"The females of Hannil's village are more slave than woman," replied Ceralt with distaste. "I enjoy the sight of obedience in a wench, yet slavelike obedience turns my insides sour. If a wench has no spirit, where is the pleasure in taming her?"

"The matter is not pleasure to all men," laughed the second male, a greater look of respect for Ceralt entering his eyes. "As you are not far distant from your rendezvous point with Hannil, will you not pass a longer time with us? We are always honored by the presence of our High Rider."

Ceralt smiled and turned to place a hand upon the other male's shoulder. "And I am always honored by the hospitality of my Headman Levanis," said he, true warmth in his tone. "Though we have, in truth, small distance yet to be covered, you must remember the presence of the wenches. It will require the balance of this fey and part of the next before we will reach the rendezvous point. Perhaps the return journey will allow for a longer visit."

"The Serene Oneness make it so," said the male called Levanis, the sound of sincerity in his tone. The other males, too, added their voices to his, showing the regard in which Ceralt was held. Each came to place a hand upon Ceralt's shoulder, and then, with all body furs replaced, saw us to our mounts.

Mida's skies had turned gray when the village was once more behind us. The cold remained as it had been, yet a lessening of the wind made it more bearable to one's cheeks. We rode as we had earlier in the fey, yet with the loss of the glare upon the snow about us, the ride had become more enjoyable. I now was able to look about myself, though the benefit in such a state remained to be seen. After perhaps a hin of travel, Ceralt left his place at the head of the formation and rode back toward my own position, yet was hailed by Lialt before he had reached his objective. Lialt and Telion continued to ride behind me, and Ceralt urged his lanthay to a place close beside Lialt's.

"I do not care for the look of these skies, brother," said Lialt, eyeing the grayness above us with displeasure. "Perhaps it would be best if I were to walk the Snows this darkness and search for the likelihood of a storm."

"No," said Ceralt, and his tone was clear with decision. "I know not how often you may need to walk the Snows upon this journey, and I will not see you lost by cause of unnecessary walking. Save your strength, brother, for the time it will most be required of you."

Lialt sighed, and the sound seemed to be one with the gray of the skies. "As you wish, Ceralt," said he in obedience. "Though I know a storm cannot be stopped by my searching it out, still I would prefer the freedom to search. I am not to walk the Snows again till we have reached Siggur's Peak?"

"I would prefer it so," replied Ceralt, "yet I fear that blindness till then will not aid us. You shall walk the Snows in a fey or two, when Hannil and his riders have joined us and our journey is properly begun."

"And our lot from the Snows unavoidable," added Lialt, his voice flattened so that all emotion might be kept from it. "Are you so eager to embrace what has been seen for you that you give no thought to its avoidance?"

"In what manner might it be avoided?" demanded Ceralt, anger and annoyance amingle in his voice. "Shall I refrain from making this journey and thereby cheat the Snows of their due? Would this be possible, brother?"

Again Lialt sighed, and I kept my eyes upon the backs of those before me, making no effort to turn again to see the faces of those who spoke.

"Such a thing would not be possible," said Lialt, his voice no longer willing to argue. "Forgive me, Ceralt, for having spoken of it. I, above all others, should know the futility of defying the Snows."

"The words were born of concern," said Ceralt, and a sound came as though he had gently clapped Lialt upon the shoulder. "Such concern means much to me, Lialt, yet we need not speak further upon the matter. Our paths have all long since been set, and now we have only to follow them."

Lialt made no further reply, nor did Telion add comment to the discussion, and a moment later Ceralt's lanthay had been ridden up beside mine. I raised my eyes to look upon the male

who was destined to lose his life at the end of the journey he had
so willingly begun, and the cold of the air dug deeper into the
flesh of my body.

"A wench's face looks best in the cold," observed Ceralt,
reaching out a hand to touch my cheek. "The blush of winter is
most becoming, yet it cannot be comfortable for you. Should the
cold increase, I will fashion a veil of cloth to cover your face and
protect it. How sharply do you feel your having gone unfed?"

Briefly I studied the calm and serenity of his face and eyes,
then looked away from him. "Jalav feels no hunger," I replied,
knowing it easier to go unfed in the dead white and dark twists
of the woods about us. Ceralt made a sound of disbelief and
reached forth a hand to turn my face to his again.

"What Jalav pretends not to feel is her punishment," said he,
a sharpness having entered his eyes. "A woman's place is beside
her man, seeing to his needs and serving him. Jalav kept to
herself rather than kneel beside Ceralt, leaving him to be seen to
by others as though he were womanless. For this, Jalav was
denied her provender, so that she might consider her actions
upon an empty belly. Consider well, wench, and ask the aid of
the gods in cooling my anger. Should you fail to do so, your
hunger may continue for some time."

He then removed his hand from my face and kicked his
lanthay to faster motion, riding ahead once more to resume his
previous place at the head of the march. My lanthay attempted
to follow his, and I found it necessary to hold my mount close,
allowing it to do no more than dance in place. When the lanthay
was once more resigned to its position, I looked ahead at Ceralt's
broad back and considered his words. How like a male to make a
warrior his captive, and then feel disappointment when she will
not do him as a slave of the cities! Had Ceralt wished such a
female, he would have done well to choose another. I looked
about at the bleak landscape once again, then silently called
down the curse of Mida upon Ceralt's head. His speaking of
having refused me provender had brought a hollowness to my
insides, recalling clearly the outrageous need my body had lately
shown. Only once before had I seen such a thing, when a warrior
of mine had been healed of a serious wound. Her appetite then
had been great indeed, and Rilas, Keeper of our clans of the
Midanna, had said that feeling so was necessary to replace lost
blood and flesh. My hunger, however, outdid that of my warrior,
and I recalled that her healing had not been as rapid as mine had
been. Perhaps the rapidity of my healing was the cause of the

hunger, yet whatever the cause, the hunger remained. I moved about upon the lanthay, causing it to dance again, and refused to consider the number of hind left to the fey.

Full darkness was not far from settling about us when the silent, gentle white began falling from the skies. It did not fall as thickly as it had in Ceralt's village, and the cold seemed lessened by its presence. No wind blew as we continued on, and I saw that each tiny bit of white disappeared as it touched my lanthay and my coverings. Although the dimness had been made much lighter by the falling white, we rode only a short time before stopping in a white-covered clearing. Lines were strung for the lanthay, tents were erected, and those of our party separated to enter their individual shelters. After seeing to my lanthay, I entered Ceralt's tent to find that the male had already lit the flame-boxes upon the walls, and had also set the black stones to burning. None other save Ceralt was in the tent, and he glanced at me when I had stepped within.

"The coals will soon be ready to cook upon," he said, poking at the black stones with a rod of metal. "Remove the trappings of a man, and prepare yourself for woman's work."

I hesitated no more than a moment, then began removing furs and leather. Though the heat from the black stones had not yet reached all corners of the enlarged tent, the warmth of the shelter made coverings unnecessary after the cold of the open. As I removed all coverings from my body, I made careful note that such coverings were unnecessary, yet the shame I felt was not much lessened. Ceralt wore all leathers and furs save body furs, yet I had been commanded to bare myself. He kept his eyes from me till the last of my leather lay upon the lanthay fur, then he turned from the dying flames to examine me closely.

"Much the better," he murmured, a faint smile upon his face. "There are few things more beautiful in a man's eyes than the soft body of his woman. Come closer to me, wench."

I had no wish to approach him, yet how might I have refused? He put aside the metal rod as I neared, and drew me into his arms.

"You are truly lovely," he said, looking down into my eyes. "Each fey you grow to be more of a woman and therefore lovelier. I look forward to the time you are all woman." He then lowered his head and touched his lips to mine, and the scent of him and his leathers brought a dizziness upon me. I was held so gently, so tenderly, and then his lips were gone and soft laughter came from him.

"More than satisfactory," he murmured, his hands astroke upon my hair. "Go now and fold your clothing and put it to the side, then prepare the meal."

His arms were removed from about me, yet a faint, pleasant tingling remained in my flesh. I brushed my hair back from my arms, more than aware of the bareness of my body, then went to see to the garments I had removed. Ceralt had turned again to the black stones, and as I knelt beside my coverings and folded them, my eyes strayed to the large male who stood so unconcernedly near. A strange feeling had come upon me as he had held me in his arms, a feeling far from the desire he had ever bred in me, yet somehow also linked with it. I knew not what the feeling meant, yet the thought of it caused me to shiver where I knelt. The shame I had felt at his command to disrobe was gone, replaced with the desire to feel his eyes upon me once again. A Midanna cared little for garments, using only a clan covering upon her womanhood to bespeak her pride in her clan, and never had I cared whether the eyes of males were upon me or not. Now, through some sorcery on Ceralt's part, I longed to show him my body and feel his approval. What had the male done to me, that I should feel so? I shuddered again, holding firmly to the thought that I was a warrior of Mida, and rose to take my garments to the side of the tent. It would be necessary to resist the doings of the male, yet I knew not which doings should most be resisted. The question would require deep consideration, and I would spend whatever time I might upon it.

Ceralt left the tent briefly, then he and the others returned by the time the provender was prepared. Each male had paused by the entrance to the tent before coming well within, and each had wiped the bottoms of his leg furs so that the snow upon them would not be brought in with their steps. The lanthay fur upon the tent floor was thick, although patches of wetness made walking and sitting uncomfortable. Lialt and Telion had come to inspect the progress of the provender, each also looking upon me with a wide grin, and then they had gone to sit at their ease and pass about a skin of near-renth. They spoke quietly to one another of trails and lanthay and snow, and when the meat had been divided by Ceralt, they accepted their portions with eagerness. I had also roasted fellin tubers to add to the meat, and with the tubers divided among them, I attempted to withdraw to the back of the tent. My middle had been knotting since first I had looked upon the raw and bloody meat to be roasted, yet Ceralt would not leave me be.

"Come and kneel beside me, satya," he called, gesturing to the fur beside his left leg. I knew not by what name he now called me, yet it made little difference. By any name I was his to command, and the thought turned my body stiff as I knelt beside him. His dagger had cut a piece of the meat I had roasted, and it was this piece which he took between his fingers.

"Eat this," he directed, holding the piece to my lips, his eyes clearly upon me. I thought then that he was again of a mind to see me fed, yet after the first piece had gone down my throat, no others were forthcoming. He returned without comment to his own feeding, cutting piece after piece, and my empty belly rumbled so loudly that all within the tent must have heard. I glanced at the other males, who seemed completely immersed in the business of swallowing, then licked my lips and looked back toward Ceralt. I could not bring myself to ask to be fed no matter how great my hunger, yet the decision was taken from me. Ceralt raised his eyes to see my face, and a smile grew as he looked at me.

"A thought has come to me," he said, his smile growing broader as I watched a bite of meat to his mouth. "Earlier, I told you that you must cool my anger before you might be fed, yet it now seems likely that you have no knowledge of how this might be done. I think it best that I instruct you in the method I prefer."

I shook my head, wishing none of his instruction, and his smile turned to broad grin and laughter.

"Heed me now, satya," he chuckled, moving his eating board to the right upon his lap. "Place your cheek there, upon my thigh, and soon, perhaps, we may see you fed."

In great misery, I lay my face upon him, knowing that shame and humiliation were again to come to me. Ceralt had removed the covering from his broad chest, yet the leather leg covering remained to bring a cool touch to my cheek. I knelt beside him, bent at the waist to lay my face upon his thigh, and his hand came to stroke my hair where it lay against him.

"It is clear that you feel great hunger," he said, "therefore you must show regret for the actions which caused your punishment. Put your lips to my leg and say, 'I should not have left you unattended, Ceralt. I ask your forgiveness'."

He sat silent after these words, awaiting my response, but my response was not immediately forthcoming. Thought of saying such words choked me voiceless, yet Ceralt had not said I might refuse them. Sooner would I have seen my body consume itself

in its need, yet I had been commanded to speak. Again I thought
of the possibility of being forsworn, although such a shame was
beyond my ability to conceive of. I struggled in the silence about
me, yet never have I been able to win a struggle with my sense
of right. My fist clenched where it lay upon Ceralt's thigh, and
I turned my face so that I might press my lips to his leg.

"I should not have left you unattended," I whispered, unable
to look upon the face of the male. "I ask your forgiveness."

Surely did I expect great laughter to come from him then, yet
no more than his hand came, to caress my hair once more.

"Forgiveness shall ever be yours, satya," he whispered, putting his lips to my hair. "You have only to ask, and it will
gladly be granted you."

In great surprise, I raised my eyes to his, finding no meaning
in his words nor in the look in his eyes. Why had he not laughed
at my humiliation, and why had he spoken as he had? And why,
in the name of Mida, did I feel none of the humiliation I had
thought to feel? The words forced from me had given pleasure to
Ceralt, much as though the ache of a wound had been eased, yet
a male's pleasure was ever a warrior's shame. This was ever so!
Why, then, was there no shame within me for having spoken so?
I whimpered with the torture of these thoughts, yet Ceralt saw and
heard not, for he was busily cutting upon what meat was left.

"Now you may eat in a proper manner," he said, a lightness
having entered his voice. "Sit up where you are and I shall feed
you."

I raised myself erect as I had been and accepted what meat he
gave me, yet my mind whirled in confusion as I gazed upon him.
I felt the need to question what had occurred between us, yet I
also felt a great reluctance to face what answers there might be. I
had many times told Ceralt that I might never be his, yet there
had been a time when I had wished this might not be so. Now,
as I looked upon the dark of his skin, the merriment in his eyes,
the joy in his movements, the strength of his body, I knew that
this wish had returned to plague me. It could not be, it could
never be, yet the Ceralt of old had returned as well, and my
desire for him had increased tenfold. To be held by him, to feel
the warmth of his lips upon mine, these were sufficient to drive
all other thoughts and desires from me, yet I remained, as
always, bound to Mida. And Ceralt, himself, was destined to
die! Was this the sole manner in which I might be freed from
him? Is his coming death in truth your doing, Mida? Have you
consigned him to the final ending so that your warrior might

continue to move slowly in your service? I spoke so to Mida deep in my heart, yet she continued to withhold all answers from me.

When the last of the provender was within me, Ceralt took me in his arms and held me upon his lap as though I were a child. I had attempted to harden my heart toward the male, knowing that Mida had refused him to me, yet the touch of his hands upon my arms sent all thoughts of hardness flying from me. I wished only to be held by him, yet the sparkle in his eyes gave hint of some definite purpose even before he stroked my side and spoke.

"Satya, there is now another thing I shall teach you," he said, grinning. "As I have allowed you to satisfy your hunger, you shall show your gratitude by saying, 'Ceralt, I thank you for having fed me.' Then you are to raise your lips to mine."

I squirmed in his grasp, knowing that this time he would find amusement in my words, yet I was unable to refuse. Seeing my agitation he laughed gently and held me closer.

"The words will come more easily when you have said them enough times," he assured me. "As you shall say them each time you are fed, in a matter of feyd you will no longer hesitate. Come now. Let me hear them."

"Ceralt, I—thank you for having fed me," I stumbled, feeling my cheeks blaze up at the grin he showed. I lay in his arms, naked and helpless, and this he knew full well.

"An excellent beginning," he pronounced, his light eyes filled with laughter. "Now offer me your lips."

Slowly I raised my lips to his, cursing my captivity, yet the strength he showed taking my kiss gave proof to the true nature of my capture. My body had been chained to his, his to do with as he pleased, mine to do only as he allowed. I submerged myself in the glory of his lips, aching deep inside as my need began to grow, yet his lips left mine sooner than I had expected, too soon to build the full blaze of desire.

"It is now time for a woman's true service to begin," Ceralt murmured, his eyes lazily upon me. "Telion must leave soon to share the watch of the camp, therefore you are to offer him your use before he departs. Go to him quickly, for time grows short."

I was then released from Ceralt's arms and placed upon the lanthay fur before him, there to sit and contain my anger and confusion as best I might. It was Ceralt I desired, not Telion, yet it was Telion to whom I had been sent. My hair lay half beneath my legs, causing a painful pull at my scalp, a thing which gave me no aid with my humor. Ceralt lay at his ease in the lanthay rur, his eyes calm, his face unconcerned, doing no more than awaiting obedience. Once he had said that I must ask to be kept as his alone, yet how might a warrior of Mida speak such words to a male? It was Mida to whom I belonged, Ceralt being no more than the male who had captured me, no more than temporary possessor of my sworn word. Males knew naught of the ways of Midanna, and this lack would be their downfall.

Angrily taking my eyes from Ceralt, I rose to my feet and looked about the tent. Lialt lay upon the lanthay fur not far from me, as bare-chested as Ceralt, yet his attention had been captured by a leather bound sheaf of white material, a thing containing black strokes which seemed to hold meaning for males. This sheaf lay beneath a flame-within-a-box, the light shed from the box falling upon the black strokes, and Lialt kept his eyes upon them, to all appearances far from the tent in which he lay. Telion stood to the rear of the tent, beside the metal container upon which I had cooked, his arms folded across his broad chest, his eyes held by the glow to be seen beneath the now gray stones. He alone wore all of his leathers, and the distraction of the two males brought me a good deal of annoyance. So usual a thing had my shaming by Ceralt become, that those others within the shelter no longer took note of it.

Telion seemed unaware of my approach to him, and as I halted beside his left arm, I studied the male who called himself warrior. Despite his capture and use by the Hosta, Telion had often shown feelings for warriors unmatched by any males I had heretofore met. He alone had shown no upset at my prowess with weapons, and he alone had kept whatever word he had given to me. It was true that he had joined with Ceralt and others in the capture of the Hosta, yet I had heard him say that he had done what was necessary to possess Larid, she whom he called the wench of his heart. Though I knew not what to make of the male, it often seemed that had all males been as Telion was, warriors might more easily find a point of truce with them. As I stood immersed in thoughts such as these, Telion grew aware of my presence and turned his eyes from the glow to regard me.

"What is it you wish, girl?" he asked, the words soft so as not to give insult. His arms remained folded across his chest, and again I thought that his leg furs gave unneeded additional height to his form. His light eyes continued to regard me as I attempted to recapture the manner in which I had once looked upon males, yet the effort was beyond me. A Midanna's desire for males would always be with me, yet I had learned to know their unbridled strength and be wary of it.

"Have you come to me merely to stand mutely and stare?" he asked again, amusement entering his tone and eyes. "It is ever a pleasure to look upon you, wench, yet if you have come to speak with me, I would have you do so."

He stood patiently awaiting what words I would utter, seeing something of the difficulty those words bred within me. Ceralt had commanded that I offer myself to him, and this was the difficulty that I faced. Not that Telion was to have me, but that the having would be by Ceralt's will and not mine, was what grated upon my pride. Too, the feelings engendered by my lack of clothing underscored the place Ceralt wished me to have: not that of a warrior seeking pleasure of her own, but of a mere female, begging the gift of manhood for her femaleness. My hands came together about my life sign, and my eyes sought the lanthay fur beneath my feet, the better to avoid Telion's calm gaze. Undoubtedly I would have stood so till I was forsworn, had Telion's hand not come to my chin to raise my face.

"I believe I know the purpose of your presence," he murmured, his strong fingers seeing that my eyes looked up to his. "Say the words, satya, and do not count the shame. Soon all sense of shame will be gone from you."

There was little comfort in such assurance, indeed the thought brought bitter laughter. What other thing than shame might a warrior find among males, even with such males as Telion? I released my life sign and stood somewhat straighter, yet still found the need to look upward toward Telion.

"I have come to ask that I be allowed to serve you," I forced myself to say, knowing that the choice of words would please Ceralt, and perhaps Telion as well. "Should you wish it, my use is yours."

Telion continued to hold my face in his hand, and a faint smile touched his lips. "I am able to find no fault with the words," he murmured, "yet the feelings behind them seem less amenable than they should be. I will, however, respond only to the words, for a man without his woman is a man in great need."

Telion released my face then, and busied his hands with removing his swordbelt and breech. I stood quietly before him, nearly resigned to my lot while I dwelt among males, and was somewhat startled when his arms drew me to his chest rather than immediately putting me to my back.

"You are indeed a lovely morsel," he said, touching his lips lightly to mine. "But for the shining black, your hair is much the same as Larid's. I find much joy in your hair and hers. As I am unable to have her beside me, I thank the Serene Oneness that it is you who warms her place. She, too, I know, would be grateful."

He took a deeper kiss then, and one so full of desire that my head turned with dizziness. Telion was truly a male fit for warriors, and was deep within me even before I had realized that he had lowered me to the fur. The pleasure he gave was intense but brief, for his name was called from without the tent when he had barely begun, and he made haste to satisfy his need before leaving me. With the spilling of his seed, his lips came to mine again, and then to my ear.

"There is no shame in giving a man pleasure," he whispered rapidly, the smell of him strong in my nostrils. "It is a woman's purpose, along with the bearing of his children. Learn this well, satya, and take joy in the joy you give others."

Again he kissed me, and then he was gone, to replace breech and swordbelt, hurriedly don body furs, and at last depart the tent. I shivered somewhat from the rush of cold air his departure brought, and moved uncomfortably in the furs where he had left me. Telion's desire had been seen to, yet mine growled hungry within me, aroused and scarcely touched. There was little joy to be found in such brevity of use, and I twisted about in the furs, commanding my hips to be still, finding myself disregarded by my own body. The lanthay fur was warm and soft, and I stretched wide upon it, my arms above my head, my body twisted to one side, the toes of my feet pointed, yet the heat refused to leave me. I raised my head to search for Ceralt, thinking to use his body to satisfy mine, and found Lialt's eyes upon me instead. The male seemed interested in my movement in the fur, and a sudden heaviness within me brought to mind the sure knowledge that Lialt, too, must be served before Ceralt would have me. I turned to my belly and put my cheek to the fur, feeling the same impatience with Lialt that I had always felt, yet unable to move my gaze from where he held it. Lialt, a male, smiled with sudden amusement, and my cheeks grew red as the knowledge which had come to him also visited itself upon me.

"I see she is capable of learning," Lialt laughed, and I knew he spoke to Ceralt. "See how she tries to hide her body, brother. She has learned that she must serve me if I desire her, and therefore seeks to hide herself from my eyes."

"I have always known her capable of learning," Ceralt chuckled beyond my sight as I twisted about in humiliation. "And now the thought comes that she may be taught other things of value upon this journey. I would much enjoy seeing her taught to read, Lialt, and perhaps your efforts would prove to be more fruitful than mine."

"The thing is not difficult," Lialt pronounced, looking at me thoughtfully as I stretched my head about to gaze at Ceralt in protest. I had no desire for this thing called "read," yet Ceralt's face seemed set and determined. Once before I had been forced to such foolishness, and the experience had not been pleasant.

"Reluctant students are often the best when finally reached," Lialt said, seeing my lack of desire. "Come and see this, Jalav, and tell me if it holds meaning for you."

Ceralt gestured briefly that I was to obey Lialt, and once again my fate was sealed. With a deep and weary sigh, I rose from the furs and went to where Lialt lay, seeing that he had moved the sheaf with black strokes so that I might look upon it. The strokes held as little meaning as ever, and knowing full well that I had once been beaten for the utterance said, "The foolishness holds no meaning for any with wit. Males alone find meaning where there is none."

Lialt glanced up at me where I stood, and rather than show the anger I had expected, his eyes were filled with a patience I had not before seen.

"All things have meaning," Lialt said, touching the black strokes gently as he gazed upon them. "In order to learn the meaning of things, one must first learn that there is, indeed, a meaning to be learned. Kneel before the book, wench, and we will begin by teaching you the names and sounds of each of these letters."

Lialt waited until I had knelt where he had indicated, then he sat himself straight beside me to point at various strokes and make odd noises. My repeating these noises seemed to satisfy the male, yet the process went on and on, finding no end. My body's needs had not diminished, and all too soon I found that the nearness of Lialt had indeed increased them to the point where I was barely able to kneel without writhing. Lialt's eyes remained upon the sheaf of strokes, therefore I turned my head to see what Ceralt was about. Had he asked it then, I would surely have begged my use without hesitation.

"You will not find the letters there," Lialt's voice came just as I had noted Ceralt's dozing form. "What is it you wish from my brother?"

I returned my gaze to Lialt and found again that similarity to
Ceralt was not as Ceralt himself. Lialt narrowed his eyes as he
inspected my face, and then some understanding came upon him.
He raised the palm of his hand to rub gently at my breast, and
smiled at the gasp that was torn from me.

"Are you that badly in need?" he murmured, setting my body
aflame with the touch of his hand. "I had thought Telion's use
too brief to see to you, and now you prove the thought true.
Widen your thighs."

I did as he bid, unable to refuse, knowing that I would sooner
have his use than no use at all, shamed by the feeling but unable
to deny it. Lialt was male and I had need of a male, yet
satisfaction was not soon to be mine. Lialt touched me lightly,
seeking and finding the flow of moisture from my body, and
then his hand was gone.

"When you have learned the names and sounds of three
letters, I will use you," he informed me, a grin strong upon his
face. "Until then, the lesson will continue, and should your
attention flag, I will increase it."

He returned then to the strokes and their calling, and I moaned
where I knelt, knowing full well that Lialt might easily have me
writhing should it suit him, for he was male and I was chained
by my need. A desperation had entered me, centering about his
promised use, forcing my attention to the strokes he pointed to,
yet I feared that all effort would be useless. Again and again I
sought meaning in the meaningless, and when the strength of my
seeking grew fainter than it had been, Lialt's hand between my
thighs renewed the desperation and the effort. At last, most
likely through the intervention of Mida, some small similarity for
certain of the strokes appeared to my eye, and Lialt pronounced
himself satisfied with my learning. Weakly, nearly sobbing, I
was taken in Lialt's arms, and my hunger was such that Lialt
was long in the seeing to it. Ceralt was again awake when Lialt
left me, and I was sent to his furs as he saw to the flames within
the boxes. I knew not where I would find the strength to serve
Ceralt's needs, yet the question was seen to of itself. Ceralt had
the strength to tend his own needs, and my body, as always, was
his to command. Ceralt commanded, I obeyed, and sleep was
long in coming.

# 14.

## A place of meeting—
## and an exchange of slaves

Although the snow had ceased before attaining too great a depth, riding the next fey proved more difficult than it had previously. The lanthay plowed through the mounds, sometimes jumping from one place to another, and more than one of the village females had to be seated behind a male to keep her from falling to the snow. Our progress was slow until we reached a rising of the ground, and then we were able to continue more easily, for it seemed the snow lay to a lesser depth there. None seemed pleased by the presence of new snow, and Lialt looked constantly upon the deep gray of the skies, his worry clear to any with eyes. Should the snow come again, and in larger quantity, the journey so eagerly begun might well end no farther than the woods we rode.

When Lialt rode ahead to join Ceralt, Telion came forward to pace his lanthay beside mine, saying no word yet looking upon me with satisfaction. With the arrival of the new light, Telion had requested my use from Ceralt, saying that thoughts of Larid during the darkness had rendered him nearly unable to ride. Ceralt had commiserated with the other male's need, yet had shocked me by pronouncing the decision mine. It would not always be mine to decide, he had said, yet at that moment, my use was mine to give or keep. Telion had turned calm eyes upon me, unangered by Ceralt's decision, and all had watched me closely for my decision. There was little to think upon in the matter, for I did not wish Telion's use, yet I was not given time to voice this decision. Telion, perhaps seeing the thoughts of a war leader in my eyes, quickly took me in his arms, saying he would allow me longer to think upon the thing, and then put his lips upon mine. Filled with indignation, I sought to free myself, yet amid the laughter of Ceralt and Lialt, Telion had little difficulty calling forth the heat in me. The decision which was to be mine then became a raging need, much to the satisfaction of Telion, who then saw well to his own need. With his hands and lips upon me, I had not been able to deny him, and thought of this disturbed me more than having been forced to his service. Was it not solely Ceralt but all males to whom my body was enslaved? Would there come a fey when I found myself unable to deny any of them? If this were so, what then would become of her who had once been a war leader of Hosta? Seated upon my lanthay, I shivered as though from the cold, yet the cold had come no farther through my leathers and furs than ever.

A short, thin gust of wind blew, seemingly alone in the area between the trees, stirring the cold and the fur of my lanthay, passing well below the motionless roof of gray in the skies. All Midanna knew that the stronger the wind, the sooner the change from fair skies to foul or foul to fair, and apparently the lands of males saw the thing the same. Mida had sent no wind to rid her skies of the grayness of clouds, and these clouds would stay above our heads till they had emptied all within them upon us.

"For a journey demanded by the gods," remarked Telion from beside me, "there seems to be little from them in the way of approval. We are barely able to travel now, yet further snow is a constant threat. Perhaps they merely wish to amuse themselves watching us founder beneath a sea of white."

The male gazed sourly upon the skies so close above us, one hand holding to his lanthay's rein, the other hand twisted within the lanthay's neck fur. Telion continued to yearn for the leather seat left behind upon his kan, and sat his current mount with little more confidence than the females of the village. I smiled at his discomfort for I felt none of it myself, and his satisfaction with his earlier actions dimmed to annoyance.

"There is little call for such smugness," he growled. "Though you ride that beast as though born to it, should the rest of us founder you, too, will cease to be."

"This set is not meant to founder," I replied, too pleased with the male's annoyance to allow it to fade. "Mida, too, speaks of the journey as necessary, therefore shall it be completed. Once completed, I shall continue in her service for I am not yet done with it."

Telion turned his head sharply to gaze upon me, and frowned in a way that seemed to have little to do with his previous annoyance.

"Again you speak of your Mida," said he, his tone displeased. "Does she continue to walk your dreams as she did upon that first instance? When will you learn that Ceralt has taken you from such things, and that they need no longer trouble you?"

Strangely, his displeasure seemed more for Mida than myself, yet his understanding was far from complete.

"That Ceralt has captured me is of no moment to Mida," said I, attempting to show him the right of it. "It is her will that I travel with this set, and it shall be her will when I am freed from it. There is a thing I must do for her, yet she was not spoken of what the thing might be."

The male's eyes turned cold, and he straightened upon his lanthay. "The only will you need concern yourself with is Ceralt's," he growled, a low, cutting edge to his voice. "It is by Ceralt's will that you ride here, and by his will alone shall you remain. Were he to hear you speak of this Mida again, he would see you soundly punished. Can you not comprehend the fact that you are his, wench? He has taken you and will not allow a return to your former, savage existence!"

Telion had kept his voice low, to disallow its traveling to those who rode before us, yet the strength of his displeasure came to me clearly. He insisted upon seeing me as no more than that which Ceralt wished me to be, and my anger at such a state of affairs loosened my tongue injudiciously.

"So I am his, eh?" I hissed, nearly spitting the words at him. "For how long am I to be his? Till he is struck down at this journey's end? And then to whom am I to belong? Pah! The plottings of males disgust me!"

Telion drew back from the blaze of my anger, a stricken look upon his face where once his own anger showed. I turned my eyes from him, studying the backs of those who rode before us in an attempt to calm myself, and his hand and voice came to me unexpectedly.

"Jalav, you were not to know that," he protested, his hand tightening about my arm. "Ceralt wished you to remain ignorant of the possibility to spare you unnecessary pain. There is ever the chance that he might live."

"How great a chance?" I demanded, turning again to rake him with the blaze of my eyes. "As he accepts the matter as though it were the will of Mida, how great can be the possibility of his survival? Have males no sense of rightness that they ride to their deaths with joyous acceptance in their hearts? Should death come to a warrior, she will accept it happily for it is her means of attaining Mida's Blessed realm, yet she will not seek it when it is not required of her!"

"Ceralt does not seek his death!" Telion growled, fingers tightening to an even greater degree. He no longer appeared stricken, and his anger had returned in full measure. "Women have no knowledge of man's ways, of the manner in which his thoughts turn. Ceralt will not seek to avoid his lot, for should he succeed in doing so, all those about him would lose their lives in his stead. Only by completing this journey and chancing his own ending might he avoid the fate so clearly seen for his people. And you are not to speak to him of this, for it would serve only to increase the burdens already upon him. Are my words clear to you, wench?"

I looked upon Telion, he who had seemed so concerned with my anger, he who had once seemed so pleased with a warrior's prowess. Had I expected a request from him to aid in the defense of Ceralt's life, my expectations would have come to naught. Wench, he called me, helpless female who was to obey all males, one whose sword was unwelcome among those of males. Ceralt had wrought well among his brothers, degrading me to them, yet his work had not been as successful with himself. Why, if I were no more than a female in his eyes, was his concern so great lest I seek vengeance for his death? Does one fear the vengeance of a city female in the same manner as one fears the vengeance of a warrior and war leader? Ceralt felt no desire to unleash my fury, yet Telion had forgotten the strength of it. In anger, I kicked at the side of Telion's lanthay, causing the unsuspecting beast to snort and rear, and Telion hastily removed his hand from my arm to grab at the lanthay's neck fur. In such a manner did I answer the demand he had put to me, and I allowed my dancing lanthay to increase its pace so that we might close the gap which had grown between us and those ahead of us. The breath came white from my lanthay's nostrils, as white as from mine, and the snow crunched beneath its hooves as we left Telion and his indignant mount in our wake. The male was not thrown as he might have been, and a moment or two later found him again at my side, yet the words were gone from him and no new demands were addressed to me. I made no attempt to look upon him, yet his silence suggested that he had found the understanding previously spoken of.

The new light had not yet reached its highest when we entered a large clearing. The clearing, ringed with tall, bare trees all about, seemed sufficient for twice our number and more, yet it was there the males halted and began seeing to the unburdening of the mounts. The females, freed from the need for further riding, dismounted quickly, handed over the reins of their lanthay, and moved away from the activity of the males. Their assistance was not required in the erecting of the tents, and the males preferred having them where their presence would not be a hindrance. Despite the threatening gray so close above their heads, the females laughed gaily as they took themselves across the clearing, some few attempting to run in the deep, unmarked snow. I watched them from the height of my lanthay's back, attempting to fathom the meaning of their lightheartedness. Perhaps they had no knowledge of the gravity of the quest we rode upon, the gravity which kept their males from the same gaiety, or perhaps they lacked the sense to appreciate such gravity. I knew not which the answer might be, yet I knew that warriors, in their place, would not have done the same.

"A wench should have the company of other wenches, Ceralt," came Telion's voice from behind me. "How is she to learn to be as they if she is ever kept from their midst?"

I turned to see Telion and Ceralt regarding me, they having dismounted from their lanthay and having tied them. Telion stood with arms afold across his chest, an unreadable expression upon his face, yet his eyes held a remembrance of anger and disapproval. Ceralt, beside him, regarded me with brows drawn together, and his head nodded in agreement.

"I fear you have the right of it, brother," Ceralt pronounced, self-annoyance tinging his tone. "How indeed is she to learn a woman's ways when her constant companions are men? Men may teach a woman her womanhood, yet womanly ways are taught by women."

He came close to the side of my lanthay, then, and his hands at my waist took me from my mount and stood me before him. I had not released the lanthay's rein, and as it jumped from our sides, Ceralt's hand shot out to halt it, at the same time pulling the rein from my grip.

"I will see to the care of your lanthay," he informed me, gazing down upon me with a softness to the light of his eyes.

"Take yourself now to the other wenches, and learn what you may from their doings. I should have seen to this much the sooner."

I attempted protest, yet such an attempt was futile. Telion, in deep concern over my welfare, urged Ceralt to discount my "shyness" with other females, a shyness which had kept me from joining their ranks sooner. The male knew well enough my thoughts upon city females, yet sought to send me to their midst for purposes of his own. Ceralt saw no covert reasons in Telion's arguments, therefore was I soon sent upon my way, Ceralt's demands for obedience ringing in my ears.

The deep snow left very little doubt as to the direction taken by the females, a thing which soured me further. Midanna are taught to leave no track which an enemy might come upon and follow, yet even Midanna would be hard put to see to the thing in the treacherous medium termed snow. Little need was there to aid any tracker with as many prints as the females had left, yet they had proceeded to leave the full story of their passage upon the ground. It came to me to wonder if those males who hunted each new light to fill the set's needs also left such an abundance of evidence as to their presence. If so, game would soon be scarce indeed.

The females were not far ahead, yet a large bush, made larger through being heavily laden with snow, kept them from my sight till I was nearly upon them. I rounded the bush, concerned with keeping my footing in the slick unevenness left by those who had gone before, then stopped abruptly to stare at the sight which met my eyes.

All of the females of the traveling set had rounded the bush, even she who was known as Famira. This was easily seen as it was she who knelt in the snow beyond the line of other females, her head covered by her arms, her body bent forward to protect her face, all of her shaking to the pelting of snow which rained upon her from the other females. The attackers laughed and shouted as they threw what was between their gloves, then bent to the ground at their feet and grasped a renewed supply of their chosen weapon. Not all threw at once, nor did all bend at once, therefore an almost constant pelting fell upon their sole target. In typical, empty-headed lack of vigilance, none heard my approach as all concerned were too enwrapped in jumping about joyfully and laughing in delight. I halted perhaps three paces from the backs they presented me, feeling the increased damp-

ness in the air from their disturbance of the snow, and folded my
arms in deep disgust.

"What do you do here?" I demanded angrily, watching as their
laughter ceased and they spun quickly to look upon me, guilt
and fear writ large upon their faces. How like all city females
they were, pleased to do a thing yet shamed when found doing
it. One or two nearly tumbled to the churned up snow, so rapidly
did they turn, yet the others quickly repented their fear and
startlement, and anger took its place.

"Why do you sneak about behind us?" one of the females
demanded in turn, brushing a stray lock of dark hair from her
eyes. "We do no more than that which we have longed to do for
many kalod! It is more your place to join us than condemn us!"

"I grow weary of being told what place is mine!" I returned,
straightening even further before the eyes of these females. "Never
have I found the need to hide behind numbers when facing a
single opponent! Should you wish to see to revenging some past
injury done you, face your enemy with dignity and with like
meeting like. For many to fall upon one demeans your motives
as well as your actions."

The females cared little for my words, and muttered angrily
among themselves as I looked upon them. Some few appeared to
be considering the merits in pelting me with snow as they had
done with Famira, yet I, with legs spread wide and arms afold,
was no easy victim for their wrath. Should they be foolish
enough to attempt the deed, they would soon discover the difference between a wench and a warrior.

The bite of the cold was sharp upon all of us, and the females
before me had had the joy taken out of their doings. She who
had spoken tossed her head as though discounting my words,
then all began to return as they had come, filing past me with
baleful looks for me and venomous ones for the female Famira.
She called Famira rose slowly to her feet, her gloved hands
brushing at the snow which covered her, her eyes upon the backs
of her departing attackers. When all of the females had slowly
rounded the bush and vanished from sight, Famira turned her
eyes to me.

"And what of you?" she called, her voice edged with bitterness.
"Do you come now to avenge previous wrongs? Your weakness
meant naught to me when we first faced one another. Come and
take what you feel is due you and have done with it!"

She stood and faced me, trembling slightly with anger, perhaps even with disgust at the actions of those about her. She had

little fear of that which I might do to her, seemingly looked upon it as merely another burden which must be borne, another indignity to be suffered before it might be forgotten. I returned the look she gave me with something of a smile, knowing a loss that she might no longer be considered an enemy. Famira the village female would have been an excellent enemy.

I turned from the lone female without speaking and reentered the area of churned up snow which had been produced by the other females in their return to the camp. Rounding the bush showed that they had nearly reached the now erected tents, therefore did I give attention to my footing till I had done the same. Ceralt and Telion saw to the unburdening and tying of the lanthay, a thing which was nearly done, and as I approached, the males bent curious gazes upon me.

"Your time among the other wenches was not of considerable duration," said Ceralt as I neared him, his hand astroke upon the lanthay he tended. "There could not have been much gained in such a brief interlude."

"Indeed," agreed Telion from where he stood among packs, perhaps three paces away. "She was to have learned from the other wenches, not merely nodded to them in passing. She will require further time among them to learn."

Telion's eyes were upon me as he spoke, his face as clear of expression as his gaze was not. He continued to seek difficulty for me, perhaps in revenge for that which I had done earlier, yet his methods were unpalatable. Had he wished to face me with weapons, he should have done so.

"And yet I have learned a thing," said I to Telion before Ceralt might speak. "For one who observes, there is ever a new thing to be learned."

"This I do not believe," scoffed Telion with a look of derision. "There is naught which might have been learned."

"Perhaps we should ask what this thing might be," said Ceralt as I stiffened with insult at Telion's words. To say that a warrior spoke other than the truth was to say that a challenge has been offered.

"It can be naught save the imagination of a female," said Telion, folding his arms. "Yet am I willing to be shown."

Ceralt seemed puzzled by Telion, yet his light-eyed gaze came to me with a smile. "You may show us that which you have learned, satya," said he, attempting to lighten my anger. He saw full well how I stood in the snow, a pace from him, my body filled with the desire to wipe insult from me. Telion stood as he had, arms afold upon his chest, doubt writ large upon his face, and I could not have refrained from acting had the safety of my very soul been in question. Rapidly, I bent to the snow at my feet and grasped two handfuls of the stuff, patted them together in the shape of a sphere as I had seen the village females do, then hurled the sphere toward Telion's head. The village females had thrown as all village females do, poorly and with little skill, yet I, as a warrior and war leader, had great skill in the throwing of rocks, which is no more than a child's game. Telion attempted to evade the throw by moving to his left, yet I had anticipated such a movement and had allowed for it. The sphere of snow struck full in the male's face as he cried out in anger and dismay, his cry mingled with that of Ceralt, who jumped quickly to my side to prevent the grasping of further snow. I had fully expected Ceralt to be filled with great anger, perhaps so great as to beat me, yet the male laughed in full amusement as he kept me from further snow, his arms about me to hold me still. Telion brushed the snow from him with loud curses as Ceralt and I watched, and when his eyes were once again able to see, he sent to me a look so black that Ceralt laughed the harder to see it.

"You see she spoke the truth, brother," he called to Telion, amusement rolling about his words. "There seems to be no need to punish her for lying."

"Ceralt, you must allow me to give her a hiding for this," Telion growled, his flesh reddened where the sphere of snow had touched. He stood to his full height, indignation all about him, traces of snow clinging here and there to his furs and hair. Telion had long been eager to use his leather upon me, and now, at last, his wish was to be fulfilled. I stood in Ceralt's grasp and awaited his utterance of approval, knowing how well he thought of the punishment, yet his decision, when voiced, brought greater surprise to me than to the other male.

"I shall not allow it, Telion," said he, his voice soft as he looked upon the male called warrior. "Her punishment is mine to mete out, and I do not feel that she has earned punishment. Was she not ordered to show that which she had learned?"

"Certainly," protested Telion, "yet—" His words broke off in great frustration, as though he were unable to support the stand he had taken, and I looked up at the male who held me so close to him. His eyes came down to meet mine, a familiar softness therein, and the cold of the fey seemed to recede behind the warmth his gaze sent. Why had he not allowed Telion his will? I wondered, but could not bring the words forth to question

him. Did he merely wish to do the thing himself? This did not
seem to be the case, yet I knew not what to make of his strange
decision.

"In future I shall first ask for a description from you," said
Ceralt, again amused. "Your eye and arm are far too good for
the safety of those around you, therefore are you forbidden to
throw snow in such a manner again. Do you understand?"

I nodded mutely, understanding his words rather than what lay
behind them, and his smile increased.

"Good," said he, his arms briefly tightening about me. "Now
take yourself into the tent and prepare our mid-fey meal. Cold
increases a man's appetite, and I look forward to something
other than our usual cold mid-fey meal."

He urged me from him then and toward the tent, he himself
returning to the lanthay he had been seeing to. I walked from
him slowly, barely seeing Telion as I passed him, barely aware
of the curious look the male warrior sent to me. Why had Ceralt
not allowed Telion to beat me? Why had he not beaten me
himself? The doings of males are strange to a warrior's thinking,
yet Ceralt continued to do that which was stranger than any of
the others. Why did he look upon me as he did—and how would
he look upon me when Mida had freed me from his capture?

Entering the tent was something of a distraction from the
turmoil of my thoughts. Though I had expected to see Lialt
within, perhaps engaged in the activity termed "reading," the
tent held naught save that which it always held, a heat rising
from the coals which had been set aglow. I removed my leg
coverings and body furs beside the tent entrance, yet the heat to
be found within the tent made my leather coverings unnecessary
as well. I hesitated as I looked about the tent, yet there was no
reason to retain coverings which had become unnecessary. It was
possible that the males would dislike my having divested myself
of garments without having been ordered to do so, yet the matter
seemed of small consequence. There was little they might do which
had not already been done, and who knew how much longer I
would be burdened with their presence? Perhaps Mida would act
that very fey to free me, and I need then no longer concern
myself with them. Having made the decision, I quickly removed
all save the breech about my middle, then saw to warming the
meat which had already been previously cooked.

The three males entered a short time later, each eager to
partake of their sustenance. Lialt chuckled as Ceralt told him of
Telion's mishap with a sphere of snow, and Telion, though still

annoyed at the incident, was also coaxed into a chuckle. The males looked upon me as I stood beside the metal holder of glowing coals, a metal rod in my hand, yet none spoke of my lack of covering. Perhaps the sight of Jalav pleased them, and they thought themselves more fully served having her so. Each showed familiar heat when looking upon me, yet this, too, was unmentioned.

With the males seated and served their meat, Ceralt, predictably, knelt me beside him. I was served from his board as always, and with all of the meat consumed, was also taken in his arms. It was then that I was reminded of that which I had been bidden to say to him, words not easily spoken by a warrior. His arms held me to the warmth of his bare chest, his eyes looked deeply into mine, and the weakness which was the curse of his nearness settled again upon me, to thin my voice to a whisper and put tremors within my body. I forced the required words from my throat, tripping upon them, then raised my lips to my captor, trembling as I awaited the touch of his own lips. How helpless a warrior feels so, held in the arms of a male, awaiting the touch of his lips which will further drain her strength. Ceralt looked upon me as he held me so, a fierceness in the light eyes of him, a greater strength than ever in his arms.

"You are mine and shall be so forever," he whispered as though pronouncing a blood oath. "Woman, do not forget the words I speak to you."

And then his lips took mine, crushing them with the strength of his desire, making my head swim. I clung to the arms of him, knowing there was naught I might do to halt his desire, knowing too that there was naught I wished to do. My body burned where his hands touched my flesh, and I writhed in his lap, consumed by the need he had brought upon me. So quickly and easily was my enslaved body made his, captured more surely than by the points of spears, held more tightly than by the weight of chains. I moaned as I twisted about against him, feeling the strength of his awakened manhood upon my body, fearing that he would laugh and push me from him as he had done other times. My fears were unfounded, however, for Ceralt's need raged as high as mine. The breech was torn away from my body, and then I was thrust to the lanthay fur and entered so strongly that a gasp was forced from me. Ceralt's body drove at mine, causing me to cry out even as I rose to him, and it was many reckid before the storm passed from him. At last I lay in his arms, still in his possession, knowing that had I not been told of Mida's wishes, I would indeed have considered myself his. The smell of him was strong upon me, marking me his as clearly as his presence within me, and had it not been contrary to the way of Midanna, I would have wept for the loss which would be mine. Ceralt would be taken from me, likely by Mida's will, and should that be so, there was naught I might do for it.

"She has truly become much of a woman, brother," came Lialt's voice from above me. I raised my eyes to see that he studied me openly with a grin, Telion also agrin by his side. "I look forward to my use of her this darkness," said he.

"I, too, feel so," agreed Telion, resting his arm upon Lialt's shoulder, silent laughter in his eyes. "Such use is greatly preferable to the hiding I had wished to give her."

The two males stood gazing down upon me, and Ceralt's eyes joining theirs in appraisal. "Is this what you wish, wench?" asked Ceralt most softly, his right hand gently rubbing at my breast, his light eyes soberly upon me. "Should it be contrary to your desire, I must hear words from you."

The lanthay fur beneath my back was not the best of resting places, for as I writhed somewhat to the stroke of Ceralt's hand and the throb of his strengthening presence, the fur seemed to whisper weakness to me, greater weakness than I had yet felt. Ask to be kept as his alone, whispered the fur, stroking my bottom as my hips began to move. Beg him to keep you from the others, it urged, tangling gently with my hair where it lay crushed beneath me. Ceralt slid slowly about within me, forcing a moan from my lips, his gaze becoming more demanding, yet I could not speak such words. Lialt and Telion watched with amusement as Ceralt extracted slave-due from the once mighty Jalav, and to add to the humiliation of such a state was beyond me.

"I cannot," I whispered to Ceralt, agonized to my soul. I knew he would leave me with need full upon me, yet I could do no other than as I did. I awaited his withdrawal, awaited the aching emptiness, yet it was not to be. A sadness touched the broad, strong face of him, and then his lips came briefly to mine.

"Patience will see it done," he murmured, more to himself than to any other. "The fey will come, and upon that fey I will be there."

Then he held me more tightly in his arms and saw to the need of both of us. It must surely be the doing of Mida that thought is impossible at such a time, for had it not been so, I would have spent the pleasure in demands for understanding. When he left

me at last and stood to see to his leathers, I lay upon the lanthay
fur, still held by the memory of his use. So strong was this
Ceralt, so filled with satisfaction for a warrior. Ah, Mida. Do
you take him so that he might be brought to your Blessed Realm
for your own use? If so, your war leader bids caution. This male
is one who might find the means to enslave a goddess.

"You have rendered her useless, Ceralt," came Lialt's voice,
more mockery than annoyance therein. "I had hoped to give her
a reading lesson, and now it must wait till her mind returns to
govern her flesh."

Lialt's words and the laughter of the other males came to me
where I lay in the fur, yet I felt no shame at the way I stretched
and wiggled about. Ceralt was a male like no other, and the
pleasure he gave belonged to a warrior. I rubbed my face and
body in the lanthay fur and smiled my satisfaction, and each of
the males laughed even further.

"She seems to find little disappointment in the loss of a
lesson," chuckled Ceralt, replacing his leather body covering.
"It would indeed be futile to attempt teaching her now, yet the
matter may be seen to later. Hannil and the others may not arrive
till darkness has fallen."

"We are as prepared as possible," said Lialt, the laughter
having left him. "Should the skies refrain from burying us in
snow, we shall be able to begin the balance of the journey with
the new light."

"There are a number of things we must discuss before Hannil's
arrival," said Ceralt, going toward his body furs at the tent's
entrance. "Walk with me, brothers, and give me your thoughts
to add to mine."

The males each donned body furs and left the tent, thinking no
more of the female who lay naked in the fur, she who had been
made to writhe to a male. There were weightier matters to
concern males than a female who had been used and left, and I
sat up bitterly, no longer in the grasp of pleasure. How was such
dismissal accepted by village females? Had they no pride, no
sense of self, that they lived no farther in the world than the
shadow of their males? Was I, war leader of the Hosta, foremost
of all the clans of Midanna, to accept such dismissal in a similar
way? A growl came to my throat and I rose to my feet to find
and replace the breech Ceralt had torn from me. To live with no
purpose in life was to live not at all, yet I had purpose aplenty
before me. Mida had spoken, and I would ride in the cause she
wished to see me tend to, and then would males be dismissed

from *my* thoughts. I put my hand to my hair and rubbed at the scalp, easing the place where Ceralt's grip upon my hair had been so tight, then turned to the clearing away of the boards which had been fed from. My thoughts turned to the males who had served *me*, and the grimness dropped slowly from mind.

The boards had been cleaned and returned to their places when there was movement at the tent entrance. I had been considering dressing and going forth into the cold once more, to walk about in the snow and lose myself to my thoughts, when the tent flap moved aside and she called Famira entered. I knew not why she should be there, yet the tent was not mine to defend against intrusion. The village female stood no more than a step within, her face flushed from the cold of the fey, her eyes startled as she took in my form, clad in no more than leather breech. I cared little for her or her startlement, yet when I failed to address her, she took it upon herself to begin.

"I would enter and speak with you," she said, the words coming slowly and with difficulty. Her hand brushed the hood from her head, and she looked upon me squarely, her gaze not avoiding mine.

"You have entered," I returned, standing straight and folding my arms beneath my life sign. "You are also speaking."

"Why must you make this so difficult?" she demanded, taking one short step forward. "I came to ask why you have refrained from doing as the others do. Why have you not taken vengeance for what was done to you? Do you mean to await your opportunity, or do you fear me?"

I could not help but smile at the thought of a war leader of Mida fearing a village slave-woman, and then the smile turned to laughter as Famira frowned. The female knew the look of herself, and even in her fur leg wrappings she stood to less of a height than Jalav. My strength was greater than hers, my skill was greater than hers, and I laughed at the audacity of the thought she had voiced. Had she been a warrior, the matter might have been near to a challenge and therefore naught to laugh at, yet she was not a warrior. I laughed as one laughs at a child, and Famira felt the barb and flushed deeply.

"So you do not fear me!" she snapped, pulling open the fur body covering her. "I had not realized how much like the men you are, looking down upon all who are not one of you! Yet you have not replied to my question. Why have you not sought me out to take vengeance?"

"One seeks vengeance from enemies who are as they were

when the insult was first given," said I, frowning at the words she had spoken. I, likened to the males? How might my actions be like those of the males?

"And I am no longer as I was," said Famira, the bitterness a great part of her. She removed the furs from her body, sat to remove her leg coverings, then stood again in naught save her leathers. Her eyes were filled with pain as she looked about herself, and a short, mirthless laugh came forth from her.

"Ceralt's tent and Ceralt's belongings," said she, walking forward to place her hand upon a leather pack. "I would know Ceralt's things anywhere." Her eyes left the pack and came to me, and an odd smile turned the corners of her lips. "Would you have the truth?" she asked, her manner strange in its friendliness. "Never have I had the wish to be drawn from the circle by Ceralt, yet I thought that to be Ceralt's woman would secure the place I had made for myself among the others of the village. Ceralt is a beast, Jalav, and I do not envy you your place with him, for I know now that he would not have allowed me a place above others. He would have used me even more brutally and casually than Cimilan does, and I would have had no more than I have now to show for it. All that I had is lost to me, and was destined to be lost from the first."

Her voice emptied of the unnatural lightness it had had as she turned her back and bent her head, grief filling her at the sight of her dreams crumbled to ruins about her feet. Her shoulders shook as she struggled to keep from falling to tears, and I recalled the similar plight of a would-be warrior of mine, one who had been taken bound in leather to the dwellings of males, there to be left to be made a slave-woman of males. The young warrior had fought the leather and the hands of males upon her, and then had turned desperate eyes to me where I sat upon my gando.

"War leader, do not abandon me here!" she had cried, a great fear filling her. "I do not wish to lose my place among you!"

"You have no place among the Hosta," I had told her, signaling my warriors to prepare to depart. "You left the cleaning and sharpening of your sword to those who were younger than you; you walked the woods in pleasure and ate berries while others hunted; you lagged behind in battle till the enemy was vanquished, then strode forth to bloody your sword in the body of one already slain. You are not a warrior but a hanger-on, a slave-female fit for naught save the bidding of males. Rejoice that we leave you with males rather than send you to face the wrath of Mida.''

"Oh, Mida, why have you taken your shield from me?" she had cried as we turned and left her to be seen to by the males of the village. She had not understood, as Famira failed to understand, yet perhaps Famira might be made to understand.

"There was naught ever in your possession to be lost to you," I said to the village female before me, causing her head to come up. "How is one to mourn the loss of a thing one has never possessed?"

"How can you speak so?" she demanded, whirling angrily to face me, her small hands closed to fists. "All in the village stepped back from my path when I walked among them! All looked upon me and knew me as their better! None dared stand to face me, and no single rider offered me the insult of his smile! Is this your concept of naught to be lost?"

"I know only that which I have heard," I shrugged, regarding her anger coolly. "The other females kept from your path out of fear of he whom Ceralt named Uncle, a male, I gather, of some note in the village. The males, those termed riders, kept their smiles from you in the belief that Ceralt wished to claim you as his own. In each instance, fear of another gave a false belief to you, a belief that it was you who generated their subservience. Such a state is not a true position of leadership, as you have already learned to your sorrow. Do you wish to deny the contention?"

Her lips parted angrily, as though to retort, yet suddenly the anger went from her and she again bowed her head. "To deny the truth would be foolish," she said, a deep sigh taking her. "You, who stand beneath the leather of Ceralt, command the awe and fear of the other women simply by being as you are. They see, as I do, a power and presence within you, having naught to do with the actions of others. I have even heard a rider say that he would not care to face you with sword in hand." Her head lifted and her eyes found mine, and a reluctant truth entered her tone. "I greatly feared that you would come to repay the pain I gave you, yet I found myself unable to sit about and await its coming. Sooner would I have had the pain than the fear of its arrival."

Again I smiled at her words, yet this time in approval. Only a fool and coward chooses to run from that which she has earned by her own hand, and whatever else she might be, Famira seemed no coward.

"I had thought you ill when Ceralt first brought you to the village," said Famira, watching as I sat myself cross-legged upon the lanthay fur. After a brief hesitation, she seated herself as I had, and when no words of rebuke came from me for her liberty, her face and eyes grew calmer. "These marks that I see upon your body," she said, "was it that which caused your infirmity?"

"Indeed." I nodded, touching the track of a Silla spear. "I have been allowed my life so that I may do the will of Mida, yet should she be pleased with my efforts, I may also be allowed the pleasure of once more facing she who caused these wounds to be given me. Then we shall see whose lifeblood flows to the ground beneath our feet."

I had spoken casually, merely voicing an oft-repeated prayer to Mida, yet Famira shivered and wrapped her arms about herself.

"Had I known what I know now," she breathed, eyes wide, "never would I have approached you, not to speak of knocking you down. Tell me what befell you, Jalav, and tell me of this other who caused such terrible wounds."

She seemed full eager to hear the tale, yet I wondered if she asked because she wished to know, or if it were merely loneliness for the company of another which prompted her curiosity. I had rarely had the time to speak with any save those warriors who seconded me and Rilas, Keeper of the Clans, yet in the place of males, there was little to do other than spend one's time in idle chatter. Inwardly I shrugged, knowing I was not kept from more important matters, and began the tale which Famira had requested. She was not one such as Tarla, however, and the end of the tale brought strong anger to the female before me.

"Such cowardly actions, Jalav!" she fumed, nearly taken completely by indignation. "That they would do such a thing to a lone woman is despicable!"

"They are Silla." I smiled, amused at her indignation. "They knew full well that it was a war leader they faced, not a slave-woman who might be looked down upon. Had I had the strength to reach the sword, the Silla's blood would have joined mine upon the ground. It is the manner in which one gives an enemy the chance to die as a warrior should."

"It is a horrible thing," said Famira, "and yet it seems kinder than the ways of the men of my village. Your Silla offer the means to death with dignity, yet the men of the village offer no such easy escape. A woman among them must suffer and continue to live, to serve them and their vile lusts!"

The female's eyes burned bright, hatred clear in the lines of her face, and I wondered at the thoughts she voiced. Had she been used so harshly and constantly that she now loathed the touch of a male? Such things were not unknown, and I thought of he named Cimilan, the male who had claimed her. His first use of Famira had been spoken of by the females in the village, yet none had mentioned what other things he had done. It was my intention to broach the subject, for I had not forgotten my time with the male Nolthis, yet before I might speak of it, Ceralt entered the tent, followed by this very same Cimilan. I rose to my feet at their appearance, yet Famira nearly flew erect, rage coloring her features.

"Am I to be followed wherever I go?" she demanded, her dark eyes blazing upon a frowning Cimilan. "Why will you not leave me be? Can you not see how unwelcome your presence is?"

"Famira, do not speak so," said this Cimilan, putting a hand out toward her. His face wore a look of pained embarrassment, yet the gesture was one of placation.

"I shall speak as I will!" snapped Famira, rounding Cimilan's outstretched hand to take her fur leg coverings and don them. She donned her body covering as well and then left the tent, sparing the male no whit of a glance. Cimilan's hand dropped wearily to his side, his head hung in misery, and Ceralt could restrain himself no longer.

"By the putrid privates of Sigurr the Dark, what has come over you?" he demanded, the oath fairly flickering in his eyes. His hand went to Cimilan's shoulder, and the second male was made to turn to face him. "What is it that ails you that you would allow your wench to speak to you so?"

The male Cimilan faced his leader in embarrassment, then lowered his eyes and shook his head. "I am able to do naught with her," said he, opening and removing his body fur. "She is beyond what skill I possess, and it is for this reason that I came to speak with you. Shall I free her to be chosen by another, Ceralt? Her hatred of me is clear, and I am unable to placate it."

"Placate it?" Ceralt echoed with a frown, he, too, removing his furs. "I do not recognize the sound of you, Cimilan. Was it not you who said the wench needed little more than a man's hand applied to her arrogance to bring the sweetness flowing from her? How could such sentiments have changed to placation?"

Cimilan shook his head in confusion, then stepped past Ceralt to enter further into the tent. His eyes fell upon me where I, stood, and he halted to inspect me closely, a faint grin eventually finding him.

"She is indeed magnificent, Ceralt," he said, folding his arms as he gazed upon me. "I have heard others say that the mere sight of her is enough to stir a man, and this is surely so. Where do you find the ability to keep your hands from her?"

"I have no need to keep my hands from her," returned Ceralt, coming to stand at Cimilan's side. "The wench is mine and I use her as I please. You continue to cause me worry, Cimilan. Why would a man find it necessary to keep himself from his woman? Seat yourself and tell me of what has so far occurred between you and Famira."

Again Cimilan hesitated, yet Ceralt had turned from him to fetch a skin of near-renth and return with it. I seated myself in the lanthay fur and stretched out upon my left side, yet the male Cimilan seemed no longer aware of me. He accepted the skin Ceralt held out to him, drank deeply from it, then sat himself cross-legged upon the fur. When Ceralt was also seated, he took his eyes from his leader and began the unburdening of his soul.

"I had never thought of myself as unthinkingly cruel," said he, his voice uneven, "yet I have caused Famira pain and terror which I had not meant to be hers. It occurred upon the occasion of my carrying her to her father's halyar, the very darkness I drew her from the circle. Ceralt, I was a fool, for I drank from the second skin knowing that she had yet to be opened. I have had women aplenty and have even opened a few, yet never have I seen such screaming and such blood. The drug blinded me to all save the need within me, and it took the coming of the new light to show me what I had done."

The male sat with head down, fist buried in the fur before him, voice bitter with shameful memory. Ceralt looked upon him as he listened, no sign of condemnation appearing in accusation. A brief silence filled the tent, as though Cimilan looked again upon the scenes of which he spoke, and then his resolute words continued.

"She lay in exhausted sleep," said he, "covered with the blood which my use had brought to her. I recalled the pain she had had, the terror she had known, saw how small and helpless she appeared in the thinness of the new light. I knelt above her for many reckid, reviling myself and my thoughtlessness, knowing how deep my love for her was, cursing the continued absence of her father, who should have been present to condemn me. She and I were alone in the halyar, and then she stirred, moaning in pain and beginning to weep. I quickly gathered her up, wrapped in furs, and carried her to the bathing halyar, where I washed the blood from her and smoothed in soothing salves. She thereafter spoke no word to me for more than a fey, at first jumping to obey each thing I said to her, later merely cringing back from even the touch of my hand. The first darkness of our first fey together, she hid herself in a corner of my halyar and screamed when I looked upon her, and I found that I could not force myself upon her. Since that time I have not been able to touch her."

Cimilan's voice had fallen to a whisper, yet even so his disturbance had come through clearly. It puzzled me to reconcile his actions with Famira's words and feelings, yet Ceralt was not puzzled. He continued to look upon the male before him, he who could not meet his leader's eyes, and then Ceralt's hand went to Cimilan's shoulder, squeezing gently in reassurance.

"Cimilan, my friend, you are not a child," said Ceralt, gentleness mixed with mild reproof. "A youth would be fit meat for such a problem; I had not expected to see it binding a man. However," and his voice gained briskness as his hand clapped Cimilan's shoulder, "as the problem is yours, we must solve it for you."

Cimilan's head raised to Ceralt with a frown, and Ceralt grinned a grin I had ofttimes seen before. "Your primary difficulty," said Ceralt, "is that you are not familiar with my cousin and her ways. Have I ever told you of the time she and I were in the woods, and she took a branch and crowned me with it?" Cimilan shook his head, and Ceralt laughed to see the beginnings of outrage upon the other male's face.

"It is true, I assure you," grinned Ceralt. "She was perhaps eight kalod in age, and I thirteen, and I had dismissed her presence behind me till I felt the branch upon my skull, swung with a good deal of energy. She had been insulted by my refusal to take her hunting, and had chosen attack as the means by which to show her displeasure."

"I do not understand," Cimilan protested, his eyes upon Ceralt. "What has that to do with—"

"Patience," counseled Ceralt, holding a hand up before the other. "The point of the story is yet to come. When the ringing caused by the blow cleared from my head, I rose to my feet, cut a switch from the nearest tree, and went seeking my beloved cousin. She had left me lying upon the ground, and when I caught her, too far from the village for screams to be heard, she knew she faced punishment she would not be saved from. Perhaps that was the first time she formulated her plans, yet it was surely not the last time she applied them. She received all of two blows from me, accepted in total silence, and then she screamed and twisted about as though her body were the victim of a bone-destroying rack. I was a child then, and thought surely I had caused her some great damage. I grew afraid and ceased the switching at once. I attempted to comfort her. I offered her sweets. I carried her to her father's halyar and placed her gently upon her furs. Mind you, she had nearly opened my skull with a branch, and I had given her all of two blows with a switch upon the leather of her skirt, and yet it was I who begged forgiveness and felt bottomless guilt. Does this injustice seem somehow familiar to you?"

"It cannot be the same!" Cimilan insisted, greatly disturbed. "The blood which came from her was unbelievable—though she did begin to accept my touch in silence."

"Aha!" pounced Ceralt, a gleam in his eye as he leaned forward toward Cimilan. "She fully intended to snare you, and had not counted upon your drinking from the second skin. Cimilan my friend, Lialt will tell you that there are some few wenches who produce rivers of blood when first broached—no matter how they are broached nor by whom. I feel certain that Famira herself felt frightened at its presence, not to speak of the pain she was given, yet she undoubtedly meant to entrap you as she has so obviously done. It has ever been her plan to rule a rider, and now her plans have come to be."

Cimilan, though struck by Ceralt's words, nevertheless leaned down upon an elbow, to consider them. He took the skin Ceralt passed to him and drank from it distractedly, then raised his eyes to meet the gaze of Ceralt.

"The matter still cannot be as you describe it," said he, shaking his head. "If it were true that all which transpired was by Famira's devising, then she would be pleased with her lot in life. She would undoubtedly pretend great fear of me to feed my guilt, not show how deeply she despises me. You saw her. You heard."

"Indeed," nodded Ceralt, "yet perhaps we each saw and heard a separate thing. You saw and heard the woman you love through layers of guilt and self-condemnation. I saw the woman who is my cousin, she with whom I grew from childhood, she who has apparently found great disappointment in the man who chose her. Consider my cousin, Cimilan, and understand that she will never feel respect for a man who is in her control. It is said, and truly, that a strong woman requires a stronger man. She expected—and perhaps hoped—to find that she would no longer be allowed her manipulations, and then you fell to them at once, allowing her to rule you. Can you imagine her disappointment, when she no longer bothers to hide her disgust? Is she to remain without a rider forever?"

"No," growled Cimilan, a hardness appearing in the dark of his eyes. "No!" he shouted then, striking the palm of his hand with a fist the size of Ceralt's. "So she planned to ensnare me, did she? She is pleased to practice her wiles, then feels herself unjustly treated when a man falls prey to them?" He rose to his feet and stood wrapped in rage, one square fist clenched before him, his dark eyes focused upon that which was not to be seen by others. "I must teach her that men are not to be manipulated," he muttered, then lowered his gaze to Ceralt. "My woman and I shall return here shortly. Though you be male kin to her, I feel you will not interfere with what is to be done to her."

He then turned and strode from the tent, failing even to pause to replace his body furs. Ceralt reclined in the fur with a soft laugh, stretching his large, hard body out in lack of concern. I gazed upon him briefly in silence, then sat myself straighter in the furs.

"The male has named you kin to her called Famira," I said, bringing his eyes to me. "Are you not bound to stand in defense of kin, as are the Midanna?"

"Indeed," nodded Ceralt, still amused. "Yet first one must consider the true meaning of defense. Should I keep Cimilan from punishing Famira as he intends, my cousin may never know the happiness which is the right of every woman. Famira desires strength in a man, the sort of strength which will force her to bow to his desires. She believes she desires pliability, yet this is not so. Patently, if it were true that she wished to rule a rider, she would now be pleased rather than miserable as she is. To defend my cousin, then, requires that I refuse to aid her against the man to whom she belongs."

"This is not clear." I frowned, regarding his strange composure with less than amusement. "Should the kin of a Midanna warrior stand in jeopardy from others, that warrior will stand beside her kin, even though she may share her fate. Apparently the matter is seen differently when one's kin is male."

Ceralt must surely have seen the disapproval I felt, however his anger appeared only briefly, before fading to naught. He regarded me as I had regarded him, in silence, then his hand rose from the lanthay fur to gesture to me.

"Come sit here beside me, satya," he said, his voice soft with patience. "That I am male and Famira female has no bearing upon my behavior. I would have you understand this."

I had little desire to sit beside Ceralt—and yet my body rose quickly from the fur to close the gap between us. He had used me no more than a short while earlier and then had dismissed me from his thoughts, yet I sank to the fur before him feeling naught of my earlier anger. I, in no more than a breech, sat before the male who had captured me, feeling his eyes touch me with pleasure, feeling much of the pleasure myself, knowing that I pleased him. His hand reached out to touch my right calf, and the warmth of his fingers spread to encompass my entire body. I sat as though I were going to recline to the left, my legs bent before me to the right, my left hand flat upon the lanthay fur, and I clasped my thighs tightly together so that I might not shame myself before him.

"Among my people," said Ceralt with a smile, "a man is required to defend his kinswomen before all others save his own woman. This is a matter of honor for men, and gladly do we discharge the obligation. Here, however, it is my belief that Famira will be better served if my aid is withheld from her. We shall see the thing through, and the results will prove me correct or in error."

He paused to stroke his hand upward to my thigh, round my knee and just above it, and my left hand closed to hold the lanthay fur in a grip which nearly tore it loose. I thought perhaps he toyed with me, yet his eyes were thoughtfully upon my face.

"Tell me," he said. "For what reason was my cousin Famira within this tent? Had she come to bedevil you with ridicule?"

"In truth, I know not," I murmured, attempting a softer voice in the hope that its unevenness would not be noticed. "She professed to have come asking after my intentions of revenge for her treatment of me, yet I feel that loneliness brought her. She is not well liked among the others."

"I have long been aware of that," he sighed, removing his hand from my leg to hang the forearm upon his knee. "She feels the difference between herself and the others, and as she stands apart from them in her own mind, so do they treat her in reality. The others are women of men, held, cherished, and made to be obedient. Famira is not."

Ceralt's mind left the tent to wander alone, enabling me to

release my grip upon the lanthay fur. Once I had thought upon holding Ceralt in my tent among the Hosta, yet I no longer considered the matter feasible. The lanthay fur against my left leg reminded me of his presence; the sight of his broad, hard body reminded me of his presence; the scent of his leathers reminded me of his presence. How was a war leader to lead her clan when all things about her brought thoughts of naught save a male? I longed to reach my hand out to touch him, to be taken in his arms and held against him, yet I kept my hand back and did not stir. Ceralt wished a village female, one who would see to his belongings, one who would not be so bold as to show her desire for him. Jalav was not such a one, and Ceralt was not hers.

Few, indeed, were the moments which passed before the sounds of struggle and displeasure heralded the return of Cimilan with Famira. The male appeared at the tent flap, the female upon his shoulder, shouts of outrage and revilement flying about his head. Cimilan strode three steps within before setting Famira upon her feet, yet his having released her meant naught of consequence. He stood, wide-shouldered and hard-eyed, between Famira and the tent flap, a thing the female saw at once. I had twisted about to observe their entrance, leaning low and to the left, and Ceralt promptly pushed me flat to the lanthay fur upon my belly, his hand in my back holding me there.

"For what reason have you forced me to return here?" Famira demanded of Cimilan, her fists clenched as she stared up to the face of the male. "Have you not already done more than enough to me?"

Cimilan received Famira's words with no expression, yet his dark eyes seemed to reflect more of the light from the flames-within-boxes. He stood in no more than his leathers, apparently not having felt the cold, and his eyes swept the body furs Famira stood wrapped in.

"I have brought you here so that you may offer apology to the High Rider," said Cimilan, folding his arms across his chest. "Your conduct before him earlier was inexcusable, and I will not allow the incident to go unnoticed. And have you never learned the proper actions of a woman? What do you do there, standing in a man's dwelling with boots upon your feet? Remove them at once, and your furs as well!"

The snap in Cimilan's voice gave Famira pause, yet she seemed to come quickly to a decision. She opened and removed her fur body covering, bent to remove her leg furs, then stood straight to face the male once more.

"As it was you who forcibly carried me here," said she in a sharpened tone, "what else was I to expect save abuse for my lacks? Have it as you will, Cimilan. The fault was mine."

A faint grin appeared upon the male's face, and his head nodded in agreement. "I am pleased to see you have the right of it," said he, bringing a brief look of surprise to Famira. "You may now prepare your apology."

The female grew furious at the words addressed to her, yet she did no more than clench her fists and glare upon the male. Then she tossed her head in angry dismissal and began to turn to Ceralt, yet Cimilan had not yet completed his instructions.

"Hold," said he, halting her turn. "I see little in your bearing of the proper humbleness an apology calls for. I think it best that you remove the leather of men before attempting a wench's apology."

"How dare you suggest such a thing?" Famira gasped, outraged beyond limit. "Do you think that I, being who I am, will do such a thing? Never!"

The female stood stiffened in fury, her eyes ablaze, her cheeks reddened in embarrassment. She faced the male who dared to speak to her so, and Ceralt chuckled softly behind me.

"You will indeed do such a thing," Cimilan returned, holding her eyes as he looked down upon her. "You are a woman who has been commanded by the man who has chosen her. Do not think you will not obey."

Famira seemed truly taken aback by the soft menace in Cimilan's voice, and also seemed at a loss as to what might be said. Her eyes moved briefly to Ceralt and me and then grudgingly returned to the male.

"Cimilan, I cannot do such a thing before others," she whispered, reluctance and desperation amingle in her tone and manner. "I will return with you to our tent immediately, and there you may do as you wish."

She then bent to retrieve her body fur, yet Cimilan's booted foot rested upon the garment, disallowing its retrieval. Her head turned to look up toward him again, and true fear showed a shadow of itself in her eyes.

"Cimilan, please!" she begged, voice aquiver with emotion. "There are strangers present! I cannot remove my garments! Allow me to return to our tent with you!"

The male's head shook in negation, no amusement to be seen

in his eyes. His bearing was calm, his mind firm, and there was little to be seen of the male who had earlier condemned himself. Famira, too, saw these things, and turned from him to stand erect before Ceralt.

"Cousin, I ask your aid," said she, choking upon words which were loathsome to her. "I, your kin, am in need of assistance."

Ceralt regarded her from where he reclined beside me in the lanthay fur. "Kinswoman, I hear your plea for assistance," said he, his tone mild yet grave. "Do you wish me to give aid in your disrobing?"

"Ceralt, do not speak so!" Famira cried, eyes wide in shock. "Take amusement from my predicament if you must, yet stand before me as you are honor-bound to do!"

"Matters of honor are those between men," Ceralt informed her, his tone having grown cold. "I will not be schooled in my obligations by a wench. Should I find that Cimilan's actions require my intervention, I will begin such intervention upon my own initiative. At the moment, I believe you have been commanded to perform a certain act. As I am filled with a kinsman's concern, I suggest that you obey—and with speed."

As Famira heard Ceralt's words, a bitterness took her. Her shoulders straightened and her head came up, and the bleakness in her eyes was painful to behold.

"So you both mock me," she said, her voice edged with all that which her body showed. Her eyes remained upon Ceralt, yet she also addressed the male Cimilan. "For many kalod I have been aware of the hatefulness of men, of their beastiality and lustfulness. I had thought, perhaps, to find myself wrong, yet your actions continue to prove my original estimations correct. Do as you will with me, I cannot prevent it, yet I refuse to contribute to my own moral degradation. I will not disrobe."

The female stood with head held high, hands clasped before her, a look upon her face which was akin to that which might be found upon the face of a warrior about to be summarily executed by enemies. I, myself, knew well the concept of humiliation before males, yet Famira showed naught of thoughts of humiliation. I stirred in the lanthay fur beneath Ceralt's hand, puzzled by that in Famira of which I had no understanding. Beyond Famira, Cimilan moved his gaze to Ceralt, an uncertain expression beginning in his eyes, yet the male must have seen a thing in Ceralt's face which hardened his resolve. He looked

again upon the female who stood before him, and reached a hand
out to her shoulder.

"The matter, then, is simple," said he, unconcern much
evident as he turned the female to face him. "As you will not
obey me, you shall be punished for the refusal and made to obey
me."

He then pulled Famira toward him and put his hands upon her
leathers, obviously with the intention of removing them. The
female uttered a sound of combined shock and outrage and
attempted to struggle and retain her garments, yet Cimilan was
not to be denied. I wondered at the manner in which Famira
struggled, for she had clearly indicated that she would offer no
resistance to the male, yet she beat at him with her fists and cried
out in dismay. Ceralt, whose hand had grown heavier upon me
as though he thought I would rise to Famira's defense, leaned
closer to me and put his lips by my ear.

"Within her, she is no more than a fearful child," he murmured,
unheard by the others above Famira's cries. "She fears men and
what they might do to her, for she has not yet truly been made a
woman. Observe her actions and recall them afterward."

He then leaned back from me, for Cimilan had succeeded in
removing Famira's leathers, just then finishing with her breech.
The city female reached at the bit of leather in desperation, yet
Cimilan threw it behind him, beyond her reach. Famira was then
nearly beyond herself, her anger gone, shock alone riding full
within her. She was not badly made for a city female, full
breasts, well turned hips, slender legs, flat belly, yet one would
wonder at her concept of herself, were they to see the expression
she wore. Her shame was not that she had been made to bare
herself by the will of men; it was that she had been made to
show her body to anyone other than herself. I marveled at the
manner in which city females grew to womanhood, to accept
selection by males as meet, to feel shame at baring their bodies.
This Famira stood as one caught in dishonor, her body bent
forward and half turned from us, her right arm stretched before
her body, attempting to shield herself from view, her left hand at
her face, disallowing sight of her pretty, red-flushed face. I knew
Ceralt looked upon her, for his hand spread wide upon my back,
moving slowly back and forth, stirring my blood as his desire
came into being. Cimilan, too, looked upon the female Famira,
yet the eyes of the second male detected a lack. He stepped to
her and reached his hands to her hair, and another moment saw the
clasps and plaits gone from it, Cimilan seeing that it fell loose

about her shoulders, dark and flowing nearly to her waist. As he stepped back once more to survey his handiwork, a sob came from Famira, as though her soul were soon to be lost. Cimilan considered her a number of reckid, yet no further sounds came to interrupt his observations, and at last he folded his arms and addressed her.

"I do not find myself satisfied with that which I see," he said, somewhat afrown. "Remove your arms from before you and straighten your body so that I might have what little pleasure sight of you brings."

Famira's head came up in wounded anger, hate filling her dark, flashing eyes, and then her arms no longer shielded her as she sent a look of daggers to Cimilan.

"You are a brute and a beast!" she hissed, leaning toward the male in her fury. "That you care naught for me I already knew, yet I thought you intelligent enough to keep the fact from others! Now my kinsman must surely face you, for you have voiced your lack of caring! Ceralt! It is the law of our people!"

She stood poised in anticipation, her eyes held fast to Cimilan, her fists clenched at her sides, yet the first words to come to her were not those she had anticipated.

"Of what law do you speak, Famira?" Ceralt inquired innocently. "No more was said before me than that the man to whom you belong is displeased with you. In that, Cimilan is correct. Your attempts at obedience are scandalously poor, and you shame me before him."

The female's head flew around to send her shafts toward Ceralt, and the color had risen truly high in her cheeks. "You low, vile, crawling sednet!" she screamed, beside herself with rage and disappointment. "To side with another against your own blood kin! You are as base as all men, Ceralt, as base and as filled with lust and decay! I despise you all and shall hate you forever!"

She then attempted to throw herself past Cimilan to the tent entrance, seemingly bent upon departing without clothing. Cimilan threw his arms about her to prevent this, and she turned to the attack as a child of the wild, claws and teeth set to commit violence. Famira had not learned, as I had, the futility of attack upon a male with no weapon save strength against his strength, yet the lesson was swiftly taught her when Cimilan forced her to the lanthay fur upon her back. The two struggled briefly less than two paces from where I lay, and then Cimilan had Famira's wrists above her head, held by his left hand, his knees straddling

her body. The female fought to free herself, head tossing back
and forth, breasts rising in great agitation, body twisting between
Cimilan's knees, yet her strength was not equal to the task.
Cimilan allowed her her struggles, a thing which brought bitter
memory to me, for Ceralt had also allowed me a time of struggle,
knowing full well how useless the attempt would be. I put my
cheek to the lanthay fur, grasping it in my fists, finding that I
also grasped strands of my own hair. Famira's desperate grunts
of struggle were much too familiar, and the ghost of shame
touched my sense of honor and fitness. For what reason Mida
had placed me there, upon my belly beneath the hand of a male,
I knew not, yet I knew how difficult it was to bear. I could not
touch the male of my own will, could not take him if desire
came to me, could not send him to a corner and silence when
matters of import required undisturbed thought. The life was not
one I might easily accept, and Ceralt's stroking hand upon my hair
brought scant comfort. The male somehow sensed my disturbance,
yet his gesture was the sort to comfort a slave. It did naught save
agitate a Hosta war leader.

"Enough of this foolishness," came Cimilan's voice, and I
looked up to see that he frowned upon Famira. "Your words and
actions are equally unacceptable to me, and I wonder that a
wench might be allowed to grow with such ignorance. This 'lust'
you speak of as a part of men is also to be found in women.
Have you never been instructed by a woman older than yourself?"

"My father has never felt the need to have me schooled in
debasement!" snapped Famira, a light sheen of sweat covering
her body. "Though you defile me with every touch of your
hand, I shall resist you forever! I shall not wallow in the filth
you and your ilk are so fond of!"

I had often wondered how city males saw to their needs when
their females loathed their touch, and therefore watched Cimilan
carefully. I had thought that some might perhaps joy in forcing
themselves upon unwilling females, yet Cimilan was not such a
one. The male regarded Famira's flushed, resolute face in silence,
then slowly shook his head.

"There is no filth to be wallowed in when a man puts his
woman to use," he said, more patience to be heard than I had
expected. "Women long for the touch of a man, for women have
been shown the pleasure a man is able to give them. You,
however, are still a girl, and the time has come for you to be
shown."

Famira frowned with lack of understanding, yet when Cimilan's head lowered to her breast, a groping desperation seized her. She writhed at the feel of his lips upon her flesh, and cried out, "Cimilan, no! Do not offer me such debasement before others! Do not soil me before my kin!"

"Debasement seems to suit your flesh," Cimilan murmured, his head raised somewhat so that he might regard the spear his lips had brought about. "Be silent a moment, and listen for the voice of your needs."

His head lowered to her a second time, yet no more than the specified moment had passed before Famira's breath came in great gasps and she again resumed her struggles.

"Release me!" she screamed, fear now clear in her features. "Do not touch me so, I beg of you! My shame is too great to bear!"

"Shame?" inquired Cimilan, his tone even yet remorseless. "Do you often feel shame here?"

His free hand went to Famira's womanhood and she gasped in mortification, then cried, "Oh!" at his touch. His fingers moved in a restless rhythm, and the woman beneath his hand could not restrain herself. She threw her head back with a moan, arched her body, then commenced weeping in a manner she had not yet done.

"No more, Cimilan, please no more!" she wept. "I fear what you will do to me. The pain was greater than any I have ever felt!"

"Do not fear, satya," whispered Cimilan, his hand leaving Famira to move to his breech. "The pain will not visit you again, and should not have been allowed to spend this much time in your memory. The fault is mine, and I must now rectify it."

He moved to her then and brought his body to hers, and again she pleaded and wept to remain untouched. The male heard her cries and responded with soothing noises, yet slowly, inexorably, he made her his. Her cries lessened when he was full within her, and her tear-stained face looked up toward his.

"There was, in truth, very little pain," she allowed, her voice low. "Yet my discomfort is great and I feel no pleasure. Might I not be released now to replace my garments?"

Cimilan laughed softly and leaned down to touch her forehead with his lips. "Your discomfort will disappear when the tightness of you is lessened," he said, his tone gentle and caring though he still held her wrists. "I am far from done with you, so your garments shall remain where they are. Do you feel this?"

"Oh!" she cried, her face reddening at the movement within

her. She stirred in Cimilan's grip, unsure of his intentions and still somewhat fearful, and then his hips began to move. Famira whimpered, feeling the strength of him, knowing his presence for the mastery it was, attempting to deny the weakness he brought upon her. His movement increased in speed and force, and her mouth opened in amazement, words lost to the unimaginable and inexpressible sensations being given her. Cimilan lowered his head and took her lips, and with a small, muffled moan, Famira began attempting to match his movement. In no more than heartbeats she leaped beneath him, crying out incoherently in response to the slave due he forced from her, lost in the pleasure of his manhood. I felt the demands of desire in my own flesh, yet my earlier disturbance had not left me. The two opposed forces fought in my body, one insisting that I beg in my need, the other demanding that I carry my pain in silence. My flesh ached from lying in one place so long, yet the distraction of the ache was not enough to overcome knowledge of Ceralt behind me. In Mida's name, I knew not what might be done, and the sound of Ceralt's voice startled me from consideration of the dilemma.

"See the unrestrained heat of her," said Ceralt, unconcerned with being heard by any save I. Cimilan and Famira dwelt in a world made only for two, and heard naught save the heartbeat each of the other. "I have always known she would be magnificent for a rider," he chuckled. "She had only to be chosen by the proper rider. True obedience will be long in coming to her, yet I venture to guess that she will no longer risk full insolence with Cimilan. Should he find the need to give her a hiding, she will thereafter pack her insolence away, no longer to be used upon men. I will listen closely for her first words when Cimilan releases her."

Then his hand came to my arm and pulled me around to my back, so that I must stare up at his face. Light eyes met mine in sober regard and silence, and it was a moment before his hand came gently to my face.

"What disturbs you, satya?" he asked, a faint echoing disturbance to be heard in his voice. "I have learned to be wary of such silence from you, and your eyes show a great unhappiness. Speak to me of that which gives you pain."

A lock of dark hair had again fallen to Ceralt's brow, and I felt the desire to raise my hand and brush it away, clearing his vision. He saw so much and yet so little, and I was helpless to do other than as I did.

"It is not a thing which might be spoken of," I replied, keeping my hand from him. "It might only be seen to should my word be returned to me."

"No," he growled, so softly that a chill touched me. "You are mine and shall continue to be mine. I see you have replaced your breech. Do you think this bit of leather will keep me from you if I should desire your use?"

"No," I whispered, turning my head from him and closing my eyes. His hand had touched the breech, solidly, possessively, and the flesh beneath it burned as though touched by the coals I cooked upon. How might I think myself other than fully in his capture when the mere sight of him made my body his? His hand moved in and about the breech, forcing a moan from my lips, and his other hand came to turn my face back to him as he chuckled.

"A man must needs be touched by Sigurr to release one such as you," he murmured, shifting about so that he might stretch out beside me. "You, too, are magnificent for a rider. Show me what you have learned in offering your lips to me."

I opened my eyes to look upon him, yet sight did naught to alter his command. I raised my face to his, parting my lips slightly as I did so, knowing the gesture was one he approved of. My lips were his and he took them fiercely, showing again that my release would be through Mida's doing and not through his. His arms held me to his body as he drew my soul from me, and Famira's cries of pleasure were as daggers twisting through my flesh. I writhed in his grip, my need growing beyond my ability to govern, and Ceralt raised his head to regard me.

"What, again?" he laughed, putting his hand to my hair. "Surely you were seen to no more than a hin ago, and yet here you lay, squirming about as though untouched for feyd. You cannot possibly require further attention, so I will consider myself mistaken."

He released me then to stretch and yawn, and then put himself flat upon his back in the fur beside me. I sat up quickly, knowing momentary shame, yet my desperation would not allow the agony to be borne in silence. It was the place of a war leader to take, yet Ceralt was no longer a male who might be taken from. I gazed upon him as my breasts rose and fell in agitation, and a comforting smile came to his face.

"Calm yourself, wench," he murmured, drawing a thick strand of my hair toward him. "Speak to me of what disturbs you, and I shall do all possible to assist you."

He waited patiently for what words would come from me, yet I was nearly beyond speech. I pulled myself to my knees and tore the breech free of my body, then put my hands upon his chest.

"I must be used," I whispered in pain, pleading with my eyes. "My need is such that I will beg if necessary."

He pursed his lips at my confession and gazed thoughtfully at the strand of hair in his hands, yet made no move to do as I had asked.

"So you are willing to beg," he murmured, keeping his eyes from mine. "When one is willing to do a thing, that thing has proven itself less distasteful than another thing. Just how high does your need rage?"

His hands released my hair and suddenly came to me, one hand behind my waist, the other to test the intensity of my desire. I cried out and attempted to throw myself upon him, yet this he would not allow.

"We are beyond the time when you may force me to your service!" he snapped, keeping me from him by his hands upon my arms. "Have you no knowledge of anything other than forcing your will or begging to be taken?"

I struggled in his grip, unable to reach him, miserable in the knowledge that he would refuse me use. I burned within me, my flesh demanded service, yet I knew this service would not be forthcoming. From somewhere in the depths of my being, I found the strength to pull from his hands, yet when I attempted to take my misery to a far corner, this, too, was denied me. Ceralt's fist came to my hair, and my head was forced to the furs.

"A question has been asked you, wench," he pursued, his voice close to my ear as my face, as I held to the fur beneath my knees. "Have you never thought upon other methods of bringing relief to your flesh than taking it or begging it?"

His hand gripped my hair with such force that my head whirled, and my own hands went to his fist in an attempt to ease the strain.

"What other methods can there be?" I choked, seeing naught save my knees and the lanthay fur they rested upon, feeling naught save the squareness of the fist beneath my hands. "One is natural," I gasped, "the means warriors have ever used upon males. The other is shameful, yet necessary when one has been made captive to males. There are no other circumstances."

"Captive!" Ceralt growled in anger, his hand giving my head

such a shake that I cried out in pain. I had no hope of loosening his grip, yet my hands went again to where he held me, resting gently against the corded strength of his fist. "Still you persist in calling yourself captive!" he ground out. "When will you no longer be a captive?"

"When Mida frees me from your presence," I whispered, knowing he would give me pain again, yet unable to speak other than the truth. "This has been promised me, and it will surely come to be. I will not forever be the captive of a male."

I had thought to hear him shout then, and perhaps see him beat me, yet no sounds came other than those from Cimilan and Famira. And then my head, held so cruelly to the lanthay fur, was slowly raised by Ceralt so that I might look upon his face. Strange did that face appear when once I knelt straight, strange in the impatience of his expression, the pain in his eyes. No anger showed from that which he had earlier felt, yet it lingered in the set of his body, the grip of his hand.

"You mistake the meaning of my question," said he, his voice held low through effort of will alone. "When I asked when you would no longer be a captive, I meant I wished to know when you would begin to know yourself my woman. I had no wish to hear the fantasies of your frustration, nor do I care to hear them now. You may tell yourself you will one fey be delivered from me, yet such soothings to your pride will only bring aches to your bottom. It will be much the better if you learn what is needful for your place with me, for you will never cease to be mine while breath is left to my body."

His eyes, the color of a vast stretch of water I had once seen, spoke to me as always of the belief he had in that which he had said. Till the breath leaves his body, he had sworn, and thus had he sealed his own fate. Each of us has the right to live her life as she sees fit, yet I gazed upon Ceralt's body, so broad and strong, the flesh so firm, and wished I might force him to withdraw those words. That he stood himself against Mida's will was plain, equally as plain as the certainty that he would fall. Lialt had seen it so, and I was indeed meant to ride free once more, and therefore Ceralt's life was forfeit in a cause which had long been lost.

"I think it best that we return to our original discussion," said Ceralt, his eyes examining me once again. "I have disallowed your taking service from me, and find no interest in having you grovel at my feet. In such an instance, this is what you must do."

He then released my hair to lay himself flat upon the lanthay fur, his broad chest no more than a handspan from my knees. I shook my head to free myself of the lingering feel of his fist forcing me to his wishes, and his hand came to take a thick strand of my hair again.

"Here I lie," said he, "toying with your hair, and there you kneel, deep in your need. I have no interest in seeing to your need, yet you cannot continue with it unseen to. What you must do is waken my flesh to feel a need approaching yours, and the way this might be done is to bring your flesh to mine, using it and your hands and lips to see to the task. You have only to remember that should you displease me with too great an insistence, I shall cast you from me to suffer in solitude. Come, now. Let us see what you may accomplish."

His fingers played with my hair, his eyes awaiting my actions, yet I knew not what his instruction might mean. That I was to touch him was clear, yet less than clear was the manner in which this might be done. All confused, kneeling beside him, I reached a hand out to touch his belly with one finger, feeling the hair that clustered there just above his breech. How much simpler it would be to merely tear the breech from his body, taking that which he refused to give. And yet, when I had first touched him I had not attempted to force him to my will with strength and insistences, but had toyed with him to build his heat. Once, in the darkness, I had thought myself back in the forest with a sthuvad before me, and had attempted to take Ceralt as I would have among the Hosta. I clearly recalled the shock I had felt upon discovering an unbound male before me, yet such now seemed foolishness. Had Ceralt never taken and used me, that shock should result from his doing that very thing? If such was my purpose—and the ache in my body swore it was so—then why would I refrain from doing that which I had done in the forests? Again I looked to Ceralt's eyes, seeing him as he watched me, knowing for how short a time I was destined to remain in his furs, and saw myself for a fool. Was I to refuse the enjoyment of his presence merely by cause of my captivity by him, denying myself as I could not deny him?

I shook my head slowly back and forth, holding his eyes, seeing the frown begin to crease his brow and then disappear as my finger trailed across his belly and down to his thigh. My left hand moved then as well, to the broadness of his chest and shoulder, and slowly, slowly, I leaned down to touch his middle with my lips. His firm flesh quivered as I touched it, lightly, gently, once, twice, thrice. My arms spread out upon his body, my lips barely touching him, I was yet able to feel how he fought to keep his breathing slow, to keep his hands from reaching for my body. I smiled to know that he sought a lost disinterest, and raised my head to send my gaze to his.

"Have you no interest in me as you are?" I whispered, keeping my hands amove upon him, in all places save where his rising hips sought to direct me. "Must I find another to quench the heat which you yourself have raised in me? What other shall I go to?"

"None other!" Ceralt growled, anger in his eyes as he raised up and pulled me to his arms. "You may not go to another save with my permission, and this you do not have!"

His lips took mine then, violently, demandingly, and soon I knew naught of what Famira and Cimilan were about. Ceralt had me, in his arms, in his possession, in the throes of a desire he had been unable to deny. I moaned with pleasure at the feel of him within me, knowing that the pleasure he gave was indeed fit for a war leader, for who else had the right to seek such? Ceralt was sthuvad beyond compare, and his loss would cut me more deeply than any other.

The joy continued for many reckid, and when I was at last released to lie alone on the lanthay fur, Ceralt, spent, at my side, I found a silence which had not before filled the tent. Yet lying upon my back, I turned my head toward Cimilan and Famira, discovering two sets of eyes filled with interest. The female sat upon the lap of the male, her arms as far about his body as they might go, he also with his arms about her, yet his hands were not unmoving as were hers. Cimilan joyed in the presence of his female, unclothed, near to his touch, and Famira, though most recently seen to, moved as though fire again began to claim her.

"There you have seen what you must strive for," said Cimilan to his female, his lips briefly touching her hair. "You saw how her body moved to meet his, how the opennness of her called him to heights of added pleasure. It is a thing all women are capable of, should their men know enough to demand it of them. Presently you will find that I demand no less."

"I will strive for its attainment, Cimilan," Famira whispered, her voice breathy with weakness. "I will give great attention in future to—oh! No, do not touch me so! You take my strength away doing so, and so soon again after having just—No, no, it cannot be done so soon again."

"Can it not?" murmured Camilan as Ceralt chuckled and put

his arm about me. "Very well, as you say it cannot be, I shall bow to your greater wisdom. Desire cannot again be raised in you, therefore shall I cease my efforts."

He then took his hands from her body, moved her from his lap to the lanthay fur, and stood to stretch his broad body to the tent's roof. Famira, having been unceremoniously placed alone upon the fur, looked up at the male above her with abrupt uncertainty, her thighs pressed tightly together. I shook my head over her foolishness as Ceralt continued to chuckle, for it seemed clear to any with eyes that Famira had been made to feel her need, yet had refused the male who might see to it. Cimilan retrieved his breech and quickly donned it, then reached down again for his leather chest covering.

"Do—do we now return to our own tent, Cimilan?" asked Famira, her tone uncertain and yet filled with considerable hope. "There is—a thing about which I would—speak with you alone."

"Oh?" said Cimilan, gazing fondly down upon her, mellow good humor having been restored to him. "You need not await our return to our tent, satya. Speak to me now of that which concerns you."

"I—I cannot," choked Famira, her gaze slipping to Ceralt and myself before finding the fur beneath Cimilan's feet. "It is a matter for your ears alone."

"Such foolishness," laughed Cimilan, crouching down beside her to touch her hair with a gentle hand. "Surely there can be no matter which may not be spoken of before the High Rider. Speak now so that we may ease your questioning the sooner."

Again Famira's eyes moved, this time to Ceralt alone, and though she seemed near to bursting, her head shook resolutely.

"The matter is not so pressing," said she, pulling her legs beneath her so that she might rise to her feet. "I shall accompany you to our tent as soon as I am clad."

"Cimilan, I insist you and your wench stay and take the evening meal with us," said Ceralt, sitting straight to watch Famira reach for the leathers which Cimilan had removed from her. "There is little to be done till Hannil and his riders join us, and no need for the time to be spent in solitude."

"High Rider, my thanks," glowed Cimilan, standing the straighter with pride as Famira stiffened behind him. "We will be pleased to. . . ."

"No!" snapped Famira, fury filling her eyes and voice, her body beginning to tremble. "I wish to return to my own tent, and I wish to go now! Perhaps another time, Ceralt!"

"Woman, hold your tongue!" growled Cimilan, turning quickly to face her. "I will not have you spit upon the honor granted me! Stand yourself before the High Rider and ask his forgiveness for your ill manners, then thank him for requesting our presence!"

"I shall do no such thing!" gasped Famira, clearly shocked at the insistence, taking a step backward from the male. She held her breech and leather shirt to her, as though to ward off Cimilan's wrath with them. "I wish to leave, and need no one's permission to do so!"

"You require *my* permission," said Cimilan, his voice grown hard and cold as he kept his gaze upon her. "And now it returns to me that you must be punished for your earlier actions, yet at this moment the High Rider awaits your words of apology."

One large hand went to her arm, the other to the leathers she held, and a moment later the female was once again bereft of leathers and quickly pushed to her knees less than a pace before me. It was Ceralt she had been knelt to, of course, yet Ceralt did not move himself before me. He remained seated upon the fur as he was and awaited what would occur.

"We await the apology, wench," said Cimilan from behind a Famira who was well taken with rage. She had been shocked to find herself put to her knees after having her leather taken again, yet the shock had quickly changed to fury. Her fists clenched, her eyes blazing hot, she attempted to regain her feet, yet this Cimilan would not allow. His hand moved quickly to her hair, tangling therein, bringing forth a cry of pain from the female.

"The words?" repeated Cimilan, his voice soft as his eyes continued to rest upon a female who now knelt rigidly, aware that movement would increase her pain. Her eyes had returned to an awareness of shock, a disbelief that she might be treated so by a male, perhaps most shockingly that it was Cimilan who treated her so. Again I shook my head, despairing of her foolishness, yet what might one expect from a village slave-woman?

"I shall speak!" Famira choked, her hands to Cimilan's fist in her hair, a tremor in her voice. "Release me and I will speak!"

"The choice of when to speak is no more yours than whether or not you may do so," returned the male, his voice as soft as it had been. "Speak the words you now understand are necessary, and then, perhaps, you shall be released."

"Perhaps?" the female whispered, meaning the word for no one other than herself. It had come to her that Cimilan need not release her if it was not his desire to do so, and her eyes, when moved to Ceralt, glistened with tears. "Cousin, I ask your

pardon," she whispered, the tremor in her voice grown greater.
"I would have you—forgive my—lack of good manners and—
also have you know—that your invitation is—most gratefully
accepted."

"Cousin, the pleasure is mine," smiled Ceralt, speaking as
though the words came freely from his kin. "You will ever find
a welcome beneath my roof."

"High Rider, we thank you," said Cimilan, his hand yet in
Famira's hair, a smile again upon his face. "In token of our
gratitude, my woman will be pleased to see to the preparation of
the provender—without the aid of your wench. Is this acceptable
to you?"

"That is very generous of you, Cimilan." Ceralt grinned,
again pretending that he had no knowledge of the stricken look
which took possession of Famira. "There is time yet before the
meal need be cooked, yet perhaps it would be wise for Famira to
familiarize herself with the whereabouts of the supplies and
utensils. I am quite sure she would be upset if our meal were
delayed by cause of her unpreparedness."

"In such an event, I have no doubt of her upset," said
Cimilan, speaking in main to the female he now raised to her
feet by the hair. "Come, Famira, let us have you inspect the
cooking facilities. You may remember such things from your
time in your father's halyar."

The female drew her breath in in mortification, yet made no
attempt to resist the male as he led her toward the holder of
glowing coals. She stumbled along in his grip, striving to keep
pace with him, and neither she nor the male were aware of my
eyes having left them to go to Ceralt. That male sat and laughed
softly as he watched the others, then suddenly became aware of
my gaze. His eyes moved to mine where I lay in the lanthay fur
before him, and his laughter softened to a smile.

"Why do you study me so?" he asked, his hand coming to
smooth my hair. "Do you, too, have a thing which must be
discussed in private?"

"It is more a matter of confusion," I sighed, doubting my
wisdom in speaking of it. "At first Ceralt would not allow Jalav
to touch him, now he demands that she do so. I do not understand why this is—nor when it shall again become forbidden."

"My poor Jalav," said he, a sigh to match mine in his voice.
"All about her is confusion, yet one fey understanding will
come. For now she has only to understand that Ceralt welcomes

the touch of her hands—as all men welcome the touch of their women. Come, Jalav mine. Stand now and replace your breech.''

My look must have told him of my new lack of understanding, for he chuckled as he took my hands and pulled me to my feet.

"I am sure Cimilan intends keeping Famira unclothed as an added punishment," he said very softly so that only I might hear. "Should this be the case, the presence of your breech upon you will increase her embarrassment and decrease her willfulness. It is more than time she was taken firmly in hand."

He turned from me to reclaim his own breech, and as I took mine in hand I again wondered at his concept of duty toward his kin. It was evident that the thought of Famira's coming embarrassment pleased him, a thing no Hosta would allow herself to feel. Perhaps one must be of the cities and villages to consider such an act a part of honor—and find pleasure in it.

No more than a hand of reckid later, Lialt and Telion entered the tent. They paused beside the entrance to remove their body furs and dry the bottoms of their leg furs, and only when they stepped full within the tent did they see Famira and she them. The female had been kneeling among the packs of provender, seeking knowledge of what lay where, hidden behind the crouching bulk of Cimilan. As the two newcomers entered within, Cimilan rose to his feet to greet them, and Famira, all unknowing, also straightened from her search to find the eyes and grins of Lialt and Telion full upon her. Her flesh reddened, from face to ankles, her breath drew in in a gasp of mortification, and she quickly placed herself again behind Cimilan.

"My leathers!" she choked, grasping at the back of the male she stood behind. "Cimilan, I cannot reach my leathers!"

"For what reason do you require your leathers?" asked the male, an easy amusement to his tone. "It is warm within this tent, and we shall not be leaving for some time yet."

"But there are others!" the female pleaded, pulling again at the male. "I cannot go unclad with others within the tent! I must have my leathers!"

"Nonsense," laughed Cimilan, closing one eye toward Lialt and Telion. "I am pleased to have other men see my good fortune. Stand here before me and give greeting to the Pathfinder and the High Rider's chosen brother."

"No!" wailed Famira, once again reduced to tears. "I cannot, I cannot, I cannot!"

Then did she whirl away from Cimilan and throw herself toward the back of the tent, in among the packs and provisions, in an attempt to bury herself among them. Telion and Lialt chuckled well as Cimilan, with a grin, followed after the female, Ceralt also watching the sport with amusement, I, alone, finding no humor in the matter. Shame touches each of us in different ways, yet even village slave-women were able, at times, to feel its pain. Famira had undoubtedly earned her shame, yet there need not have been such—complete amusement—in the giving of it. The original doing had not been through her efforts alone.

The male Cimilan, full bent upon his amusement, drew the female from her hiding place with an arm about her waist. Her voice rose in a wail of pleading, she kicked and fought to remain hidden, yet naught moved the male from his purpose. In no more than a moment was she placed upon her feet among the three males, they having made a loose circle about her, seeing that they gave her no place to run. She stood with head down, weeping, attempting to hide herself with her hands, making more of the thing than any save a city female would have done. The males examined her with their eyes, yet Cimilan found himself dissatisfied.

"Remove your hands from before you, satya," he directed, his voice not unkind. "Should it be necessary, your wrists may be bound behind you."

Famira raised her head to look upon Cimilan, her eyes widened in denial of belief, her arms slowly dropping from before her. The female now knew, beyond doubt, that she was bound to males, theirs to do with as they pleased. Should Cimilan wish it, she would be bound tightly with leather, displayed before others or left untouched in a corner, to pull at the leather and struggle in vain. She dared not disobey his commands, dared not even consider such, and I folded my arms beneath my life sign, struggling to see the matter as Famira saw it. It is possible for any to fall captive to males, yet how might one give over dignity and freedom with no more than token protest? Had Famira been beaten near to death her fear might be understandable, yet naught had been done to her save the suggestion of a possibility, and there she stood, fearful lest she be bound in leather, a fate too horrible to contemplate. Much did I struggle for understanding, yet such was not meant to come to me.

"A lovely morsel, Cimilan," said Telion with a grin, causing Famira to redden further. "It is good of you to allow us to look upon her."

"Indeed," agreed Lialt, also with much of a grin. "I had not known my cousin to be so much of a woman. My congratulations on your good fortune."

"You are horrid, all of you!" wept Famira, her hands now before her face, her head lowered to them. "You shame me with every word and care naught for doing so! I shall never forgive you, never!"

The males looked upon one another with a twinkle Famira saw naught of, and again I shook my head at her foolishness. To berate those with power over you may be done only when one cares naught for the consequences.

"So you feel you have been given shame," said Cimilan with a sternness his eyes belied. "I think, my girl, you have not yet learned the meaning of shame. Men have complimented your appearance, and you have returned them discourteousness. The insult must be wiped away. Lialt, Telion, please take seat and make yourselves at ease."

Cimilan did as he had bade the other males do, and all looked up toward a Famira who now stood warily apprehensive, her hands no longer before her face, the tears running unheeded down her cheeks. Ceralt came to stand beside me, his face expressionless, his eyes amused, yet Famira no longer looked upon him. She looked only upon Cimilan, sparing not even a glance for the other males.

"Now," said Cimilan sternly. "Hold your arms away from your body and turn to face Lialt and Telion. Do not return your arms nor face away from them without my permission, else you shall be punished on the spot."

A lack of understanding showed in Famira's eyes as she slowly did as she was commanded, yet the movement was not lost upon the males she stood before. Her arms, bent at the elbows, held away from her body, beckoned the males toward the sweetness of her form, the large breasts, the small waist, the obvious presence of her womanhood. A murmur of approval arose all around, from Ceralt as well as the others, and startlement at last came to Famira, to see such desire in the eyes of males. She looked upon Telion, then upon Lialt, seeing the heat sight of her brought, and then a feeling came to her which I was able to recognize from also having felt it. When Ceralt looked upon me with pleasure and desire, I often found that I wished to show myself to him even though the heat rose high within me at his gaze. I wished to show myself to him yet did not wish it so, for the desire I felt then was near to crippling, nigh unto agony. Famira stood with her long legs at ease, the left one straight, the right one somewhat bent at the knee, gazing at Lialt and Telion as they gazed upon her, and then, as though in curiosity, her head turned to Cimilan where he sat. Naked desire shown from the male's eyes, pleasure and heat and pride bound together, and Famira suddenly shuddered, drew her legs tightly together, then threw herself to the fur at his feet.

"Cimilan, take me back to our tent!" the female wept, clawing her way to his lap and arms. "I beg you, Cimilan, I cannot bear the pain!"

"There is a way your pain might be eased, satya," the male murmured, drawing her close to his chest. "Here, now, without the need of returning to our tent."

"No!" the female whispered, twisting about in his arms. "You could not use me before these others! You would not!"

"Do you feel the act would shame you?" the male asked, moving his hands upon her body. "As badly as you have thus far been shamed?"

"Oh, much more!" Famira moaned, knowing naught of where Cimilan's hands went till she cried out as though in fear of her soul. Her screams rang out again and again as she attempted to force Cimilan's stroking from the center of her being, yet the male was not to be denied—nor was her flesh. It took no more than the briefest moment before she began to beg her use, there, upon the spot they sat, out upon the snow, anywhere possible that it might be done immediately. Cimilan laughed to see the change in her, put her to her back in the fur, and soon had full, deep possession of her. Telion and Lialt chuckled as they rose to their feet, and Ceralt stirred beside me.

"So much for the shame of use," said Ceralt, stretching his broad body hard. "How quickly a wench may be made to change her views."

"From whom were such views learned?" I asked as Telion and Lialt stopped beside us. "Should all village females glory in their use by males, who might be left to instill such beliefs in those not yet touched?"

My question had been for Ceralt, yet he himself made no answer as he looked to Lialt and Telion, who quickly avoided his gaze as they coughed into their cupped hands. Ceralt glared upon the two he called brother, then returned his gaze to me.

"Famira had the ill luck to be daughter to one who delighted in the unhappiness of others," said he, his voice showing difficulty with the words. "In his attempts to protect his daughter from men with no honor, he, perhaps inadvertently, instilled too great a mistrust in her. It is, after all, a man's duty to protect his daughter from unwelcome advances. How else might she be protected save with cautions deeply instilled?"

"Would it not be simpler to slay those without honor?" I pursued, frowning at the concept presented me. "The innocent are cruelly handicapped so that those without honor might live in peace? No Hosta would countenance such a thing."

"Perhaps the Hosta are not mistaken in all of their views," murmured Telion, drawing unreadable glances from Ceralt and Lialt. "In our civilized lands, the innocent do indeed suffer for the guilty."

"I dislike straying from so fascinating a subject," said Lialt, his haste causing him to speak before my own words might be uttered, "yet I feel that Ceralt should know that Hannil's group has been sighted. They will be here well within the hin, and should be properly greeted."

"By me," nodded Ceralt, already turning toward his leg coverings. "We will take our evening meals separately, yet Hannil will expect our presence afterward. You two will, of course, accompany me."

"Of course," agreed Lialt with a nod from Telion. "Do you wish us with you now?"

"No," denied Ceralt, taking himself toward his body furs. "I have rested and refreshed myself, and so must you do as well. Hannil is not one to visit with an unguarded tongue. Should you feel up to it, Lialt, you may give Jalav another reading lesson."

By then Ceralt was well covered in furs, therefore did he take himself from the tent to see to the matter he had spoken of. Lialt and Telion looked upon one another with shrugs, removed their leg coverings, then found a skin of near-renth to share. Famira continued to writhe and cry out beneath Cimilan, causing Lialt and Telion to gaze musingly upon me, yet their musing looks no longer disturbed me. Were I to be used by them it would be so, for Mida had not freed me from my capture. I would accept their use as the trial it was, knowing my capture would one fey come to an end. I sat myself upon the lanthay fur, cross-legged as became a warrior, and awaited the end of my capture.

Perhaps half a hin passed in quiet as the males shared near-renth, and then did Lialt fetch the sheaf called book which contained black stokes called letters. Again I was made to kneel before the sheaf, and again did Lialt point to various strokes and pronounce their calling, yet this time was not as the time before. I immediately saw a stroke I believed I knew the calling of, and when I pointed toward it and spoke its name, Lialt was much pleased. He told me the stroke was the letter ''see,'' the letter which began Ceralt's name, and then I paused, recalling the silent speech of the Midanna, which was taught to all warriors-to-be. So long had it been since I had learned it that nearly had I forgotten, yet all first signs taught to warriors-to-be had but a single sound. The sound ''see'' was made by all the fingers of the right hand, cupped in a semi-circle, as though measuring a small distance. The sound, the sign and the stroke, then, all had the same calling. I asked the stroke for Lialt's name and the one for Telion's, and each appeared somewhat the same though differences were apparent after inspection, each sound matching a sign I knew. Lialt became eager at my interest, near excitement in his manner, causing Telion to come close to watch our doings and speak a word or two of his own. It became apparent the strokes were much the same as tracks in the forest, identical to those with no knowledge of them, easily differentiated by one who has studied the matter. Jalav knew each track and print, each scent and habit of each child of the wild; was she to allow mere strokes upon thin leather to best her?

Much did I labor till the evening meal was prepared, Lialt and Telion by my side. Lialt had wished to end the session considerably earlier, yet I had pressed him to continue till all the sounds of all the letters had been shown me. There were less than six hands of such, nearly all the same as the signs I already knew, yet I found it as difficult separating one from the other as a new warrior finds separating the track of the hadat from the track of the zaran. It was this at which I labored, the separating of the strokes, till Telion stretched and stirred where he sat.

''It seems our meal has been prepared,'' said he, gazing back away from the sheaf toward the metal holder of glowing stones. ''I am pleased to see our stomachs need not suffer due to Jalav's new-found zealousness. I had not thought it would be so.''

''The High Rider kindly accepted my woman's efforts,'' said Cimilan, causing Lialt and myself to turn toward him as well. He lay at his ease upon the furs, his breech and leggings and leg furs having been replaced, his expression strong with satisfaction. Famira knelt beside him, three cuts of meat upon the board she held, the aroma of cooked flesh only then coming to me. The female remained completely unclothed, her hair falling free down her back, her head bent so that the blush on her cheeks might partially be hidden, though the blush on her body showed clearly her awareness of the attention of males. Lialt and Telion grinned as they looked upon her, causing her to further lower her head in misery, and Cimilan chuckled as he sat up and reached over to stroke her hair.

"I feel you now know yourself to have been punished, satya," said he to a Famira who seemed near to tears. "Should you wish to disobey me again, should you attempt to force me to your own selfish ends, you will in future know what the attempt will bring you. Do you understand?"

"I understand," whispered Famira, tears glistening in her eyes as she raised her head to gaze upon Cimilan. "Indeed, all is completely clear to me now."

"Such understanding should be shared with Jalav," said Ceralt from the entrance, having entered in time to hear Famira's words. "I often feel understanding is a total stranger to her."

"In this matter, my understanding is complete." I shrugged, turning about to sit cross-legged upon the fur. "Males may give shame and pain to see their desires brought about, yet females are forbidden to do the same. The reason for this is that males have greater strength and size, therefore, they are free to do as they please. The matter is called, 'concern' or 'civilizing' or possibly, 'love' or 'generosity,' and is clearly a male thing. None save males might act so in the name of honor."

A moment of silence passed, broken only by the rustle of Ceralt's furs being removed, the eyes of all those within the tent resting upon me. The males gazed upon me with frowns, Famira stared with pained yet silent agreement, then Ceralt dried the bottoms of his leg furs and came forward.

"Such sentiments are nonsense," he asserted, removing his leather chest covering before crouching to face me. "Would you prefer seeing men give women true physical pain to see themselves obeyed? Would you have them beat their women with a lash to spare them the discomfort of embarrassment? Should these women be struck down with swords for the crime of insolence or haughtiness? Men are indeed larger and more powerful than women—yet they need not be brutal in their strength. It is enough to do only that which must be done to see themselves obeyed."

"And who is to decide what must be done?" I countered, looking up into his light, serious eyes. "It is, of course, the male himself. Surely it is more brutal to lash a female than to shame her to the point of wishing for death, says he, therefore do I show great generosity in doing no more than giving shame. That she may no longer hold her head up in dignity is of no moment, for surely she is more appealing to males with her head lowered and her eyes upon their feet. Surely does the male feel more a male with his female cowering upon her knees, a living tribute to his prowess as a male. How difficult it is, to put a small frightened, unarmed, female to her knees before you! How great is your concern for others, and how noble!''

"Enough!'' growled Ceralt, putting his hands to my arms to shake me. "It is bitterness which speaks within you, not reason! The dignity you speak of is no more than foolish female pride, a pride now pinched to tenderness. It galls you that you may not be served by those about you, but must instead serve them, and as a woman. Women do indeed serve men because they are the smaller, the weaker. Those who serve well need fear neither pain nor embarrassment, a fact which you seem to have overlooked.''

"Ah, they are free, then, to obey,'' I nodded into his anger. "How may one not envy such freedom, such glory? Indeed is Jalav wrong to bemoan her lot when such freedom may be hers as well.''

"What has gotten into you?'' demanded Ceralt, releasing my arms to send a frown toward me. "Why do you suddenly speak so when heretofore the words must needs be torn from you?''

"I have learned a thing from males,'' I shrugged, putting my hands to my arms where his fingers had dug so deep. "To shame a female gives a male great pleasure, the more he desires her, the greater his pleasure. Too, her silence in the face of his great generosity does no more than convince him of her fear of him and her approval of his actions. Jalav is a warrior born, bred to fear no male living or dead. She shall never find aught save shame and pain at the hands of males, for such is the trial imposed upon her by Mida. To remain silent to avoid such shame and pain is the act of a coward, a thing she has, till this moment, failed to see. Ceralt may beat her or shame her as he wishes, yet no longer will she remain silent in cowardly escape. She shall speak as she sees fit till commanded to silence by he who holds her captive.''

"Yet, even then, the sentiment shall remain, the words merely unspoken,'' nodded Ceralt, his eyes flat, his expression veiled. "No matter how I speak upon the matter, no matter what kindness I show you, still will you see naught save your own views, hear naught save your own beliefs. In your own thoughts you remain a captive—and a warrior. You have previously been warned concerning such attitudes; now shall you be punished. Come with me.''

Ceralt again stood erect in the silence about us, then turned away to walk to the center of the tent. The other males appeared most sober-faced as they watched me rise to follow him, yet none spoke a word as Ceralt seated himself cross-legged in the fur, then indicated a place at his feet.

"My captive may now kneel here, before her captor," said Ceralt, gazing up at me where I stood. "Remove that breech and place yourself at my feet, where you belong, and speak not another word till you have my permission to do so. As you care so little for what is done to you, the position should cause you neither pain nor shame."

My hesitation at his command was brief indeed, yet the lack of understanding which caused it was longer in duration. Fully had I expected to be beaten for my words, yet Ceralt, it seemed, was not of a mind to do so. He watched as I removed the breech and threw it from me, his light eyes showing little anger. It seemed more like pain which lurked in the pale, deep pools, yet naught had been said which might have caused such pain. I had spoken naught save the truth, yet the male felt pain from the words. Did he truly think himself blameless that the truth would put such a look in his eyes? As I knelt before him I would have spoken my questions, but I had been commanded to silence.

"You do not yet seem the proper captive," mused Ceralt, studying me where I knelt, then his hand came swiftly to my hair. "I believe it would be best if this warrior's head were bowed in proper humility. Bend yourself so, Jalav, and do not move till I release you."

His fist in my hair put my head to the furs, forcing my body forward toward him as though I bowed in his presence. I knew a moment of anger and humiliation, then forced the feelings from me. The shame given me was by the will of Mida, no more than another trial her warrior must endure—yet the need for endurance was a trial in itself.

"Now, let us eat," said Ceralt, a thick heartiness in his tone. "Come and join me, brothers. Cimilan, is your wench prepared to serve us?"

"Certainly, High Rider," replied Cimilan, his voice somewhat subdued. "Famira, my heart, see to the others first."

"Yes, Cimilan," replied the female, the sound of her rising lost in the sound of the others taking their places. There was much moving about, murmured comments and questions, and then all seemed at last to be settled with their provender. I knelt as Ceralt had placed me, my head to the fur at his knee, my eyes seeing naught save the fur and my own knees.

"How went the arrival of Hannil?" asked Lialt after a few moments of silence. "Surely their tents already stand about the clearing with ours."

"Their tents stand," agreed Ceralt about a mouthful, then he paused to swallow before continuing. "Hannil himself stands with anger, for he is far from convinced of the wisdom of the journey. We must see to it that he does not return immediately from whence he came. When our meal is done, we are invited to visit his tent."

"Surely, his own Pathfinder has seen the necessity for the journey," protested Lialt. "Why does he continue to hesitate?"

"I know not," muttered Ceralt, once again at his provender. "Perhaps we shall soon find out."

The meal continued in silence, telling me little of the doings of others. I knew not whether those seated upon the lanthay fur looked upon me, yet it mattered not. Should the males press Ceralt for my use, they would show they had looked upon me. I knew the meal as having been concluded when the sound of movement betokened someone's rising.

"We will now return to our own tent, High Rider," said Cimilan, his voice as subdued as it had been. "I thank you for your assistance, and wish you success in your dealings with Hannil. Famira, replace your leathers."

Soft footsteps hurried through the lanthay fur to do Cimilan's bidding, and again the silence descended till Cimilan himself donned his leather chest covering and went toward his body furs. Then came the sound of footsteps close to me, and Famira's voice above me.

"Ceralt—cousin—I beg of you not to be too harsh with her," she whispered, a catch in her voice. "I feel sure she spoke as she did primarily on my behalf. I would not wish to see her punished because of me."

"Do not be concerned, cousin," Ceralt replied, his voice as soft as hers. "Jalav must reap what she sows—else she feels herself free to do as she pleases. Would you see yourself punished for insolence while Jalav goes free?"

"She and I are not the same," the female replied, a wistfulness in her voice. "I would deny it if I were able—I have never before felt another woman superior to myself—yet denial would be idle. She is more than I shall ever be able to become."

"You speak foolishness," snorted Ceralt, an impatience entering his tone. "The wench is no different from you, no different from any other. She kneels at my feet, obedient to my wishes, and may be put beneath me as easily as you were put beneath Cimilan. Where, then, lies the difference?"

A brief moment of silence came, underscoring the heat of Ceralt's demand, and then a stirring sounded, accompanied by a sigh which was half sob.

"Ah, cousin, my heart aches for you," whispered Famira, her voice muffled as though against Ceralt's shoulder. "I see now how greatly you desire her to be yours, so greatly you attempt to deny the evidence of your senses. May the Serene Oneness hear your prayer for aid and assist you to victory; I fear she will never be mastered as easily as I."

"Famira," Ceralt began, his voice softened again so that it nearly faltered. "Cousin, I thank you for your thoughts on my behalf. You make me proud before the man who has chosen you. Go with him now, and feel no further concern. All shall be well."

A sound came as though they embraced, and then the female rose to her feet and departed the tent, the amount of cold entering saying two left at once. Stirring dotted the silence, and then Ceralt spoke again.

"No, Telion, do not say you agree with the wench," he growled, all softness having left his tone. "A female may be thanked for uttering muddleheaded foolishness; a man should know better."

"I intended saying nothing of the sort," replied Telion with a yawn. "I merely intended pointing out that our wench here has felt herself responsible for all wenches about her for quite some time. Perhaps it is too soon to expect her to witness another wench's punishment without the bitterness of being helpless to prevent it."

"Perhaps," Ceralt conceded, his voice unconvinced. "She may indeed be bitter for such a reason, yet a reason does not dispense with the need for punishment. If naught else, she must learn her old responsibilities are no more."

"Such a thing may take more time than we currently possess," Lialt sighed, rising to his feet. "I feel the Times pressing, the Snows demanding their due. There shall soon be room for thought of naught else. Is Jalav to accompany us to Hannil's tent, or remain behind?"

"She must accompany us," Ceralt replied, also rising to his

feet. "Hannil must be shown every bit of evidence we possess to convince him of the necessity for the journey. How may we do so without the presence of the hadat? Jalav, straighten yourself now and replace your leathers. All of them."

I raised my head from the furs in obedience to Ceralt's word, yet found the need to kneel in place till the lightheadedness and whirling left me. The males, including Telion, all moved about fetching their leathers and furs, yet soon were able to stand and watch as I donned mine. Their interest in me seemed other than usual, with no word spoken even as we left the tent.

Without the tent the cold seemed to draw the life from one, a small wind sending it deep within one's leathers and furs. Through the strange, lightened darkness and snow we trudged, toward a set of tents which had not stood about the clearing earlier. One tent, larger than the others as it was like that of Ceralt, three tents as one, was that to which we walked, all hurrying to the urging of the wind and cold. In but a few reckid we had reached its entrance, and Ceralt led Lialt within, Telion's arm urging me in before him.

The new tent appeared no different from Ceralt's, yet the smells within were strange and unattractive. Ceralt and Lialt paused to remove their furs, as did Telion behind me, yet it took a nudge of some strength from Telion before I was reminded that my leg furs must be removed with the rest. I did so most unwillingly, uneasy in the atmosphere which lay heavily all about, then Lialt and Ceralt moved more fully into the tent, and I was able to see those who occupied it.

Three males sat in a line upon the furs, two reclining at their ease, the third seated cross-legged as he drank from a skin which undoubtedly contained near-renth. Dark of hair and eye were these males, like all village males save Ceralt and Lialt, large, broad and strong like the others, yet somehow less alert, less alive. Each male was attended by a female, slight, dark, unclothed—and chained. The females knelt beside their males, their wrists, chained together, held close to their throats by yet another chain which circled their throats, their faces tense, their eyes filled with misery and fear. It was this fear which stained the air, fouling it so that to breathe it was to breathe terror and defeat, despair and hopelessness. Ceralt and Lialt moved as though reluctant to enter, and Telion made a sound in his throat, too low for others to hear. Had it been possible, I would have left on the instant.

"Ah, Ceralt!" boomed he with the skin of near-renth, wiping

his mouth upon the back of his hand. "Thinking you would be longer in coming, we were about to begin a sport with our wenches. See, they have already been chained."

"What a shame our arrival has caused you an inconvenience," murmured Lialt, looking down upon the females. "The sport would undoubtedly have been an extraordinary one."

"Not at all," laughed the seated male, putting his hand to the female kneeling beside him. "Deela has many times played at the sport, therefore do the other two wenches lose to her with regularity. Perhaps it is time to devise a new sport, one which is equally unknown to them all."

The female Deela, kneeling beside the male, had seemed as fearful as the other females—till one looked into her eyes. Secret triumph lurked within the large, dark orbs, twisting the female's beauty to pleasured cruelty. At the male's words her skin paled and terror came to her eyes, and immediately she bent farther and began putting her lips to the male's belly and thighs.

"I see Deela wishes no part of a new sport," laughed the male, putting his fist to her hair to hold her still. "To the rear of the tent with you, wench, on your knees and head to the fur. Serious business is now at hand; sport must wait for another time. All of you wenches, go!"

The three females struggled to their feet, hurried to the packs at the rear of the tent, then knelt with heads down as they had been commanded. Little relief had shone in their eyes, for their torment had merely been postponed.

"Does that one not know herself female?" asked the seated male, his eyes of a sudden resting upon me. "Did I not say all females were to obey me?"

"Hannil, this is Jalav," said Ceralt, turning to regard me without expression. "Do you forget the words describing the hadat of our journey? This one is hadat in truth, as opposed to accompanying us as would be one which walked upon four legs. She obeys none save me, for I have made her my woman."

"Her eyes show little obedience of any sort," muttered he called Hannil, displeased to a large degree. "How is she beneath those leathers? Worth the taking?"

"She is scarred," said Ceralt, returning his gaze to the seated male. "She was near death when we retrieved her from the forests to which she had fled. She will wear the marks upon her for all of her days."

"Indeed," murmured the seated male, leaning back at his ease. "And yet, how badly wounded might she have been, that she now stands before us? I understand you claim the intervention of the Serene Oneness, preserving her solely to allow her to make this journey. Perhaps I had best see these scars you speak of, so that I, too, may be certain of the matter of intervention."

Ceralt gazed down upon the male Hannil, his face expressionless, his body unexplainably more tense than it had been, unaware of the look Lialt sent him, unaware of Telion's stirring beside me. No more than a brief instant did Ceralt stand so, and then he nodded as though naught had occurred.

"Certainly," said he, something of a smile upon his face. "Let us by all means make certain of your belief. Jalav, remove your leathers."

The eyes of the seated males came to me at Ceralt's words, and I disliked their stare in its entirety. They anticipated more than the sight of the tracks of Silla spears, a thing obvious from the gleam in their eyes, the licking of their lips. They seemed more youthful than their appearance would indicate, mere children all aglow, about to indulge in forbidden pleasures. These males were males in appearance only, as some Hosta captives had proven to be, fit only to have lips curled when warriors looked upon them.

"Remove that look from your face!" Telion hissed in my ear, unnoticed by the others as they inspected my legs where I had begun taking the leather from me. "Would you force Ceralt to punish you here, before these others, to salve their pride?"

I made no reply to the male, merely removing the covering from my upper body, seething within at the battle my mind fought. Was I to hide my disgust at these new males to keep from being shamed before them? I could not bear either thought, wishing only to be shut of the entire lot of them, gone about Mida's business as I was destined to go. How long, Mida, how long?

"Surely those are spear scars," frowned one of the seated males, moving his eyes about me. "It seems unbelievable that she walks and uses her hands. I have seen riders permanently crippled with wounds less severe."

"Yet they do naught to distract from the femaleness of her," said Hannil, his eyes resting upon my breasts. "Have her remove the breech as well, Ceralt."

"There are no further scars to be seen beneath her breech," replied Ceralt, folding his arms across his chest. "Do we speak as those who shall ride together, Hannil, or do we merely nod in passing, each going his own way alone? Have you come here merely to see another wench stripped before you? Your own wench seems attractive enough to satisfy the wants of any man. Must we exchange wenches to have your agreement to the journey?''

Ceralt spoke sharply, deriding the other male, seemingly out of patience with the foolishness presented him. Hannil turned his head sharply toward Ceralt, nearly angered at having been spoken to so, and then he laughed.

"We had best not quarrel, brother," said he, something distasteful behind his amusement. "The journey ahead of us will take much effort—if it is to be successful."

"You will go then?" Lialt pounced, gladness in his tone. "You believe in the journey?"

"I have been forced to believe," grimaced Hannil, reaching again for the skin of near-renth. "My own Pathfinder spoke to me of it before the arrival of Ceralt's messenger, a dozen feyd before. I was also told of the hadat, what her appearance must be, how she would respond to the journey—and the certainty that death awaited us should the journey not be made. I wished only to see this wench of yours, to assure myself she was indeed the one spoken of by my Pathfinder. Take seat and let us drink together now, for who knows how much longer we will be able to do so?"

The three males about me looked upon one another, then took their places upon the lanthay fur, facing those who already sat. He called Hannil drank from the skin he held then passed it about, seeing that each of the males did as he had done. Once the drink had been partaken of by all, the females were ordered from the back of the tent, touched and kissed briefly by the males to whom they had run, then sent to the three males who were guests within their tent. She called Deela threw herself upon Ceralt, squirming and kissing at him, causing him to laugh in delight as she attempted to please him with her wrists chained near to her neck. I alone stood where I had been, arms folded beneath my life sign, body straight, head held high. The males had come for serious talk, yet there they sat, arms about the females who had crept to them, laughter in their voices, desire in their eyes. After some reckid of sport the talk again turned to the trail, a matter which should have been seen to at once. These males made mighty warriors indeed.

Surely more than a hin passed in talk of formations and march times, supplies and hunting, how many would remain behind with the females, how many would continue on. The males seemed intent upon the talk, yet how may one discuss possible battle amid the giggling and wheedling of slave-women? Ceralt and Lialt and Telion seemed pleased with the distractions pressed upon them, a thing Hannil did not fail to note. Many times did his eyes come to study me where I stood, and at last he leaned back once more in the lanthay fur.

"I see, Ceralt, that Deela pleases you," said he, showing a pleasure of his own. "I find it odd that your own woman fails to kneel by your side, allowing, instead, another female the task of seeing to her man's pleasure. Have you instructed her to act so?"

Ceralt raised his eyes to regard me, listening to Hannil's words without expression, his hands spread out upon the female Deela, who pressed nearer and ever nearer to him. A moment passed in silence after Hannil had completed his observation, then Ceralt shook his head.

"No, I have not instructed her to act so," said he, all inflection gone from his voice. "She continues to refuse acknowledgment of her position as a man's wench, and I grow weary of it. Your wench's welcome is a pleasant change."

"Yet you must continue to keep the cold wench by you, for her presence is critical," nodded Hannil, sober concern and complete understanding clear in his manner. "A pity you, who labor in the cause of all, must suffer while others make merry about you." Hannil's head shook in commiseration, and then his face lighted as his hand smote his thigh. "No, by Sigurr's putrid breath, it need not be! You, too, shall have pleasure, for this darkness at the very least! You may use Deela, and I shall keep watch over this silent statue."

"That is very kind of you, Hannil," Ceralt began, his hands amove upon the female he held, "yet it may not. . . ."

"No, no, I insist!" interrupted this Hannil, his face pleased and full of friendship. "You need not protest out of a sense of propriety, for I shall hear none of it. As there be two other wenches in the tent, I will not find myself bereft. Take her, brother, and find the joy in her you have so valiantly earned."

Ceralt hesitated, and then his eyes touched me again, staring as though he searched for a sign which might guide him. I took my gaze from his and looked toward the tent wall, already knowing which way he would decide. Ceralt wished a village slave-woman for his own, one who knew naught of being a warrior. Jalav was not one such as that.

"You see, she makes no protest," said Hannil, his voice as

pleased as it had been. "To an unwilling wench, one place is as distasteful as another."

"Apparently you see the thing more clearly than I," said Ceralt, and then came the sound of his rising to his feet. "Had she desired to return with me, she would have spoken of it. I accept your kind offer, Hannil, and shall find some means by which to repay you. Remove the chain from this wench so that she may find her leathers and furs. Jalav, as my company is so distasteful to you, you will remain here."

Further sounds came, of rising and dressing and preparations for departure, yet through it all I continued to look upon naught save the far wall. Ceralt had the female he desired, clearly his free choice in the matter, yet had he attempted to show the choice as one forced upon him by my actions. Was I to believe he had no memory of commanding me to silence, that he spoke of the lack of words from me? Perhaps the male spoke to confuse the others, yet it mattered not. Again had I been given to a strange male, to face the trials imposed upon me by Mida.

Ceralt and the others, accompanied by the female Deela, at last left the tent to a considerable silence. Hannil and his males sat in silent contemplation of me, eyes hooded and faces thoughtful, and then, after a full hand of reckid, Hannil rose to his feet to approach me. His face showed naught of what he was about, yet suddenly was I taken and held by male strength, his arms about me and holding me still, till the chains taken from the female Deela were firmly closed upon me. About my throat was the largest secured, to that one the two upon my wrists attached, all holding me as Hannil wished, confining me as though I were a slave. Hannil laughed to see the manner in which I struggled, useless as always against the metal of males, then his fist found my hair to force my gaze up to his.

"It is now time for sport earlier begun, wench," said he, stroking his hand down my belly to the breech about me, then tearing the breech away. "Now you seem much the same as any other wench, save perhaps a bit more to pleasure a man's hands and eyes. Truly are you well made, well made indeed."

His hands, free of the breech, came to fondle and stroke my breasts, quickly bringing them to eager points. Again I struggled against the chain which held me, shamed to my soul that the touch of one such as he would reach my blood.

"You are quick to heat for one so cold," he laughed, taking the points he had made between his fingers. "It is my sincere hope that you will be first to lose the game, allowing me rapid access to this body of yours. Taking you now would be pleasant, yet entirely against the rules of the game."

The other males asprawl upon the lanthay fur laughed with the one before me, then was I pushed to the center of the tent, a moment later joined by the other two females, propelled in the same manner.

"For the benefit of the newcomer, I shall explain again the rules of the game," said Hannil, coming to stand before myself and the two who cringed in fear beside me. The male now let cruelty stare from his eyes, now that males who knew him not were gone. "The matter is simple, Jalav, in that there are the bodies of two forest scarm hidden within this tent. You wenches must search for them without use of your hands, and immediately upon finding one must take it in your teeth and bring it forth to lay it at our feet. She who fails to find a scarm is the loser, and must then pleasure my riders and me till our desire is spent. We, of course, take the loser together, that she not feel undesireable and unwanted. Do you understand?"

His eyes again moved about me, his grin strong as he stood with fists upon his hips. I said naught to that which I had been told, for I had not been given instruction for my own benefit. These males held to a twisted code, one which demanded that they give warning to their intended prey, a warning which would nevertheless prove useless. Though I failed to acknowledge their instruction, their codes were satisfied, as Hannil's nod immediately showed.

"You may now all begin," said he, stepping back and to one side. "We bid you good hunting."

The other males laughed softly with their leader as the two females beside me looked fearfully about, then moved in opposite directions to begin their search. I continued to stand as I was, declining even to look in the places where the scarm must lay hidden. A smell of dead things came from two places to the rear of the tent, one which should have been clear even to those of cities and villages. Though Jalav continued to be captive to those about her, her senses had not yet died as theirs had long since done. The males looked upon my refusal, glanced at each other and to their leader, then those upon the lanthay fur rose to join Hannil in standing before me.

"Unwilling and unbending," murmured Hannil, a hand to his face, his eyes calculating. "Shall we declare her loser now, or wait till the others have found their scarm?"

"If she will not search, she cannot win," said one of the others, putting out a hand to stroke my thigh.

"And yet, the insolence in her gaze annoys me," said the second, staring deep into my eyes. "As though she might win easily should she wish to make the effort."

"Aye, there is much insolence to be seen in her," nodded Hannil, his eyes aglow. "I feel she will make no effort to please us as she is, therefore must we give her reason to make the effort."

He then turned away from me to go to his belongings, and when he straightened to face me once more, his hands held a lash. Those females who had been searching the tent froze where they knelt, terror filling their eyes, a terror I, myself, could feel in no small part.

"See the look in her eyes now!" Hannil exclaimed, pointing with the coiled, heavy leather lash. "The bite of the sednet has not even reached her, yet she knows and fears it. Once she has felt its kiss, her service will be eager indeed. Hold her."

I turned to run from the males, from the pain they intended for me, yet escape was not possible. With my wrists fast to my throat, I was caught easily before I might gain the opening of the tent flap. The two males turned me roughly back to the center of the tent, threw me to my knees, then forced my head to the fur with their fists in my hair. I fought them uselessly, near mindlessly, recalling again and again the touch of the lash, the fire of its track, the scream of its presence. I writhed in the males' grip, feeling their amusement through the relentlessness of their hold, hearing when Hannil shook out the coils of the lash as Bariose had done so long ago in the city of Bellinard. I shook to the fear which held me even more tightly than the males themselves, trying in vain to keep my voice still.

"No!" I screamed, the word forced from me, though my insides came forth with it. "No! Ceralt!"

"Ah, the wench speaks," laughed Hannil, pleasure much in evidence. "A pity her words are wasted on one who lies elsewhere, sporting with a gift. He does not hear you, my pretty, nor would he care even if he were to hear. Let us begin."

I screamed the scream of a wounded hadat, fear and hatred and pain co-mingled, trapped by those who would savage my soul. I twisted about in helplessness, awaiting the first stroke of fire, and then a voice spoke, startling all within the tent.

"You are mistaken," came the soft, menacing tones, fury held carefully to feed the softness. "Ceralt does hear and does indeed care. Release her now or face me with weapons. I care not which you choose.''

The hands of the males, so tight to my arms and hair, quickly disappeared, allowing me to straighten upon my knees. Within the tent stood Ceralt, Lialt and Telion entering behind him, all staring with deep anger at Hannil and his males.

''Remove the chains from her,'' said Ceralt, looking as though he kept himself from speaking further only with great difficulty. Hannil stood where he had been, the lash in his fist, fury upon his face, without words to counter Ceralt's demands. One of the two males who had held me removed the chains from my throat and wrists, and Ceralt gestured to my leathers and furs, indicating that he wished me to don them. I rose to my feet and did as he commanded, sickness filling me over that which I had done. When completely clad, Lialt and Telion held the tent flap for me, then they and Ceralt followed my track into the cold and darkness.

I walked across the snow, surrounded by the males, so completely filled with shame that I could not bear my own company. I had been a fool to think no further shame could touch me, a fool to believe no worse could come to me than at the hands of males. I had shamed myself more than the males had ever done, a thing I had not thought possible to do. And yet the why of it eluded me, the reason for its having happened. Never before had I sunk so low, and I knew not how a warrior might bear it.

''Those vermin!'' snarled Telion suddenly, no longer able to keep silent. ''It is now no wonder that those wenches cringe when near them! Do we truly require their presence, Ceralt?''

''Unfortunately, yes,'' replied Lialt when Ceralt did not speak. ''The Snows demand their presence as they demand ours. Should matters change, I will speak of it at once.''

''Jalav, were you hurt?'' asked Ceralt, abruptly stepping beside me to put his arm about me. At the shake of my head his arm closed more tightly, his free fist rising before him. ''Through no fault of mine!'' he spat, his anger directed elsewhere than at me. ''Sigurr take my wits, for surely I, myself, have never used them! To leave you there. . .!''

''Gently, Ceralt,'' soothed Telion, coming to place a hand upon his shoulder. ''Even I failed to see the truth at first. A man cannot be blamed for being blinded by pain and disappointment. You thought she wished none of you, forgetting her inability to show her true emotions, thought she refused even to speak to you, forgetting you commanded her to silence. Be thankful we saw the truth in time to correct the error."

"Barely in time," muttered Ceralt, yet he gave over railing at himself for the balance of the walk. When we reached his tent he thrust me first within, then he and the others followed. I immediately began removing my furs in the heat, and was startled by the abrupt appearance before me of the female Deela, who had earlier been taken from Hannil's tent by Ceralt.

"No!" snapped the small female, seemingly in great anger. "You were to remain in my place while I took yours! You may not return here this darkness!"

"Do not fear, wench, you shall not be so quickly returned," said Ceralt, coming to stand beside me. "There are other furs to be filled in this tent aside from mine."

"Let *her* fill them!" spat the female, tossing her head in fury. "I am too beautiful and desirable for any man not a High Rider! Hannil allowed the others to toy with me, yet only he took me! I am meant for the High Rider of the Belsayah, and so it will be!"

"I see," murmured Ceralt, stepping forward to look down upon the small, pretty female. "I also see that the fear you felt in Hannil's tent is no more. Why should this be so, wench?"

"What is there to fear here?" The female shrugged, looking uninterestedly about the tent. "All know Belsayah men are weak, too weak, even, to own a lash. I am weary from the fey's ride, Ceralt, and wish to be taken to your furs now. We may not dally long, of course, for Hannil will insist upon an early beginning come the new light. Should you intend to use me at all, it must be now."

"Must it indeed," murmured Ceralt, his head high as Lialt and Telion joined him about the female. The poor, foolish slave-woman saw naught of the manner in which the three gazed upon her, for she seemed more interested in her own appearance than in the thoughts of males. She stood somewhat turned from them, her hands to her hair, her body held gracefully beneath the leathers she yet wore. As the three males exchanged glances of annoyance and anger, I turned from them all, went to the far side of the tent, removed my leathers, and sat. I cared not how the discussion would be resolved, so filled with shame and dismay was I.

"Brothers, we have been ordered to our furs," said Ceralt,

looking not upon the other males but upon the unseeing female. "Think you we dare do other than obey?"

"Certainly not," said Lialt, folding his arms across his chest. "Belsayah riders, in their weakness, dare do naught other than obey."

"Yet, I am no more than a visitor among the Belsayah, a lowly warrior of the cities," said Telion, also with arms afold. "Perhaps I, alone, might be permitted to disobey."

"Have you truly such courage?" asked Ceralt of Telion, watching as the female at last turned to regard them with a frown. "I, myself, am too fearful, too beaten down."

"Should Telion do such a thing, I, too, may find the wherewithal to act so," said Lialt, looking, like the other males, no place other than upon the female. She, seeing their stares, slowly began shaking her head, slowly, wide-eyed, began backing away, yet the realization of her true position came far too late. Telion and Lialt moved no more than two easy paces before the female found herself trapped between them, her leathers the most immediate object of their hands. She struggled and screamed as though being torn limb from limb, indignation high within her, yet so quickly were the leathers removed that she stood bare before them in no more than a moment.

"This may not be!" the female fumed, attempting to pass the two males and approach Ceralt. "I am not meant for the likes of them!"

"You may be correct," Ceralt nodded most soberly, looking upon the female's body with pleasure. "Should they touch you and find you completely unresponsive, they will allow you sleeping furs of your own, where you may lie undisturbed. If, however, they find a spark of warmth within you, they will encourage it till you politely request your use. Belsayah men allow a large measure of freedom to wenches who do not belong to them. If it is this which you mistook for weakness, you will not mistake the two again."

The female cried out in anger as Lialt and Telion, having removed their leg and chest coverings, took her to the far side of the tent, Telion holding her arms as Lialt unfolded two sets of sleeping furs. The three were quickly down upon the furs, Ceralt doing no more than removing his chest and leg coverings as he watched Lialt and Telion begin to give the female their attention. The female truly seemed to dislike their touch, yet was she female and they male. They touched and stroked her body, kissed and caressed it, demanded and took; when next she cried out it was with desperation, a look of disbelief strong upon her face. Her body writhed to their smallest touch, showing it would not be long before she begged her use. Ceralt stood and chuckled as he watched, and I turned away, too ill to scorn or commiserate.

It could not have been more than two hands of reckid before the female began screaming in her need, causing laughter among the males. I barely knew when one of them began giving her release, knew naught of the approach of Ceralt till his hand touched my arm. I opened my eyes to see that the flames-within-boxes had been extinguished, and was glad of the darkness which hid me within it.

"Come to my furs, satya," Ceralt said softly, a shadow rising straight beside me. I, too, rose to my feet, made my way through the darkness in his wake, then lay myself down beside him. His hands touched my body, found the breech I yet wore, quickly removed it, then drew me more closely to him. I had not resisted, could not resist, yet his lips touched mine only briefly before his head drew back.

"What disturbs you, satya?" he whispered, a concern to be heard in his tone. "Are you yet disturbed that I was so foolish as to leave you with Hannil?"

I shook my head, dismissing the suggestion, knowing there was a thing of greater moment concerning me.

"Your misery is so strong that I feel it in your flesh," said Ceralt, moving his hand upon me. "Speak of that which disturbs you, so that I may share it and perhaps ease it."

"Do not ask me to speak of it," I whispered, closing my eyes even against the sight of his shadow form. "Have I not shamed myself enough that you would have me add to it?"

"Shamed yourself?" echoed Ceralt, confusion in his tone. "In what manner have you shamed yourself? I bid you speak, woman, for I would hear of this."

I writhed briefly in his arms, consumed with the need for silence, achingly aware that I could not disobey, then choked out, "Why do you force me to this? You yourself heard my shame, the weakness and fear so great within me that I called upon a male sooner than face it. How am I to call myself a warrior, knowing I behaved so? How am I to think myself a war leader, who must know no fear? And how am I to bear being forsworn, from speaking my cowardice after having been bidden to silence? Truly have I shamed myself more than any effort of yours."

I attempted to twist from his arms, to take my shame further away into the darkness, yet he pulled me tight to his chest and held me there, stroking my hair with a gentle hand.

"You are not forsworn," said he, sounding much like a war leader correcting the misconceptions of her warrior. "Were you not told, long ago in the forests between Bellinard and Ranistard, that should someone again offer you harm you were to raise your voice and shout for my assistance? To obey my command is not to be forsworn."

I paused in my agitation, suddenly recalling the time he spoke of, yet the discovery did little to ease my upset. I had not had memory of such instruction, had not recalled it and purposely acted to obey. If not forsworn I remained much shamed, for such a thing could not be faced with other than the truth.

"Ah, Jalav," Ceralt sighed. "Still does the misery hold you. The strictness of your codes continue to give me pain—and your adherence to them as well. You spoke of shame, yet I failed to see what shame there might be for you in a thing which gave me such joy. Do you not know, woman of my heart, how long I waited to hear you call upon me in need, rather than bear the load yourself, alone and in silence? My heart leaped with greater joy than it had ever known—and you found naught save shame therein? Can there be shame in giving another such joy?"

"How can there be joy in another's fear?" I whispered. "How can there be joy when that fear should never have been voiced? Why must males forever find joy in that which brings a warrior agony?"

I spoke these words, aching within, caring naught for what Ceralt might do upon hearing them. Should he end my life in his anger, the world would be the better for it.

"Why must such fear be unvoiced?" he demanded, suddenly less than gentle. "Are you so different from others that you, alone, must feel no fear? Men feel fear, and wenches too, and all gain in the feeling of it. How can there be bravery if fear is never felt? To overcome such fear is the mark of a man, not the denial of its very existence. When the thing feared is worthy of fear, there is no shame in the voicing of it."

"There can be no bravery without fear," I echoed, my hand reaching to touch his arm, my mind, though well confused, recognizing the truth in his words. "Yet I cried out to you, like a craven, begging the aid I should not have needed. I showed no bravery, and the words cannot be called back."

"When fear and need are so strong that one cries out, to whom does one call?" he asked, gentle yet not to be denied.

"Does one call to a stranger, to the one offering harm, begging their lenience? Such a thing would indeed be weakness—yet this was not what was done. You called to one who holds your trust despite the witless things he does, despite the pain he has caused you. You called to one who holds your heart as you hold his—to one who is forever a part of you. Is there shame, my heart, in calling upon another part of you?"

I fell silent in confusion, knowing his words mistaken, yet knowing not how they might be denied. And a peace stole over me, a peace which might have come from words Keeper-spoken, one which soothed the distress and took all trace of it. Again his lips came to mine, gently demanding, softly taking, and this time the male scent of him came as well, causing my head to whirl as ever it seemed destined to do. My hands touched him as his touched me, and the female Deela and her moans and pleadings were quickly lost for all of the darkness.

# 15.

## *A cave is found— and a carving of evil*

The new light brought an early beginning for all, seeing us well upon the trail before the gray threatening had strengthened to its brightest. Hannil and his Neelarhi rode before those called Belsayah, yet few of Ceralt's Belsayah would have had it otherwise. Though the Neelarhi alone seemed little different from the Belsayah males, Hannil's presence turned them overly concerned with position and order of march. Ceralt gave them the lead with a gesture of disinterest, spending his concern, instead, upon the skies. The smell of the air, windless and calm, promised new whiteness to add to that through which we struggled, an event none looked forward to.

My lanthay once again moved beside that of Telion, this time at Ceralt's direction. I was to remain with Telion or Lialt when I could not be beside Ceralt, for Ceralt mistrusted Hannil and his intentions. Those who called themselves brother to Ceralt seemed pleased with the duty entrusted to them, saying they would see me safe or themselves in Sigurr's grasp. I dwelled as little as I might upon this, for it was all one with Ceralt's thoughts and actions.

Telion hummed to himself as he rode, a distracting sound with little pleasure to it. When he and Lialt had awakened after the darkness, they had done no more than stretch before assuring Ceralt he had missed naught of consequence by not having bedded the female Deela. She, who had been made to sob and writhe far into the darkness, had flown into a fury, looked toward me with a promise of death, then had dressed herself and fled the tent. The males were more amused than I, for the female had not sent her venom toward them but toward me, undoubtedly considering me less than the males. At another time the thought would have annoyed me, yet my own actions and Ceralt's replies remained to plague my waking hind. Did I truly consider him as he had said, and if this were so, how might I rid myself of so foolish a notion? I knew not—in Mida's name, I knew *naught*— and wisest would I be to leave the matter for another time.

The fey continued to a dark, lowering gray, then grew no brighter. Upon halting for our mid-fey meal, Lialt approached me with a sheaf and proclaimed that I had been too silent of late. Perhaps another reading lesson would take my mind from what depths it had plunged to. At first I disliked the idea, then the lure of the thing took me, nearly against my will. Ever has there been a part of me demanding to *know*, and this part refused to be denied. I entered the lesson with more interest than Lialt had expected, then rode beside him the balance of the fey, reciting the letters' callings and describing their shapes. Though I erred more often than I cared for, Lialt pronounced himself extremely pleased, as was Telion. The two males then bound me to secrecy, for they wished me well able to read before Ceralt learned of my progress. Why this was so I knew not, yet both assured me Ceralt's pleasure would be greatest should I do as they demanded. I shrugged the matter off as a thing of males—without sense and without reason—and gave my word to abide by their request. It seemed a small thing to give those who had pledged themselves to my safety.

The snow came no more than lightly at the end of that fey, yet a hand of feyd farther saw our set halted for more than another fey. The snow fell so thickly then that one was unable to see the rider before her, not to speak of the direction in which one rode. The cold decreased, as did the wind, yet the tiny bits called snow swirled all about, making one squint in an attempt to see, turning one's cheeks cold, then colder, then numb, encasing each rider in a low, narrow world of white. We fought to find one another in the stuff, fought to tether the lanthay and erect a tent, then fought to take the numbness from our bones with warmth. Ceralt chafed at the delay, pacing the tent with long, impatient strides, demanding of the air to know where the balance of his people might be. None were able to answer him till the storm was spent, then, by twos and fours, was the set reformed to discover the loss of one male and female of the Belsayah, two each of the Neelarhi. All seemed sobered by these losses, Ceralt and Hannil nearly asnarl, yet I thought the losses not unreasonable. Battle had been joined with the land through which we rode, and where does one find battle without also finding loss?

The second heavy storm, seven feyd past the first, found us already within our tents and fully prepared. Ceralt had relented and allowed Lialt to walk the Snows none other might see, that we might have warning soon enough to face the falling whiteness without loss. This Lialt did with eagerness, yet was I sent to the tent of Cimilan and Famira till the Clouds of Seeing had blown themselves to nothingness upon the cold about us. I grew angry with Ceralt for refusing me the opportunity of again walking the white lands, yet Ceralt would not allow me anger either. When once again the snows whistled chillingly about us, he punished me for my anger by contesting with Telion and Lialt to see which of them might use me the longest—and most often. They each saw that I was given no pain, yet the humiliation of finding my body slave to each male in turn was stronger than I had thought it would be. Though I had thought myself resigned to use by males till Mida freed me from them, the impatience of freedom-soon-to-be made my capture much the worse.

Another hand of feyd went by beneath the hooves of weary lanthay before the males discovered themselves nearly to their goal. Our vision had been constantly hampered, if not by snow swirling from the skies, then by snow blown about by the wind;

the gradual rise of the ground was not noted till the skies briefly
cleared to show us the looming bulk of that which males called
Sigurr's Peak, closer, by far, than any had expected. Ceralt
sought out Hannil, the two conferred, then the march resumed
toward the snow-covered foothills perhaps a fey's ride from
where we stood. Had the ground not risen before the approach to
this Sigurr's Peak, our attempt to reach it would have been much
the longer in the doing.

The new fey brought us to the foothills we had sought, yet the
unevenness of the ground caused the males to push farther on,
seeking a level place where the females of the set might be left in
safety and comfort. Again I thought their actions foolish, for
naught save Lialt's seeing had brought us to our destination;
should we and he fail to return to those left behind, seeking the
return trail would likely cost the females their lives. And upon
the matter of provender, none would speak nor dwell overlong.
We had fed less and less well as the journey went on, little
edible to be found around us, little left of that which we had
brought. Should our quest prove an empty one, the females
would find themselves unable to feed upon lanthay and continue
their trek afoot—as a warrior would do. Ceralt cared little for the
thought of warriors, yet should survival have been possible,
warriors would have survived.

Our lanthay struggled through the mounds of snow, the hind
passing fruitlessly, and then a shout rang out, calling our attention to a large, dark gap in the whiteness. Word passed quickly
of a cave having been found, and all in the set turned their
lanthay toward the haven. The thought of so large a cave cheered
the males and females alike, after having been so long amid
naught save gray sky and white ground. Jalav alone disliked the
look of the place, yet Jalav was not consulted—nor would the
males have heeded her disquiet had she spoken. Jalav was a
savage, and a captive, and knew little of that which males knew.
Jalav was now able to make out small, simple words in the book
Lialt taught her from, yet such was very little in the eyes of a
male.

Gaining the cave was more difficult than the males anticipated.
The snow before it, for some fifty gando-strides, had turned to
ice, making our approach treacherous in the extreme. Many
lanthay slipped and fell, spilling their riders or the load they
bore, some plunged through the ice to rocks and hard-packed
snow, some balked and refused to travel farther upon the uncertain footing. Surely I thought to see lanthay legs and human

necks snapped before all stood within the dryness of the cavern yet, despite all falls and slippings, the entrance was gained without a single loss of life. Ceralt grinned and moved about, ordering torches to be lit, taking one of his own, then leading a hand of males deeper within the darkness of the cavern. Before long many torches were lit, and Ceralt reappeared with confidence restored.

"The cave is perfect," said he, speaking to Hannil yet looking about at those females who crouched against the cave walls, weary nigh unto death at battling snow and frightened lanthay and cold with no roof above them. "We shall leave the wenches here, comfortable and guarded, and return for them when we have found Sigurr's Altar."

"And where might this Altar be found?" rumbled Hannil, much subdued from when he had first joined us. "Should it be much farther, we will not survive to see it."

"It cannot be much farther on," said Ceralt, at last giving Hannil his attention. "It is said to lie in the heart of the Peak, not the head but the heart. Lialt will seek out the trail to this heart, saving us from having to search for it."

"I like this not," grumbled Hannil, throwing his hood back to shake his head. "The Pathfinder is yours, speaking words you wish to hear. Are we to take a trail, knowing naught of where it might lead, leaving our wenches to what might be their fate?"

"Do you propose we join them here?" demanded Ceralt, patently keeping himself from taking offense. "What then of the journey we began—and the people left behind us to face the coming strangers?"

"Perhaps the journey was ill-conceived," muttered Hannil, rubbing a large hand across his face, avoiding Ceralt's eyes. "Perhaps the strangers will go elsewhere, leaving us to live in peace. I am weary of battling snow and cold, lack of food and adequate shelter, illness and discontent. And I do not care for the look of this mountain. It somehow bodes evil—for all of us."

Ceralt's face worked, as though he wished to reply heatedly, yet his temper was soon taken in hand and he nodded toward Hannil.

"I fear we are too weary to discuss this rationally," said he, letting his own weariness enter his tone. "We shall all spend the darkness here, taking our ease, restoring our strength and purpose. The new light will shine on clearer thoughts and stronger wills. Let us enter farther into the cavern, for the bowels of the earth warm it as though it were spring."

All seemed pleased with the thought of warmth, and soon were we entering a large room of a cavern, deep gloom chased to corners by the torches held high by males. The lanthay were left near the entrance, and once the torches were set in hastily chopped niches, the males returned to the beasts of burden to fetch sleeping furs and provender and that which the females deemed necessary. No more than four paces within the cavern I had found it necessary to remove my body furs, and soon all had done as I, retaining no more than leathers.

We all moved about upon the center of the wide floor, yet were the walls of greater interest to one who disliked the place. Amid stone growths from floor and ceiling, a hand of side caverns seemed to beckon with dark mouths, whispering of things which hid from our sight and watched us. Perhaps my dislike of the place peopled the farther darkness with enemies, yet the thought was not an unreasonable one. When one has the care of others to consider, one does not settle down to sleep with unconcern. Some males moved about placing things they had fetched, the females chattered happily to one another, other males stretched and laughed and sported with one another, some females fussed and straightened and unpacked that which they could not survive without. No other save Jalav thought to look about her and wonder upon the fate of any others who had perhaps come first to the cavern. The shelter had been easily found—perhaps too easily—yet no sign of earlier visits remained to be read.

The black coals were quickly brought to heat, meals were cooked thereon, and all settled down to feed, converse, then take their ease—of the males, that is. The females were first required to see to the remains of the meal, the cleansing of boards, the desires of their males. Ceralt, having conferred with Lialt and Telion, took his ease with us, far from Hannil, his eye close upon me to see that I did as the other females. He seemed intent upon finding distraction, grinning well when I removed my leather leg coverings. The warmth was such that I would have preferred also removing my boots, yet the sharp, pebbled rock which floored the cavern disallowed so sensible a course. I had nearly removed my chest covering as well, but this Ceralt had refused to allow. The other wenches would protest such immodesty, he laughed, especially as their men might demand the same of them. Best leave well enough as is, said he, and Lialt and Telion, also with laughter, approved his decision.

With all slave chores seen to, Lialt came to demand my

attention to another reading lesson. I truly had no desire for such, with unlighted, unguarded openings about us, yet Lialt would not hear of refusal. He took my arm and led me to sit upon a lanthay fur thrown beneath a torch, and soon we were immersed in the effort to show me the sight of words I already knew well, yet only to hear. Some words, I learned, though exact in all respects to another just like it, nevertheless were spoken differently at different times. The need for this escaped me till Lialt thought to speak of them as male and female, exact to one who sees no more than shape, different to one who knows the place of each. I grasped the thought with some difficulty, chewing it with the teeth of my mind, and the cavern grew still in the time we sat beneath the torch.

At last I raised my head to see that all those village folk save Ceralt, Lialt and myself lay upon furs in deep, soul-weary sleep, females beside their males, sharing their furs. Perhaps two or three females yet moaned to the touch of their males, softly so as not to bring the eyes of others to them, helpless even in their embarrassment. Ceralt lay awake in his furs, watching as Lialt and I rose to our feet, then gestured that I was to accompany Lialt to his furs before coming to him. Lialt hesitated before removing his leathers, gazing down upon me as though considering refusal, but the sounds of those who continued awake disallowed his refusal. I was taken in his arms beneath his furs, used softly yet well, then sent to Ceralt with a last, deep kiss. Ceralt, heated more than Lialt had been, filled my soul to overflowing, so much so that I failed to stay awake as I had intended, instead finding sleep in the circle of his arms.

I must admit to surprise when I awoke to find all as it had been. The cavern showed little to the eye to cause unease, yet I liked it not. Some few males were also awake, seeing to the replacement of the torches set upon our arrival, a thing which should have been seen to sooner. No more than a handlength remained to most, some already having sputtered out in their niches. I moved about in the furs beside Ceralt, feeling a deep desire to don leather and furs and leave that place, even should the snow fly in the air without, burying all beneath it. Surely there are worse fates than to lie dead beneath the thing called snow, and I somehow felt that my dreams through the darkness had hinted at such.

"Satya, what ails you?" asked Ceralt of a sudden, his voice no more than a murmur in the deep silence. "Throughout the darkness you tossed in sleep, now you continue to toss when awake. Has something disturbed you?"

I lay upon my side, facing away from him, considering the possibility of explaining what I felt. The track of lenga or falth may be easily shown to another in the forest, yet how may one show a track upon the mind, a faint hint upon the breeze, a broken leaf, a knowledge that speaks of the lenga's presence even without evidence one may point to?

"I am uneasy here," I groped, turning slowly to face him. "This place is not what it seems, and none should linger here. Do you truly mean to leave your females behind in this place?"

"We have found no other place to leave them," said he, a frown creasing his brow. "This cavern seems no different from any other to me. What do you see that I do not?"

"There is naught to *see*," I pressed, shaking my head. "One must feel this place to sense that which is here. It is much like a cage for souls which are lost, their bodies no more, their spirits unable to reach a final glory."

"Such is foolishness," he snorted, smoothing my hair with his hand. "Your superstitious nature leads you astray, my girl. There is naught here to cause harm to any."

"So *you* say," I jibed in turn, shaking his hand from my head. "There is a hint of the white land about this place, a lack of sign where there should be, portents where there should be none. Is even Lialt blind and deaf in this place of innocence—or merely at Ceralt's command?"

"Woman, you overreach yourself," he growled, closing his fingers upon my arm. "That I allowed Hannil to speak so does not mean you may take the same liberty. Lialt will walk the Snows before our departure, and then will your theory be tested. Should he find anything, I will be greatly surprised. For now, go and see to Telion's needs, for he has awakened."

Ceralt's hand left my arm, yet the anger did not leave his eyes. He was pleased to speak of my beliefs as superstitions, yet disliked the reminder that Lialt would do exactly as his brother wished, no matter the cost to himself or others. He now attempted to punish me for what he considered insolence, sending me to Telion when he knew full well how I disliked being forced to the service of a male. For a moment I gazed upon the darkness of his face, his light eyes clouded, then did I turn from him and leave his furs to move to Telion's, little more than a pace away. A greater number of males and females stirred about the cavern, some few rising to their feet, others no more than awake in their furs. Telion raised a corner of his furs in invitation, then chuck-led as I lay myself beside him.

"I thank the Serene Oneness that your tongue remains unbridled," said he, gathering me to him. "Was it not such a constant burr to Ceralt's temper, I would have long since found myself deprived of your use. What was the subject which this time caused such disagreement?"

"I merely remarked upon the blindness of males," said I, putting my hands to the broadness of his chest. "Telion. Does naught cause you uneasiness in this place?"

"Uneasiness?" he echoed, losing the grin he had been showing. "I feel naught save a faint closeness which is natural in caverns such as this. Do you sense more?"

"Aye," I nodded with a sigh. "Ceralt calls it superstition and dismisses it, yet do I feel that Mida sends me warning against that which only she might see. Wisest would be to leave here, and that right quickly."

"There are times when wisest is not best," said Telion, matching my sigh. "It is almost certain death for us out there, from cold and snow, if not starvation. Are we to choose certain death over that which may occur? Ceralt thinks not, and I am forced to agree."

"There are many things worse than death," I said in deep disgust, taking my hands from him. "A pity city males have not yet learned this truth."

I began to turn from him, annoyed with myself for believing he would see where others gazed blindly, yet this the male would not allow. Though often seeing more deeply and having greater understanding than other males, Telion yet remained a male within him, displeased with hearing that which he did not wish to hear.

"Jalav is ever so sure in her beliefs," said he, continuing to hold me to him, anger beginning to grow. "To leave the safety of a haven on no more than vague feelings of unease is little more than female foolishness, not for men to indulge in. Take your fears in hand, wench, lest they bring you punishment in the midst of the safety you so earnestly seek."

His hands and lips came to me then, taking the use Ceralt allowed him, using the easing of his needs to mask the thoughts my words had brought. Telion used me hard and well, giving the punishment he and Ceralt wished for me, bringing me greater distress than shame would account for. Throughout the time of my use by Telion, I felt that another watched and waited, his lips dry with the thought of using me, his loins athrob, his fingers curled to claws upon the body of another whom he used in my stead. Soon, said the silent, whispered thoughts of this male, soon it will be you beneath me, woman. Never have you had use as that which I shall put you to. You will survive long enough to know me your master.

I wished to shout defiance at these thoughts which assailed me, yet Telion was deep within me, taking my strength and will, refusing to allow me to do other than that which he demanded. A female in use is a female mastered, said Ceralt in my thoughts, his grin before my eyes, his dark hair reaching down toward the light of his eyes. I moaned and cried out in Telion's arms, feeling a fear like a cloth upon the head, suffocating, strangling, debilitating and terror-making. Telion murmured in pleasure, thinking I, too, felt the pleasure, then the soft cry of his release brought me promise of imminent freedom, then the freedom itself. He held me no more than a moment past his spending, then moved to my side and released me.

"Your leathers now lay upon the stone behind you," said he, smoothing hair from my forehead before putting his lips to it. "Do not arise till you have clothed yourself, else Ceralt will be angered. It was he who placed the leathers there as I took you."

I turned my head to see the leathers he spoke of, afrown that I had not myself seen Ceralt approach. Or had I seen him, merely believing that his face was no more than in my thoughts? Was this confusion one with the belief that another had spoken to me in silence, all born of a great dislike of that which surrounded me? Could the males be correct and I in error? I reached a hand out and drew the leathers to me, so deep in confusion that knowledge of naught else approached me.

Once in breech, chest-covering and boots I rose to my feet, seeing that all those within the cavern were now awake. Females moved about conversing with one another, and some few males of Ceralt's and Hannil's took themselves toward where the lanthay had been left, perhaps to see to their welfare, perhaps to see how the snow and weather fared. I, too, was considering the preparation of provender when those who had gone to the lanthay returned hurriedly in much agitation.

"Ceralt!" shouted one of the males, arun toward his leader. "The lanthay are gone—and the entrance as well!"

"Gone?" echoed Ceralt in shock, amid the gasps and exclamations from all those in the cavern. "They cannot be gone! You and the others must have taken a wrong turning!"

"There *is* no other turning!" the male protested, stopping before Ceralt. Hannil, too, stood with those of his males who had gone to the lanthay, then the second High Rider looked toward the first. They both nodded in mutual decision, then moved off in the direction from which the harried males had run. All knew they went to see the thing for themselves, and many of the males hurried to accompany them. The females gazed upon one another in fear, tears and sobs quickly coming to them, yet tears and sobs avail naught. The decision was easily made that I, too, would accompany Ceralt, yet not so easily seen to. Telion's hand took my arm as I began to pass him, forcing me back from the heels of Lialt.

"What do you think to accomplish there?" he demanded, his light eyes cold. "Do you go to say how evil a place this is, now that we may no longer leave it? Do you wish to see yourself beaten savagely, a victim to the fear of men entrapped? Will you never learn your place is among wenches, far from the doings of men?"

"I merely wished to see the thing for myself," I replied, attempting to loosen the pain of his hold. "To repeat a warning when the attack has been launched is the doing of a fool. Far better to seek out weapons and stand prepared."

"Weapons are not for females," Telion grated, loosening his hold though his eyes remained bleak. "I shall see the thing for both of us, then perhaps speak of what I see. Or fail to see. One may hope those men are indeed in error."

He took himself after the others at no great pace, reluctant to learn an unpalatable truth. I remained where he had stopped me, considering following, then shrugged and crouched instead. Ceralt's fate was not yet upon him, this I knew without having the why of it; following to see a thing I already knew as truth would be idle.

The males returned with far less vigor than they had shown when leaving, proving our difficulty more thoroughly than with words. The females hugged one another and wept their fear and desolation, and the males gathered in the center of the floor to gaze upon one another in anger.

"We are trapped," said Hannil to Ceralt, putting all blame upon the second male. "Where now do we seek Sigurr's Altar, now that we languish in his maw? What now of the journey so necessary to our people? What now of our own lives, lost beyond redemption?"

"Our lives are not yet lost!" snapped Ceralt, all patience with the male gone away. "To take the lanthay could be the work of any, yet to take the entrance as well must be the work of the dark god! Had he wished our lives they would already be his, our bodies struck down more easily than the removal of so large a cavern entrance! That we live must mean that we shall achieve our goal!"

"Yet at what cost?" snarled the other male, his dark eyes wild with fear. "Should Sigurr demand the living death of each man here as his price for that which we have come, who shall deny him? You? The Serene Oneness? Why then was it not the Serene Oneness to whom we spoke our need? Why must it have been Sigurr?"

"The why matters not," growled Ceralt, gesturing a dismissal with one hand. "Surely it was the Serene Oneness himself who demanded our approach to the dark god. Who else may write upon the Snows? Who else would see the thing so far in advance of its happening? We need not trouble ourselves with why, merely with how."

"I shall not trouble myself in any manner," said Hannil, drawing himself up in an attempt at dignity. "Perhaps Sigurr will know those who come unwillingly from those who come to do some mischief. My riders and I no longer count ourselves among you."

With such words did the male take himself off, followed at once by those two who had been with him in his tent, more slowly by those others called his riders. These latter looked upon Ceralt as though wishing they might remain, yet their words undoubtedly belonged to the craven Hannil. Ceralt's eyes followed them away, then his gesture brought his own males closer, so that they might continue their discussion in lower tones.

"Jalav, what are we to do?" whispered a voice, and I turned my head to see Famira bent beside me. She attempted a crouch such as I had taken, yet her balance was too unsure to keep it. She knelt, instead, upon the rock of the cavern floor, and raised large, anxious eyes to my face.

"There is little any may do," I replied in answer to her plea. "We remained when we should have fled, now Mida must see to our safety."

"Within the bowels of Sigurr?" pressed the female, no scorn to her manner. "Is Mida truly that strong?"

"I have stood behind her shield for many kalod," I shrugged. "I shall not doubt till that shield fails me."

"How are they able to sit there so calmly?" the female

demanded, low-voiced, her eyes upon Ceralt and his males who now sat in a close circle, undoubtedly discussing the dilemma and all manner of ways of solving it. "I cannot bear to merely sit here, awaiting the Serene Oneness knows what! I have eaten naught since arising, yet the thought of food is as ashes in my mouth! Is there naught we may do save sit and speak of what has happened?"

"I had thought the next thing to be done would be obvious," said I, rising to my full height to glance about the cavern. "Naught may be done concerning what has happened; however I doubt the thing was done without reason. As Ceralt has said, we yet have our lives; does it not seem likely that we are left as we are that we may search out another passage from this cavern, one we would not have sought had the entrance been kept as it was?"

"Of course!" breathed Famira, rising to her feet to stand beside me, her eyes now bright. "Jalav! We must tell the men at once!"

"While they find themselves so seriously enmeshed with the problem?" I snorted, looking toward the males. "See you there as well; even Hannil and his ilk sit apart, speaking words meant for males alone. Females are not welcome in their midst."

"They cannot refuse to listen to reason!" insisted Famira, her pretty face stubborn. So soon had she forgotten the doing of Cimilan, to teach her her place as a female. "As you do not care to disturb their talk, I shall do it for you!"

Quick as thought she had left my side, marching in determination toward the males. She had gone perhaps three paces when Cimilan discovered her imminent arrival and quickly rose to his feet, stepping away from the males to halt her upon her way and keep her from the others. She attempted speech to him, he interrupted and disallowed the thought, she again attempted to speak, and then did he interrupt for the final time. His dark eyes gazed sternly down upon her as he spoke, undoubtedly reminding her that she was bound to obey him else be punished and before the others. He turned her about and sent her upon her way with the flat of his hand to her seat, not ungently yet with more force than Famira cared to face again. Her fists clenched as she glanced over her shoulder to see Cimilan reclaim his former place, and then she was again before me, tears of anger in her eyes.

"He would not hear a single word," she choked, looking up

to meet my eyes. "How do you know them so well, you who know men so little and so poorly?"

"It is all one with the balance of their actions." I shrugged, putting my hand to my life sign. "How else might they continue to think themselves masters, save they keep their thoughts from their slaves?"

"Well, are we to stand here and await the revelation to strike them?" she demanded. "Can we not look about on our own, finding that which is to be found and showing them their foolishness?"

"It is an action to consider," I allowed, again looking about the cavern. "Let us begin by walking about as though in conversation of our own. Perhaps the proper trail will present itself to us."

"Excellent," nodded Famira, also looking about. "Let us stroll to the right, to the first of the openings in the wall there. It is possible our search may be that easily begun and ended."

There was little reason to disagree, therefore did we make our way across the cavern floor, idly, as though we walked to no real purpose. The females had done as their males, huddling together in groups to weep and seek support from one another, and none seemed to look upon Famira and myself with more than passing interest. The males, deep in the import of their conversations, gave us no whit of their attention, therefore were we soon before the narrow gap in the wall which was our goal.

"Shall we go in?" asked Famira, peering uncertainly through the crevasse to the darkness beyond. "How are we to see where we go?"

"In such a way," I murmured, stepping quickly to the nearest torch upon the wall. No eyes rested upon us, of this I had made certain, therefore was it best to act quickly. I took the torch, returned to the crevasse, and stepped within.

The light of the torch showed a small, stone-rubbled room, much like the cavern we had come from, yet smaller. With Famira close upon my heels we circled the small area, seeking other crevasses which might lead to that for which we searched. A barely seen fold in the wall, hidden by the shadows cast by our torch, formed a private nook from which even the torchlight failed to seep, yet the nook went no farther and was not repeated other places about the wall. We had discovered no more than a dead ending to our hopes, therefore did we take ourselves back to the main cavern.

"Best we replace this torch and later seek another," I said to

Famira, suiting action to words. "We would not wish our doings to arouse curiosity."

"Indeed," murmured the female, gazing past my arm. "A woman of Hannil's comes to join us, yet I am sure she saw naught of where we went. Should she ask about the torch, say we borrowed its use to comfort us."

I turned slowly to look where Famira looked, pretending unconcern, and therefore saw the approach of Deela, she who had been used by Telion and Lialt. The female came with a smirk of private amusement, her steps of a slowness to allow her hips a lazy swing. Though no male masters gazed upon her, still did she move in a manner to give her masters pleasure.

"Ah, the High Rider's wench," said she, halting some two paces before me to widen her smirk. "I was pleased to learn you are indeed less than I, even in your man's eyes."

"No creature is less than a slave," said I, letting my eyes run slowly over her. "Why do you fail to wear your chains where all might see them? Do you believe none see their mark?"

"I am a woman of men, not a slave!" she hissed, all amusement gone away. "It is you who is more the slave! Those Belsayah found it necessary to force me to their pleasure, I, who am meant only for the highest! You, however, are meant for all, which was clear when the High Rider sent you from his furs to the side of another! The red-haired rider used you till you wept, I saw, with Ceralt's full approval! Hannil would never do me so, for I am his alone!"

"Perhaps Hannil does not care to allow opportunity for comparison," murmured Famira, seeing the way my chin rose at Deela's words. The slave-female spoke words of deliberate insult, perhaps thinking herself safe from my wrath. The wrath she thought herself safe from had been long in building, yet venting it upon the small slave female would have given little satisfaction.

"Ceralt knows his worth," continued Famira in a purr, "yet Hannil seems uncertain of his. You say our riders forced you to their pleasure. Was your own pleasure so much less than theirs, so much greater with Hannil? I somehow think not, else you would be less filled with venom at having been returned to Hannil."

"You lie!" hissed the female, much like the venomous sednet, her fingers curled to claws. "Hannil is Ceralt's superior, and all will be shown this when it is he who frees us from the conse-quences of Ceralt's foolishness! I will then throw your lies in your face, for I will be the woman of the only High Rider!"

The female spat her words, then turned and hurried away before Famira or I might show our contempt. We watched her join those other two females of Hannil's tent, then Famira turned diffident eyes toward me.

"Did Ceralt truly give you to the one called Telion?" she asked, a hesitancy in her question. "I had thought Ceralt wished you for his own."

"Ceralt felt he had cause to give me punishment," I growled, then smoothed the growl from my voice when Famira flinched. "It is a thing done by males when they find themselves displeased or disobeyed. Telion, however, was far from displeased. Shall we try the next crevasse?"

"I think it would be best," said Famira, a small quiver in her voice. "I prefer other subjects than punishment."

I took another torch and entered the second crevasse, seeing immediately in the light spilled forth that this second was not like the first. A wide corridor opened before us, bound on either side by walls of stone, leading away into the darkness beyond the reach of the torch. Famira gasped and urged me forward, eager to see where the corridor led, yet I took the time to examine the corridor walls before continuing. A warrior does not turn her back upon unknown stretches, yet the walls yielded no more than further nooks such as that in the first crevasse. Knowing my back secure I continued on, through the corridor and to its end, Famira close by my side, perhaps half a pace behind. Upon reaching the far end we both halted, Famira with a larger gasp, I with a frown.

The chamber which confronted us had no relation to that which had gone before, save that it, too, was taken from the rock about us. Nearly as large as the cavern without did it appear, forcing me to raise the torch so that I might see ahead toward the far side. The walls and floor appeared smooth and polished, untroubled by the rubble of stones which lay elsewhere, colored black and gray by that which had smoothed and polished them. Symbols of some sort appeared in the floor before us, as though sunk into the stone and covered over so that smoothness was retained even over their presence. The symbols held no meaning for me, nor for Famira, yet I felt they held great meaning for others, perhaps the others I felt all around, their eyes unseen yet seeing all. In the midst of the chamber, all lines drawing toward it, stood a carving of stone, a large seat upon which sat a figure, unmoving and immobile, yet somehow poised for movement—of evil. The figure was male, unclothed and in great heat, its arms

up and hands clasped to make a circle, its stone manhood
enraged and quivering, eager to plunge deep within its intended
victim. Famira moaned in fear at the sight, adding to the trembling
which I, myself, felt, and quickly did we leave the entrance to
return up the corridor.

"Was that where we must go?" whispered Famira at last,
visibly shaken. "If so, I believe I shall beg to be left behind.
What was that monstrosity?"

I felt I knew who the carving represented, yet I said naught,
perhaps to hide the unsteadiness of my voice. I, too, would have
difficulty in passing that figure, yet refusal would only bring
death. I was preparing to speak on the subject, but a sound came
from the outer cavern which intruded upon thought.

"Do you hear that?" asked Famira, turning her head in the
direction of the sound. "What could have happened out there?"

I, too, was curious, yet I felt it wiser to keep the torch from
the crevasse entrance while Famira hurried to see the source of
the disturbance. She, in shadow, peered out into the main cavern,
then immediately turned and ran back to where I waited.

"Hannil and his riders come with torches!" she gasped, pale
and obviously frightened. "That sleek varaina of his leads them,
pointing the way with glee! You can be sure she means us no
good!"

"Then we shall have to disappoint them," I said, looking
about myself. "Were you able to see the torch when I entered
the largest of the nooks, the one over there?"

She followed the gesture of my finger, her face lighting, her
head ashake. "No," she breathed with a small laugh. "Not even
when I stood directly beside it. Shall we return there?"

"At once," I said, hearing the voices and footsteps of many
males grow louder. I hurriedly led the way into the nook, Famira
following after, finding little room for the two of us together in
the slight, wrapped-around place. I knew not what had made me
run from the males rather than stand and face them, yet I felt no
doubt about the wisdom of my choice. To run was not a warrior's
way, yet the cavern we had found stood all previous doings in a
new light.

"Are you certain she came this way?" said a voice not far
from us, muffled by the stone yet Hannil's without doubt. "I see
no light ahead."

"I am completely certain," came Deela's voice, oily with
satisfaction. "She seeks to bring Sigurr's vengeance down upon
us, of that I am equally certain."

"Perhaps she went ahead, to the far end of this corridor," said another male voice. "The wench seems as foolishly without fear as Ceralt himself."

"We shall see," said the voice of Hannil, and muffled footsteps began again. Famira and I waited, the torch held high above us, till no further sounds were to be heard, then did we edge carefully from where we had hidden. Many torches could be seen at the far end of the corridor, yet before I could decide upon either following the males or returning to the cavern from which we had come, new torches entered the crevasse.

"Jalav, what do you do here?" demanded Ceralt in a hiss, Lialt and Telion beside him, his riders, with torches, in his wake. He strode to us with anger clear upon his features, yet Famira did not hesitate.

"We do that which you should have done!" said she, placing small fists upon rounded hips. "We search for another exit from this cavern, cousin. Had Hannil's wench not sought harm to Jalav, we would have called you long before now."

"What harm?" rasped Ceralt, then listened as Famira described that which we had found, and then that which we had heard. A murmur arose among the males, yet Ceralt silenced it with a motion of his hand.

"It is clear we must see the thing for ourselves," said he, gazing toward the flickering torches in the distance. "And also see what Hannil is about. Let us proceed."

He and the others moved ahead, up the corridor, leaving Famira and myself where we had stood. Famira hurried toward the crevasse, obviously pleased to be away from the doings of males, yet I could not dismiss the goings on so easily. Silently, with as little noise as possible, I followed the track of the males.

I came up behind the males as they paused in the entrance to the farther chamber, struck by the sight of the carving seated within it. I could not easily see beyond their shoulders, yet soon found the problem solved for me. A hand touched my shoulder then reached for the torch I carried, and I turned my head to see a disapproving Telion. The male was not pleased with the fact of my presence, yet chose not to make an issue of it. His broad hand pushed those before us aside, and I was able to see within the chamber again.

Hannil's males moved about the chamber in search while Hannil himself stood before the carving, lost in contemplation of it, his female atremble behind him. The male seemed fascinated by the carving, lost in it till one of his males spoke.

"There are other corridors, yet none seemed tenanted, Hannil," said the male. "Shall we continue to search for the wench?"

"Has a wench been lost?" asked Ceralt before Hannil might reply, causing the males to whirl to face him. "Should you need our assistance, we would be pleased to give it."

"We search for our freedom!" rasped Hannil, angered at having been discovered. "Your wench seeks to bring Sigurr's wrath down upon us, and when we find where she has hidden herself in this chamber, we shall offer her up to Sigurr!"

"Ceralt's wench has not been in this chamber," said Telion, drawing Hannil's eyes to himself—and to me. "She has been engaged in a task I, myself, set her, and now stands among us. How could she have entered first, when here she stands, having entered with us, behind you?"

"She did enter first!" shrilled Deela, beside herself with fury. "I, myself, saw her enter here, and followed to be sure! She entered here first!"

"Hannil, see what we have found!" called one of the males, and Hannil, in a fury of indecision, turned from the grins of Ceralt, Telion, and the rest to examine what his male had found.

At the base of the stone carving, below the figure and its chair, were letters sunk deep in the stone and covered much as the symbols upon the floor. It was to these letters that Hannil's male pointed, and Ceralt and his males moved forward, the better to see the message written therein. I, too, moved forward with them, overcoming a great distaste to do so, and presently gazed down upon the message others read with such ease. I struggled with each letter and sound, fighting to bring sense from them, and at last succeeded in doing so. The males had remained silent the while, considering what they had read, for the message, black upon gray, went so: "I am Sigurr, the Dark God, and to me belongs what I would take. Offer up the first among your females or feel my wrath."

"It now seems clear why yonder wench so insists upon having followed Jalav," said Telion when none other spoke. "Were she to convince us she followed another, she would not be first."

"I have not lied!" insisted Deela from where she stood, having been left behind with the advance of the males. Only she had failed to read the message on the carving, her next words proving her ignorance. "And I am first among all the women, not only that Jalav! Jalav is used by many men, Deela used only by Hannil! Who, then, is first between them?"

"Perhaps the savage wench may read the words first," muttered Hannil, not yet caring to comment upon his female's insistences. "She would then be wise enough to hide her prior presence from us."

"The thought is logical," nodded Ceralt, meeting Hannil's eyes. "Unfortunately, Jalav is unable to read. Lialt strives to teach her her letters, yet her resistance is incredible in its strength."

"Then she could not have known," said Hannil, his voice weary with defeat. "It is Deela herself who is demanded of us, on pain of punishment for refusal." His voice, and Ceralt's, had been held low, yet now he raised it. "Deela, you are indeed first among the wenches. Come here and join us."

Upon hearing these words the pretty female smirked and preened herself, then came forward with swinging hips. She glanced a look of triumph toward me, then passed to stand herself beautifully before Hannil. This male placed his hands upon her shoulders, then turned to show her the inscription. Deela read the words more rapidly than had I, and suddenly her breathing quickened to frightened gasps.

"No!" she moaned, attempting to back from the inscription and the male who yet held her shoulders. "He does not wish *me*! It was Jalav who was first! Jalav!"

"And yet you stood and declared yourself first among all the wenches, Jalav included," said Hannil, closing his fingers the tighter upon the female. "How else were we to know the first among our women, save that that one spoke out in our need? It matters not who came here first. She who was chosen was made to speak out."

"No!" screamed the female, truly frantic with terror. So strongly did she struggle that two others of Hannil's males came to assist in the holding of her.

"What do you propose to do?" asked Ceralt of Hannil, drawing that male's eyes to him. Ceralt's voice was disturbed, and he had moved to stand beside me.

"We must give her to Sigurr," said Hannil, a wildness in his eyes unmatched by the calm in his voice. "One female is a small price to pay for our freedom, and if she pleases him, he may perhaps keep her for use."

"You are insane," breathed Ceralt, sickened by what Hannil intended. "How can you believe. . .?"

"I do believe!" Hannil blazed, hand to the dagger at his silvered belt. "I will do as the dark god commands and save us all! The wench is mine and you may not interfere—as I have not

interfered in that which was done with your wench! Stand back
now and do not seek to halt us!''

Ceralt stirred as though to move against the other male, yet
many hands came to hold him where he stood, Lialt's and
Telion's among them. That he failed to struggle proved he knew
the futility of such an act, for Hannil's males moved feverishly
about the female Deela, who screamed and wept as the leathers
were cut from her. The males moved in great haste, as though
having made their decision, they now raced frantically to see the
thing done before promised wrath fell upon them.

It was but scant moments before the weeping, naked female
stood before the carving, the hands of males keeping her from
fleeing her fate. I had no clear understanding of what that fate
would be, thinking perhaps they intended spilling her blood upon
the carving, as tribute to he whom they called dark god. That no
battle was to be involved was somewhat unseemly, yet Hosta,
too, will take the lives from enemies slowly, in retribution for
acts performed against the Hosta clan. That these males offered
up the female was clear, yet the next of their actions also
clarified how she was to be offered up.

''No!'' I cried, seeing three of the males, Hannil included, lift
the female toward the waiting arms of the carving. They clearly
intended placing her for use by the carving, and I could not bear
the thought. So evil that face was, so sunk in pleasured cruelty,
not even the pretty, foolish, female Deela deserved being done
so.

''Jalav, hush,'' said Ceralt, holding me by the arms to keep
me beside him. I had attempted to move to the female's aid, yet
he and Lialt and Telion would not allow this. Their arms circled
me and held me as I struggled, impossible to escape, impossible
to deny. None had heard my outcry, for all had eyes only for that
which occurred upon the carving.

Deela screamed as though possessed, throwing herself about,
terror in every fiber of her being. The three males who held her
lifted her from her feet, raised her above the circled, outstretched
arms of the carving, then lowered her within them to the lap
below. The carving's manhood seemed to pulse in the flickering
torchlight, evil and expectant, poison-filled and demon-raised.
Slowly but inexorably was Deela's womanhood slid toward it till
her body blocked its view, her screams unending echoes in our
ears. Hannil himself moved before her, his hand between her
thighs, and truly could I see his positioning of her upon the cold,
stone shaft. The carving's desire was too large for her, far too

large for any female of flesh, yet Hannil took her thighs, his males her bottom, and as one, pulled and pushed her upon the spear that cleft her body. Deela choked as saliva dripped from her opened mouth, her eyes wide and staring, her screams abruptly cut off. She choked again, and a third time, and then her hands went to the stone arms about her, clutching them in madness.

"It moves within me!" she choked out, and then her screams returned increased twofold. "It moves within me! Merciful heavens, it lives within me! Hannil! Hannil!"

The males released her and took a shuddering step backward, yet Deela had not been freed. She had been given over to the circling stone arms, from which she was never to escape. Her body began a movement in rhythm, as though she were truly being used, and I cringed back against Ceralt's chest, sunk in a fear the likes of which I had never before encountered. All thoughts of warriorhood were gone from my mind, all fear felt till then no more than a child's small dream. Sooner would I face a lashing of a thousand strokes than approach that carving, and had Ceralt's arms not held me to him so tightly, I would have run from that place though every Hosta war leader ever to live stood about me in judgment.

Surely all those who stood about thought to see a rapid ending to the gift they had placed upon the carving, yet such was not to be. Deela's movement continued on and on, her voice now screaming, now choking, now whispering hoarsely, now laughing. The sight was enough to cause madness in the watchers, the sight of a female's use by a carving. No word was spoken by any in the group, till a shifting torch shone redly upon the stone.

"See there!" said Hannil of a sudden, his finger apoint toward the carving's knees. "Sigurr's use has returned her virginity and taken it all in one stroke! She gives him her virgin blood, her use now his alone for all eternity!"

Hannil's voice rang out in a laugh, madness clearly to be heard, Deela's maddened laughter adding to his. I could bear no more of those sights and sounds; tearing myself from Ceralt's arms I ran stumbling toward the corridor we had come by, my hand to my mouth to hold my insides within. After no more than a step or two, Ceralt was again beside me, his arm about me in support, his broad face as pale and sickened as mine must have been. I clung to him in my illness, faintly aware that many others followed us, knowing little of what occurred about me till we had again passed into the main cavern. The females stood about, and those few males who had remained to guard them, and all drew back from us upon seeing our faces.

"What has happened?" demanded Famira, the only one to immediately approach us. "Ceralt, Cimilan, Jalav—what has happened?"

"We have begun to pay Sigurr's price," said Ceralt, his voice thicker than usual. "Famira, help me with Jalav."

Though the words would once have given me insult, no thought of refusal came when Famira approached to offer her aid. I trembled in Ceralt's arms, my head awhirl, my thoughts in chaos. Deep within I knew what lay ahead of me, yet my mind refused to consider the possibility, my flesh shrank from the very hint of it. Was my fear, then, to be the cause of Ceralt's loss, a fear before which I was no more than a child or a slave-woman? Fear should be thrown off and denied, faced and conquered; this fear was one which I could not even begin to think of in such a way.

I lay for many reckid upon Ceralt's furs, my eyes closed, my arm across them. Famira sat near, prepared to aid me should I need her, unspeaking other than that. The males had gathered in the center of the cavern, all of them together save the two who had been Hannil's closest. They two had attempted to take Hannil's riders from Ceralt's side, yet the other males had refused to hear them. Hannil was High Rider no more, and none other was able to stand in his stead.

I lay unmoving and unthinking upon the furs, attempting to deny that which had happened, attempting to put it from my memory for all time. It was an action no warrior was well used to, and slowly, slowly, the fact returned to me that I was a war leader, pledged to the service of Mida. It mattered not what such service might be, only that I performed it, and well. Few were called to Mida's service to perform tasks easily done. That I wished to remain unmoving with the lanthay fur cradling my back had no bearing; were I to continue in Mida's service, naught save that service must concern me.

It took an effort, yet I soon sat in the fur upon which I had lain. Famira clucked and berated me for failing to continue the rest Ceralt had decreed, yet Ceralt had said I must lie still till the illness was gone. The illness had gone as far as ever it would; lying longer in place would accomplish little good. No longer than a moment did I sit considering what next action must be taken, yet in that moment I saw four males returning with torches, obviously having been about examining the crevasses

Famira and I had begun upon. I felt it needful to hear what word they brought, therefore did I rise to my feet and walk to where the balance of the males sat.

". . . no other openings," said one male as I reached the group. "Further corridors lay only through the chamber where Sigurr sits, delighting in Deela's use and Hannil's madness."

"We cannot return there," said Ceralt, hand amove through long dark hair in a gesture more than weary. "We cannot take our wenches through a place such as that."

"We must return there," said I, drawing the eye of every male, causing Ceralt to rise quickly to his feet. "Our path leads forward, no matter the cost."

"Satya, how do you fare?" asked Ceralt, coming close to put his arms about me. "With all that has occurred, you must rest till the shock has passed."

"I have no further need of rest," I assured him, putting my hand briefly to his face. "We cannot remain here, Ceralt. There is further to come should we attempt it."

Ceralt's face turned pale with my words, undoubtedly remembering the last warning I had spoken. I knew not how the certainty of further ill had come to me; I knew only the truth of the words I uttered. The other males muttered and stirred where they sat and stood, unable to face the possibility of further distress, unable to gather the strength of decision to depart the seemingly peaceful surroundings. The decision, however, was not theirs in any event. Ceralt's color returned, yet the shaking of his head seemed to take the life from him.

"We cannot depart till we hear Lialt's words," said he, nodding toward a far corner of the cavern. The other male sat surrounded by the Clouds of Seeing, his eyes upon a scene other than that which his sight presented him. Telion sat near to Lialt, his attention full upon the other male, his body far from relaxed. "There has been enough of blind movement, enough of thoughtless flight and doing."

"The delay will not aid us," said I, speaking the words yet seemingly hearing them for the first time. It was as though another spoke through me, putting the new knowledge in my mind and upon my tongue. The thought gave me no discomfort, for it was undoubtedly Mida who acted so, seeing, as ever, to the safety of her warrior. Again Ceralt looked grave at that which he heard, yet his light eyes remained determined. I shrugged at the decision which in reality delayed decision, moved from his arms, and crouched down to await what would come.

Time passed, and all those within the cavern ceased pretending they engaged in necessary activity. The males sat as they had been, only now their females sat beside them, making no sound save an occasional sob of fear and despair, most seeking the arms of their males in an attempt to find comfort. The torches sputtered in their niches around the cavern, yet it seemed as though the edging darkness had begun an advance, creeping stealthily upon us where we waited. Ceralt had sat deep in thought awhile, yet now he paced back and forth, much like a lenga in a pit, seeking a way out where there was none. His eyes constantly sought the dreaming Lialt, desiring an awakening, seeing naught save the movement of pipe to lips, naught save the emptiness of unblinking eyes. At last he could no longer stand the stretch of endless time, and strode with determination to where his brother sat. Enlisting Telion's aid, the two began working to rouse him who was called Pathfinder.

Returning Lialt to our presence was not an easy thing. The male resisted all attempts for quite some time, yet at last Ceralt was rewarded with blinking eyes and low, protesting groans, bringing murmurs of relief from all who now stood about watching closely. Only I had been warned away from the area which yet contained traces of the Clouds of Seeing, an unreasonable demand with matters as they stood. Had Ceralt been less foolishly male in his outlook, I might have fetched Lialt forth much the sooner.

"He stirs!" said Famira, who stood by my side. "He has returned to his body and soon will speak to us!"

"Doubtless with words of wisdom," I murmured, looking about the cavern. Sand and small bits of rock dribbled down from the entrance through which we had originally come, near silent in its descent and small in its beginning. Soon other slides would join the first, perhaps eventually becoming a river, yet there we stood, awaiting Lialt and the salvation he would bring.

"Lialt, what did you see?" demanded Ceralt, holding his brother to a sitting position. "What signs do the Snows send us?"

"I—" Lialt began, then fell to a fit of coughing. When the spasm passed he continued. "I understand naught of what I have seen. There were no signs."

"How is that possible?" frowned Ceralt, well aware of the mutterings behind him. "The Snows have ever given us signs."

"It must be this place," groaned Lialt, fighting from Ceralt's arm to struggle erect and look about himself. "The Snows are covered with clouds of fog, disallowing all seeing, as though the future may not be. I walked as far as I was able, hoping to pierce the fog, and soon became lost. Had you not roused me, I might never have returned."

Many cried out at this, male and female alike, and some began weeping with a hopelessness born of self-defeat. Famira, too, moaned with despair, yet how might one consider oneself defeated with life remaining and Mida uncondemning?

"Should we fail to depart soon, none will return," I called across the cavern to Ceralt, causing him to jerk his head around. "Do you propose to wait till all of the roof has fallen to the floor?"

He and the others followed the direction indicated by my arm, and again gasps and moans of fright echoed about. I was much out of patience with males, and surely this had been heard in my voice. Ceralt gave no more than a glance to the slide, then left Lialt to walk to the center of the cavern.

"Gather up no more than food and drink," he commanded the others, speaking to them yet looking only upon me. "We must leave here within ten reckid. Jalav, come here to me."

Famira hurried to do as the others did, frantically and with great misery. I stood where I was no more than a moment, then went to stand before Ceralt as he had commanded. His face showed no expression, yet the light eyes gazing down upon me were cold with anger.

"Again you disapprove of my actions," said he, his voice menacingly soft. "You are not the leader of this expedition, nor even second in command. Tell me what you are."

He stood with arms afold, awaiting the words his eyes commanded, yet I could not again profess myself wench beneath a male. Even should he beat me before the others, I was able to speak no more than the truth.

"I am a warrior," said I, meeting the anger in his eyes. "A war leader of Mida, ever about her business. You may not deny this."

"I do deny it," he growled, showing the increase in anger no place save in his eyes. "It is only my business which you may be concerned with—now and forever more. Kneel before me."

Again I hesitated to obey him, yet there was naught else I might do. Slowly, reluctantly, I went to my knees upon the graveled stone floor before him, nearly feeling the male's pleasure at my actions and the reluctance behind them.

"Perhaps it now returns to you whose word must be obeyed,"

said he, looking down past his folded arms. "Should it be my wish, we shall remain here till this floor is covered with sand and rock. The decision remains mine alone. Now put your brow to the floor."

Beneath his eyes I did as he commanded, then heard the sound of his footsteps, taking him elsewhere. The fury was high within me that he would treat me so, and I raged silently as I knelt, feeling naught of the stones beneath my knees and head. And then sounds came to me of the movement of others about the cavern, others who saw what Ceralt had done and perhaps paused in their hurry to smile. While the male held my word I was bound to him, constrained to obey his every command as though I were the lowest of slave-women, the meanest of females. The flames of rage died to burning coals of shame. So much for the folly of a warrior's tongue, when speech will bring no smallest taste of glory, no more than a punishment fit for a girl.

Ceralt had decreed departure in two hands of reckid, yet twice the number of reckid passed before I was ordered to my feet and given a large leather sack to carry. My eyes met Ceralt's as the sack was given me, his stare entering and penetrating to my soul. Perhaps he saw the shame I had felt, perhaps he saw the difficulty I found in continuing to hold his eyes; whichever the truth, a smile touched his lips, faint and thin yet warmer than a grin of satisfaction. His hand came to smooth my hair, then his arm went about me, to lead me to the gaggle of others who stood before the crevasse which led to our only escape. My step did not falter as I walked beside him, yet the thought came again that there were many things one might face which were worse than death.

"The rock slides grow worse with each passing moment," said Telion to Ceralt as we reached him. Telion was engaged in assisting Lialt, whose dark skin appeared pale from beneath, drained in some manner from within. He seemed stronger than he had been when first awakened, yet the strength of Telion's arm remained necessary to him.

"We leave now," said Ceralt, looking about at those who stood and awaited his commands. Each female held a leather sack matching mine, each male wore a sword which had not been so much in evidence earlier. "You men keep your wenches close," continued Ceralt, still looking about. "The chamber beyond the upcoming corridor will be difficult for them, yet they may do no more than keep close. They may not cling. Should we find it necessary to use our swords, push them behind you and form a circle of protection. Those I have assigned as rear guard may now take up their positions. The rest of you follow me.''

Ceralt took a torch from a nearby male, nodded to Telion, then entered the crevasse. Telion indicated that I was to walk beside him, then he and Lialt followed Ceralt's path. I, too, followed, as did the others, and soon we trod the stone of the corridor taking us to the chamber beyond, no sound save that of our bootsteps breaking the silence of the rock.

Ceralt paused at the threshold of the chamber, staring within, then immediately continuing toward where the carving stood. We none of us understood the uncertainty of his pause till we, too, stood at the chamber's threshold; naught save the carving was to be seen, no sign that any other had ever visited the place.

"No more to be seen than traces of fresh blood," came Ceralt's voice as he and some others walked about the base of the carving. "Save for that, all that passed might well have been a dream. Where are those who earlier explored this place?"

The males in question came forward to speak with Ceralt, leaving their females clustered about the chamber's entrance. Each female who saw the carving gasped with shock, even Famira who had seen it before. I merely entered the cavern with Lialt and Telion, looking about myself, keeping my eyes from the carving. All had been decided and naught would keep me from that which awaited; I had only to meet it when it came— and endure.

A crevasse on the far side of the cavern was soon discovered to be the one through which we would pass. Some three of the crevasses possessed corridors behind them, yet these corridors were narrower than that which led to the cavern we stood in, narrower than that through which we would pass. Again were all of our set commanded to follow, again did Ceralt start out before us, again did we hurry along in the flickering of torches.

The second corridor led to a third cavern, much like the first save for the presence of a floor pressed to shininess, beneath which symbols might be seen. No carving brooded from this third cavern and we paused before continuing on, finding it necessary once again to choose from four crevasses which contained corridors. Corridor after corridor we walked, passing chamber after chamber, the hind moving past us with no sign of salvation. Once we paused upon a pressed, shiny floor, seeking sustenance in the sacks we carried, and afterward when we continued on Lialt walked without assistance. Aside from this, all remained unchanging.

Surely the fey without must have been near to ending when we entered another cavern, no different from the others save that its walls bore drawings beneath pressed shininess, just as the floor did. Upon the floor were again unknown symbols, yet the walls were more easily read. Upon one side males knelt before a dark male, one who held a female by the hair, preparatory to using her. Upon the opposite wall stood a golden female, surrounded by other females wearing sword and dagger, all standing above a male who had been staked out for use. So much did the golden female seem like Mida that I stared in wonder, failing to see that the males stared in such a way at the dark male.

"It is undoubtedly Sigurr," came Lialt's voice, and I turned to see where he gazed. "We have been moving ever downward in this maze, and now I begin to wonder. Is it possible the Altar we sought was that which was first passed, the chamber with the carvan figure? Should we now approach the true base of the mountain, its heart must be above us."

"I sincerely hope not," said Ceralt, looking upon the drawing with distaste. "The sole demand about the carven figure was a demand for a female, a gesture I could not repeat even should it mean our end. It is not my way to bargain above female blood. Let us continue on in hopes of finding a more palatable Altar, one where we need only do battle to gain the ear of the god."

With the other males murmuring assent they turned from the drawing—and every torch suddenly sputtered and went out. Males shouted, females screamed, bedlam reigned till suddenly there was light again, the light of hundreds of torches rather than mere hands of them. The walls we had gazed upon were now gone, the roof no longer immediately above us. We stood in a cavern as vast as a forest, stone sky stretching far above us, stone walls lost in the distance. This there was time to see and little more, for armed males rushed toward us from all sides, obviously bent upon attack. With a shout, the riders formed a circle of defense, backs to those females put behind them, swords out and readied though they knew not what they faced. When the attacking males closed with them the battle was begun, a battle none had anticipated—and none might avoid. Unsurprisingly, it took little time for the battle to be over.

# 16.

## *A battle is joined—*
## *and the dark god encountered*

I stood to the left of the line of huddled, weeping females, placing myself as close to the males as possible. Some stood, yet many more sat or lay upon the shininess of the floor, their leathers slick with the redness of blood. Telion and Lialt crouched, paying no heed to their own wounds, for Ceralt lay on the floor between them, his face pale from the gaping wounds in his chest. My fists clenched as I crouched as the males did, staring at Ceralt's life ebbing away. So swift the attack had been, and so completely overwhelming; eight or nine had faced Ceralt alone, their swords tasting his blood, their voices demanding his surrender, their anger striking him down when he refused to yield. There had been no time to reach his side before he fell, little time to remain there afterward. With so many riders wounded Lialt had called out their surrender, and once all swords had been taken, the females had been separated from them, to form a ragged, pathetic line. I had attempted to remain with Ceralt, yet the victors would have none of it; had I persisted in defying them, Ceralt's throat would have been cut. I crouched in silence as near as I might be, perhaps three paces from where he lay, burning with fury and kill lust. Had Ceralt been accompanied by Hosta rather than males, his life would not have been forfeit.

"Ah, captives!" came a voice, a female voice filled with great satisfaction. "Our males will need to be healed of their wounds first, of course. How stand the wenches in your eyes, Tastil?"

"Well enough," answered a male, and I turned my head to see the two standing to my right, examining the weeping females. The male was large and light of hair and eye, clad in leather breech and leather boots, a swordbelt firm upon his hips. The tall female also wore the same, her large breasts unashamedly exposed, her brown hair worn loose and long to her thighs.

"Could there be one in which I would find interest?" murmured the female, moving her dark eyes over the village females.

"Vanin, leave them be!" snapped the male called Tastil, his annoyance clear as he looked down upon her. "The females are ours to toy with, not yours!"

"There will obviously soon be one male lost to me." She called Vanin shrugged, gesturing unconcernedly in Ceralt's direction. "I am therefore entitled to choose one of yours, to test my blade or wet it. Do you wish to protest before the Golden One?"

The female had turned to lock eyes with the male, mockery and supreme confidence clear in her manner. The male regarded her in silence a moment, then made a gesture of disgust.

"To what purpose?" he growled, resting hand upon sword hilt. "All know you to be the Golden One's favorite. Take what wench you will and be damned."

The female Vanin grinned, her mockery increased, then she turned from the male to look again upon the females lined before her. Each wept and shook and clung to another, all appearing wide-eyed and miserable—save one. Famira stood perhaps a pace to my right, dry-eyed and nearly calm, no more than concern for Ceralt filling her large, dark eyes. She stood alone as she had stood alone for all of the journey, refusing to mix with the village females, unwilling to disturb my silently demanded solitude. Vanin, grinning, moved slowly till she stood before Famira, causing the village female to look up into her eyes with bewilderment.

"You seem the largest here," remarked Vanin to Famira, examining her with an insolent gaze. "How long do you feel you might stand against me with sword in hand?"

"I do not understand," stumbled Famira, her skin paling. "I do not know the wielding of a sword."

"You will soon wish you had studied the matter," laughed Vanin, pleased with Famira's fear. "The largest is ever my choice as opponent, and you are largest."

"You are mistaken," said I to Vanin, rising from my crouch. "She is not the largest among us."

Vanin's head turned quickly toward me, her grin becoming a frown. She and I stood eye to eye, obviously of a size. Even with a pace separating us this was clear, and then the female's grin returned.

"Much more to my liking," said she, leaving Famira to stand herself instead before me. "I dislike striking down the small and the helpless. There is little effort needed and little sport to be found. How am I to prove my prowess when she who stands before me cowers?"

"To strike the small and helpless requires no prowess," said I, folding my arms. "It requires only fear."

"Fear!" raged this Vanin, immediately taking insult. "I fear no mortal being! I am a warrior, and not to be spoken to so!"

"Warrior?" I echoed with raised brows, allowing a faint smile to touch me "In what manner have you proven yourself warrior? Through the murder of innocents? In the swagger of your walk? In the dishonored blade you wear at your side? Such are not the qualities of a warrior."

"I am a warrior!" screamed Vanin, her fists raised high, a madness in her eyes. "You will die slowly for those words, horribly cut to ribbons by my blade! That you will have a blade of your own matters not! You will fall before me! Tastil, give her your blade!"

The female stepped back, nearly foaming in her fury, allowing the male Tastil to approach me. He drew his sword and proffered it by the guard, the look in his eyes calling me fool for having spoken so. I turned my head from him to look toward Ceralt, seeing anger and fear on the faces of Telion and Lialt, pain and distress upon Ceralt himself. Armed males stood close about them, preventing Telion's attempt to intervene, preventing Lialt's attempt at protest. Again I smiled, partly at the fact of Ceralt's continued existence, then looked again at the male Tastil.

"I choose not to take the sword," said I, continuing to keep my arms folded. "Proceed with this farce in any manner you wish."

"Take it, you fool!" hissed the male, again proffering the sword, yet his anger was naught compared to that of Vanin. The female shouldered by him, bringing a small growl to his throat which she took no note of, and put herself again before me.

"You will not refuse!" she shrilled, nearly beside herself with rage. "Take the sword! Take it!"

"I do refuse," said I, unimpressed with her anger, and then her hand flew toward me, striking me across the face, sharply, with a good deal of strength. I staggered, caught off balance, and her other hand came, striking even harder in the backswing. I went to the ground, a buzzing in my ears, a blurriness in my sight, a trickle of blood at the corner of my mouth. I shook my head to dislodge the difficulty, angered almost beyond bearing. The female begged to have her blood spilled, yet it was not I who would be privileged in the doing of it. Sounds of dismay came from all about, sharpening as I prepared to regain my feet, and then another sound came, no more than a whisper, no more than a rustle of nearly dead leaves.

"Jalav," called Ceralt, all strength gone out of his voice. "Jalav, I release you from your vows. Do not allow her to harm you."

I turned quickly to search Ceralt's face, disbelieving the words I had heard, seeing only that the effort to speak had cost him consciousness. Lialt quickly sought the spark of life in his sprawled, motionless body, seemed to find it, yet wept at how low it was. The chill of the shining floor entered me, feeding my grief and anger, driving me again to my feet. Vanin stood but two paces distant, impatiently awaiting the return of my senses. When she saw I had regained my feet, she gestured toward the male Tastil.

"Bring her closer to me," she commanded a male who stiffened in anger. "I will beat her to bloody ruin if necessary, to convince her to take the sword. Then I will strike her down!"

"Such is to be seen," said I, my voice harsh, the blood-lust tinge in it keeping Tastil where he stood. With one motion I removed my leather chest covering, hurling it from me in disgust, leaving me with breech and boots, just as Vanin wore. Again a muttering arose all about, and Vanin sneered.

"Do you think emulating my dress will save you?" she asked, placing fists on hips. "My skill with a sword does not depend on it."

"Nor mine," said I, walking forward to take the sword Tastil yet held. The hilt fit well in my long-deprived hand, its balance easily to be found. The male smiled as he walked to stand with others, and I turned full to face Vanin.

"It is time," I informed her, keeping my point low. "You spoke earlier of warriors, therefore allow me to introduce myself. I am Jalav, war leader of the Hosta, foremost of all the clans of Midanna—who are *warriors*. I spit on your concept of warriorhood,

on your concept of honor. Face me if you dare, for I mean to
have your life.''

"War leader?" she scorned, reaching to her sword and unsheathing it. "Of the Midanna? What a fool's tale you tell,
wench. *I* am of the Midanna, chosen favorite of Mida the
Golden. I shall soon have your blood upon my sword, dedicated
in whole to the glory of Mida.''

"Such is to be seen," I said again, advancing to where she
stood. "Do you mean to slay me with words?''

The jibe brought her anger as I knew it would, causing her to
cut at me as though I stood weaponless. It was a fool's move,
easily blocked and easily riposted, leaving her with a thin line of
blood down her arm as she retreated.

"You fiend, I will have your life!" she screamed, the fingers
of her free hand finding the blood I had caused to be. She rushed
at me again, swinging her sword all about, much like a young
warrior-to-be, determined yet unskilled. Again I met her flurry
of swings, turning them with little effort, again I left a line of
blood on her, felt deeply when she retreated.

"Where is the skill you spoke of?" I demanded, seeing her
chest rise and fall with agitation. "Am I expected to be as you
and strike down the helpless? Do you mock me with pretense at
sword skill? If such is the case, go to your knees now. Should
you attack me again, I will claim the balance of your blood.''

"You cannot defeat me!" she shrilled, wildness heaving her
chest. "You speak only to frighten and I will not be frightened!''

Again the fool of a female came at me, clearly believing
desire for a thing would win that thing for her. She swung left
and right as she had before, her teeth gritted, her eyes blazing, at
last reaching the bottom of my patience. I caught her swing on
my blade and stopped it clean, jarring her to the teeth, then
began a swinging of my own. Had I faced one of skill my edge
would have sought the flesh behind the blade; with Vanin it was
enough that I struck her weapon. Back and back I forced her, she
hard pressed to retain her footing, fear clearly beginning to enter
her eyes. When I saw she knew she faced a superior warrior, I
struck her blade from her hand, sending it spinning and clattering
away. The female then sobbed in despair and threw herself to her
knees.

"I yield!" she cried, putting her face in her hands. "I cannot
best you and do acknowledge it here before all these others!''

"It is not enough," I said, causing her to raise her head to see
the point poised before her throat. "Earlier I offered you your life

and you chose to throw the offer in my face. I do not choose to make the offer again."

"You cannot slay me!" she choked, her widened eyes on the point so near to her. "I am Mida's favorite, chosen above all others!"

"Not quite above *all* others," said I, feeling more disgust than amusement. "Send Mida your final greeting and prepare yourself."

"No!" she screamed, throwing herself backward. "Mida, I beseech your aid!"

I began to step after her, to spit her where she lay, yet a golden haze began to form to the right, beside the female craven's body. I halted to watch the golden haze, hearing gasps and moans from those who watched behind me, feeling the pulse quicken in my body. Surely the time of my release from capture was at hand, for the haze quickly formed about the person of Mida, golden and glorious in her presence.

"Mida, send her from me!" screamed the female Vanin, attempting to crawl to the golden presence. "Do not let her slay me!"

"Greetings, Mida," said I, standing proud and straight before her. "The blood of this one is soon to be yours."

"Greetings, Jalav," said Mida, sending golden radiance all about with the smile coming to her lips. "I am pleased to see you here at last."

"Mida, no!" gasped Vanin, cringing where she lay. "Do not give her my life, I beg of you!"

"Vanin, Vanin, my foolish daughter," crooned Mida, turning gentle, concerned golden eyes upon her. "Did you not announce yourself the equal of any of my wild daughters? Did you not beg the presence of one to prove the contention? I fear you and your sisters have dwelt here overlong, making of yourselves more pets than warriors. The war leader Jalav stands before you, greatest warrior of all my wild daughters. Why do you not best her?"

"Mida, I cannot," whispered Vanin, paler by far than she had been. "She fights as a male might, not as a warrior."

"All warriors fight as I do," said I, looking down upon her with Mida. "Those who fight as you do are called wenches."

"No!" Vanin howled, throwing herself about upon the floor. "I am a warrior, not a wench! Mida, take me from her!"

"Jalav, you are the challenged," said Mida, turning from the form upon the floor. "As you have bested her, her disposition is yours. Do with her as you will."

I looked from Mida to the female Vanin, howling and screaming in a frenzy upon the floor. I touched the life sign which hung between my breasts, seeing that Vanin wore none. To slay the female would be fitting and satisfying, yet little honor would adhere to the act.

"I cannot leave an enemy behind me," I mused, speaking to Mida. "Nor do I care to sully my sword upon one such as she. I have learned a thing from males, Mida, a thing termed mercy. Do you wish to see the cruelty of it?"

Mida smiled, a smile filled with full understanding, therefore did I turn to those others who stood watching us.

"Is there one among you who would have a female pretending to warriorhood?" I called. "She is no more than comely to the eye, as yet to be taught obedience in the furs. Is there one who would teach her such a thing?"

"I am one," the male Tastil called back, grinning amid the laughter of his males before coming to stand beside me.

"No!" shrieked the female Vanin, sending venom toward the male with the single word she apparently still possessed. "No, no, no, Mida, no!"

"Ah, but yes, little one," laughed Tastil, advancing to where she lay upon the floor. "As the Golden One's favorite you were untouchable, yet now that you have fallen from grace—I have waited long for this moment."

Vanin turned and attempted to scramble to her feet, thinking, perhaps, to run from the male. He, however, had no intentions of allowing her escape. As she turned he moved quickly to put his hands upon her arms, pushing her to the floor with the weight of his body.

"There is another thing I have long wished to do," he said, gathering her thigh-length hair in his hands. Once captured, he held her hair in one hand, drew a dagger from his boot, then proceeded to cut the hair from her at shoulder length. The female screamed and twisted beneath him, yet her hair was cut, each strand in its turn, till all hung in a knot from his hand. "I shall bind your hair and braid it," said he, thrusting the mass through the sides of his breech. "The whip I form will be used each fey to teach you your new lot in life, that of a wench subject to a man's will. You will find yourself much beaten and much used— and well repaid for every insult ever given me."

He then rose to his feet, drawing her up with him, taking her from the spot by a fist in her shortened hair. Her wailing cry to Mida could be heard far across the vast chamber, even when shadows no longer showed their forms. I took a breath of

weariness, remarking again upon the mercy of males, then turned
to see how Ceralt fared.

"No, Jalav," said Mida, before I might begin a step. "I have
waited long to speak with you, and wish to wait no longer.
Come with me."

I was about to ask but a moment's time, yet before I was able
to do so, the golden haze about Mida spread to encircle me as
well. The air itself glowed golden about me, filling my lungs
with the color of life. I felt I floated there, in the golden haze,
between one step and another, and then it was gone and a
chamber stood about me, Mida's chamber beyond doubt. All
was golden, the cloth beneath my feet, the silks upon the walls,
the seats, the platforms, the furs upon the thing called bed. Mida
herself seemed to step from the haze of gold, sending it elsewhere,
turning at last to face me. Her skin and hair and eyes were gold,
soft and radiant, giving her a beauty beyond all others. Her
large, full breasts were bare, and about her hips was draped a
golden covering, long to her ankles, much like that which Keep-
ers wore. She gazed upon me in silence for a moment, then
gestured toward a seat.

"Divest yourself of that sword, war leader, then sit yourself
there," said she. "There are many things to be discussed between us, not the least of which is my reason for calling you
here. There is much for you to do and I would have you begin as
soon as possible."

"I shall be pleased to do so," said I, cleaning the blade I had
used upon my thigh before throwing it to a corner. "However,
there is first the matter of the male Ceralt. Is his life yours or
mine, Mida?"

"His life?" she frowned, meeting my eyes. "Of what interest
is his life? His life has served my purpose and is now no longer
necessary. In another hin it will be gone."

"I do not wish it to be gone," I persisted, watching as she
turned from me to walk to a tall, golden seat, much like that
called throne. "I wish his life to be mine."

"For what reason?" she demanded, turning to seat herself and
once again gaze upon me. Her eyes probed deep, spearing me
with golden radiance, and then a smile returned to her lips. "Ah,
I see," she breathed, placing her arms upon the seat arms as she
leaned back. "The male has bred the desire for revenge in you,
raising a fury I feel clearly. You mean to hold him captive again,
or perhaps give him to a sister clan for use. I approve your
intentions, Jalav. A pity they cannot be."

"Cannot be?" I frowned, diverted from correcting Mida's impressions. I had often thought of Ceralt as she had described, yet not for some time had those intentions been mine. "Naught is impossible to you, Mida. Heal him as you healed me."

"The matter is hardly that simple, Jalav," she laughed, in some manner pleased. "You are a warrior and a daughter. The male is a male—and primarily in Sigurr's province, who is unlikely to give up his blood. He has had me bring you here for other purposes than to give you the gift of a male."

"He?" I blurted, again feeling the whirl of confusion. "Mida, I do not understand."

"You soon shall," said she, no longer seeming pleased. "The matter begins with the pending arrival of these strangers from the stars. They think to take you from us, yet it shall never be! Never!" A great anger had taken her at mention of the strangers, yet she soon had control of her voice again.

"All you need know is that these strangers are evil, beings who must be fought with and conquered," she continued. "Sigurr and I, between us, hold the obedience and loyalty of the two greatest warrior forces on this world, the Midanna and the Sigurri. As it was long ago destined that you make the journey here, Sigurr considers the decision to send you forth to his Sigurri, raising them in his name to battle beside my Midanna. It is his thought that his males will triumph over all about them, and after the victory over the strangers, my Midanna as well, yet this will not be. After victory is ours, it is his Sigurri who will fall, never to rise again. It is for this purpose that I have prepared you, Jalav. Are you prepared?"

"How have I been prepared, Mida?" I asked, standing, yet, in the clouds of uncertainty. "Through being the war leader of your Hosta?"

"Not that." She laughed, humor apparently restored. "Your position as leader of warriors held by males will allow you to be war leader for all of my Midanna. Nearly all of the Hosta carry the quickened seed of males, rendering them unfit for battle. The sole Hosta will be you, Jalav, a war leader without partiality, a war leader all may follow without prejudice."

"Then how have I been prepared?" I whispered, ill to know the Hosta would not be beside me in battle. Ever had my clan sisters fought by my side, yet now I was to abandon them to their fate. Though Mida had not said so, I knew this to be in her thoughts.

"You have been prepared by your captivity by males," said

she, great amusement evident upon her face. "Do you now feel
a proper hate for males, Jalav? Are you able to remember the
shame given you at their hands? Many times you called to me in
your misery, demanding to know why I allowed the capture to
continue. It was for this reason, that you would learn to hate and
despise males, all males, even those you will fight beside. When
the battle is done, you will take all their lives, giving me their
blood as you have ever done."

I turned without words and went to a seat, turning again to
numbly seat myself. The reason Mida spoke held little reason for
my mind, for was I not a Midanna warrior? Had I been bidden
by Mida to end the lives of certain males, would I have hesitated
in the manner of a city slave-woman? In the full flush of battle
lust, what need has a warrior of hate?

"Sigurr will soon present himself to speak with you," said
Mida, a small, pleased smile upon her lips. "We will, of course,
say naught of our true intentions, allowing him to believe all is
as he wishes it. Do not allow his manner to disturb you—you
stand beneath my protection."

"What of the two left at his Altar?" I asked of a sudden, not
knowing why I spoke the question. "The slave female and the
male—what has become of them?"

"The female Sigurr tasted to her soul," laughed Mida, much
pleased with the thought. "He holds her close to death in his
domain, continuing her use, disallowing her end The male is
here in my domain, already having felt his use, burning in the
throes of the sthuvad drug. His use is mine alone, therefore does
he burn with none other to see to him while I concern myself
elsewhere. He has long since begun to beg my presence; he will
live long enough to do more."

I nodded slowly, somehow having come to expect naught else.
My hand went to my life sign, feeling the worn wooden carving,
communing with the guardian of my soul. My mind whirled in a
manner I was unused to, with thought rather than confusion.
All about me seemed suddenly clear, yet I knew not what might
be done about it.

"Ah, Sigurr comes," announced Mida with a purr, sounding
much like a city female anticipating the arrival of a suitor. The
golden air to my left began to darken, a thick black fog surrounding a growing presence. My flesh chilled as a male formed in the
fog's depth, his body and face as dark as Mida's was golden, his
eyes so black and hungry they made one want to flee his sight. I

darted a glance to where I had thrown my sword at Mida's behest, and Mida's laughter rang out, light and golden.

"You threaten my warrior's peace of mind, Sigurr," said she, speaking to the fully formed, black-misted male. "Yet, see how her thoughts go, to a weapon rather than to fearful homage. Are not my warriors here mere children in comparison?"

"She laughed at my displeasure," breathed the male, a deep, low, breathy chill to his voice. "When she thought she lay dying, she laughed at my desire."

"She is wild and untamed," smiled Mida, finding no discomfort in the male's ice-tinged fury. "Would you have her behave as do those who are chosen to satisfy your lusts? Would you have her grovel at your feet, shuddering in terror?"

"Yes," breathed the misted male, his eyes taking the measure of my soul. Mida laughed to hear the single word, yet I found the need to grasp the arms of my seat, the desire to cry out in fear beating a mad pulse in my body. The male stood upon the mist covering Mida's golden floor, his form larger than any male I had ever seen, his desire covered with the blackest of breeches. As he gazed upon me his hand moved to the breech, and Mida stood quickly out of her seat.

"In my domain, your lusts will remain covered!" she snapped, cold authority in the command. "You now see Jalav before you. Do you accept her as courier to raise your Sigurri?"

"They will take her and sell her as warrior-pleasure," growled Sigurr, his large, square hand yet at his breech. "They will tie her by that thigh-length hair to a post and ravage her body as it is meant to be ravaged. They will not heed the words of a squirming wench, hot in her need."

"She will require a sign of sorts," mused Mida, deaf to the balance of the male's words. "A sign your Sigurri cannot doubt. It will be necessary to think upon what this sign should be."

"With a sign it may perhaps be done," grudged the dark male, his eyes continuing to rest upon me. "These wenches of the forest have knowledge of my warriors, yet know naught of where they dwell. Will she go to raise them to fight by her side, or will she lead others in attack upon them? It is difficult to know what a foolish female may do."

"Jalav is a warrior above all else," said Mida with scorn. "Her desire would be to attack, yet her obedience is to me. Should she give her word to raise your Sigurri, she will not be forsworn."

"Is this so, wench?" asked the male. "Do you stand ready to give me your word?"

"Perhaps," I allowed, not knowing how my voice had achieved such steadiness. "For this service, however, you have not yet asked my price, male."

"Your price?" the dark male breathed, the blaze heating in his eyes. "You dare to put a price on service to me?"

"You are naught to me," I answered with flatness. "For what reason would I do you service without a price?"

"For your life," growled the male, "for your soul and sanity. All are mine should I wish to take them."

"Take them, then," I shrugged, forcing my body to lean at ease in the seat. "Find another to raise your Sigurri to meet the strangers."

Mida laughed at the male's silence, seeing that he realized death held no fear for me. That she would not allow him my capture was also clear, for madness peered from his eyes as he fought to speak.

"So I must meet a wench's price," he breathed, the breathiness ragged. "What will you have, wench? Jewels for your fingers and throat? Silks for your body? A beauty greater than any other wench may possess? What small, puny thing will you have?"

"Jalav is a warrior," I growled, angered by the male's manner. "It is no city slave-woman thing I desire. I will have the lives of the males and females who accompanied me, that and their health. They are all to be healed and released, clad against the cold, armed against danger, mounted and with their possessions intact. They are to be given adequate provender to allow them to return to their village as they left it, healthy and whole."

"For what conceivable reason do you ask this?" demanded the male, eyes narrowed with lack of understanding. "Mida has assured me you do not suffer from this mortal disease of concern for those not of your clan."

"It is not a matter of concern," I shrugged, using the gesture to hide my discomfort over speaking other than the truth. Truth, in that instance, would have doomed them all. "The females look to me as leader, therefore are their lives mine to consider. The males I wish to have free and whole, for a debt stands between us that only swords will see to. When this matter of the strangers is done, I will lead my warriors against their villages."

"Ah, it is their blood you wish," said the male with a breathy chuckle. "Once free they will think themselves safe, then you and yours will swoop down upon them, burning, torturing, raping and killing. I had not expected so worthy a purpose."

"You will meet my price, then?" I asked, showing naught of the burning hurry I felt within me. Less than a hin of life did Ceralt have, too little to be wasted in talk.

"Perhaps," chuckled the dark male. "Their terror would be amusing, their capture and torture and use most diverting. Were they pledged to me you would not have them, yet as they are—perhaps. For I, too, have a price."

The words had been spoken, the words I had feared above all others, yet I sat as I had been, seemingly unconcerned. The thing would require my consent—would the strength be mine to see it through?

"A price for a price?" I murmured, speaking low to keep hidden the tremor in my voice. "For my price you receive a service. What am I to receive from yours?"

"For my price you will have their minds," he laughed, a deep breathy laugh of black pleasure. "Without my price you will have no more than that which was asked for—their bodies whole just as they were when they left their village. They will believe they have not yet sought my Altar—and will come again in search of it, placing themselves again in my power. Without my price, their lives will yet be mine."

His laughter spread and pushed upon my ears, insolent, demeaning, arrogant and evil. Mida, too, laughed at my plight, at the way the male had snared me in his trap. Should I insist upon my price, his, too, must be paid.

"Jalav, give over the thought of the male," Mida urged, amusement sparkling in her golden eyes. "There are other things before you, things of greater moment than the capture of a male. When you are victorious I will give you many males."

"Yet none who first had the capture of me," I said, nearly faint with the need to dissemble, the need to appear calm. "What is your price, male?"

"You know my price," he answered, growing larger in the mists of black, his hot, black eyes boring into me. "I whispered my price when another lay upon you, taking your use as mere mortals do. Do you pay my price or do you fear to meet it, mortal wench? Your survival is no sure thing."

Again his figure grew in the mists, throbbing as his carving had seemed to throb. I felt the silk and wood of the seat beneath and behind me, felt the smoothness of the wood beneath my hands, and yet it seemed the black mists spread to envelop me, touching and clinging. Sigurr it was who grew before me, dark god feared by all who knew of him, justly feared, justly shunned.

"Speak to me, mortal wench," he breathed, so close, the smell of his desire made my head spin. "Do you meet my price, or do I, alone, meet yours?"

I sat in the chair, caught in the gaze of the male, my tongue like leather in a sand-filled mouth, terror beyond description consuming my insides. Had my muscles not been locked full tight, surely I would have soiled myself. Had another asked the deed of me, I would have fled to show my refusal, yet no other had demanded the act of me, no other would have considered the asking. For that other, then, one who never would have asked, did I swallow the sand and force movement upon the leather.

"First their wounds," I croaked, finding it impossible to back any farther. "First heal their wounds and then your price . . ."

"It is done," breathed the dark voice in exultation, moving forward with the mists. "And now my price."

The mists surrounded me, smothered me, lifted me from the golden room to another place, one I dared not look closely at. Hands touched my arms, the breech was torn from me, and then was a price paid in full.

# 17.

## *A sign is fashioned—*
## *and a final warning given*

I know not how many feyd passed as I lay in delirium, or, in truth, if feyd passed at all. Perhaps no more than hind passed as I lay curled upon furs, my body aflame with agony, my mind near to madness. When sight returned to my eyes there were slave-males about, true slaves with fear in their eyes, apology clear in their movements. They brought wet cloths to bathe my brow, fanned me with feathers half the size of the males themselves, fetched tall pots called flagons filled with daru. This latter I attempted to drink, to soothe the rawness screaming had brought to my throat, yet my insides would not hold it. Spasms threw it back to the floor, beyond the furs, then darkness took me again, a soothing darkness in which my mind did no more than weep.

Sight came again after a time, bringing greater knowledge of the room I lay in. Large it was, nearly the size of Mida's, draped in many shadows of green, predominantly Hosta green. I stirred upon the furs beneath me, finding little strength, knowing more than a shadow of the pain I had been given. My body ached, both inside and out, yet my mind ached more with the memory of what the thing called Sigurr had done. He had taken his price fully, causing me shame and humiliation and fear as well as pain. He had done things which, had they been done before my capture by males, would have driven me mad. I had been used, and made to serve, and used again and again to heal an unnatural

389

need, one even larger than that felt by males filled with sthuvad drug. I knew not how long a time I had spent in red agony, nor would I ever know. The thing was endless as it went, unforgettable in its aftermath.

I stirred again upon the furs, turning my head here and there, seeing the male slaves ranged upon their knees before a side wall, heads deferentially down, shoulders bowed, eyes upon the floor before them, bodies draped in scanty cloth of green which failed to cover that which made them male. Had I need of one, I had only to summon him with word or gesture. That had been whispered to me when first I had opened my eyes, wildly fearful, much in pain, prepared to continue screaming. The sight of such slavey males sickened me, yet relief was there beside the illness; had the males been free and proud, I could not have faced them.

Two hands of reckid and more passed as I lay upon the furs, my thoughts darting about here and there, touching my time with Sigurr fleetingly, lightly, as one would touch tongue to mouth sore, testing to see if pain remained. At last I could bear the shock of testing no longer, therefore did I turn to one side and force myself to sitting, using strength of arm to keep myself so. Dizziness touched me, whirling round and round in brief sport, then did it go elsewhere to bedevil another. I had no true wish to examine my body, yet when I moved to pull my hair from beneath me, my eyes found the bruises which marked me well. Upon breasts and thighs and belly were they, round and black and set within my flesh to show how he had touched me, that god of males. The slave males had been about washing me when I had first awakened, yet I felt the need to bathe in deep, clear streams, full with scrubbing sand, far from the caves I sat in.

And then my eyes were drawn to the life sign I had worn since first I had become a warrior, the life sign I had carved with my own hands from the tree which had been marked as mine at my birth. The sign of the hadat which hung between my breasts as ever it had done, its lines full familiar to my eyes, yet no longer made of wood, stained in enemy blood. It had now become like Mida's Crystals, light and clear as dream substance, filled with uneasy roiling. I stared at the gray, swirling mists, disbelieving the sight of my eyes, and then the swirling changed of its own, growing deeper and more throbbing, till at last it turned and moved in blackness. My eyes closed as I nearly shuddered but I felt a great leadenness, an understanding of how deeply I had been fouled. Sigurr breathed within my life sign, soiling my soul as he had soiled my body, marking me as his for all to see. This, then, was the sign he and Mida had spoken of, the sign of his touch upon me. I lay again upon the fur, curled up tight in a ball, all feelings of fear and loathing numb within me. Sigurr had become a part of me and would remain so forevermore.

Some time later a golden haze began forming not far from me, speaking, I knew, of Mida's impending arrival. I considered continuing to lie as I was, then thought better of it and sat upon the fur. When Mida had formed completely within the mist, her lovely golden eyes moved closely all about me.

"I see you have returned to yourself," said she, her voice light and lovely and concerned. "Have you memory of that which was done to you?"

"I have memory of it." I nodded, holding her gaze. "His price was met."

"And withstood," she murmured, a strange glow touching her. "His sign and mine you now find on you, showing our approval, our confidence, our acceptance of you. More, Sigurr finds himself—taken with you, in a manner of speaking. Never before has a mortal female given him such strength, such release. Should you survive the raising of his warriors and the following battle, I believe he will seek you again."

"What more might he do that has not already been done?" I shrugged, truly unconcerned. Pain is pain, to be borne in silence; one's soul may be tainted no more than once.

"Perhaps he may do a thing never before done," said she, again in a murmur, then passed to other matters before I might ask her meaning. "When you leave here, you will first come upon my Midanna, led to the land of males by the Keeper Rilas, as yet unsure of what their actions should be. You will find them in the vicinity of Bellinard, for there comes the first work to your hand. The strangers will appear not far from Bellinard, and the city must be ours when they do. The males who dwell there would give up whatever asked for."

"In fear," I nodded, recalling the look of the male called High Seat in that city. "They are of a low sort, to be easily taken by warriors."

"Good," said she. "In that city, now held captive by them, are certain Sigurri warriors. It is these warriors who will guide you to their brothers who must be returned to the city you will then hold. From there may the final battle be faced."

Again I nodded, then leaned back in the fur upon one elbow. "So the Hosta were given into capture by males to allow Jalav to lead all the Midanna," I said, watching Mida carefully. "Jalav herself was given to males to breed hate within her for the selfsame males. All was done with this final battle in mind."

"Certainly," smiled Mida, pleased with the understanding I had attained. "Jalav is my finest warrior, most beloved of my daughters. How might I have chosen another?"

"How, indeed?" I murmured, seeing all most clearly. Mida had placed me among males to learn hatred of them, yet it had only been memory of these meant-to-be-hated males that had kept me from madness at Sigurr's hands. Memories of gentleness and laughter, care and comfort had held me during terror and pain, bolstering me to face the devastation of my soul. Never would I feel the hate Mida had wished for, not for those males, yet I remained bound in blood to Mida—and Sigurr as well. It would be foolishness to dwell upon what feelings I had for them.

"When may I leave this chamber to walk about your keep?" I asked, returning my gaze to Mida. "I would see what there is to see before my departure."

"You may leave as soon as you are able," smiled Mida, gathering her golden mist about her. "I will have guides awaiting you in the corridor without your door. We will speak again before you depart."

The mists thickened, masking her smile, and soon she and her mists were gone once more. The male slaves, upon their knees by the wall, had put their heads to the floor at Mida's appearance, straightening again only when her mists were gone. I gestured to one, telling him to bring provender, then slowly levered myself to my feet. Movement remained an ache and an effort, yet was it necessary that I ignore such things. Once again was I Jalav, war leader of Midanna, soon to face attack and battle. In battle there is room for thought of naught else.

A glance about the chamber showed my breech neatly folded by my fur boots, most likely returned to me by Mida and prepared against my need by the slaves. I went to don both, and only then saw clearly what lay beyond them, upon the fur of the floor. With breech in place and boots upon my feet, I bent to that which I had been too long without: a silver handled dagger complete with leg bands, and a leather scabbarded, silver-hilted sword. I drew the blade from its sheath to examine it, and found it to be an exact mate to the dagger; both were made of pale gold metal, chased with deep-set strokes of black. The strokes spoke no letter I had learned, yet did I feel they spoke in another tongue, one I had no knowledge of. It was a matter to be considered, yet of no real moment. The slave returned with the provender I had requested, therefore did I turn my attention to filling the hollow within me.

When I was done with feeding, I rose to my feet to consider the slaves. They knelt as they had earlier, beside the wall, heads bowed till they might be needed. A full hand of them were there, well-made males broad in the shoulder and chest, tall and seemingly strong, yet with fear and trembling clear in their eyes when those eyes dared to look upon me. What thing had taken their manhood from them I knew not, and though it continued to sicken me to look upon them, there was a manner in which they might serve me other than in obeying my commands. I chose two, one dark of hair and eye, the second red-gold haired and pale of eye, and with them following obediently behind me, left the chamber.

Without the door stood three dark-haired females, each clad in breech and boots of leather, each with sword at hip, each with hair as long as mine. They started nervously when I appeared, dark eyes going large and round, each straightening where she stood in an attempt to match my height. None of them was within a hand of her called Vanin, therefore did they fail in their attempt to match me. I looked upon them more directly than they looked upon me, wondering if their boots hid dagger and leg bands as mine did, and one of their set found courage enough to face me.

"We are here to guide you, war leader," said she, a girlish quaver in her voice, her hands nervously before her. "Will you follow us?"

"No," I denied, unable to cover my displeasure with the three. "A war leader does not follow. You are of those who call themselves warriors?"

The females behind she who spoke exchanged fear-filled glances, yet the female before me did not join them. Much did she seem numb with fear, unable to do more than nod woodenly. The disgust in my expression caused them all to cringe, so much like the male slaves who stood silently behind me that I felt a growl rising to my throat.

"Show me where those who were taken with me are being kept," I said before I might further frighten these children who played at being warriors. Indeed were they the pets Mida had spoken of, too long kept in safety and comfort, far from the harshness of true battle.

"At once, war leader," nodded the female before me, tripping

upon her words and her own feet in her haste to obey. She and
the other two moved carefully past me, to my right, glancing
quickly at the male slaves behind me, then made their way up
the corridor in which they had waited. The corridor was smooth,
pressed stone, black and white with gold, floor, walls and ceiling.
I walked to a wall and touched my fingers to it, feeling a
coolness unmatched by the warmth of the air. The three females
waited the same number of paces ahead of me, the two male
slaves followed obediently after, all wondering why I sought to
learn what thing it was which made the walls of that keep, none
speaking of their curiosity. Had they been warriors they would
not have wondered, yet had they been warriors, I would not have
acted as openly as I did. After a moment I moved toward the
females, and they, again in haste, once more took up the task
given them.

Through the corridor we moved, passing many doors, till at
last we came to its end, where it moved through a doorless
doorway and widened into a large cavern, wherein stood perhaps
four hands more of females such as those who guided me. The
females held sword and shield, facing each other in pairs, one of
each pair attacking with sword the shield of the other. The smell
of sword oil came clearly to me, that and the smell of sweat, and
those who walked before me paused to look upon their sisters.

"It is here that we practice and perfect the use of swords, war
leader," said she who had spoken earlier. "We are proud of our
skill, and proud to have you witness our efforts."

"Pride should be kept for that which merits it," I said,
looking from one to the other of pairs of females. "They do well
in attack upon shields, hacking and swinging in true abandon.
Have they never been told that the object is to reach the flesh of
she who stands behind the shield?"

"I—I do not understand," stumbled the girl, her eyes again
widened. "We have been taught to keep our opponents behind
their shields, to prevent the use of the swords they hold."

"Till one or the other of you falls from hunger and thirst?" I
demanded. "What if you and your opponent hold no shield? Do
you then attack an imaginary shield? Pah! True warriors are long
blooded by your age, having both taken and lost blood in true
battle. None here could hope to stand before the least and
youngest of Hosta, not to speak of the puniest of males. Let us
continue before I lose that which I have fed upon."

The shaken female nodded, her lip atremble as though she
held back tears, and we passed from that place into another

corridor, one which led downward. Torches stood upon the walls in all of these corridors, burning steadily, giving the air a strange smell as though sunlight were unknown there. I felt a great anger within me, as though I had been gulled out of that which I had ever considered mine, yet I kept my mind to the odor of the air, my disgust for the male slaves, my impatience with those who dared call themselves warriors. The place was not one where unbridled thought was wise, not if I wished to ride free on my way again.

Three further hands of reckid were filled with walking, and then we came to a widening of the corridor which did not become a chamber. Of a sudden there were doorways to either side of the corridor, doorways closed off with lines of metal, much like those rooms in the dwelling of the High Sea of Ranistard. I could see, behind the lines of metal, males and females of the set with which I had traveled, males to the left, females to the right, three to each enclosure. The females sat huddled together with sobs much in evidence, the males stood with fists clenched in anger, yet all broke off their doing at my appearance, coming forward to stare in silence. As my eyes swept them the females shrank back with gasps, they having noticed my guides and the slaves who dogged my steps. The males growled low to each other, displeased at what they saw, yet I cared little for what they thought. It was others I had come to find, and those others were not far. Four enclosures farther on, I found those I had been seeking.

Unsurprisingly, Telion, Lialt and Ceralt were enclosed together. Ceralt lay upon furs, cloth bound about his body, his face pale from loss of blood, yet he lived. Wounded and unconscious, prisoner to those about him, yet his life had been reclaimed. Lialt sat by his side, ever vigilant for the least change in breathing, the least stirring of limbs, his face lined from lack of sleep. Telion sat apart from the two, back against a wall, knee up to support an arm which in turn supported his head. At my appearance Lialt and Telion looked up, then rose quickly to their feet to come to the metal.

"Jalav, where have you been?" demanded Telion, circling two lines of metal with his fists. "We thought you taken and forever lost!"

"And yet, here I stand," said I, meeting the male's eyes. "Mida wished to speak with her warrior, therefore was I taken from your midst. Her powers are strong for one who is only— how did you call it?"

"A superstition," Telion ground out, teeth clenched in anger, light eyes flaring. "I see she has done well by the one who has ever remained faithful."

"Perhaps not so well as all that," said Lialt, eyes amove about me. "What caused those bruises upon you, Jalav? You seem badly used for one who is a favorite."

"The bruises are naught." I shrugged, stepping closer to the metal. "I see your wounds have been tended to."

"Indeed." Lialt nodded, his eyes continuing to hold to me. "Even Ceralt moves farther from the dark gateway with every breath he takes. Perhaps there is that in the air here which promotes healing."

"Yet, it is not merely healing which we require," said Telion, drawing my eyes. "We also require our freedom, Jalav. Is there naught a favorite of the goddess may do to accomplish this? Have you forgotten so soon how close a bond we share?"

His voice had softened with the disappearance of his anger, and abruptly one hand left the metal to draw me close, while the other moved to caress my breast. Much did I expect my flesh to melt and harden at his touch, just as he expected the same, yet the expected did not occur. My flesh remained as it had been, cool both without and within, and after some reckid, Telion removed his hands from me in confusion. I, too, had no understanding of what had caused the change, yet the meaning was clear: no longer was my flesh slave to any male who touched me, no longer theirs to do with as they pleased. Perhaps it had been the touch of Sigurr, shriveling my senses as well as my soul; should that be so, it was the one thing for which I might feel well pleased.

"Apparently the bond no longer exists," Lialt observed, searching for signs that he was in error. "I feel sure, Telion, that she has not come to free us."

"You are correct," I said, stepping back farther from the metal. "We are destined to meet again, male, yet the time will be when you, too, are able to take weapon in hand. Jalav has not forgotten your doings, nor shall she ever forget them. Should you wish to see what the future holds for you, look here."

I turned from them then to the male slaves I had brought, gesturing them to their knees before me. With my finger pointing downward I bade them press their heads to the floor, clearly marking them as slaves chained to my bidding. I looked again upon Telion and Lialt, who stood behind the metal thin-lipped with rage, and smiled a smile of challenge.

"Such is the fate which you shall find, should we ever meet again," I informed them. "When that one awakens, give him the greeting of Jalav, war leader of all the Midanna, and bid him return to his simple village and the life he once knew. Jalav shall see to the coming strangers with warriors of worth, warriors who well know the spilling of blood. Should we ever meet again, there will be swords drawn between us."

I ordered the slaves to their feet again, then turned and walked away, much aware of eyes upon me. Telion and Lialt had been warned away, and Ceralt, too, would be given my message. I felt anxious to be about the work before me, yet felt, deep within me, the loss of the male called Ceralt, he who had come to mean so much. Not again would I know his arms about me, not again would I feel the ecstasy of his touch. Were Mida to discover my true feelings for the male, his life would be taken as easily as it had been saved. My life was Mida's, as was my sword, and naught in all the world would take me from her service save death, which, I knew, would not be easily attained. I retraced my steps up the corridor, my hand arest upon the silver hilt of my sword, knowing death—and peace—would be difficult to find indeed.

## TANITH LEE

"Princess Royal of Heroic Fantasy and Goddess-Empress of the Hot Read."

—**Village Voice** (N.Y.C.)

- [ ] DELUSION'S MASTER        (#UE1652—$2.25)
- [ ] THE BIRTHGRAVE         (#UE1776—$3.50)
- [ ] VAZKOR, SON OF VAZKOR    (#UE1709—$2.50)
- [ ] QUEST FOR THE WHITE WITCH  (#UJ1357—$1.95)
- [ ] DON'T BITE THE SUN       (#UE1486—$1.75)
- [ ] DRINKING SAPPHIRE WINE    (#UE1565—$1.75)
- [ ] VOLKHAVAAR           (#UE1539—$1.75)
- [ ] THE STORM LORD         (#UJ1361—$1.95)
- [ ] NIGHT'S MASTER         (#UE1657—$2.25)
- [ ] ELECTRIC FOREST        (#UE1482—$1.75)
- [ ] SABELLA              (#UE1529—$1.75)
- [ ] KILL THE DEAD          (#UE1562—$1.75)
- [ ] DAY BY NIGHT           (#UE1576—$2.25)
- [ ] THE SILVER METAL LOVER    (#UE1721—$2.75)
- [ ] CYRION               (#UE1765—$2.95)
- [ ] DEATH'S MASTER         (#UE1741—$2.95)
- [ ] RED AS BLOOD          (#UE1790—$2.50)

**THE NEW AMERICAN LIBRARY, INC.,**
P.O. Box 999, Bergenfield, New Jersey 07621

Please send me the DAW BOOKS I have checked above. I am enclosing
$_____ (check or money order—no currency or C.O.D.'s). Please
include the list price plus $1.00 per order to cover handling costs.

Name _____

Address _____

City _____ State _____ Zip Code _____

Please allow at least 4 weeks for delivery

**BOOKS**

Have you discovered . . .

### JO CLAYTON

"Aleytys is a heroine as tough as, and more believable and engaging than the general run of swords-and-sorcery barbarians."
—*Publishers Weekly*

The saga of Aleytys is recounted in these DAW books:

- [ ] **DIADEM FROM THE STARS** (#UE1520–$2.25)
- [ ] **LAMARCHOS** (#UE1627–$2.25)
- [ ] **IRSUD** (#UE1640–$2.25)
- [ ] **MAEVE** (#UE1760–$2.25)
- [ ] **STAR HUNTERS** (#UE1871–$2.50)
- [ ] **THE NOWHERE HUNT** (#UE1874–$2.50)
- [ ] **GHOSTHUNT** (#UE1823–$2.50)

THE NEW AMERICAN LIBRARY, INC.,
P.O. Box 999, Bergenfield, New Jersey 07621

Please send me the DAW BOOKS I have checked above. I am enclosing
$_____ (check or money order—no currency or C.O.D.'s). Please
include the list price plus $1.00 per order to cover handling costs.

Name _____

Address _____

City _____ State _____ Zip Code _____.

Please allow at least 4 weeks for delivery

Presenting JOHN NORMAN in DAW editions . . .

| | | |
|---|---|---|
| ☐ | HUNTERS OF GOR | (#UE1678–$2.75) |
| ☐ | MARAUDERS OF GOR | (#UE1676–$2.75) |
| ☐ | TRIBESMEN OF GOR | (#UE1720–$2.95) |
| ☐ | SLAVE GIRL OF GOR | (#UE1679–$2.95) |
| ☐ | BEASTS OF GOR | (#UE1677–$2.95) |
| ☐ | EXPLORERS OF GOR | (#UE1685–$2.95) |
| ☐ | FIGHTING SLAVE OF GOR | (#UE1681–$2.95) |
| ☐ | ROGUE OF GOR | (#UE1710–$2.95) |
| ☐ | GUARDSMAN OF GOR | (#UE1664–$2.95) |
| ☐ | SAVAGES OF GOR | (#UE1715–$3.50) |
| ☐ | BLOOD BROTHERS OF GOR | (#UE1777–$3.50) |
| ☐ | KAJIRA OF GOR | (#UE1807–$3.50) |
| ☐ | TIME SLAVE | (#UE1761–$2.50) |
| ☐ | IMAGINATIVE SEX | (#UE1546–$2.25) |
| ☐ | GHOST DANCE | (#UE1633–$2.75) |

With close to four million copies of DAW's John Norman
books in print, these enthralling novels are in constant demand.
They combine heroic adventure, interplanetary peril, and the
in-depth depiction of Earth's counter-orbital twin with a special
charm all their own.

---

DAW BOOKS are represented by the publishers of Signet and
Mentor Books, THE NEW AMERICAN LIBRARY, INC.

---

THE NEW AMERICAN LIBRARY, INC.,
P.O. Box 999, Bergenfield, New Jersey 07621

Please send me the DAW BOOKS I have checked above. I am enclosing
$_____ (check or money order—no currency or C.O.D.'s). Please
include the list price plus $1.00 per order to cover handling costs.

Name _____

Address _____

City _____ State _____ Zip Code _____

Please allow at least 4 weeks for delivery